THE
SCARLET DEATH

ALSO BY DAVID DELEE

THE SCARLET DEATH

A PARKER QUINN ARCHAEOLOGICAL THRILLER

DAVID DELEE

Dark Road
PUBLISHING

COPYRIGHT

For more information about new releases, special events, and exclusive content only available to subscribers, sign up to get David DeLee's newsletter.

https://www.subscribepage.com/daviddelee

Thank you for purchasing this book. We hope you enjoy it.

THE
SCARLET DEATH

PROLOGUE

Baghdad National Museum
Iraq - August 2011

A SENTINEL TO HISTORY, behind its sandstone and wrought iron barrier, the National Museum of Iraq still bore the scars of violation. A cruel reminder of the chaos that accompanied the U.S.-led invasion begun in 2003. Resilient against the ravages of senselessness and war, the structure is an intricate blend of neoclassical and Islamic architectural styles. Despite its notable wounds, its smooth, cream-colored stone created a solid foundation for the building, projecting an unyielding sense of formidable endurance.

In the aftermath of Operation Iraqi Freedom and the subsequent fall of Saddam Hussein's regime, the once-sacred sanctuary of art and antiquities was transformed into a chaotic scene of broken glass, shattered display cases, and empty pedestals. Priceless artifacts, many dating back to the cradle of civilization, were stolen or destroyed, igniting international outrage over the irreplaceable losses to history and culture.

Now, under the moon's steely-gray glow, its grand façade was bathed in a silver-amber mix of light, softened by the ever-present desert dust. The museum glittered like an impeccable sandcastle against the black velvet night sky. Its rows of towering columns, their surfaces illuminated by spotlights, framed the façade with classical elegance. The main entrance was a grand portal flanked by monumental pillars intricately adorned with carvings of ancient motifs. The doors were framed in rich, dark wood and elaborate metalwork that depicted scenes from Mesopotamian history.

The distant sounds of traffic and occasional sirens beyond its protective walls a constant reminder of the city's ongoing military unrest.

Dressed entirely in black, Maximilian Stahl stood in the shadows of a doused streetlamp strategically damaged the day before. A tall, lean man with sharp features and piercing blue eyes, he projected an air of quiet authority. His brown hair cut short and slicked back. He wore a thin mustache and goatee.

With a forced patience, only consulting his watch once—a Patek Philippe Sky Moon Tourbillion—he waited in the sultry warm air despite the late hour. Heavy with a blend of earthy scents from the Tigris and Euphrates rivers, the musky aroma of desert flora, and the lingering smells of grilled meat from the day's street vendors.

Precisely on schedule, Anton Kuznetsov emerged from the gated shadows surrounding the museum. A stout man of only five-five. He appeared to be nearly as wide as he was tall. Muscular and thick, from his bullet-shaped bald head to his powerful legs, Stahl thought of him simply as a beast.

"The team is in place," he said, his Russian accent thick. An orphan from the town of Tolyatti, in the Samara Oblast, before being conscripted into the military, Kuznetsov had spent little time outside Russia other than his involvement in the Chechen Wars.

Stahl patted his shoulder. "Well done."

They crossed the road and strolled down Al-Sa'adoon Street along the eastern side of the museum. The wrought iron gate at the rear of the building stood open. A chain and open padlock wrapped around the bars. Raking the lock's pins and tumblers would be child's play for any of Stahl's people. A trio of individuals meticulously chosen for their exceptional talents. They were huddled in the shadows by a back door.

Li Xinru, Lilly, a twenty-three-year-old Chinese hacker with an uncanny ability to dodge digital surveillance and infiltrate impregnable computer networks. Then there was Mike Harper, a seasoned American mercenary and former U.S. Marine from Dallas. He boasted an unparalleled mastery in the art of electronic security systems. Finally, their Swiss Army knife ace in the hole, Nico Müller. A man renowned for his safecracking finesse and ability to dismantle both physical and electronic defenses with precision and finesse.

Kuznetsov rewrapped the chain around the gate and snapped the padlock closed, locking them within the confines of the museum's receiving area before joining Stahl and the others at the back entrance. A set of steel double doors.

Each member was dressed in black. One-piece jumpsuits. They carried a backpack on their backs or slung over their shoulders. Müller crouched on one knee, a small hand-held black pouch resting open on his thigh.

He disengaged the heavy deadbolt lock using a standard lock pick set before raking the lock embedded in the standard doorknob below. Once he opened the door, they would have ninety seconds to move inside and disable the perimeter alarms at the control panel to prevent an alarm activation involving lights, sirens and police response.

Feeling the last pin about to click, he nodded to Lilly and Harper. "Got it."

He swung the heavy door open, revealing a dimly lit interior stairwell.

Led by Harper and Lilly, the team moved swiftly inside. Guided by the silvery glow of the moon seeping through a set of arched windows, they moved quickly and silently to the alarm panel in the corner of the vast space.

Kuznetsov closed the doors behind them, sealing off the outside world.

"Ninety seconds," Stahl announced.

Harper stared at the alarm panel. His eyes narrowed in assessment. With a confident grin, he declared, "A Securix Quantum Guard 500. Piece of cake."

He unslung his backpack and dropped it to the floor, nodding to Müller.

The first order of business was to disable the box's tamper alarms. Different systems utilized different tamper switches to prevent intrusion, such as pressure-sensitive buttons, magnetic sensors, or micro switches. The Quantum Guard employed a dual pressure-sensitive switch and microswitch system.

Once Müller picked the panel's lock—little more security than one would find on a standard filing cabinet—he held the panel door closed. Seconds counted.

Harper withdrew a DPE device from his jumpsuit pocket. In his skilled hands, he snaked the device between the panel door and the lip of the panel box, manipulating it into position. A second passed while the Digital Pressure Equalizer gauged the switch's calibration, calculating the proper amount of pressure needed to maintain the switch's integrity.

Holding the DPE in place, he fished out a leather-covered meter the size of a small cell phone from his backpack on the floor. One-handed, he manipulated the dial with his thumb, selecting the proper low-frequency electromagnetic field harmonic necessary to defeat the microswitch.

Lilly Xinru hovered nearby. Her attention focused on the unfolding operation.

Having done its work, the disruptor beeped quietly.

At the sound, Müller stepped away from the alarm panel. His work there was done.

Holding the DPE in place, Harper whispered to Lilly, "You're up."

Stahl said, "Sixty seconds."

Lilly swung the panel door open, revealing a tangle of wires and circuits. Her nimble fingers worked like a blur as she plugged the USB-C connector of a Stealth Decryption Interface (SDI) into an available port. Her fingers danced across the SDI keypad, entering information at a rapid pace. The LCD screen glowed red, displaying five numeric digits running in a blur, like a sped-up clock, sifting through tens, hundreds, thousands of combinations of passwords. Searching for one of just six passcodes programmed into the alarm system, the codes authorized to disarm it.

Stahl's voice cut through the tension. "Thirty seconds."

Lilly threw him an annoyed glance.

He, Kuznetsov, and Müller moved to a set of closed doors across the lobby. Harper remained by her side, prepared to assist.

With a mere three seconds to spare, the digital display froze on a number. With slender gloved fingers, she keyed the numbers into the panel. Holding her breath, Lilly waited until the alarm panel blinked from red to green.

"We're in," she whispered, exhaling in relief. Swiftly, she disconnected the SDI, and Mitch removed the DPE, resecuring the alarm panel door.

Prepared for the next step in their mission, Stahl and Kuznetsov stood by the interior doors. They'd donned black hoods and goggles. At the ready, they were armed with Russian AK-74s. Successors to the famed 47.

Müller, once again, skillfully used his lock-picking set to unlock the next physical barrier. Hearing the whisper of a click, he grinned.

Stahl nodded. "Open it."

Müller stepped back and pulled the door open.

Stahl and Kuznetsov rushed inside. Across the dimly lit corridor was a bank of wire-embedded glass windows. They framed an open door leading to the security office. Inside, a guard sat at a desk. His brow furrowed while examining a bank of computer screens before him. Another guard stood leaning over his seated companion. His finger pointed to a particular screen.

Though the team's illegal entry had successfully avoided setting off alarms, the disarming and rearming of the panel did create an entry notification on the computer board.

Not expecting any visitors, the guards were puzzling over the alarm system readout. Wondering who had arrived... and why.

The standing guard's gaze lifted from the display.

He was met with Kuznetsov's cold, calculating stare from behind his goggles. In an instant, a single muffled shot rang through the corridor. The bullet found its mark in the center of the standing guard's forehead.

He fell back and crumpled to the floor with barely a sound.

The hushed stillness carried an ominous certainty as the seated guard looked up. His fear etched in his features. Without hesitation, Stahl fired. The second shot struck the man in the forehead. The guard slumped unceremoniously out of his chair.

With practiced efficiency, the team took over the security office, making it their own.

Müller, Harper, and Kuznetsov grabbed the dead guards and dragged them to a back room, leaving trails of wet blood across the tiles in their wake. Lilly took her position at the computer console.

With paper napkins found on the desk, she wiped a spatter of blood from the screens. Her gaze took in the expansive array of monitors before her. The soft glow of the screens cast a gentle illumination on her delicate features.

The system was a sleek amalgamation of dark metal shelving, housing a multitude of controls and interfaces with blinking LED lights and display graphics. Each button and switch a gateway to the museum's sophisticated alarm and security infrastructure.

The bank of monitors provided a mosaic of information.

Lilly's skilled eyes darted across the grids, rapidly interpreting the data. A digital tapestry of information that she deciphered effortlessly. Various camera feeds captured different angles and perspectives within the museum. The high-resolution displays rendered the exhibits and corridors in vivid detail. Adjacent to the camera feeds, a series of grids displayed the surveillance network. GPS-tagged green blips denoted the locations and movements of the roving security patrols.

This allowed Lilly to call up various camera feeds and track them in real time.

"You're good here?" Stahl asked, a hand on the young Chinese girl's shoulder.

Her smile up at him read like a kid let loose in a candy store.

To the rest, Stahl said, "Comms in."

They each inserted small, black earpieces into their ears.

"Move out." Stahl took the lead. "There are six more armed guards on roving patrols. I want to be in and out without any confrontations."

While remaining in the security office, Lilly's mission was to keep tabs on the patrols and monitor the team's progress using the collection of camera feeds, alarm systems, and other elements of the security network. Within the confines of the National Museum, their continued success would not be without its challenges. In addition to the patrols, there were motion detectors, laser grids, sound, and proximity sensors demanding her meticulous attention and expertise to either deactivate or avoid—requiring split-second directions to the team as they progressed toward their ultimate goal.

"Ten minutes, and it'll all be over," Lilly whispered. A countdown for the critical moments ahead.

IN THE MAIN CORRIDOR of the National Museum, the team moved with calculated precision, listening to and heeding Lilly's directions over the comms as she worked to disable active and passive alarms, keeping one step ahead of their progress as they pressed deeper through the hallowed halls.

Moonlight filtered through arched windows. Their night vision goggles brightened the dimly lit expanse in a grainy, ethereal, monochromatic green glow. Stahl whispered directives, leading them through the museum's labyrinth.

He had the structure's floor plan imprinted in his mind. The location and layout of every room, every display, all down to the smallest detail. He should. He'd paid handsomely for the information, in money and in blood.

They passed various exhibit halls, ignoring the vast fortunes of valuable treasures contained within. Art and antiquities from bygone eras whose worth was beyond measure. Priceless. And while the weight of history hung in the air, to Stahl, that meant nothing. He was singularly focused on three very specific items.

From the security office, Lilly's voice crackled over the comms. "Be advised, there's a patrol currently on your floor. They are moving away from your present position."

Any errant sound in the hallow corridors would be enough to alert them. They would need to remain alert. Diligent. "The others?" Stahl asked.

"One team is in the break room in the basement." After a momentary pause, she said, "The other is on the top floor."

Stahl acknowledged her report with a tap of his comm. To the others, he said, "Almost there."

He advanced the team through a secondary corridor, past the Mesopotamian Gallery. Pale moonlight shone through large windows. Majestic arches cast ominous shadows on the polished floors. Every step brought them closer to their destination.

The Assyrian Hall—the coveted centerpiece of the soon-to-be re-opened museum.

They reached their target.

Stahl raised his hand.

He fisted a halt before a display sign and velvet rope ceremoniously barring access to a vast room filled with glass-encased artifacts. Art pieces hung on the walls. Antiquities representing the mythical gods of Aššur, Ištar and Šamaš, revered creatures such as Ušumgallu and Kur, and worshiped idols like the crescent of Sin sat on display pedestals. All treasures recovered over decades from the Royal Library of King Ashurbanipal.

"Lilly," Stahl said. "Guards?"

"Team one is still on break. Team two is completing their sweep of the top floor. Team three, closest to you, is in the southwest stairwell, descending to the next level down." She added, "You are clear."

"Stay on it," Stahl said. The urgency in his voice underscored the tension.

Many exhibit rooms had their own dual, redundant alarm system, separate from the central security network under Lilly's vigilant domain. These independent systems were equipped with a myriad of detectors—motion and heat sensors, laser eyes, proximity and contact points on the display cases. Pressure switches beneath objects weighing more than one kilogram, presenting them with a unique challenge.

Nico Müller and Mitch Harper shed their black coveralls.

Underneath, they wore skin-tight, silver-metallic suits lined with aerogel, an insulation material specifically designed to conceal body temperature and circumvent the heat detection alarms. They covered their heads with hoods, pulled silver booties over their shoes, and put on matching gloves.

They look like astronauts.

They then replaced their night vision goggles with infrared laser mapping ones with LiDAR technology. These would render the otherwise invisible light beams in the exhibit hall visible. A crisscross of bright lights against the white polished marble floors, aimed at odd and different angles, making it impossible for a human body to navigate.

From his backpack, Harper extracted two wearable Photo-Spectrum Disruptors. He handed one to Müller. They attached them to their suits. The PSDs were integrated with the suits' nanoscale sensors and calibrated to detect the wavelength, intensity, and trajectory of the laser lights. After a real-time analysis of the grid, the devices would project a counteractive photo-spectrum field and redirect the beams, letting Müller and Harper pass through the field undetected.

Another challenge was the motion detectors.

For that, Stahl pulled out a small object the size and shape of a large cigarette pack. Matte black, the device was called EchoShade. An ultrasound signal jammer designed—and stolen from—MAFAT, the Israeli Directorate of Defense Research and Development. Designed to emit a disruptive field of ultrasonic waves calibrated to the same frequency but at a slightly different phase. It would create a destructive interference, thus canceling out the alarm's sensors, rendering them blind.

Once activated, Harper and Müller advanced with confidence to the center of the room.

At the exhibit's entryway, Kuznetsov removed six duffle bags from his backpack and moved through the adjacent exhibit rooms. There, he began pilfering items from drawers. Using an old school glasscutter—the glass break sensors already defeated by the EchoShade—he cut through display cases and snatched up various stone and clay tablets, sculptures of winged human-headed bulls and serpent dragons, amulets, small plaques, cylinder seals, necklaces, earrings and bracelets. Bagging them all.

Harper and Müller had reached their final challenge.

A black onyx pedestal with a satin pillow under a glass display case. Centered on the pillow was an Assyrian Bronze Guardian statue. Ashur. A chief deity of the Assyrian pantheon. It stood a meter tall and weighed fifteen kilograms. Exquisitely crafted, the guardian held a massive, double-edged sword with large, majestic wings extending from the figure's back.

Carefully, Harper removed the glass case.

Müller gingerly inserted a flat, inflatable bladder made of graphene-enhanced polymers under the statue. Harper's hand poised over the artifact while Müller set and monitored the attached load scanner, nodding to Harper. The American gingerly pinched the head of the statue, carefully lifting it while Müller watched the sensor inflate the bladder in microsecond increments, precisely matching the weight being removed.

Harper pulled the statue clear. "Got it."

Müller let out a held breath.

Clear of the laser eyes and other active alarms, Stahl accepted the offered statue and held it with reverence. "Give Kuznetsov a hand. Take as much as we can carry, and let's go."

Harper and Müller removed their headgear and cumbersome gloves. They split up and moved through the remaining Neo-Assyrian Exhibit, aiding in the pilfering of dozens of additional items. More clay seals, pieces of artwork, jewelry, and statuettes. Anything they could quickly grab and shove into their bags. When the six duffel bags were filled, Stahl checked his watch.

"That's it. Let's move."

With the black bags lumpy and brimming, hanging heavily from their shoulders, they gathered at the entryway to the exhibit.

And froze.

Lilly's voice over their comms. "You have company."

"Where?" Stahl hissed.

"Elevators."

Stahl stared at the bank of elevators directly across the corridor from where they stood. "Damn."

An arriving elevator pinged.

Kuznetsov handed his two duffels to Harper and Müller and unslung his AK-74. He knelt, using the archway for cover. "Go."

Stahl watched the elevator doors part. The car's interior light knifed across the darkened corridor. No time for a plan B. No time to argue. "Five minutes," he instructed Kuznetsov in a hushed tone. "No more."

"Understood."

Stahl and the others slipped down the corridor, silent and unseen, swallowed by the darkness. Stahl paused. He glanced over his shoulder as two heavily armed security men dressed in black tactical gear stepped from the elevator.

They wore sidearms on their hips and carried American-made M4 rifles. They spoke amicably between themselves, unaware of Kuznetsov's presence as they began to sweep the area, checking various exhibits and displays, moving closer to where the Russian lay in wait.

His gun barrel aimed in their direction.

Stahl urged Müller and Harker to keep moving. He whispered into his comms to Lilly. "Rooftop. Five minutes. Then we're gone." It was also a reminder to his old friend Anton.

"On my way," Lilly replied.

The team hurried down the dimly lit corridor, putting distance between them and the threat of discovery.

KUZNETSOV STILLED HIS BREATHING as the guards came closer. His sights on the taller of the two. The men chatted in Arabic, unsuspecting. He had picked up a few phrases from his many combat postings over the years but little else.

Their conversation was just gossip and small talk.

Through his comms, Lilly said, "Bad news. Two more guards heading your way."

He heard the sound of a stairwell door opening.

The guards greeted each other. One pounded another on the back. Their voices got louder. Boisterous. Their conversation became more animated.

One guard glanced toward the Assyrian Exhibit. His jubilant expression faltered.

From the corner of his eye, Kuznetsov could see what caught his attention. The display where the bronze statue had stood. The glass cover on the floor. The inflated bladder still in place, highlighted in the pedestal's spotlight.

The guard said something to the others and stepped toward the exhibition entrance.

Kuznetsov fired.

His bullet pierced the man's eye, exploding it in a bloody spray of gore.

The others reacted with stunned inefficiency, ducking, darting away. Crying out, they scrambled for cover while trying to unshoulder their rifles.

Kuznetsov thumbed his weapon's selector switch, dashed around the arched entryway, and sprayed a round of fully automatic bullets. He caught one guard in the thigh. The man cried out and dropped to the floor. In Arabic, another guard shouted into his radio. Kuznetsov ran down the corridor, zigzagging away from a staccato of gunfire behind him as the guards got their act together.

THE SHARP CRACK OF gunfire shattered the tranquility of the quiet, dark museum. The shots boomed through the empty corridors. The need for stealth was gone. Stahl and his men broke into a run. They hit the door to a stairwell that led to the roof. Pushed through, sounding an audible alarm.

"Up! Up! Up!" Stahl shouted, covering their rear.

Harper hesitated at the doorway. A former U.S. Marine, if discredited and disavowed, he'd lived his whole adult life under the credo that you don't leave personnel behind, even as a mercenary. "We should go back. Help Kuznetsov."

Stahl pushed him upward. "He's capable. Move."

The team ascended the stairs quickly. As the lower door swung shut, the stairwell provided a brief respite from the chaos they left behind.

They burst onto the rooftop and were greeted by a blast of hot, gritty wind. The sparkling lights of Baghdad stretched out below them. Above, a clear night sky was ablaze with white twinkling stars on a black velvet backdrop.

Müller and Harper dropped their bags to their feet.

Harper looked around. Desperate. "What now? What?"

KUZNETSOV REACHED THE WEST end stairwell. He turned and squeezed off a short blast of automatic gunfire down the dark corridor, not caring if he hit anyone. He just needed to brush his pursuers back. He pushed through the stairwell door. He paused, looked around, wanting something to jam in the door handle. A wedge of some kind. Barricade the door, if only for a little while.

The sound of running feet and labored breathing from the stairs below caused him to swivel. He brought his weapon up to bear. His finger on the trigger twitched, only stopping a second before it was too late.

Li Xinru appeared, pointing a small Norinco NP-22 9mm handgun at him. Both her tiny fists wrapped around its grip. She breathed a sigh of relief.

"Behind me. Two guards. Coming up fast."

"Go." Kuznetsov pointed to the roof.

He abandoned his search for a wedge and followed Lilly up the stairs. They burst out onto the roof just as Müller was pointed to the east, shouting, "There."

Kuznetsov heard the soft chuff of the approaching Mil Mi-8 transport helicopter before he saw it. The rhythmic thumping of the helicopter rotors drew closer, cutting through the night air. The team's collective gaze shifted toward the soft, blinking running lights in the sky. Their eyes traced the silhouette of the matte black helicopter with no markings coming into view in the distance.

"We've got company!" Harper announced as the stairwell door slammed open.

Crouched by the door frame were two museum guards. Two more lay prone on the stairs. One stood several steps behind them. Low. Only his shoulders and head were visible to those on the roof.

The team scattered to the right and the left.

Lilly and Müller ducked behind an HVAC vent. Harper found a covered pile of bricks, an overturned wheel barrel, and other construction tools to hide behind. Kuznetsov dropped into a prone position on the roof. All parties opened fire.

Stahl crouched by the parapet, shouting at the helicopter, ordering them to ignore the gunfire, to come in and complete the extraction.

Amidst the ongoing firefight, Kuznetsov and Lilly provided cover, keeping the guards pinned down. The chopper approached, sleek and black, and hovered overhead. Its powerful rotor wash created a tempest of wind, kicking up a sandstorm of dust and debris.

When the chopper had reached a height of just one and a half meters off the roof, Stahl, Müller, and Harper tossed the loaded duffle bags through the open cabin door. Bullets pinged off the chopper. The pilot, visible through the cockpit, signaled for haste.

"Let's finish this," Harper declared with grim determination.

He leaped. From inside the cabin, he laid down a line of suppression fire, giving Müller a chance to hop aboard. Its powerful engines drowned out the staccato rhythm of gunfire as the team continued to brush the guards back.

With the stolen artifacts stowed, crouched by the chopper's struts, Stahl shouted, "Lilly, get aboard."

She broke cover and sprinted for the helicopter.

Kuznetsov fired from behind the air duct.

A guard yelped and fell back, tumbling down the stairs.

Müller and Harper pulled Lilly into the chopper, ensuring her safe escape.

"Go, Max! I'll cover you," Kuznetsov shouted.

"No," Stahl shouted back. "Together."

Inside the chopper, Harper and Müller fired at the stairwell, pinning down the remaining guards.

Harper shouted, "Get a move on!"

Kuznetsov ran for the chopper. He joined Stahl, waiting for him. Together, they dove for the open cabin door.

"GO! GO! GO!" Harper shouted, pulling Stahl and Kuznetsov inside.

The helicopter's engines roared, lifting them off the rooftop. It banked smoothly and ascended into the moonlit night sky.

From the open door, the team watched the guards emerge from the stairwell as the rooftop dropped away. Wind whipped at their jumpsuits, at Harper and Müller's silver spacesuits.

The defeated guards watched helplessly from below. Frustrated, they fired a spatter of useless gunfire as the chopper banked and faded into the night sky. Only the distant hum of the disappearing helicopter lingered in the air.

And a good old Texas whoop and holler from Harper.

CHAPTER ONE

Starrett-Lehigh Building
New York - Present Day

PARKER QUINN SAT AT her desk.

The New York City skyline filled the windows of her seventh-floor office at the Department of Homeland Security in the iconic Starrett-Lehigh building. A special agent assigned to DHS's Cultural Property, Art, and Antiquities program, her office was unlike most agents working for the government's law enforcement bureaus.

The floor-to-ceiling shelves behind her were carefully organized with reference books, artifacts, and history tomes: books of cultures ranging from Europe to Asia to the Middle East and even Native American lore. The walls were covered with meticulously labeled maps and other art. Minor artifacts and cultural knick-knacks filled every flat surface. Some were replicas, but others were actual works of renowned and cultural art.

In her late thirties, Parker had draped her suit jacket over the back of her chair and kicked off her shoes. Stretching and wiggling her toes brought her blissful relief. She wore her hair free and loose. A full mane of bouncy flaming red curls.

She cradled her phone between her cheek and shoulder.

A laptop computer in front of her. A wireless printer across the room spitting out papers. Her desk was laden with dozens of open case files. A testament to the backlog of the work they did.

Created in 2007, the DHS's Cultural Property, Art, and Antiquities program was a specialized operation tasked with the protection and preservation of cultural heritage, art, and antiquities. Their mandate was to investigate illicit trafficking and recover stolen or unlawfully removed artifacts, relics and objects. To accomplish this, they worked with law enforcement and intelligence agencies worldwide, with experts, scholars, and others in government and academia to document and authenticate the legitimacy of lost, stolen, and recovered cultural artifacts.

Exactly what she was attempting to do at the moment.

The focal point of her attention, amid a host of open files spread across her desk, was a photograph of the legendary Honjō Masamune sword, known as Japan's Perfect Sword. Lost to history after World War II. It was the most prominent item of a cache of recovered artifacts in a recent case she concluded on the Isles of Shoals, off the seacoast in New Hampshire.

Its timeless beauty was captured in the photograph. But that paled to seeing it, holding it in real life. Yet, she stared at the photo, remembering the feeling. Its weight. Its perfect balance in her hand.

On the other end of the phone was a representative of the *Nihon Bijutsu Token Hozon Kyokai*. Their name defined their purpose and goal: The Society for Preservation of Japanese Art Swords.

A knock on her open door caught her attention.

She looked up and waved. *Come in. Come in.*

Parker's immediate supervisor, Chaz Mazzarelli, head of the DHS's Cultural Arts program, entered with a smile. Wearing a business suit sans jacket, his white dress shirt was wrinkly and disheveled. His tie was yanked away from his throat. Worry lines permanently etched his otherwise youthful face. Over fifty-five, he could retire, but he had nothing to retire to… or for. Never married. No kids. Just a twenty-one-foot Sea Ray SPX 210 sport boat with a fishing package, he docked out at City Island in the Bronx.

A typically easy-going guy with a quiet demeanor and laid-back attitude, he dropped into the chair, facing her. He propped his foot on the edge of her desk and waited for her to finish her call.

Her expression was a mix of curiosity and interest at his sudden appearance. She concluded her conversation in Japanese.

"どうもありがとうございました。またお話しできるのを楽しみにしています。." She hung up. "Hey, boss. What's up?"

"Welcome back from the Granite State. How was it?"

"The commute home was a lot easier than from where you usually send me."

He leaned forward and took the photo from her. "The Honjō Masamune. Think it's the real deal?"

"That's what I'm trying to find out. That was NBTHK. They've assigned two experts to examine it. It will be a few days—and probably not without much disagreement—before we know for sure."

"Be a big feather in Uncle Sam's cap if we can return the real Perfect Sword to the Japanese people after all these years." He handed her back the photo. "How was it working with Grayson's two coasties? Bannon and McMurphy?"

"I had my trepidations going in. I won't lie."

"Their reputations precede them," Mazz said with a laugh. "A couple of hotshots, I heard."

"Whatever stories you heard tell about those boys," she said, "they probably don't come close to doing 'em justice."

"That would make them the stuff of legends."

Parker smiled, reflecting on her recent adventure with the Secretary's small, elite team from New Hampshire. "Yeah. They're good people. I'd be tickled pink to work with them again."

Mazz shrugged. "This business? You never know."

"Oh, I'm supposed to say howdy for an old friend of yours. Thaddeus Michael Perry."

Her boss grinned. "Thad! You ran into him? How is that old sea dog? Still running that broken-down tourist trap he calls a museum up there?"

Parker smiled. "In Kittery. He sure is. Though it's not much of a tourist destination."

"Ain't much of a museum either." Mazz laughed. "I need to take a trip up there one of these days. Drop in on that crusty old son-of-a-gun."

"He'd like that. Now, it's a mite early for you to be pestering me about my reports yet, so what's got you wandering down to my little hovel?"

The question shifted the mood in the office.

Suddenly, all business, Mazz sat forward. He waved a hand at her desk. "You'll need to delegate all this to someone else. I need you on something," he said. "Something way more important."

CHAPTER TWO

PARKER FRESHENED UP AND met Mazz at the large conference room usually reserved for big-wig pow-wows. She'd sprayed and fluffed her hair, dashed on a bit of deodorant, tucked in her blouse, and donned her jacket. Mazz had done the same—probably not the hair stuff—but looked spit and polished as he swung the door inward, ushering her inside.

Dominated by a polished mahogany table and bathed in subtle lighting, the conference room had eight leather chairs arranged four across either side of the table. The walls were covered with gray, sound-absorbing panels. The windows along the exterior wall provided a view of Eleventh Avenue below were tinted brown, and a twenty-by-ten-foot interactive display screen filled the front wall.

Seated at the table were two women and a man.

Parker knew the women.

The Secretary of the Department of Homeland Security, former Army General Elizabeth Grayson, stood up. A thin, handsome woman with gray hair, Grayson smiled. As head of DHS, Grayson was their ultimate boss, responsible for Customs, ICE, TSA, FEMA, the Secret Service and Coast Guard, among others. She reported directly to the President of the United States.

Parker had only actually met Grayson in person for the first time during the recently concluded Isles of Shoals investigation. "Good to see you again, Parker."

"You as well, ma'am."

"Sorry to throw you in the soup again so quickly, but it can't be helped."

"Whatever you need, ma'am. What's up?"

"First." Grayson indicated the other woman in the room. A Lebanese woman. Her skin was a warm olive tone, and her dark hair was done up in a sophisticated updo. Her navy pantsuit was well-tailored and complimented the solid pink blouse underneath. "You know Amal Haddad, President Kingsley's Chief of Staff."

"Of course."

They shook hands.

"And this is Special Agent James Reynolds of the FBI," Grayson said, continuing the introductions. A dark-haired man in his late fifties. Wearing a charcoal gray suit and red tie, he appeared trim, suntanned, and confident. He had sharp but world-weary blue eyes.

Mazz closed the door. "A long-time investigator with the Bureau, Agent Reynolds has made a career successfully closing complicated art crime investigations around the world. His first-hand knowledge and experience will come in handy regarding this case."

"Which is?" Parker asked as everyone pulled out chairs and sat.

"How much do you know about the National Museum of Iraq heist that took place in 2011?" Grayson asked.

"Only a little." Parker forced a smile. "I was a rookie at the time. Just cutting my teeth with cultural properties. As I recall, the museum had been ransacked and pilfered at the onset of the Second Gulf War in 2003. In the years during the occupation, the museum remained closed to the public but went about the business of renovating and rebuilding. As I understand it, in that time, they'd amassed a new collection, repaired many damaged pieces, and were in the process of re-opening at the time of the burglary in 2011."

Reynolds jumped in.

"All true. They were hit by a sophisticated group utilizing state-of-the-art tech. Dozens of items were stolen, primarily from the Neo-Assyrian Hall Exhibit. What would have been the center showpiece of the newly opened museum. Priceless artwork and artifacts which had been recovered from the Royal Library of Ashurbanipal. Items not lost to the looting and damage during the initial invasion, only to be stolen later. During this heist."

"Those responsible have never been caught," Mazz said.

Parker noticed the downcast look from Reynolds. Read his discomfort. Being here, rehashing a case he had failed to close, clearly ate at him. Maybe it was his white whale? All investigators had one.

"Why the sudden interest now?" she asked.

"We'll get to that in a moment." Grayson nodded to Reynolds to continue.

He manipulated a remote control in his hand.

The lights in the room dimmed, and the glass windows showcasing the panoramic view of Manhattan frosted over. The large screen on the front wall flickered to life, casting an ethereal bluish glow on the faces of those gathered around the table.

An image of an ancient cylinder seal appeared on the screen. Small and black. The artifact measured just two centimeters in height and diameter. Alongside the main photo, three more pictures appeared. Each showed a different side of the cylinder.

Reynolds clicked his remote, replacing the photos with a 3-D rendering of the seal. It rotated slowly, as if floating in space, the backdrop white.

A remarkable work of art and craftsmanship, Parker thought.

"This cylinder seal," Reynolds approached the screen, "is called the Guardian of Secrets. Made of hematite. A dense, iron-rich mineral often used due to its durability and, as you can see, its striking appearance."

The polished hematite gave it a lustrous, metallic sheen. A series of wedge-shaped impressions and intricate symbols were etched across its surface, likely carved into the stone with a stylus. Parker knew they often depicted mythological, religious or royal motifs.

"Seals were not just pieces of artistic work," Reynolds said. "They were practical tools used to make impressions in clay and other materials. These impressions were used to seal documents, containers, and objects, affirming their authenticity and protection."

Parker had a passing familiarity with the period and its history. She recognized the marks of the language, though she could interpret none of it. Written in Imperial Aramaic, the *lingua franca* of the Assyrian Empire after the mid-eighth century BC. And yet, something about the seal appeared… off.

Before she could question it, the image on the screen changed.

Now displayed was a cuneiform tablet.

A clay slab with a rough-edged V-shape chunk missing along the top edge. At first, a large singular image. Reynolds clicked, and two smaller pictures appeared alongside. The added visuals displayed the tablet's back and thickness.

According to the photos, it measured eighteen by nine centimeters. Its surface was covered with wedge-shaped impressions similar to those on the seal.

By no means an expert. Again, the script seemed off to Parker.

Some of the symbolic motifs seemingly depicting gods and mythical creatures and other shapes and patterns she could not readily identify. They were mixed in with the more conventional Assyrian cuneiform markings she was familiar with.

"The script," Parker said. "There's something not right about it."

"Good eye," Reynolds said. "This tablet is called the Chronicles of Kings. Our experts haven't been able to completely decipher it."

"Why not?"

"As you say, Agent Quinn. The script appears to be... corrupted by other influences."

"Other influences?" Grayson asked. "What does that mean?"

"Much of the text is not standard Imperial Aramaic. At least not what our experts associate with known Assyrian writing from the time, Madam Secretary," Reynolds said. "There's tremendous disagreement among those we've consulted on what these other writing symbols might be. Old Akkadian. Old Babylonian and Middle Assyrian."

"Ancient varieties based on geography and history," Parker said.

"Sure," Reynolds agreed. "But also Sumerian logograms, syllables, phonetic complements."

"Explain," Grayson said.

"Logograms are picture-based characters representing entire words while a phonetic symbol might disambiguate word characters with multiple meanings."

"I'll admit," Mazz said. "You just lost me."

"Certain symbols are used to further define a word or concept. Provide what we'd call context clues today," Reynolds said. "For example, the word 'bank' can mean both a financial institution and also the side of a river. So we might say or write river bank to better clarify for an audience."

"In mixed logographic-phonetic scripts," Parker said. "Like we see in Egyptian hieroglyphs, early Akkadian cuneiform, Japanese, and Mayan samples often spell out the first or last syllable of a word, or may instead abbreviate an adjective to modify the logogram."

Grayson pressed her fingers to the center of her forehead and closed her eyes. "Perhaps we've wandered too deeply into the weeds."

"The point being," Reynolds said. "As we've attempted to apply these other possible languages, incorporate known theories of language pairing and issues of dialect, regional differences, and other geographical influences, our translations come out like gobbledygook. Conflicting and meaningless."

Grayson waved her hand. "Bottom line it, Agent."

"Ma'am," Parker jumped in. "It would be like doing a jigsaw puzzle with similarly shaped pieces all the same size and colors, from dozens of different puzzles, all jumbled together."

"Without the picture on the box to go by," Reynolds added. "The combination possibilities are staggering. After all this time, what the tablet and seal say is still mostly conjecture. Mostly a mystery."

Grayson sighed. "Moving on. What do tablets of this type usually signify?"

"Typically, they tell a story," Reynolds said. "Of conquests. Or they record the annals of the empire. Often identifying the kings, the years they ruled or significant accomplishments. Sometimes, they're legal documents, religious texts, scientific, educational, or medical transcripts—"

Haddad held up her hand. "You said mostly a mystery. Expand on that?"

"Definitively, we know the items detail a particular period in the rule of King Ashurbanipal II. The last ruler of the Neo-Assyrian Empire, which ended in 609 BC. On that, we've gotten a majority consensus from the experts and scholars we've consulted. We do have some other ideas, more speculative, which we can get to in a moment."

He clicked the remote.

"Bringing us to our final item of interest."

On the screen, a bronze sculpture appeared. A meter tall. It represented a formidable and majestic figure with a powerful and muscular physique. Its face framed by a dignified beard. His gaze appeared resolute and unyielding. A guardian. The elaborate details of his attire were exquisite. His heavily layered robe was embellished with ornate patterns and textures. His breastplate was covered in delicately carved symbols. His forearms were encased in intricately detailed armlets, and armored greaves shielded his legs.

The statue exhibited some of the finest craftsmanship Parker had seen in a while. Most eye-catching, in one hand, he held a massive, double-edged sword and large, majestic wings extended from the guardian's back.

"Meet Ashur," Reynolds said. "A chief deity in the Assyrian pantheon. A symbol of strength, protection, and the enduring legacy of a once-mighty empire."

The screen changed again. This time, all three items were shown side by side.

Parker's eyes flitted across the images, absorbing every detail. The artifacts weren't merely objects. They were windows into humanity's past. A time over two thousand years ago.

Still, Parker wanted to know what was so special about these three items. "What's the significance of these, Agent Reynolds?"

"Of the items stolen in 2011—that we're aware of—all have resurfaced over the years. They've been tracked down, recovered, and returned to their rightful owners." Reynolds pointed at the screen. "Except for these three. Despite my... the FBI's best efforts, they remain at large."

Parker remained skeptical. There had to be more to it.

"We often find private, aka illegal, collectors or enthusiasts hold on to treasures they've pilfered rather than selling or re-selling them. Perhaps the point of the heist was to grab these items for a specific buyer. The rest of the stolen objects were used to mask that fact. Maybe sold for their monetary value. Often, the proceeds are used to finance the heist itself. Compensate the crew."

"A reasonable assumption," Reynolds said. "But we've come to believe these three pieces represent something more, which brings us back to some of our speculative theories regarding the tablet and seal. We know they cover a period during King Ashurbanipal's rule, likely related to the waning days of his reign of power. To give you a little background, he ascended to the throne in the 9th century BC. As ruler, he expanded the empire's territory through a series of military campaigns at a rate previously unseen. His tactics were ruthless and brutal, instilled fear among rival nations."

"I still don't understand the importance of—" Parker started.

The lights came up.

Haddad took charge of the remote as Reynolds sat down. "Before we go any further, there's something you need to be aware of, Agent Quinn. Recent intelligence sources have picked up chatter over the last several months. Credible intel suggests these items may represent more than just stolen and missing artifacts of historical significance. They may tie into an unknown yet impending terrorist plot."

"In what way?" Parker asked.

"Undetermined at this point," Grayson said.

"There is a long-standing practice to acquire and sell high-value art and relics on the black market to finance terrorist operations," Parker offered.

"We fear," Haddad said, "they're more instrumental than that. An integral part of some actual, larger terror event."

"What sort of event are we talking about?" Parker asked, pressing for details.

"That's unclear at this time," Grayson said. "Reportedly, an unidentified terrorist group is making plans for a major attack. One that, according to sources, would be more devastating than 9/11 or the *Tōhoku* earthquake and tsunami in Japan."

The casualties from 9/11 were well-documented, and Parker knew the death toll from that particular natural disaster in Japan was nearly twenty thousand people.

Parker sat back in her seat. "How could these artifacts play that kind of role?"

"Here's where the speculation comes in," Reynolds said. "On the tablet and seal, we've found several references to something called the Breath of Ashur. They appear fairly consistent throughout, along with other terms like 'forbidden knowledge' and a phrase meaning 'locked away.'"

"But you don't know what they mean? What they refer to?"

"No," Reynolds said.

"What we do know," Grayson said. "These same or similar phrases are coming across in the chatter we're picking up with increasing and disturbing frequency."

"As a link, that's… " Parker said. "Weak."

Grayson smiled, appreciating Parker's candor.

"Perhaps," Haddad said. "But the tone and increased frequency of all this is alarming. The President is taking the threat very seriously. He's determined not to have this level of terror event occur on his watch."

The room fell silent.

"Where do I come in?"

Grayson said, "We need you to find and recover these items. And, if possible, determine what potential threat they represent. This is an at-all-cost situation."

Parker looked over at Reynolds. He sat with his hands clasped on the table. Staring down at them. This entire brief and operation was a recrimination against him and the FBI. When the case had reached critical mass, it was being yanked away from him. His failure front and center.

Parker felt the eyes of everyone in the room on her.

Find artifacts that have been missing for over a decade and stop a potential terrorist attack that might be on a scale larger than the world had ever seen. Sure. No pressure. Feeling that weight suddenly thrust on her shoulders, Parker wanted to scream; *Why me?*

Instead, she said, "When and where do I start?"

Mazz slid a file across the table.

Parker stopped it with her hand.

Reynolds said, "That's everything our analytics department and experts—outsourced and otherwise—have on the artifacts." He slid a thick file of his own over to her. "This is everything my team and the FBI have gathered during

Operation: Baghdad Nights. Our investigation into the 2011 heist. All the details regarding the items we have recovered since. Where, from whom, etc."

Grayson slid a third file at her. "This is the compiled dossier from the DoD, NSA, and various worldwide intelligence agencies detailing all the chatter we've received. Their threat assessments, action plans... you get the idea. Needless to say, this is all top secret clearance stuff."

Parker said, "I don't have top-secret clearance."

In unison, Grayson and Haddad said, "You do now."

Mazz said, "Agent Reynolds can be a resource for you once you've reviewed the material in the files." He looked around the room. "With that, I think we're done here."

Grayson settled her gaze on Parker. "Good luck, Agent Quinn. We're counting on you."

CHAPTER THREE

Houston Hall Brew Pub
Houston Street, New York

PARKER QUINN SETTLED IN on a corner stool at her favorite bar. A cavernous, industrial-chic craft beer pub. It was happy hour at Houston Hall in the heart of the West Village. A hazy IPA in a glass mug in her hand. A platter of guacamole and chips with a side of salsa in front of her. The place was abuzz with people laughing and drinking and enjoying life. Blissfully unaware of the global dangers that simmered around them, capable of igniting in devastating ways at a moment's notice.

After the briefing, Mazz told her he'd taken the unusual step of putting a team together for her.

Parker had bristled at that. While she had no trouble working with others, hers had been a career of solitary contribution. Unencumbered by a team or even partners, she'd had the autonomy—the freedom—to come and go as needed, do what needed to be done without much oversight. This last part was especially true as her years of service working for Mazz had gained her tremendous leeway to run ops as she saw fit.

To his credit, he'd apologized for having done so but explained the threat level had escalated exponentially while she'd been on assignment in New Hampshire. There'd been no time for her to meet and vet a team.

She took a bite of guacamole and a sip of beer before she pulled her tablet from her backpack and signed in. "Time to see what Mazz's has saddled me with."

Before she could enter her passcode into the secure, encrypted DHS system, Agent James Reynolds settled into the stool next to her. She glanced over and scowled.

He ordered a Golden Lager. "Agent."

"Agent."

"Call me Jim."

She clicked off her pad and plopped it down on the bar beside the guacamole. "Why are you here?"

"To give you this." He handed her a thick, official-looking folder.

"Another file. Terrific." She unwound the string, opening it.

"It's everything we have on the persons we suspect— but could never prove—pulled the Iraqi museum heist back in 2011."

Parker extracted stacks of paper files.

Marked confidential, she quickly fanned through the included documents: investigative reports, photographic and forensic evidence analysis, correspondence between agents, and other legal documents such as court orders, search warrants, and subpoenas. Most of those were marked denied. Many of the documents were heavily redacted. Thick black lines obliterated the text.

"Well, spill the sweet tea, darling."

"Huh?"

"Don't make me read all this right now. Tell me."

Reynolds sipped his beer. "It's long been my feeling the person responsible for the heist is a man named Maximilian Stahl."

Parker wasn't familiar with the name, which surprised her. After a decade-plus in this game, she thought she knew most of the major players in the illicit art and antiquities world. Especially the high-end, high-tech talent a job like this would've required. Yet Stahl wasn't on her radar.

She said this to Reynolds.

"Because that's not Stahl's bailiwick per se," the agent told her. "Comes from a family with roots that go back to the Holy Roman Empire. Politically powerful and wealthy. For generations, the Stahl's have maintained a façade of respectability while playing a crucial role in East German intelligence gathering. During the Cold War, they worked closely with the Stasi and the Soviet KGB."

He scooped a guacamole-laden chip through the salsa and chewed.

"Sure. Have some." Her voice dripped with sarcasm.

"Thanks."

He wiped his mouth with a paper napkin. "In the early 2000s, according to my CIA sources, Max gained notoriety in the world of clandestine intelligence. While much of his early life is shrouded in mystery, his upbringing seems to be marked by strong discipline, strict training, an exceptional education in military strategy, cyber and psychological warfare, information manipulation."

"Trained to be a spy?" Parker said. "Some family business."

"Not just any spook. A master spy."

"For the East German government?" Parker asked, knowing the political landscape had shifted quite a bit since the bad old days of the Cold War.

"Reportedly, Stahl's loyalties are a bit more fluid than that." Reynolds dug into the guacamole until Parker moved the bowl away. "His ambitions appear to have expanded beyond his family's geo-political interests."

"He's become some kind of rogue agent?"

Reynolds shrugged. "Beats me. According to some." He pointed at the file. "That's as far as I got. Every piece of information I could get my hands on after begging, borrowing, and stealing from every known law enforcement and intelligence agency I could think of. FBI. CIA. INTERPOL. MI6. Iraq's NIS. The *Bundesnachrichtendienst*. Even Russia's Intelligence Directorate."

Parker arched a thin eyebrow. That would be the stolen part?"

Reynolds smiled and sipped his beer.

"Enlighten me. How'd Stahl get to be a boil on your bum? Your report says the security system was wiped clean. All CCTV recordings erased."

"More like fried." He looked wistfully at the bowl of guacamole. "Fore they left, they planted a virus bomb, programmed to wipe everything off the hard drives, the back-up and the redundant back-ups to the back-ups."

"Doesn't tell me what I asked."

"Back, about five years now. MI6 picked up a hacker. A Chinese nationalist doing a job for North Korea. The crown was very mum about the details. But, I learned they were holding this young girl in custody. Li Xinru. Went by Lilly. Not yet thirty, she saw her life heading down the tubes. She cut a deal. Spilled everything she knew about anything she'd ever done. According to my source, she admitted to being the hacker on the museum heist."

"She named Stahl?"

"Yup. And his number two. A Russian thug named Anton Kuznetsov. Along for the ride were two others, a German, Nico Müller, and an American mercenary named Mike Harper."

"Where's the merry band now?"

"Müller and Harper are dead. Less than a year after the heist. Müller in a car crash on the Autobahn. Harper in a military action in Libya. Part of the Arab Spring uprising."

"The other two?"

"They became ghosts. I spent time trying to track them down. Thought I got close a few times, but then… " He spread his hands. "Nada."

"And the girl?"

"That's interesting. Held and in custody, but MI6 lost her."

"Lost her? What was she to them, a puppy?"

He shrugged. "I've several theories. Shipped her off to some black site to pay for her crimes, maybe force her to use her talent for good. Put her in their equivalent of our WITSEC… "

"Or?" Parker prompted.

"She slipped away. Escaped. Only way I see that happening had to be with help."

Parker sipped her IPA. "Does any of that tell me what Stahl's interest in these artifacts is or how they are key to this supposed large terror threat?"

Reynolds frowned. "Nope. Like I said, Stahl and Kuznetsov became very elusive after the heist. Off the grid. A presence, according to CIA and INTERPOL, active, but much more behind the scenes. Now, you know as much about all this as I do. The rug's been yanked out from under me."

And why was that? Parker wanted to ask but didn't. Not yet. Keeping Reynolds talking was more important at the moment. She closed the file, ordered two more beers, and slid the guacamole back to him.

"What more can you tell me about these artifacts?"

"The bronze statue is Ashur," he said. "According to Assyrian mythology, he was born to the god Anshar and his consort, Kishar, the divine embodiment of the city that bore his name. Ashur became the patron deity of the Assyrian people. His birth marked a celestial alignment. A moment of cosmic significance that would foreshadow the rise of an empire.

"His influence extends beyond myth. In the mortal realm, the Assyrian Empire, guided by the divine might of Ashur, embarked on a series of conquests that would reshape the political landscape of the ancient Near East. Under the rule of powerful kings, the Assyrians sought to expand their dominion and establish Ashur as a deity worthy of reverence and fear."

"You sound like a university professor."

"I was. Before the FBI recruited me," Reynolds said.

"Ashur was often depicted as a warrior god, armed with a bow and arrow, symbolizing the might and military prowess of the Assyrian forces. The conquests led by the Assyrians were marked by strategic brilliance and a formidable military machine, believed to be inspired by the divine guidance of Ashur.

"Driven by that divine mandate, the Assyrian rulers acquired a thirst for territorial expansion, economic dominance, and the assertion of Assyrian supremacy. Cities fell, and as the Assyrian Empire reached its zenith, the worship of Ashur became deeply ingrained in the culture and daily life of the people. Temples dedicated to the god dotted the landscape, and the Assyrian kings proudly proclaimed their divine devotion to Ashur."

"That's all very interesting," Parker said. "And it really is, but it doesn't help me much."

Reynolds sipped his beer. "From what we've managed to ascertain from the artifacts in question, they're all connected to Ashurbanipal II. The final king and his story during the downfall of the Neo-Assyrian Empire in 609 BC."

"Go on."

"According to our deciphering of the tablets and the seal—and there is vast disagreement among the experts and scholars we've consulted—together, they tell a story—or part of a story—about the glorious military might and decisive victories and expansion under Ashurbanipal's rule."

"A return to the glory days? Jihad in the name of the Breath of Ashur?"

"True believers have rallied behind less," Reynolds said. "Inspiration can come from very strange places."

"Which brings us back to inspiration, not an actual bomb that goes boom."

Reynolds shrugged. "There might be more to what the tablet and seal say."

"Which we don't know because we can't translate it. Forbidden knowledge. And whatever's locked away." Parker gave that a moment's thought, eating and drinking before ordering more beer. When they came, she asked, "Why aren't you part of this anymore?"

"Ask your boss."

The political and bureaucratic infighting between federal law enforcement agencies was the stuff of legends, infamous and otherwise. Petty jealousy, competitiveness, one-upmanship, and back-stabbing were the norm in the hallowed halls of the U.S. government.

The Department of Homeland Security had been created specifically to eliminate that very dysfunction. An umbrella agency to ensure the lack of inter-agency cooperation and refusal to share data and intel never again adversely affected the United States. The way it had leading up to the attacks of 9/11.

In truth, the department's creation had only partially succeeded at that mandate.

Yet, Parker knew General Grayson. A seasoned and recognized military woman and politician who garnered respect from both political sides of the aisle. She typically wasn't the cause of such rifts and powerplays. Not usually one to freeze others out. Not unless she had a reason.

"What are you saying," Parker asked. "Without saying it?"

Reynolds shrugged. "I got told my team and me, we're out. Debrief you, turn over everything I had—which I've done—and we're out. Move on." He sipped his beer, adding. "All I know."

"Parker," the bartender said. "This came for you."

He handed her a sealed manila envelope.

Parker took it. "Came for me... how?"

"Back door. One of them bike courier guys. Asked if you were here. Said to give it to you."

"Thanks."

The bartender moved down the bar, taking drink orders from other patrons.

"You regularly get mail service here?"

"No."

There were no markings on the plain envelope save for her name. Written in heavy black marker across the front. Printed. She ripped through one edge of the envelope and extracted a single sheet of common, white, unlined copier paper.

"What is it? What's it say?"

She handed the paper to Reynolds.

On it were two groups of numbers. 410018.60 and 285828.79.

Reynolds gave her a quizzical look. The numbers meant nothing to him.

That wasn't the case for Parker. She checked her suspicions with an app on her phone. Even without the traditional marking of degrees, minutes, and seconds, she recognized the numbers for what they were. The app confirmed it.

"Latitude and longitude. They're coordinates."

"To where?"

"Hagia Sophia."

"Who's that?"

"Not a who," Parker said. "A what. And a where. A Greek Orthodox Christian Basilica built in 537 AD by Byzantine Emperor Justinian I. Since then, it's been a mosque, turned into a museum in 1935, then reconverted into a mosque again in 2020."

"Look who sounds like a university professor now."

Parker ignored him. "Built in the capital city at the time. Constantinople. Today—"

"Modern-day Istanbul," Reynolds said. "Turkey."

The note was signed:

EBON SPARROW

CHAPTER FOUR

Teterboro Airport
Teterboro, New Jersey

EARLY THE NEXT MORNING, on a remote airstrip at the far end of the airport, a black SUV pulled up to a solitary jet sitting on the runway. White with black and orange stripes, the Dassault Falcon 8X had a sleek and aerodynamic design with clean lines, large windows, and the iconic Falcon winglets.

Parker exited the rear of the SUV without acknowledging the chauffeur, who silently drove away. Dressed in a charcoal gray pantsuit, she carried a single carry-on suitcase and a laptop bag. Parker checked out the plane from behind oversized, dark sunglasses. Her mane of red hair framed her face, loose and free. It shimmered with gold highlights in the early morning sun cresting the eastern horizon.

Familiar with the Dassault Falcon line of aircraft, she knew the jet had an impressive range of sixty-four-hundred nautical miles and a max cruising speed of Mach zero-point-nine—six-hundred and ninety miles per hour—with a superior ability to navigate challenging airports and shorter runways.

The jet and its pilots were on loan from a defense contractor whose assignments usually involved ferrying CIA operatives around the world. General Grayson's range of influence never ceased to amaze Parker.

The pilot stood at the foot of the rolling airstairs. A lean, thin black man dressed in military boots, bloused black trousers and a black Marine Corps woolly pully sweater with reinforced shoulder and elbow patches. He wore black sunglasses and a Sig Sauer in an exposed shoulder holster.

"Jason or Jared?"

"Jared, ma'am." No last name was offered or asked for. "Ms. Rodriguez is on board. We're still waiting on the others."

He checked his watch, appearing annoyed.

"They won't be late for another ten minutes," Parker said.

No less annoyed, he gave her a tight smile. "On time is ten minutes late. Your bags, ma'am?"

"I can handle them, Jared. Thanks. And Parker works just fine."

"Yes, ma—Parker."

She smiled and headed up the stairs.

With its three-zone cabin layout, the jet had defined areas for work, relaxation, and a meeting space. Appointed with premium leather, fine wood veneers, and high-quality fabrics. The interior was spacious, comfortable and upscale.

Seated midway in the main cabin was a young woman Parker knew from her file photo to be Elena Rodriguez.

The young Latina with dusky skin sat staring at two laptops open on the table between a cluster of four plush leather chairs. Beside her was a battered black backpack with a bold red Oracle database management system logo stitched into it. A cluster of anime and manga keychains dangled from the zipper. Listening to noise-canceling headphones, Lena had short-cropped raven-black hair. By that, Parker meant chopped, like it had been cut with hedge trimmers. Yet, the style suited her. The twenty-six-year-old woman, who looked a decade younger than that, was the youngest of the three-person team Mazz had put together for the mission.

On loan to DHS, Lena was an academic with zero law enforcement or investigatory field experience.

"Ms. Rodriguez, I'm Parker Quinn."

No response.

Parker put her suitcase and laptop down. Louder, this time. "Ms. Rodriguez!"

The woman, startled, looked up. She whipped off the headphones and jumped to her feet. She wore funky-patterned leggings, a black and white plaid mini-skirt, and an oversized graphic Shakira t-shirt. The collar draped off one shoulder.

With only a trace of her native Mexican accent, she said, "Oh, Ms. Quinn. I'm sorry. I didn't hear... It's a pleasure to... meet you. I'm Lena, but you already know that. Sorry."

"It's fine, Lena. Call me Parker."

They exchanged handshakes over the low table.

"Please. Sit." Parker took the seat across from her while Lena snapped her laptops closed. For one so young, Parker had been impressed with the woman's resume and accomplishments.

"So, a Ph.D. in Linguistics from the University of California, Berkeley, and another from MIT in cryptography and linguistic studies. You attended the Sorbonne in Paris. Concentrated in their cultural studies program. Afterward, you explored advanced studies in deciphering ancient scripts at Cambridge in the U.K. You've been published in the *Journal of Cryptology, Computational Linguistics, Cryptologia*, and the *Magazine of Linguistic Inquiry.* Your work and peer-reviewed papers have garnered high praise—and some spirited debates—among the top echelon academics in the field."

Lena appeared uncomfortable and at a loss for words following the praise. "Yes, ma'am."

"That's all quite impressive," Parker said, "But, let me ask you, how did you come to be so prolific in linguistics and ancient language studies while coupling that with your expertise in computer science, programming and cryptographic algorithms? Those aren't fields often mastered together, especially at such a high level. What made you bridge these seemingly disparate disciplines?"

"I've always been good with language, picking them up easily. My mamá says I have a natural ear for them. But I also have a fascination with puzzles."

"Puzzles?"

"Yes. Whether in language or in code, they tell a story—sometimes hidden for centuries. Yet, we often lack the knowledge to interpret and translate those inscriptions, markings, symbols. Unable to decipher the stories they tell. Unsolved puzzles."

"Until you solve them," Parker said.

Lena smiled. "My work and experience in linguistics gave me some tools to interpret ancient symbols and forgotten scripts but fell frustratingly short, even as new 'old' languages are discovered. I found existing computer programming, devised algorithms, even those incorporating cutting-edge AI technology were... inadequate for the task."

"So you created your own?"

"Learning computer science helped me create models to analyze data, information, at a scale others hadn't achieved."

Parker leaned forward, intrigued. "You're saying you see language and code as two sides of the same coin?"

"In a way, yes," Lena said, warming up to the subject. "Language is the original code, after all. Every civilization left behind a trail of data encoded in its writing systems. Whether working with cuneiform tablets or modern encryption protocols, I'm essentially solving puzzles—deciphering the unknown, making it known."

Parker smiled. "Impressive. Sounds like you're just what we need—"

Raised voices from outside the plane drew Parker's attention. She glanced out the window.

On the tarmac below, she saw a heated exchange between Jared, his co-pilot, a Caucasian man she knew as Jason, and a large black man standing beside a motorcycle. The new arrival wore a leather motorcycle jacket, jeans, and a skull-and-crossbones black t-shirt. He held a black helmet under his arm. His hair was a dark scrim against his brown skin. An old Colt 1911 .45 autoloader holstered on his hip.

This had to be Captain Jacques "Jack" Jackson.

To Lena, Parker said, "Excuse me." At the top of the airstairs, she stared down at the three men. "What is the problem, gentlemen?"

Jared and Jason were a formidable-looking duo. Faced against Jackson, who stood defiantly beside the motorcycle, the veteran Army man showed no sign of backing down. Visibly frustrated, the pilots turn their attention to Parker.

"This guy wants to put his motorcycle on the plane," Jared said. "We can't accommodate that."

Jackson pointed at the pilots. "They're being ridiculous! Warhorse goes with me on every mission. Who charters a jet that can't—"

"What kind of joker names his damn motorcycle?" Jason asked.

"We've got weight restrictions. It's a safety concern," Jared insisted.

"Don't try to pee on my leg and tell me it's raining, gentlemen," Parker said with authority. "The jet accommodates twelve passengers. You've got four. The weight's not an issue."

"Fine." Jared sighed. "Carrying it isn't the problem, ma'am. Storing it is. Won't exactly fit in the overhead luggage bins."

"Plus, we've no way to load it," Jason added. "There's no cargo ramp or room to store the damn thing."

To Jackson, she said, "It's mission essential?"

"I'd tell you, but I ain't been briefed on the mission yet, so no clue. But either Warhorse is on that plane, or I'm not."

Parker narrowed her gaze, sizing the man up. "The bike gets loaded. Figure it out. Captain Jackson, up here. Now."

Victorious, Jackson smiled. "Yes, ma'am."

He grabbed a black duffle from the bike's luggage rack as the pilots exchanged seething glances. Jackson ascended the airstairs, removing his sunglasses and wearing a smirk.

"A 2019 BMW *Gelände/Straße*," she said. Translated from the German, it meant 'Off-Road/Road.' A rugged and versatile adventure-touring motorcycle. Known for its off-road capabilities and long-distance comfort.

"You know your bikes," Jackson said, impressed.

"As a young lass growing up, I rode a little." Then, under her breath and with an icy stare, Parker said, "Wipe that smile off your face, Captain. This had better not be the kind of shenanigans I'll need to deal with going forward."

"I'm all in on everything I do, Agent Quinn. I do what is and will be best for the mission without a second thought about how it makes you feel. This is what you get, Quinn. Don't like it? Talk to Mazzarelli before we're wheels up. Otherwise, yeah, you're stuck with me."

With an unwavering air of arrogance and a head taller than Parker, Jackson stared her down. She read in his green eyes a look, not challenging her authority but assessing her ability to suss out character and worth, to weigh the value of an asset and manage it without necessarily controlling it.

Like the others, she'd read his file the night before. Studied it. Studied them all.

A former Army Green Beret who saw extensive fighting in the Middle East. Jackson's confident stare exhibited the quiet strength and command of a man comfortable with himself and what he had to offer. Lines etched around his eyes were more than wrinkles in his weathered face. They told the tale of a four-tour combat veteran whose whole adult life was spent in unforgiving landscapes and on countless dangerous missions.

A seasoned warrior born from a lineage of military honor. He'd inherited not just his father's name but also the legacy of a decorated U.S. Marine. An upbringing in a military family shaped him into a man steeped in discipline, duty, and sacrifice, according to his file and psych-eval.

Parker could sense those values in the measured cadence of his movements.

Beyond the stoic exterior, Jackson's file revealed a combat strategist par excellence. A man who could—and had—navigated the intricacies of action and danger with the finesse of a field-tested commander.

Parker's thoughts were interrupted by the roar of a high-performance vehicle racing across the tarmac toward the plane. A sleek, silver Jaguar I-PACE SUV. The bold front grille—with its signature J-blade LED headlights—and flush door handles were unique features contributing to the vehicle's aesthetic. With a low, wide carriage, the Jag projected a sense of agility and performance. The roofline sloped gently toward the rear, giving it a sporty and stylish appeal.

With a swerve and locking brakes, the Jag fishtailed dramatically to a stop two feet from Jack's *Gelände/Straße* and the two CIA-hired pilots, still trying to dope out how to get the motorcycle on board.

Jared pointed at the car. "Uh-uh. No way. That is *not* coming on board."

The Jag's engine cut off, and the doors on either side opened. A tall man with slicked-back black hair and a pencil-thin mustache, wearing a rather dapper black tuxedo, stepped from the driver's side. From the passenger side emerged a statuesque woman with dusky skin, long, straight black hair, and a runway model's exotic Asian features. She wore a long, flowing, white, shimmering dress with a plunging neckline. A slit up to her hip revealed a toned and shapely dark leg.

"Who's the James Bond wannabe?" Jackson asked.

He reminded Parker of a young David Niven but said, "Sebastian Davenport. MI6."

Jackson harrumphed, clearly unimpressed, and ducked into the plane.

Davenport met the woman at the front of the Jag, kissed her passionately, then proceeded to the trunk. He retrieved a large, black duffle and two over-the-shoulder computer bags. After another prolonged kiss, the woman slipped behind the wheel of the Jag. She drove off in an even more reckless manner and at a higher rate of speed than had Davenport.

At nearly forty, Davenport had fifteen years in with MI6. Recruited from the British Army SAS, where he'd attained the rank of Major and served as a squadron commander for five years. Exemplary didn't begin to do his military record justice. Late in the Iraqi War, he worked alongside American Delta Force and SEAL Team 6 as part of Task Force Knight, conducting operations in Baghdad, Basra, and other areas. He'd led special reconnaissance and direct action missions in Afghanistan against Taliban strongholds. He won numerous awards and citations, including the Victoria Cross, a Distinguished Service Order, a Queen's Gallantry Medal, and even a US Legion of Merit and Bronze Star for his contributions and exceptional service in joint operations with US special forces.

Born into a well-to-do family from London, Davenport was reportedly fluent in French, Spanish, Arabic and Mandarin. He'd excelled in academics and extracurricular activities during his university years before joining the British Army. He graduated from Oxford University with top honors in international relations and criminal psychology.

He'd progressed rapidly through the ranks of MI6 to field officer, with a recognized specialty in counter-terrorism, counterintelligence, and cyber operations. His rapid ascent through the ranks was attributed to his ability to blend in with high society, where he utilized his flamboyant personality and charisma. Reportedly, he had elite combat skills and a capacity to analyze situations quickly, make split-second decisions, and successfully close complex global cases that others could not.

The man had played crucial roles in several high-profile operations. Significant missions that involved uncovering a clandestine Chinese research facility developing dangerous AI-powered cyberweapons, infiltrating a Monaco black-market art auction, dismantling their smuggling ring responsible for funding dozens of terrorist cells, and extracting a North Korean defector with detailed information about a planned cyber-attack targeting the London Stock Exchange.

At his age and exceptional experience, having yet to achieve station chief or even team leader status, Parker wondered if the man's elaborate lifestyle, his reported penchant for a high-profile, jet-setting habits had held him back professionally. Perhaps rising questions of conflicted interests or even compromise.

Davenport had been spotted at exclusive, invitation-only events at posh locations around the world—glamorous galas in Monte Carlo, private soirées in Ibiza, and high-stakes poker nights in Monaco, often mingling with influencers, business moguls, and fellow intelligence operatives. His nightlife shenanigans reportedly involved frequenting chic rooftop bars, dancing at upscale nightclubs into the wee hours of the morning, and attending exclusive underground parties at clandestine after-hours locales.

Often not work-related, according to his file and discipline history.

The opposite of low-key. Something Parker would've thought of as being of vital importance for a spy. Davenport ascended the airstairs. "You must be Agent Quinn. It is lovely to make your acquaintance."

He put his hand out. Parker clasped it to shake, but the Brit brought it to his face to kiss.

Parker pulled back sharply.

"The others are in the cabin. Settle in." Her voice frosty. She raised it, calling out to Jason and Jared. "We're wheels up in ten, gentlemen."

The two pilots glared at her, still puzzling over how to get the damn motorcycle onto the damn plane.

CHAPTER FIVE

Dassault Falcon 8X
Somewhere over the North Atlantic Ocean

THE LUXURIOUS STATE ROOM of the Falcon 8X conveyed a quiet air of expense and elegance. The subtle hum of the jet's engines permeated the space decked out with delicate wood veneers and plush leather seats so soft they cradled the occupants in comfort. A large oval table in the center of the room filled the space with just enough room to accommodate a rich, dark brown leather sofa under the row of windows.

On the table were three file folders. All marked classified. Each contained mission-critical information.

Parker Quinn stood at the head of the table as her team filed in.

Lena Rodriguez sat to Parker's left. She set up a laptop in front of her. Now wearing dark-rimmed glasses, she slurped from a paper straw stuck in an energy drink can.

Jackson had changed into a pair of dark slacks, a light blue turtleneck shirt, and a summer-weight jacket that didn't conceal his Colt .45 autoloader as well as he probably thought. He took the seat to Parker's right.

Sebastian Davenport remained in his tuxedo. He had removed his bow tie and opened his top collar button. He grabbed one of the files from the table and plopped onto the rich leather sofa. Stretching out his legs, he kicked off his thousand-dollar shoes and casually flipped open the file folder.

His air of nonchalance annoyed Parker almost as much as his pencil-thin, Clark Gable mustache. She made the introductions.

"Let's get started," she said. "I know you've all been plucked from your lives at the last minute and haven't yet had a detailed mission brief. That changes now."

She clicked a remote.

The plane's window shades lowered, and the lights went out. On the screen behind her appeared pictures of the three lost Assyrian artifacts. The cylinder seal. The cracked cuneiform tablet. And the bronze sculpture.

These were the same slides Reynolds had presented to her less than twenty-four hours earlier.

Parker pointed at them one at a time.

"The Guardian of Secrets. The Chronicle of Kings. And the Bronze sculpture of Ashur. A deity of the god Anshar and his consort, Kishar. Over twenty-six-hundred years old, these artifacts were originally recovered from the Royal Library of Ashurbanipal in the capital city of Nineveh, near present-day Mosul in Northern Iraq. Part of an Assyrian Empire collection in the National Museum of Iraq in Baghdad. They were stolen, along with dozens of other priceless artifacts, before the museum's scheduled re-opening in 2011. Information detailing that heist is in your packets."

Parker continued. "Our mission is clear—locate and retrieve these three stolen artifacts, and if possible, identify those responsible for stealing them."

"Why are we interested in these old trinkets?" Jackson asked. "Now? After all these years."

"They are hardly trinkets, Captain," Parker said. "The theft of these important and priceless items denies Iraq and the world the significant historical and cultural importance they represent. But to answer your question, over the past decade, the FBI has had a team dedicated to recovering all the items stolen that night in 2011. All of them have been recovered or at least accounted for, except for these three pieces. They remain at large."

Jackson scoffed. "That can't be the only reason." He looked at the others. "I don't know about y'all, but I got pulled out of a pretty extensive op to be here."

"GI Jack is right," Davenport said. "My superiors acted like the world was on fire cause of this. There's got to be more."

"There is," Parker admitted. "Recently obtained intel, chatter, indicates these three artifacts play an important part in a potential terror threat."

"What sort of threat?" Lena asked.

"We don't know, specifically. Only that the threat is credible, potentially large scale, and possibly imminent."

"Sounds like a lot of potentials and possibles to me."

Davenport's unimpressed demeanor irked Parker. "This is coming straight from the Oval Office *and* from 10 Downing Street, Agent Davenport."

Jackson shrugged. "Orders are orders." He looked around the conference room, listening to the low vibrating hum of the plane's engines. "Better accommodations than I get on most of my assignments, I'll grant you that."

Lena bounced in her chair like a school-aged girl going on a field trip. "It's all very exciting to me."

"Might as well get on with it," Davenport said, sounding bored.

Parker put a new slide up on the screen.

It was a photo of the note slipped to her at Houston Hall in New York. The longitude and latitude coordinates. And the name... EBON SPARROW.

"This note was delivered to me anonymously just hours after I was briefed about this assignment. The timing of that can't be a coincidence. The numbers. They're—"

"Coordinates," Jackson said. "A set of longitude and latitude—"

"The Hagia Sophia. It means Holy Wisdom," Lena said, staring at her open laptop. Its bluish glow bathed her grinning face. The young woman's fingers danced across the keys of her computer as a detailed map of the Hagia Sophia and an aerial view of its surroundings popped up on the screen.

Parker stared at the image, open-mouthed. It wasn't one of hers. "Did you just hack my computer? The DHS's top-notch, cutting edge, NSA-encrypted government software?"

Sheepishly, Lena squirmed. "Sorry?"

Parker did her best to withhold her smile. Impressed didn't begin to cover how she felt. Mazz had chosen well with this one, she thought.

"It's a UNESCO World Heritage site now," Lena said, refocusing the conversation. "A museum recently reclaimed as a mosque. What's there?"

"Ebon Sparrow. Obviously," Davenport said. "Whatever or whoever that is."

"Sounds like a codename made up by someone who's read too many spy novels." Jackson offered.

"Or," Davenport said, "someone who's into birdwatching."

"My thoughts exactly," Parker said. "Not the birdwatching part. Ebon often means or refers to black, but there's no specific references to sparrows of any significance in Middle Eastern religions or cultures. Nothing came back as being meaningful from the intelligence community."

She glanced at Lena, silently suggesting maybe she could find something.

Lena typed the name into her computer.

"Regardless," Parker went on, "I believe this Ebon Sparrow holds crucial information about these artifacts. The coincidence of getting the message is too... coincidental to ignore. Our first objective is to get to the Hagia Sophia. Determine who or what Ebon Sparrow can offer us. Follow the threads from there."

Parker switched off the screen. "In the meantime, we are six hours out. Lena, I need you to start examining the Guardian of Secrets seal and the Chronicle of Kings tablet. After nearly a decade, the FBI's best experts haven't been able to decipher them in any meaningful way. In your packet is everything they've pieced together, with a list of the outside academics and scholars they've consulted with. Contact whoever you think can help you figure out what they've missed. I'm relying on your unique combination of linguistic and cryptography skills to get those things properly translated. I believe that's mission critical to identifying what's so important about them, and maybe, stopping whatever terror threat they're supposedly a part of."

"Yes, ma'am."

"It's Parker. All of you. I hear one more ma'am out of any of you. You're off this plane—before we land."

Lena grinned. "Understood."

"Agent Davenport," Parker said. "Agent Reynolds says they've identified a man named Maximilian Stahl, believed to be behind the Baghdad Museum heist. The FBI worked it pretty hard but couldn't link him in a way that would support warrants or international cooperation. All their reports are included in your packet. One avenue to pursue will be checking out the various art dealers, auction houses, and private collectors who received the other items stolen that night. That should lead you to—"

"I know how to do my job," Davenport said. Adding, "Parker."

"And I'm saying the Bureau did a pretty thorough job. You'll have to dig deeper. A lot deeper. Be better than they were."

"That's why I'm here. I am better than they are."

Parker narrowed her gaze. "Then prove it. I want to know everything about this man, Maximilian Stahl. Who he is? What's his interest in Assyrian artifacts? What's his involvement, then and now? Where is he eating dinner tonight? Dazzle me with your brilliance, mister-I'm-better-than-they-are."

Davenport snapped to his feet. He slapped the file against his leg and stalked from the room, muttering something that sounded like witch.

Parker gave him a tight smile.

Lena closed her laptop and smiled, uncomfortable. "I'd like to work in the cabin… if that's okay?"

"Of course. Wherever you're most comfortable. Let me know if you need anything."

When she was gone, Jackson leveled Parker with a stare. "Well, he's some piece of work, ain't he?"

"We're not here to gossip, Captain. He'll do his job. From what I've read in his file, he's pretty good at it. That's all that matters."

Jackson raised his hands, palms out, surrendering. "Just saying. What about me, boss? If it's alright to call you that?"

Parker considered the man's exceptional military record, the list of medals he'd won during his three campaigns in the sandbox. The group's muscle and combat strategist.

She smiled. "Get some rest, Captain. Since you're here to keep me out of trouble, I suspect you'll have your hands full soon enough."

Jackson harrumphed. "Well, that'll be a switch 'cause usually, I'm the go-to guy for getting everyone *into* trouble."

Parker smiled warmly. "I got that sense, darling. We touch down in Turkey in six hours. Be ready to go then."

CHAPTER SIX

Sabiha Gökçen International Airport
Istanbul, Turkey

ALMOST TO THE MINUTE, six hours later, the Falcon 8X landed on a remote runway at nineteen-fifteen local time. The team deplaned and stretched while Jason and Jared, using a pulley system they'd rigged up, lowered Warhorse down the airstairs under Jackson's watchful eye.

Like late summer weather in New York, the heavy, humid air hung over them like an oppressive wet blanket. The sun dipped low in the sky. Its fading rays painted the horizon in pink, orange, and purple hues. Brilliant colors seamlessly merged into the evening sky's deepening blue. Heat waves shimmered off the concrete surface, distorting the view of hangars and taxiing aircraft in the distance. The hum of a plane taking off or landing reached them.

"Did you know Sabiha Gökçen was the first female combat pilot in Turkey?" Parker asked Jackson. "The first ever female fighter pilot in the world."

"I'll try to remember that for the next military trivia night with the boys back at base," Jackson said. "Riveting times."

Smiling, Parker shook her head.

To Davenport and Lena, she said, "You two remain here and continue your work. Captain Jackson and I'll go to the Hagia Sophia. See what we can find out about this Ebon Sparrow. Once we know what we're dealing with, we'll see where that leads us next."

She read the disappointment in their faces.

"Don't worry, kids. I'm sure there'll be plenty of chances for you two to be more involved before we're done."

With Warhorse safely on the ground and disengaged from the ad hoc pulley system, Jackson handed Parker a black helmet. She slipped it on and quickly jumped onto the motorcycle.

In the driver's seat.

With a twist of the key, she started it up and revved the engine.

Jackson stared at her, his helmet still in his hands. "I... um... no one drives Warhorse... but me."

"You snooze, you lose, Captain. Coming?" Parker grinned before snapping her visor down. "Times a fleeing."

Jackson shook his head but put on his helmet and climbed on behind her. He hesitantly put his hands on her hips.

Parker gunned the engine and popped the clutch. They sped off across the tarmac, her flaming red hair billowing from under her helmet. They neared the gate. Over the throaty roar of the machine, Parker hollered.

"Whoo-hoo!"

PARKER BLASTED THROUGH THE tight city streets. She leaned left and right, zoomed into and out of traffic, ignoring a series of angry horn blasts. She felt Jackson's grip on her waist tighten as they zipped between cars, weaving left then right. Her head down and smiling behind the helmet's tinted face shield.

Jackson shouted over the wind and engine noise, "Where'd you learn to ride like this?"

"Oklahoma. Since I was knee-high to a hen. Dirt bikes to start with. Off-roading with ATVs before turning to street racing."

"Misspent youth."

"You have no idea, honey."

The streets of Istanbul were alive with a vibrant energy. The cityscape blurred past. The warm hues of the setting sun cast long shadows, accentuating the architectural beauty of the buildings that blended its robust history with modern architecture. Vehicles rushed through the crowded streets, emitting the occasional beep beeps of car horns. Pedestrians milled about in the twilight. The city sounds were a symphony of rushing traffic, distant calls to prayer, and the lively chatter of locals and tourists, creating a vibrant tapestry of cultures and languages.

Narrow cobblestone streets wound through the older parts of the city, lined with shops selling spices, textiles, and intricate rugs. The aroma of traditional Turkish delights wafted through the air from street vendor carts and stalls.

As night approached, colorful lanterns illuminated the streets, adding a magical nuance to their surroundings.

The Hagia Sophia loomed in the distance. Illuminated by soft lights showcasing its majestic domes and intricate architecture, they cast an ethereal glow upon the iconic structure. The impressive mosque appeared even more remarkable as darkness fell.

"Got any thoughts about our mysterious Ebon Sparrow?"

"Arriving in one piece to find out would be nice," Jackson said.

Parker zipped around two slowing vehicles, making left-hand turns. She laughed. "Fair enough."

She slowed and found a place to park Warhorse along a tree-lined sidewalk near a park. They put their helmets on the seats. Smiling, she said, "She's a sweet ride."

"She is."

They joined a streaming queue of people converging toward the ancient monument. Tourists from around the world, their faces filled with awe, snapped photos and marveled at the grandeur of the historic site.

"So, Jacques. Not a name I'd expect from a Gen Y African-American—"

"Black," he said. "Got no use for that PC crap. And it ain't accurate."

Parker nodded. "Black kid from Harlem."

"Moms was French, from Argenteuil," Jackson said. "Small town outside Paris. Pops' is from the south, third generation. The family's originally from Barbados. Hooked up with my moms when he was assigned to Fort Hamilton for a year. After 9/11, we were everywhere. Settled in Harlem when he retired."

Parker and Jackson blended seamlessly with the diverse crowd, swept along until they reached the steps to the entrance. Parker tensed as they ascended the old steps. "Got a bad feeling about all this yet?"

"I'm paid to have a bad feeling about everything," Jackson said.

It was near closing time as they stepped inside the Hagia Sophia. A wave of cool air enveloped them, carrying the scent of burning incense. The remnants of daylight, filtered through the ancient stained-glass windows, painted kaleidoscopic patterns on the worn stone floor.

They wandered through the main chamber.

Originally built as an Eastern Orthodox cathedral in the Byzantine Empire, the Hagia Sophia was converted into a mosque during the Ottoman period. Eventually transformed into a museum in 1935, it was reconverted into a mosque again several years ago. A popular destination for tourists interested in both the Byzantine and Ottoman periods of history.

One of the most iconic features of the Hagia Sophia is its massive dome.

Constructed in the 6th century, the dome is supported by pendentives, triangular sections that allow for the transition from a square base to a circular dome. An **architectural marvel at the time.** Intricate mosaics adorn the interior of the Hagia Sophia, depicting various religious scenes. **Each tile telling a story of empires that had risen and fallen,** including representations of Christ, the Virgin Mary, and other saints. Written in Ottoman calligraphy, large medallions with verses from the Quran were displayed on the walls.

The day's last visitors dispersed, leaving the monument in near silence. The echo of their footsteps resounded beneath the colossal dome. The vast interior took on an intimate, almost sacred ambiance. The hues of gold and azure streaming across the interior imbued the space with a sense of wonder in the fading natural light.

"Impressive, isn't it?"

"Yeah. I guess," Jackson said, looking around. "I wasn't ever much for all this old stuff. But I do get a sense of my own... insignificance."

"Fear not, Captain. I believe history will judge your contributions with the proper amount of reverence."

Jackson harrumphed. "Your lips to God's ear or something like that. How are we going to know what this Ebon Sparrow is?"

"I'm hoping we'll know it when we see it."

"Like pornography?"

Parker laughed. "Let's hope not."

As the crowd dissipated, Parker and Jackson continued their exploration. Absorbing the historical tapestry—a testament to the Hagia Sophia's rich and diverse past, Parker felt herself getting swept up in all the wonderment surrounding her. She tried to push past all that, needing to focus on the mission, on what Ebon Sparrow might be.

Parker studied reliefs and other carvings, looking for birds depicted throughout various pieces. She found falcons perched high atop pillars carved from precious marble... Eagles soaring over domes made of bronze... Even butterflies flitting amongst flowers...

Doing the same, Jackson said, "No sparrows that I can see. Black or otherwise."

"Excuse me." An elderly man emerged from a back room. He wore a robe and turban. His beard was streaked with gray. His slippers whispered across the floor. Approaching them, he stopped and held his hands clasped before him. "We'll be closed to the public momentarily. I don't mean to seem rude—"

"Yes," Parker said. "We'll be on our way shortly."

The man bowed his head. He started to move away.

"Excuse me," Parker said. "You're the imam, are you not?"

"I am. Yes."

"Imam. Does the term Ebon Sparrow mean anything to you?"

He paused. Parker swore she saw his lips curl into the slightest of smiles. He held an arm out, guiding them toward the back where he'd emerged from the shadows. "I believe you'll find that which you seek this way."

The imam led them to an area cordoned off by a velvet rope. He moved the stanchion aside. Beyond it lay a stone staircase. He nodded toward it.

Parker and Jackson exchanged glances. Both feared a trap. She tilted her head toward the staircase, arching an eyebrow.

Frowning, Jackson said, "Why we're here." Clearly, not thrilled.

They descended the stone stairs, spiraling downward into the depths of the Hagia Sophia. The air around them shifted. Got cooler and dank. Their footsteps echoed with a soft, haunting resonance.

Parker's apprehension grew when she realized the imam was not accompanying them. The hairs on the back of her neck bristled. She tried to read Jackson's body language. Checking to see if his concern had intensified as well. His entire demeanor had changed. He'd stiffened. His body had become tense, coiled.

It's his job to be worried, she thought. Trying to reassure herself they weren't plunging headlong into danger.

"Do you... hear something?" he asked.

"Music." So soft. Barely heard.

They continued their descent. The candles in sconces along the wall flickered, casting elongated shadows on the stone walls and across the shadowy steps the deeper they went.

At the bottom of the stairs, the haunting melody persisted, getting louder. Following it, they were guided through a labyrinthine of corridors.

The lower levels revealed a hidden world—a network of chambers filled with ancient relics and old manuscripts. Artwork and antiquities. The air became heavy with the scent of aged parchment and the mustiness of forgotten history.

The music led them to a massive wooden door. The haunting melody flowed from the other side.

Parker slowly eased the door open, revealing a dimly lit chamber.

They stood on the threshold of a clandestine sanctum. As was true throughout the mosque, intricate patterns adorned the walls. A black hooded figure in the center of the room was hunched over an ancient instrument.

As they entered, the musician continued to play.

Parker recognized it as a duduk. A double-reed woodwind instrument that produced a haunting and soulful sound. Its origins traced back centuries with ties to the Armenian culture and others.

Softly, Parker said, "Ebon Sparrow. We got your message."

The musician paused, acknowledging their presence.

In the silence, the figure turned, pulling back a headscarf. A woman. She had black hair tied in a long ponytail. Her complexion suggested either Middle-Eastern or Mediterranean heritage. She was quite beautiful.

"I am Isabella Arroyo. It pleases me you made it, Agent Quinn. Now, quickly. There isn't much time."

CHAPTER SEVEN

ISABELLA SET THE DUDUK down beside her and stood. She wore a long tunic in an earthy brown color and a modest scarf draped over her shoulders with a subtle pattern that she'd used as a headscarf.

"This chamber," she said with a wave of her hand. "It's called the Cryptum Harmonium. It has served various purposes throughout history. As a secret sanctuary during periods of political unrest or persecution. A clandestine space where musicians, artists, and intellectuals could gather to share their work discreetly. A hidden space for individuals practicing alternative or forbidden forms of worship. Scholars and philosophers have utilized this chamber as a place for intellectual discussions, debates, and the exchange of information. A strategic hub for espionage."

"Thanks for the history lesson," Jackson said. "But what are we doing here today? You said we've got to hurry."

Isabella frowned at the interruption but nodded, conceding his point. "You are in pursuit of the Guardian of Secrets seal, the Chronicle of King tablet, and the bronze statue of Ashur. I think I can be of assistance."

"Who are you?" Parker asked, not ready to just trust anyone and what they say. "How do you know we're—"

Isabella offered a sad smile. "Too complicated or time-consuming a tale for today. What you and your anxious friend need to know is I possess information that will aid you in your search for the Assyrian artifacts you seek."

"Great. Let's get to it," Jackson said. "This place gives me the creeps."

The woman smiled. "I often forget how impatient and... blunt Americans can be. The items you're after. They've never been sold, traded, bartered, or even seen in public after their theft in 2011."

"That's not news," Jackson said.

"True. What the FBI doesn't know—or has never put together—is that in the years since the National Museum heist, dozens of linguistics, cryptologists, and other art historians with extensive knowledge about the Assyrian people and the contents of the Royal Library of Ashurbanipal have disappeared or met with tragic, mysterious ends. Or members of their families have."

Parker's eyes narrowed with intrigue. "Dozens of experts? Why haven't we heard about this before?"

"A handful of scholars and academics in innocuous fields that don't garnish a lot of outside interest go missing or die from curious but natural or accidental causes over nearly a dozen years internationally. With no apparent connections. It's not the sort of thing overburdened law enforcement or inept investigative journalists will invest time and effort into, I'm afraid."

"Not without a public outcry or some sensationalized element to them." Jackson frowned. "You're saying they *are* connected? They were targeted. Why?"

"Agent Reynolds informed you the seal and the tablet you seek, they've not been properly translated, yes?"

"You're awfully well informed about a meeting you weren't at," Parker said.

"Where do you think Agent Reynolds got his intel?"

"You work for the FBI?"

Isabella smiled. "I'm what you would call freelance. But yes. I work closely with the FBI. Also, your CIA. MI6. The Mossad. Dozens of other intelligence agencies around the world. As well as certain interested private parties."

"What do you do for them?" Parker asked.

"Same as you," Isabella said. "My passion is to find and recover lost or stolen items and return them to their rightful owners."

"No," Jackson said.

Isabella arched an eyebrow. "No?"

"I know people like you," Jackson said. "Been around them my whole life. You're not some good Samaritan pining over the loss of art and cultural artifacts."

"I'm not?" Amused, she said, "What am I then?"

"A spy," Parker said. "And a very good one. With a tight cover. Or covers. Reynold said he didn't know what Ebon Sparrow was."

"Spies lie," Isabella said.

"Or are kept in the dark," Jackson said.

"You knew I'd been assigned to this case," Parker said. "Made contact with me only hours later. Know details of a classified top-secret meeting. You're much more than a simple—"

"We're wasting time on questions without merit."

"And we're not dealing with someone we don't know," Parker said. "Who do you work for? Why are you doing this? How can you know all this stuff you shouldn't… can't know?"

Isabella sighed. "I am like you, Parker Quinn. I'm from a wealthy family. My young life was one of privilege and money."

"That's not like me at all," Parker said of her upbringing on a small ranch in Oklahoma. Dirt-poor where every day was a struggle just to get food on the table.

Isabella bowed slightly. "Forgive me, I wasn't referring to your humble beginnings, but rather your passion for bringing awareness and justice to the issue of black-marketed and smuggled art and antiquities. I've followed your career, Parker Quinn. Some would say, your escapades."

Parker wasn't sure if she should feel insulted or flattered.

Before she could reply, Isabella continued. "The Arroyo family of Madrid were well-connected with deep ties in politics, international business, and the art world. I grew up surrounded by and with an interest in antiquities, art and relics of all kinds. I went to university and studied archaeology and history."

Jackson said, "Can we fast-forward the trip down memory lane? You said we needed to move quickly."

"Which do you want, Captain? To know who I am or for me to get on with why I've brought you here?"

"Both. Just faster."

"Go on," Parker said. A hand on Jackson's arm gently backed him off.

"Returning from university, I learned a dark secret about my family. Their—our—businesses and political interests were intricately woven and built from criminal activities such as the international distribution of illegal guns and drugs and other stolen contraband. We were heavily involved in the black marketing of stolen artifacts, art, and other treasures for personal profit and gain. The harm we've caused is immeasurable."

"You decided to do something about it?"

"First as an informant, then more actively as an agent, as I said, for the CIA, FBI, CNI."

"*Centro Nacional de Inteligencia,*" Jackson said. Spain's primary intelligence agency.

"Yes. Among others. Over the years, I've worked to recover hundreds of stolen artifacts. I've brought down unscrupulous collectors and black marketing dealers. I've dismantled entire criminal networks with the information I've provided authorities."

"Okay," Parker said. "Why are art, history, and cultural experts disappearing or being killed? How does that link up with our three missing relics."

"Agent Reynolds told you the FBI has been working with experts for years, attempting to decipher what the seal and the tablet say. They have only photographs and other scans or images to work with. We believe the people who possess the artifacts are doing the same thing. Only in a more persuasive way."

"Decipher the artifacts' meaning. Properly translate them."

"Except," Jackson said. "With an offer they can't refuse. Help us, or we kill you."

"Or your families," Isabella said. "Friends. Loved ones."

"What could possibly be written on those chunks of rock worth that?"

"It is the belief of many," Isabella said, "the secrets to a terrible weapon of mass destruction. The likes of which the modern world has never seen before."

"Come again," Jackson said. "Something from thousands of years ago so powerful it can destroy the world? Sounds a little too Indiana Jones for me."

"I'd say the same thing," Parker said. "Except Tomb Raider."

At Jackson's confused expression, she added, "Lara Croft. Tomb Raider?" She shook her head. "Never mind. Isabella, do you believe the seal and tablet are the key to some sort of doomsday scenario?"

"What I believe, and however skeptical you are, does not matter. Those possessing these artifacts believe in the secrets they may bestow. The power. In the hands of fanatics, it is a belief they are willing to kill to understand, to discover. We need to get these stolen relics back. It is the only way to prevent the loss of additional lives."

Parker and Jackson exchanged glances. "Do you have something we can use to find them? To stop this?"

"I am not sure. There is a man you need to meet. He is in possession of... an item that may be of help. I believe it to be crucial to unlocking the translations of the seal and the tablet."

"An expert neither the FBI nor our lethal recruiters have found yet?" Parker asked.

"No. This man... Assyrian history is not, how-do-you-say, his forte."

"How's that help us save the world?" Jackson's voice dripped with sarcasm.

"What this man has, this secret," Isabella said. "He is unaware of the value it might hold."

"What is it?" Parker asked. "What does he have?"

"The tablet you seek, the Chronicle of Kings, conveys a story. As best anyone has been able to translate it so far."

"Of King Ashurbanipal. His empire," Parker said.

"Yes," Isabella said. "What this man has... He possesses a second tablet."

"A tablet no one knows about?" Jackson asked.

"No. It is no secret he bought it. At auction. What is not known is its possible link to the Chronicle of Kings."

"Who is he?" Parker asked.

"A collector. But one of modest means. He owns a small collection of antiquities, all legally obtained and purchased. I can attest to that personally."

"A part two of a stolen rock from the Iraq museum," Jackson said. "How can that possibly be legal for him to have?"

"This item was not a recovered artifact from the Royal Library. Never a part of their inventory. This tablet has not been associated with the Assyrians or Ashurbanipal by the scholarly community. I think, mistakenly so. Its origins are far from Iraq. As for its possessor, I assure you, this man is ignorant of the true value or importance of the tablet, and his integrity is above reproach."

"Okay. Fine." Jackson said. "Who is he? Where do we get *this* hunk of rock?"

"He lives in Greece. Athens, specifically. His name is Ioannis Karas, and he is an old friend. I wish that he not be associated with this affair. I believe it would be dangerous for his well-being."

"We're not interested in causing any more collateral damage. He's willing to talk to us?"

"I have... paved the way, as you Americans say. Ioannis is happy to cooperate."

A thrill of excitement coursed through Parker. The idea they could recover a piece of the puzzle their enemies didn't have. A key to unlocking the message imprinted into the soft clay all those thousands of years ago. A message their adversaries are also desperate to discover.

The race to figuring this all out had just taken an enormous step forward.

CHAPTER EIGHT

A SUDDEN COMMOTION FROM above reverberated through the Cryptum Harmonium.

The sound of rushing footsteps and muffled voices had suddenly shattered the quiet, serene atmosphere. They were familiar sounds to Jackson. Soldiers. Issuing quiet instructions. The muted tap of metal buckles against plastic stocks. The rhythmic, disciplined cadence of trained personnel advancing in formations across ancient boards and the stone floor overhead.

"What's that?" Parker drew her agency-issued Sig Sauer, fearing she knew the answer.

"Soldiers." Similarly armed, Jackson's Sig was chambered with 9x19mm NATO rounds.

The commotion got louder. Drew closer.

Isabella pulled her scarf up, covering her head. "We must go. Now."

She reached the door of the Cryptum Harmonium, only to have the imam rush at her. Breathless, he stumbled into her arms. The color drained from his face. His robes were stained red. Fresh blood where he clutched his side.

A gun or knife wound, Jackson guessed.

"They're here. I could not stop them. You must go, *serçe*. Now."

Jackson took the weight of the dying imam from her arms. He gently laid him on the floor. Propped him against the wall. The man's head lulled to one side.

"This place got a back door?" Jackson asked.

"In fact, it does."

The imam clawed at Jackson's hand, leaving it bloodied. "Your gun. Give it to me. I will... buy you time."

Jackson hesitated, but Parker nodded. She was still armed.

Isabella knelt beside the old man. "Forgive me, old friend."

He patted her hand. "It is as we always knew it would be. Be safe, child. Continue to do... your good work."

"I'm sorry," Jackson said. "But we've got to get."

Isabella nodded. She rose and swiftly moved to an intricately patterned tapestry at the back of the chamber. Drawing it to one side revealed a concealed entrance to a narrow passage.

Jackson grinned. "Now we're talking."

Whispering, Isabella said, "Quickly, through here. It leads to a network of tunnels beneath the Hagia Sophia. They lead into the city."

Parker, Jackson, and Isabella slipped through the hidden passage. Dropping the tapestry back into place, they left the Cryptum Harmonium and the imam behind.

Guided by Isabella's familiarity with the secret passages, they navigated the dark and winding tunnels. The stone-built passageway felt cold and tomb-like. It stank of old death. Illuminated only by Parker and Jackson's cell phone flashlights, the bobbing lights cast long, ominous shadows.

"This way," Isabella urged.

Gunshots shattered the oppressive quiet. A spat of rounds followed by a barrage of automatic weapons fire. The deadening silence that followed left no doubt the imam was dead. Brutally executed.

Jackson wondered how many people had used these tunnels to escape over the centuries. Persecuted religious worshippers, refugee seekers, artisans fleeing prejudice for their works…

They reached a junction. Isabella hesitated, then said, "This way."

The tunnels seemed to twist and turn endlessly. The distant echoes of footsteps and shouted orders behind them were getting closer. The trio froze when they heard the harsh clang of metal against stone up ahead.

"They've cut us off," Jackson said

"How can that be?"

"Doesn't matter. This way," Isabella said, a trace of panic in her voice.

They reversed course, backtracking until they reached a junction they'd initially passed by. Down the way they'd come, Jackson saw the jumble of flashlights and red laser scopes of the advancing death squad.

Parker had seen it as well. "We need to move faster."

Taking the alternative route through the oppressive tunnels at a run, their breathing grew heavy as the air thickened with a damp, earthy smell. The sound of their pursuers filled the air behind them, getting closer.

They emerged into a larger chamber. Isabella gasped.

The exit was in sight, but before they could reach it, the ominous silhouette of armed soldiers danced across the curved stone chamber. Closing in. Jackson dropped to one knee and signaled to Parker to give him her gun.

He hissed, "Get that door open."

Parker and Isabella crowded around a wrought iron metal grate covering a set of stone steps leading upward. Grabbing it, they tugged. The gate barely moved, giving them only a resistant groan.

"Pull," Parker said, grunting.

"I am pulling," Isabella said. "You pull."

"I am."

Isabella set her jaw. "Pull harder."

The first soldiers crossed through the opposite archway.

Jackson took one out with a shot to the cheek. The second one collapsed with a grunt when Jackson's second bullet pierced his thigh. The shots rang in the chamber, as did the soldiers' cries.

"Door! Now!" Jackson shouted.

Parker panted. "Got it!"

She pushed Isabella through and then turned, waiting for Jackson. He raced across the room, ducking fire, reached where Parker was and placed a hand on her shoulder. He pushed her forward, covering her back.

"Go! Go! Go!"

They raced up the stone steps, wet and slick with moss.

The soldiers gathered around the base of the stairs. After losing two of their own already, they were hesitant to charge up the narrow stairwell. None wanting to be the first.

Parker and Jackson emerged from the stairs, finding Isabella waiting for them. She had a small handgun of her own. A .32 Beretta 30X Tomcat. She'd had it concealed under the loose robes she wore.

"Where are we?" Parker asked, taking a deep breath of fresh air and looking around.

"Sultanahmet Arkeolojik Park," Isabella said. "Known as the Blue Mosque Park."

"Great to know," Jackson said. "We need to move."

A shot punctuated his statement.

Isabella cried out and clutched her leg. The gunfire had come from the stairwell, but lights and shouting alerted them to a second threat. A team of soldiers were rushing toward them, making their way through the park. Flashlights and red lasers crisscrossed the manicured grass and trees.

"Can you walk?" Parker asked, holding Isabella's arm draped across her shoulders.

Isabella winced, taking two more bullets from the approaching ground troops. One hit her high in her chest. The other was a stomach shot. She collapsed in Parker's arms.

Jackson returned fire, slowing the advancing soldiers who now scrambled to take cover behind the sparse trees the park offered.

Leaning heavily on Parker, Isabella said, "The fountain."

Illuminated in blue light, the water geysers framed the mosque behind it, lit up in a contrasting yellow-orange glow.

"Set me down. I can hold them off from there."

"No," Parker said.

The spy known as Ebon Sparrow clutched at Parker's sleeve, leaving it wrinkled and bloodied. "My wounds. I will not survive. You must go."

She opened her hand. Her palms were filled with slick, wet blood. Isabella pushed a small package wrapped in brown paper and tied with string into Parker's hand. It was the size and shape of a common hardcover book.

"I can give you a chance. You must... must stop what is coming. I fear..." She winced. "What is sought... will bring catastrophic horror. It must be stopped."

Jackson pushed Parker away. There wasn't time to waste arguing. He scooped Isabella up in his arms and deposited her behind the low wall of the glowing fountain. The spray of the fountains wetting them. He exchanged guns with her. Parker's Sig had a fresh, full clip.

He grasped her hands. "We won't let you down."

"No," Parker shouted.

Jackson grabbed her arm. Shook her. "Move! Now!"

The urgency in his voice punctuated by a spray of gunfire.

Isabella aimed and fired back. With impressive accuracy, she picked off soldiers that ventured from their cover.

Jackson and Parker ran for the nearby street and zig-zagged toward where they'd parked Warhorse. Reaching the motorcycle and seemingly having shaken any pursuit, Parker shook her hand from Jackson's grasp.

"How could you leave her back there?"

"She was already dead. If we'd done anything else, we'd be dead, too." He handed her a helmet. "I'm sorry. But that's the way war is."

"We're not at war."

A bullet tinged off Warhorse's fender. Parker and Jackson ducked.

"Keep telling yourself that, Parker."

He scanned the streets around them. A contingent of soldiers leapfrogged toward them, darting from trees to benches, from cars to other cover. Red laser scopes and barrel-mounted flashlights crisscrossed the dark lawn and the paved streets.

"Can you shoot as well as you drive?"

"Better."

"Then I'm at the wheel."

He handed her Isabella's gun and mounted Warhorse. He revved the engine.

He knocked back the kickstand as she jumped on the motorcycle, facing backward.

"Hang on," Jackson shouted. "And kill anything that comes close to us."

CHAPTER NINE

THEY ROARED THROUGH THE open gate and across the airport tarmac. In the distance, far corner of the airport, away from the bustling terminals and out of sight of the hangers and cargo transfer facilities, the Dassault Falcon 8X sat shrouded by slowly drifting clouds blotting out the moonlight. A few of the tiny cabin windows were lit. Dull, yellow rectangles.

Jackson sped along a narrow access road, cracked and overgrown with weeds, evidence of how little this area of the airport was used. A single chain link fence topped with barbed wire edged the roadway.

The air was heavy. Thick with moisture from an approaching storm and the smell of jet fuel. Over the roar of the motorcycle, Parker could hear the distant hum of aircraft engines warming up, preparing to depart. It all felt eerily disconnected from their current plight. A touch of normalcy, a world away from the chaos around them.

Doing her best to pick off the drivers pursuing them in two old Volvos. Parker managed to star, but not shatter, one of the windshields.

They'd made their escape from the city, having blasted through the streets of Istanbul at breakneck speed. Using the motorcycle's superior maneuverability to navigate through narrow alleys and gaps between cars gave them a substantial lead, which they lost on the highways and straightaways where the overpowered Volvos could run full out unimpeded.

Jackson had radioed ahead.

He grinned now as the plane's running lights snapped on and the beautiful, high-pitched whine of the Falcon 8X's three Pratt & Whitney turbofan engines roared to life. The pilots—accustomed to CIA operations going south—were readying the plane for departure. One of them, Jared, Jackson thought, knelt by the open door, a sniper rifle in his hand.

Davenport was positioned at the base of the airstairs. An American-made M16 at the ready.

"Trouble," Parker shouted.

"What?"

"Missile!"

Jackson twisted around. "What!"

"Don't look. Drive."

A soldier leaned out from the back seat of the lead Volvo.

With only a glimpse, Jackson recognized the weapon their assailant struggled to aim from the moving vehicle. A Russian-manufactured Igla-S. Also known as the SA-24 Grinch.

On the plus side for the good guys, Jackson thought, aiming and firing a handheld missile launcher while hanging out of the back window of a speeding car was extremely difficult to do. Not so lucky for them, the Grinch fired advanced, infrared-homing-beacon equipped missiles designed to lock onto a target's heat signature.

"Hold on!" Jackson yanked the handlebars to the right. He veered sharply off the narrow road and onto the airstrip asphalt. "Lean with me!"

He put Warhorse into a tight, high-speed turn. The engines whined in protest. The tires skidded, losing traction on the gravel-spewed macadam.

Parker fired off two shots. She shouted, "I'm out."

The lead Volvo's windshield shattered. Thanks to well-aimed shots from Jared and Davenport.

The black sedan swerved, the driver fighting for control. It wasn't enough.

Jackson heard the familiar whomp of the Grinch launching its missile.

He banked hard to the left, zigzagging the motorcycle into a low, serpentine pattern, aggressively swaying left, then right, and back again in quick succession.

The missile swerved, following them.

"You can't outrun it!" Parker shouted.

Jackson knew better than to try. He swerved back to the left, maintaining his reckless, breakneck speed. Leaning deep into the turn, his knee nearly scraped across the tarmac.

"On my signal," he shouted. "Get ready to jump."

"What?"

Jackson put Warhorse into a skid. "JUMP!"

He leaped off the bike, twisted, and grabbed Parker in a bear hug. They flew through the air then hit the pavement hard. Jackson enveloped Parker in his protective grip. Head down, he pulled her tightly to his chest. They rolled away from the skidding bike, spinning like a top on its side and spitting up waves of sparks as it skittered across the tarmac, away from the plane.

The missile struck Warhorse.

The explosion deafened Parker and Jackson as the bike blew up in a fiery red and yellow ball of heat, fire and shrapnel. Black smoke roiled skyward. The smell of burning plastic, rubber and various fluids fouled the air.

The pilot, Jared, and Davenport kept firing at the approaching vehicles.

One of them hit the backseat gunner.

He gasped and slumped, hanging halfway out the window. Dead.

The missile launcher dropped from his lifeless hands and tumbled across the tarmac.

As the second Volvo raced toward them, Jackson got to his feet. He pulled Parker up. Her ears ringing. "You okay?"

She stared at the car still racing toward them. "Later. We need to get out of here."

They ran for the airstairs.

Under covering fire from Jared and Davenport, they reached the airstairs and scrambled up the steps. Inside the doorway, Jackson grabbed a second M16 and provided additional firepower, giving Davenport a chance to retreat up the airstairs and into the plane.

"Thanks, mate."

"Don't mention it, English."

Once he was safely inside, Jared and Jackson kicked the airstairs away.

Parker shouted to Jason in the cockpit. "Get us out of here!"

The engines whined, powering up.

Jared raced past her, getting to the cockpit. A muted vibration filled the cabin.

Jackson and Davenport pulled the Falcon's door closed.

The engines revved. The plane turned and rumbled down the runway, gathering speed. A higher whine, a more focused tone as the engines reached full power. The plane raced across the tarmac with the two Volvos in pursuit.

The ping of small arms fire across the plane's skin could be heard inside the cabin as Davenport, Jackson, and Parker tumbled into seats and strapped in.

"Go. Go. Go," Parker murmured.

The Falcon shuddered.

Jackson felt the aircraft angle back, the nose rising. Gaining lift, they ascended. He glanced out the side window, seeing the Volvos giving up the chase as the Falcon climbed steeply, the running lights blinking along the wings. The soothing sound of airflow rushing over the fuselage replaced spitting gunfire and his pounding pulse in his ears.

Quickly out of range, Jared glanced into the cabin from the cockpit. "Just out of curiosity. We got a destination in mind?"

"Greece," Parker said. "Athens, Greece."

CHAPTER TEN

Dassault Falcon 8X
Somewhere over the North Aegean Sea

ONCE THEY WERE SAFELY airborne, Parker retreated from the main cabin. Sequestering herself in the conference room.

There, she kicked off her shoes, sat on the sofa Davenport had so casually occupied earlier, and curled her legs up under her. She stared out the window. The plane's blinking lights reflected off the clouds around them in the night sky. Feeling the soft, rhythmic hum of the plane, she pinched at her lower lip and watched the clouds drift by.

Her hand trembled. Not from guilt or fear.

In anger. With unrequited fury.

In her lap, she clutched the plain-wrapped package Isabella had thrust into her hands. A dying gesture from a woman Parker had gotten killed.

She didn't know how much time had passed before she heard a knock on the door. "Come in."

The door eased open, and Jackson slipped into the room. He closed the door behind him. "You okay?"

"Yes." A pause. "No."

Jackson pulled out a chair from the conference table and sat. "Wanna talk about it?"

"No." Parker offered a weak smile. "Yes."

When she didn't elaborate, with his eyes on the package in her hand, he said, "What's that?"

Parker held the twine-wrapped package up. "I don't know. Isabella gave it to me... before she died."

She untied the string and carefully peeled back the folds of the brown paper it was wrapped in. Inside was a weathered, tattered, leather-bound book. Well worn, many of the pages were marked with thin tabs. Parker flipped through the pages.

"Looks like some kind of journal."

The paper was yellowed and coarse. Lined with delicate scripted handwriting in various colors of red, blue and black ink, indicating the entries had been made at different times dating back almost a dozen years.

"What's it say?" Jackson asked.

Parker pointed at different entries, flipping through the pages and then pointing again. She read: "The Crimson Lotus. Stolen from a museum in Bangkok. And here. The Celestial Scrolls in Japan. The Serpent's Eye Diamond. The golden Scepter of Horus. That one was only recovered about a year ago by Chinese authorities. And this one here. My God. She recovered the Jade Elephant of Enlightenment. It was one of the most talked about art thefts for years."

She looked at Jackson. "If this is all true, this woman was a legend. She should have been an international superstar in my world. And yet I've never heard of her."

"I bet most people haven't," Jackson said. "Which is more than likely how she accomplished what she did. Anonymity. No fanfare."

Parker continued to flip through the pages. "You're right. The circumstances around how most of these items were recovered are as mysterious as were their thefts. That's not all."

She looked up at Jackson. "There's also leads here to dozens of other important stolen and lost artifacts. Relics still missing. Not recovered. Why did she give me this?"

"You know, for a pretty bright broad, you're a little dense."

Parker shot him a look with a single raised eyebrow.

He smiled. "It's obvious, Parker. She gave you the journal so you could continue her work. Take on what she started, and finish it."

Parker felt overwhelmed by the sudden burden Isabella Arroyo had thrust upon her. Honored the woman believed she was worthy, but the responsibility? It felt daunting. And yet she clutched the journal to her chest. Vowing to be a suitable successor, tears filled her eyes.

Jackson misread her emotions. "First time you had people die on a mission?"

Parker turned back from the window. "What? You think this is my first rodeo, cowboy?" Realizing she had snapped at him, she softened her voice. "Hurts the same as the first one. And each time since. Especially when it's my fault."

"Hey. Not your fault."

Parker twisted on the sofa to look at him. "I wish I could believe that."

"First rule," Jackson said. "The casualties. The people who die doing what we do. That's on the bad guys. Not you."

Parker pressed her lips into a straight line. "You think that's what this is about? I'm consumed with guilt? Feeling sorry for myself? Second-guessing what I've done or not done?"

He cocked his head. "Looks like it."

With a humorless laugh, she said, "You couldn't be more wrong, Captain. I entered this business because people died. Innocents ruthlessly murdered in front of me. I was too young. Too inexperienced to do anything about it. Then. I am now."

"Meaning?"

She turned and leveled a hard stare in his direction. Her green eyes were ablaze with anger. "I know damn well who's responsible. Not specifically, but that'll come. This isn't grief or feeling sorry for myself. It's not even sadness for the imam and the Sparrow. That'll come later. This is focus, me channeling my anger, my rage, my need for justice. Back there, you said this is war. Do you believe that?"

"I do."

"Good. Because I do, too. What this is," she said, "is me gearing up. Taking all the anger, all the wrath, and balling it up, collecting it, consuming it so it's a part of me." She climbed off the sofa. "This is me preparing to unleash a storm of retribution and vengeance and revenge. Scorched earth aimed directly and solely at those responsible for what has happened. And for what will happen if we don't stop it."

Her expression was one of fierce determination. "Isabella gave her life for this work. I won't let it have been in vain."

With an encouraging smile, Jackson said, "Never suspected you would."

"I guess we have work to do then." Parker hit the intercom. "Davenport. Come in here, please."

The dapper English spy entered the room with Jackson still seated and Parker standing tall at the head of the conference table. He'd changed into a well-tailored, dark gray suit with a white dress shirt, red power tie and matching pocket square.

"What have you got for us?" Parker asked.

He looked from her to Jackson, his expression one of confusion. "Got for you?"

She snapped her fingers twice. "Over here. Agent. When I left, I gave you an assignment. Dazzle me. Maximilian Stahl. What have you got?"

"It's only been a couple of hours."

Sternly. "What have you got?"

Davenport sighed. "Maximilian Stahl. Born to Vicktor and Katarina Stahl. The Stahl family rose to prominence in the early 20th century. Part of the Prussian aristocracy. Known publicly for their wealth. It was their association with German military intelligence during World War I that set the stage for what would become the family business for the next hundred years."

"Which was?" Parker asked.

"An empire of influence, wealth, and control over both the criminal underworld and into the highest echelons of political power structures. Their specialty, specifically, is global espionage. Fast forward to the next world war. The Stahl family established deep connections within the Nazi regime. However, they were pragmatists as well. Understanding that betting solely on the Third Reich might lead to ruin, they covertly hedged their bets by secretly collaborating with both the Soviet Union and Allied nations. This duplicity ensured that no matter who won the war, the Stahls would remain in power."

Davenport paced, reciting from memory.

"After World War II, the Stahls fully committed to working with Soviet intelligence, having positioned themselves as valuable assets to the KGB. However, their operations were never entirely beholden to Moscow. Their ultimate goal was always to strengthen their family's grip on global power. More than willing to work both sides if it benefited them. They were rumored to have played pivotal roles in the Berlin Airlift, the tensions that led to the Cuban Missile Crisis, the Prague Spring and deeply entrenched in the Afghan-Soviet War."

Circling the conference table, Davenport tapped the surface with his finger. "Like any self-respecting crime family, their true wealth came from worldwide trafficking of arms, drug smuggling, art theft and forgery, and money laundering."

"Where's Maxie fit into all of this?" Jackson asked.

"Groomed from an early age, word is he led a sheltered life. Locked away, without friends and having little contact with the outside world, he studied warfare, strategy and global conflicts. Taught to him by former military officers and intelligence operatives. He reportedly excelled in battlefield command, logistics, and planning and execution of complex military campaigns. His education included hands-on training in special operations, tactics, guerrilla warfare and sabotage. They say he became an expert in clandestine intelligence, spy craft and combat training."

"A Soviet super soldier," Parker offered. "The perfect spy."

"I'm not sure about perfect," Davenport said. "But pretty darn good. Unconfirmed reports have him infiltrating a major Western European defense contractor at the tender age of twenty-one. He stole valuable intel on classified defense projects, trade secrets, and government contracts, passing that information on to both Russian and Chinese intelligence communities."

"By passing on," Jackson said, "You mean sold?"

"Yes. And that's just one example," Davenport said. "During the chaotic years after the collapse of the Soviet Union, Stahl set up shop in Moscow, where he reportedly orchestrated high-level arms deals and resource extractions. His most notable achievement came when he brokered the sale of advanced Soviet-era weapon systems, including surface-to-air missiles and cutting-edge radar technology, to rogue states and private military contractors in the Middle East and Africa.

"A real up-and-comer," Parker said.

"We're thinking this whole terror thing is Russian-backed then?" Jackson asked.

"Not necessarily," Davenport said. "Like his family, Stahl is an opportunist first and maybe a bit of a futurist. By the late 90s and early 2000s, Stahl had amassed a significant fortune and extensive experience in corporate espionage, arms trafficking, and covert operations. His next move, reportedly, and here's where intel on him begins to get fuzzy, was to expand his influence by creating a global, private intelligence network—a shadow operation operated independently of any state or government."

"Mercenary for hire?"

"But at the highest level imaginable. Max's private network specialized in gathering intelligence for corporations, governments, and criminal syndicates, seeking information about competitors, political opponents, or high-profile targets. His reputation in the intelligence community soared. He was thought to be able to provide any information, execute any operation, or eliminate any threat—as long as the price was right. He began influencing world events in more significant ways. Orchestrating political coups, manipulating markets, and destabilizing governments, building a reputation as a power broker who could shift the geopolitical landscape but also secured his standing in the spy and espionage community as a player whose influence extended far beyond traditional state boundaries."

"I've been around geopolitical hotspots my whole career," Jackson said. "How come I've never heard of him?"

Parker had the same question.

"Have either of you heard of the Odessa Incident? In 2005?"

They shook their heads.

"It was a Kremlin operation, organized by Stahl through intermediaries, involving the sale of advanced missile systems to a pro-Russian separatist group operating in Eastern Europe. Officially, the transaction was meant to bolster Moscow's regional influence, increasing its leverage in post-Soviet conflicts. Unofficially, it was another extension of Russia's covert support for proxy wars, a typical operation for Stahl's family business.

"However, the deal unraveled in ways no one expected. Unbeknownst to both Stahl and his Russian handlers, unknown forces looking for an opportunity to destabilize key players in the arms trade carefully fed false intelligence to the separatist group, leading them to believe the Russians were setting them up. The shipment was sabotaged, and in the ensuing chaos, a three-way firefight broke out between Stahl's operatives, the separatist group and Ukrainian military forces. The separatists were decimated. The weapons shipment was destroyed. The incident led to the arrest of several key figures in Stahl's network. Public exposure seemed imminent. The Kremlin was furious, and Stahl held them responsible for the failure."

Davenport pulled a chair out and sat. "After that, Stahl's almost legendary paranoia kicked in. He circled the wagons and went to ground, so far off the grid as to become invisible. But, he never relinquished control over his extensive operations. Instead, he relied on a small, tight-knit network of only his closest friends and advisors."

Jackson glanced at Parker. His bemused expression said: *not bad.*

"How did the FBI connect Stahl to the heist?" Jackson asked. "Why's Agent Reynolds's so insistent Stahl's behind it?"

Parker knew the answers. The Chinese hacker. But she kept silent, curious to see what Davenport had uncovered.

Davenport shrugged. "Good questions. A significant portion of Stahl's criminal enterprise's finances do, or did, come from illegal art and antiquities sales, thefts, and forgeries. The practice of his family for generations. But I'm not seeing much of a connection between the family's known allies and associates and the various Assyrian artwork the Bureau recovered up until now. However, Stahl has raised the bar of distancing himself from such transactions to an art form. The man is literally a ghost."

"It's good intel," Parker said. "But none of it helps us figure out any connections between the still missing artifacts and whatever this so-called imminent terror threat is," Parker said.

"Other than ideology," Jackson said.

Davenport nodded. "Stahl has a deep-seated disillusionment with the Russians and a festering belief nation-states are ineffective in an emerging new world order. Creating chaos and upheaval to destabilize—in his view— weak and corrupt governments would be an opportunity to manipulate and gain control over global events."

"With him sitting at the top," Jackson said.

"So it would seem." Parker felt like they were missing something. She wasn't seeing the full picture yet. "Good work, Sebastian. I mean that."

Over the intercom, the copilot Jason announced, "We're approaching Eleftherios Venizelos airport now." Athens International Airport. "Prepare for landing. We'll be on the ground in ten minutes, people."

CHAPTER **ELEVEN**

Undisclosed Military Manufacturing Plant
St. Petersburg, Russia

THE HARSHLY LIT UNDERGROUND facility reverberated with the low hum of machinery. Maximilian Stahl strolled along the catwalk overlooking the manufacturing floor. He ran his hand along the cold metal handrail. Dressed in a dark Armani suit, he looked more like the CEO of a large industrial corporation than the master spy that was his stock and trade.

Below him, sparks flew from a welding torch as two engineers supervised the installation of a missile guidance system into a pod that would eventually be embedded in one of five missiles, the centerpiece of the work being done here. Power tools and the clang of hand tools against metal echoed in the vast chamber. Harshly lit with fluorescent and bluish light, various computer screens and control panels blinked with colorful displays.

An alarm buzz pierced the air. The warning sound of a conveyor belt system activating. A forklift rumbled across the smooth concrete floor. It paused, then its backup alarms beeped as it reversed into a charging station. Armed security personnel manned each entryway, and the ever-present red lights on dozens of active surveillance cameras dotted the shadowy corners of the vast facility.

A small, dainty woman with black hair and a severe expression watched their work from a monitoring station on a second-floor platform behind large glass panels. Several white-coated technicians and engineers milled around the manufacturing floor, seemingly performing functions and duties above Stahl's understanding.

Constructed long ago, the facility was concealed within an unassuming industrial complex five stories above them. The legitimate business of manufacturing innocuous aerospace components for Russia's less-then-robust space program perfectly camouflaged the comings and goings of personnel, materials and equipment from prying spy satellites overhead.

"Welcome back, Gospodin Stahl," greeted Dr. Nikitin, the lead scientist selected to head the top-secret missile development project. A rotund man with a halo of graying dark hair and wearing black-framed glasses. His subtle accent suggested the man originally hailed from the Baltic states.

"Doctor."

Nikitin waved a hand. "This way."

He led Stahl to a steel door that swung open silently on hydraulic hinges as they approached. Behind it was a high-tech security checkpoint manned by stern-faced security guards. After IDs were checked and a full body scan similar in design to the metal detectors found at every airport around the world, they were passed through. Stahl nodded curtly, appreciative of the guards' thoroughness and lack of intimidation by the presence of a man of his stature.

Nikitin led him down a series of metal stairwells, taking him to the heartbeat of the facility.

Stahl took in the high-tech surroundings. Sleek consoles and monitors lined the walls, displaying complex schematics and data readouts. The air was filled with a mix of anticipation and tension. And the smell of various fuels.

Men and women in lab coats and dark blue jumpsuits moved efficiently throughout the chamber. Electronic pads in hand. Plastic ID badges clipped to their pockets.

Entering a vast chamber, Stahl paused in awe. In cradles, five colossal missiles hung suspended in a secure holding bay. The rockets were painted with a matte black stealth finish. Red stripes encircled their tails just above the stabilizing fins.

"Gospodin Stahl, allow me to present the R47 Chimera. The culmination of years of research and development. The epitome of Russian science and engineering," declared Dr. Nikitin. His expression gleamed with pride.

The missiles' design concealed its true purpose: to deliver a potent aerosol-type chemical-biological agent. Stahl's expression remained impassive as he absorbed the technical details. The scientist droning on about the missiles' many capabilities and features, such as variable warheads and target selection algorithms based upon multiple factors, including satellite imagery analysis, ground surveillance video footage collected remotely via drone aircraft, or Internet-acquired field intel from across the globe. These advanced systems allowed for instant response times anywhere across Eurasia…

Listening to him droll on like a parrot repeating factoids it had memorized between asking for crackers, Stahl resisted the urge to rub his temples to alleviate a growing headache.

He asked the one question he needed answered. "What will the dispersal range of the weaponized agent be?"

Nikitin coughed as he adjusted his glasses nervously. He said in a rush, "That's a complex question dependent on variables we've not yet received. An aerosolized agent would require us to factor particle density, viscidness, and evaporation rates. For liquid agents, the viscosity, volatility and droplet size will need to be considered. Gaseous agents, we'll need to account for molecular weight and reactivity."

Stahl held a hand up to halt him, but Nikitin was on a roll.

"Then there are the external variables. Time of year, geographical location, wind speed, prevailing weather patterns, and temperature gradients at both the release altitude and the ground level are critical components. A payload deployed at high altitudes will likely encounter more turbulence and temperature fluctuations, potentially reducing precision or spreading the agent across a wider, less predictable area. Conversely, a low-altitude release could be more controlled but would depend heavily on local wind patterns and surface obstacles."

Stahl pinched the bridge of his nose. "Understood, Doctor." He gave the man a reassuring smile. "All the information you need will be forthcoming... soon."

STAHL RETURN TO THE surface.

As he strolled through the parking lot outside, he slipped on dark sunglasses. While the visit hadn't yielded much in the way of new information, he felt reassured the hardware aspects of the operation were proceeding along on schedule. And yet, as he walked, a subtle tension settled between his shoulder blades. A constant reminder the weight of the project rested heavily on Stahl and his ability to complete his part of the mission.

Waiting for him was a nondescript, dark-colored sedan with tinted windows.

Leaning against the fender was Anton Kuznetsov. His short, compact frame was encased in a civilian business suit a size too tight. He wore sunglasses of his own. Favoring the American aviator-style Ray-Bans.

Stahl approached him.

"Our team in Istanbul was unable to secure the woman identified as Ebon Sparrow."

"Yes, Anton, news of your failure has traveled fast."

"The Sparrow is dead, as is a local imam."

Stahl glanced around the parking lot. He ground his back teeth in frustration. "Tell me, Anton. Have you any news that was not the lead stories on CNN, Fox, and the BBC this morning? Tell me something I do not know."

"The woman, Parker Quinn, and her team are en route to Athens, Greece."

This piqued Stahl's interest. "For what purpose?"

"Unknown at this time," Kuznetsov said. "Perhaps you'd like to ask the reporters at CNN and Fox?"

Stahl smiled. Anton Kuznetsov was one of few people on the planet that could speak to him in such a manner. Stahl reached for the back door handle. "I've every confidence I won't have to, old friend."

"I've made arrangements to deal with them once they arrive," Kuznetsov said over the sedan's roof.

"Very good." Few things took Stahl by surprise. This did. To his old friend, he emphasized, "It's important we learn why they went there."

"Understood," Kuznetsov said.

Stahl slipped into the backseat.

Kuznetsov took the wheel.

They drove away from the complex with Stahl wondering, *What could possibly be of interest to them in Greece?*

CHAPTER TWELVE

Home of Professor Ioannis Karas
Vouliagmenis Avenue, Koropi, Greece

THE GREEN HYUNDAI RENTAL navigated the gently winding streets through the quaint neighborhood of Koropi. Vibrant bougainvilleas cascaded over whitewashed walls. Tall trees stood like sentinels along the roadside, casting dappled shadows on the pavement. The streets were lined with modest family homes. Their pastel-colored facades reflected the warmth of the Greek sun. Occasional glimpses of distant mountains caught Parker's attention. She allowed herself a moment to reflect on the picturesque backdrop the serene suburban landscape provided.

Jackson drove.

Lena sat in the back, focused on a GPS app on her cell phone. "It should be just up ahead. On the right."

A minute later, from the passenger seat, Parker pointed at a single-story building with a tiled roof and large windows covered with ornate wrought iron grills. A low wall surrounded the pretty little home.

"It's that contemporary Greek revival there."

Jackson shot her an arched eyebrow look. "The what?"

"The yellow one."

Once parked, the three of them strolled through the front gate.

A modest but well-tended garden filled the space on either side of the walkway. A delightful aroma of rosemary, thyme, lavender, and an earthy, sweet scent of jasmine wafted about them as they made their way to the front door.

A little gnome of a man who could barely be five feet tall greeted them. He pushed the wrought-iron outer door open with a big grin. Wearing baggy slacks and a cardigan sweater, his blue eyes sparkled with the intensity of a man in his thirties rather than nearing seventy.

"You must be Ms. Quinn. And friends. Come in. Come in." He beckoned them past the threshold and into the shadowy, cool interior.

Led to a small front living room. It flowed seamlessly into a dining area and a small but functional kitchen. The walls were olive green and sandy beige. Shelves abounded with old pottery, sculptures, vases, and other artifacts. Mixed in were books on art, archaeology and history. Parker had many of those same tones on the shelves in her office at work. The furniture was sturdy and functional, with worn but comfortable-looking chairs, a sofa, and a large marble coffee table.

"Sit. Sit. I'll make tea. You must have tea."

The old man shuffled into the kitchen without waiting for an answer. From there, they could hear the clicking of porcelain cups and the rattling of metal spoons.

"I was so excited to hear from Isabella." He returned to the living room carrying a tray with a teapot and four cups. "How is Isabella? She's such a sweet woman. So dedicated to her work, to the arts."

Parker waited until the old man settled the tray on the coffee table. Once he sat in the chair across from the small sofa she and her team had squeezed into, she said, "How much do you know about Isabella's work, Mr. Karas?"

"Professor, actually, but please call me Ioannis." He crossed his legs and perched his cup and saucer on his knee. "Little, of course. She's quite the private person. Especially since—"

"I'm afraid we've got bad news, Professor. Isabella. She's been killed. I'm sorry."

Visibly shaken, Karas' hands shook. The cup and saucer precariously balanced on his knee jiggled. Lena leaned forward and took them from him, gently setting them down on the end table next to his chair.

"Killed? How?"

Parker hesitated. Not sure how much she should reveal.

"Her work, wasn't it?" he said. "Chasing art poachers. I told her it was dangerous. That the risks were too great... The people she exposed were too powerful. That it would be her undoing."

"We're sorry for your loss," Parker offered.

"Do you know who did this?"

"Not those ultimately responsible. But you have my word, we will find out."

"It was over this damn cuneiform tablet I have. It's what got her killed."

"We don't know that for sure," Parker said. "But we do believe it's important. Isabella believed it was important."

"Do you have it, Professor?" Jackson asked.

Karas hesitated for a moment. Then, he stood up, having reached a decision. He looked as if he had aged considerably since their arrival. "Remain here. I'll be back in a moment."

Parker and her team watched the elderly gentleman shuffle across the room toward the rear section of the house. They exchanged worried glances.

Jackson sipped his tea and grimaced.

Karas returned, carrying a small glass display case. As he approached, Lena leaned forward and moved the tea tray and cups aside to make room on the low marble coffee table. The case was roughly the size of a shoe box and appeared heavier than it looked. Inside were two stone fragments, sandstone in color.

Parker leaned forward, curious.

Lena looked like a little kid about to dig into her first ice cream sundae.

With weathered, age-spotted hands, Karas lifted the glass case from its black lacquer base. He handed blue latex gloves to Lena and Parker. Jackson declined the offer. The women snapped them on, and Lena lifted the smaller of the two pieces from the base. She held it up to the light shining through the living room window.

Bored, Jackson stood up and began to pace the living room.

"How did you come to be in possession of these cuneiform tablet fragments?" Parker asked.

"I was at an art auction about a year ago. I was interested in a carved ivory statuette of the goddess Umay. It dates back to the era of Genghis Khan's Mongol Empire around 1227 or so. Artifacts depicting her are extremely rare. It was a time of great political and military power for the Mongols, marked by vast conquests and cultural exchanges. Artifacts like that—but I digress."

He returned to his chair. His face had regained some of the color it had lost earlier. "I was quickly outbid, unfortunately. But, while I was there, I noticed these fragments on a display table—not up for auction—but rather offered for direct sale. I recognized some of the script as Assyrian cuneiform, which was unusual in itself, but also that something about it was... off."

He leaned forward. With his pinky, he pointed at some of the etchings on the fragment Lena held, careful not to touch it with his ungloved hand. "These symbols here. They are known and established Assyrian markings. But these here? They are not."

"You've a very good eye, Professor," Parker said. "What is your academic specialty?"

"I taught archaeology and art history at the University of West Attica. Retired now. Specifically in the ancient territories and cultures of modern-day China, Central Asia and Persia."

Lena carefully put the smaller fragment back on the display board and picked up the larger piece. She examined it again in the light even as Parker watched Jackson nervously pace.

"Everything alright, Captain?" she asked.

"Yeah. Yeah. Hunky-dory. Just stretching my legs." His focus was on something beyond the front window. "You know. Since I'm useless around all this, think I'll go out and get some fresh air." At the front door, he slipped on a pair of sunglasses. "Be back in a jiff."

Parker felt uneasy, probably perpetrated by Jackson's paranoia. But she was grateful for it. After Istanbul, she decided a position of heightened diligence was certainly warranted. Still wondering if her casual approach there had contributed to how things went sideways. She forced those thoughts away and returned her attention to the discussion about the cuneiform tablet fragments.

"Another curious anomaly about the tablet," Karas said. "It was discovered in Mongolia. I wasn't made aware of the details surrounding its recovery, but an Assyrian piece found in Mongolia? That's unheard of."

"When did you learn of the value these items might possess?" Parker asked.

"I wasn't. I'm not. I simply mentioned to Isabella, in passing, telling her I'd acquired them. And that I found the etchings to be quite unusual. She became quite animated as I described the markings. We discussed the odd symbols that seemed out of place. She made me promise not to tell or show anyone these fragments until she could get to Greece and see them for herself."

He smiled sadly, knowing he would never see his old friend again. "She didn't make it here."

"How do you know Isabella, Professor?" Parker asked.

"She was a grad student of mine. Many more years ago than I care to admit. A brilliant woman. Smart and beautiful and with a sass well beyond her years. I knew she would go on to do great things. It wasn't until several years later we would get together regularly. Two or three times a year."

"And you learned what she was up to? What she did?" Parker asked.

"She never said specifically, but an old man can read between the lines. She led a fascinating life, Agent Quinn. Did so much good in the world."

His sad eyes began to well up with tears.

"To clarify, she never saw the fragments?"

"Live? No," he said. "But she saw them. Insisted I send her detailed photographs. Of every angle, every conceivable lighting imaginable. It took me by surprise how excited she became examining them."

"But she never told you the significance of these pieces?" Parker asked. "Why they were important to her?"

"No. She said it was in my best interest that I not know. Only to keep them safeguarded and to tell no one I had them. I knew whatever it was, it was dangerous. Perhaps if she'd told me more, if she had opened up to me, maybe she'd still be alive."

"No, Professor," Parker said gently. "I am afraid the opposite would have been true. If anyone knew you had these, they would have killed you both."

Karas shook his head. "It is so hard to fathom the lengths these art thieves and unscrupulous collectors will go to to own something... The greed involved."

Lena returned the second fragment to the case and replaced the cover, resealing it.

"I am afraid, Professor," Parker said. "There's more at stake here than merely possessing collectibles and run-of-the-mill greed."

Before she could elaborate, the front door swung open.

Jackson rushed into the room, closing the door behind him. "People, we've got a problem."

Parker jumped to her feet. "What is it? What's wrong?"

"Astryomia."

"The police?" Karas said. "Why are they here?"

"Damned if I know," Jackson said. "But it's not the welcome wagon. Something's rotten in Athens, Parker. Is there a way out through the back?"

"Of course," Karas said, now on his feet too. "The kitchen. There's a back door."

As Jackson moved through the house, Parker glanced out the front window. Through the wrought-iron gate between the two sections of whitewashed wall, she saw their rental car parked at the curb, now boxed in by two marked police cruisers and one nondescript brown sedan.

Jackson poked his head back through the dining room archway. "We've got to move. Now!"

Lena came to her feet and scooped up the display case.

From the street out front, a voice with a distinctive Greek accent, amplified by a bullhorn, called out.

"Αστυνομία! Το κτίριο είναι περικυκλωμένο. Δεν υπάρχει διαφυγή. Βγείτε ειρηνικά και δεν θα πάθει κανείς κακό." *Police! The building is surrounded. There is no escape. Come out peacefully and no one will be harmed.*

CHAPTER THIRTEEN

AMPLIFIED BY THE BULLHORN, the cop said, "Αν δεν βγείτε ειρηνικά, δεν θα έχουμε άλλη επιλογή από το να μπούμε μέσα. Σας διαβεβαιώνω ότι αυτό δεν θα τελειώσει καλά."

Parker looked to Karas for a translation.

"Surrender or bad things are about to happen here. I'm paraphrasing."

She glanced at Jackson, silently communicating this was his wheelhouse. He was to take the lead. They would follow. Jackson nodded, but he lacked an immediate, viable tactical retreat strategy.

"What have you got for us, Captain?" Parker asked.

"The car out front is out of the question. We need some sort of distraction. I'm open to suggestions."

Parker glanced from him to Lena and even to Karas. "Anyone?"

"My car is in the garage. A Volkswagen Golf. But I'm afraid the battery is dead. I don't drive much in retirement."

"Don't sweat it, Professor," Jackson said. "Even if it were a tank, it wouldn't be much help to us. The cops have the garage barricaded with two more squad cars. Five more officers in addition to the seven I counted out front."

"Seems like a lot for just the three of us," Lena said.

The bullhorn boomed again, but no one paid much attention.

"Professor," Parker said. "I believe you are in danger. I'm afraid you'll need to come with us. With the fragments, of course."

There was no question in Parker's mind. Their enemies—whoever they were—had orchestrated the police raid. Enemies that were very powerful and had significant influence and reach. An enemy that was disturbingly well-informed about their actions.

Leaving the professor behind would surely mean one more death would be on her conscience. "At least for the time being."

"Of course," Karas said. "Isabella told me to trust you explicitly. That is enough for me."

"Great. Now, if we could figure a way to get us all out of here," Parker said.

"Without getting ourselves killed would be nice," Jackson added, gripping his Sig.

Parker's sidearm remained in her holster at the small of her back. She didn't know what the police had in mind or how far they would go to secure their prisoners, but she was sure she did not want to shoot her way out of this situation.

Her cell phone, placed on silent before the meeting, vibrated in her pocket. She pulled it out. The only people with that number were in this room, the CIA-provided pilots and Sebastian Davenport.

She glanced at the screen. She opened the line...

"Parker."

"Seems you Yanks got yourself in a bit of a pickle," Davenport's clipped British voice said.

Annoyed, she put him on speaker. "Unless you have a solution to said pickle, Davenport, we could do without the banter."

"Be prepared to move on my signal. The back door would be best."

"What will the signal be?" Parker asked.

Her answer came in the form of a large explosion. It vibrated through the floors and rattled the windows. Outside, they heard glass shattering and car alarms suddenly blaring over police sirens.

"I'm gonna go out on a limb and say that was the signal," Jackson said. "Let's move people."

He waved them through the dining room and into the kitchen. There, he held them up while he opened the back door. He surveyed the walled-in backyard beyond.

Parker noted his raised pistol. "Without bloodshed, if possible."

Jackson nodded. He raced across the narrow walkway through a flourishing garden similar to the one in the front yard. At the gate, he could hear police radios and officers shouting over the sirens, car horns, and alarms.

With Parker directly behind him and the phone connection with Davenport still open, Jackson said, "You got any other tricks up your fancy sleeve, English?"

"Count to five," the MI6 agent said. "Then come out, running like hell."

Jackson counted down silently in his head. His hand was on the throw bolt of the gate covering Karas' driveway. Waiting. A second explosion rocked the neighborhood. They all caught sight of a fireball and black oily smoke rising in the air.

He tossed back the throw bolt and pushed the large wooden gate open. Jackson took in the carnage Sebastian Davenport had created with a quick, practiced and reluctantly appreciative glance.

The two police cars he had spotted earlier during his walk around the house were both blackened, chard husks of the vehicles they once were. The police officers had moved away from the cars and the house, trying to maintain a perimeter but not too close to where the explosions had occurred, clearly concerned more were to follow.

Jackson spotted Davenport at the end of the street.

He stood on the running board of a black SUV. He held a shoulder-fired LAWS rocket launcher aimed and loaded at where the police officers had crouched behind a civilian vehicle and a grouping of trash bins.

"Come on! Let's move!" Jackson shouted.

They ran down the sidewalk alongside Karas' privacy wall. Karas and Lena—carrying the case under her arm like a football—hunkered closely behind Jackson. Parker brought up the rear. Her Sig out and aimed at the offices down the street in the opposite direction.

Reaching the end of the sidewalk, Jackson threw open the rear door of the SUV. Karas, Lena and Parker dove into the back seat. Jackson slammed the back door closed and opened the passenger door while providing cover fire for Davenport.

Purposely shooting over the heads of the cadre of cops, as per Parker's wishes.

Once everyone was safely inside the vehicle, Davenport passed the rocket launcher to Jackson and hit the gas hard, spinning the tires and leaving behind burnt rubber and clouds of blue-white smoke, even before his open door slammed shut.

"Everyone okay?" Parker asked.

Lena nodded.

Karas grinned like a kid on a rollercoaster. "I've not had this much fun since looters attacked us at the Qalat Al-Rahma site in '02."

Driving erratically, Davenport zigzagged through the winding streets. "Glad you're having so much fun,' mate. Cause the excitement isn't over yet."

The three backseat passengers spun around to look out the window even as they heard the distinctive wail of pursuing police vehicles.

"I'm hoping you have an idea for evading them that doesn't include blowing up yet more police cars," Parker said.

"You're concerned about a little vehicle damage now?"

"I'm concerned about the living, breathing police officers inside the vehicles now."

"Fair point," Davenport said.

Three cruisers pursued them. The two marked cars and the plain brown sedan from the front of the house. More were sure to join.

"I think I know where we can lose them," Jackson said. "Take a right at the next block."

The directions brought them back along the same route they had taken to enter the city on the way to Karas' residence earlier.

"Where are you taking us, bloke?"

"I noticed a construction site on the way into town. There, we can try and lose our police escort, or if we must make a stand, the risk of casualties and collateral damage will be reduced."

He glanced over his shoulder and met Parker's gaze.

She nodded, approving of his line of thinking.

Familiar with the city streets, the pursuing police officers steadily gained on them.

Davenport, while driving well, navigated without the benefit of knowing where he was going. Jackson shouted instructions, but he too was unfamiliar with the city's layout, trying his best to remember from only passing through once where he had seen the construction site in the first place.

He pointed to the left and shouted, "There!"

Parker leaned forward between the two front bucket seats for a better look.

Entering the construction site, Davenport drove fast. They bounced violently over the rutted dirt road as they sped past a trailer that served as the project's office. A cement mixer parked beside it. Near the trailer was a large sign that mapped out the future development of the complex, a residential community, including two additional exits at the far end of the property.

Parker quickly committed the map to memory.

She shifted her gaze to the rear window. Through it, she saw the three police cruisers pursuing them through a rolling cloud of dirt. Their flashing lights and grim expressions diffused by the swirling brown maelstrom of dirt, pebbles and debris.

"I have an idea. But things are going to get bumpy," Davenport said. "Hang on."

The site was dotted with concrete foundations and wooden frames. A few had progressed to having the roofs framed out. Davenport aimed the dark SUV toward the right, where there was a fork in the road. Ahead of them, Parker saw a mound of gravel and rock to the side of the dirt road.

To her amazement, and shock, Davenport appeared to be aiming them straight for it.

She gripped the back of the two bucket seats and twisted around to see how close the police cars were.

They were closing the gap.

Jackson said, "You're not going to do what I think you're going to do, are you?"

Davenport's thin lips twisted into a wicked smile.

"Aw, crap, English." Jackson pressed a hand to the car's roof and tensed.

The front end of the SUV started to rise as Davenport drove halfway up the incline of rock and gravel before quickly twisting the wheel to the left and moving back onto the road with a bang and a thump. Their back end fishtailed.

The closest police car zoomed up the incline.

They had been too close and shrouded in the swirling dust cloud kicked up by the SUV to see where they were going until they hit the incline. Too late to spin away.

The cruiser sailed over the rock pile. Its engine whined as it caught air.

The vehicle nose-dived into the ground. Its grille smashed into the dirt, crumbling the hood, while the back end, high in the air, came crashing down. The vehicle spun off to the right. Its tires dipped into a gully beside the road. The car ground to a stop and sent a hubcap spinning away.

"That's one down," Davenport said.

Jackson rolled the passenger side window down and twisted in his seat. Awkwardly, he struggled to pull the rocket launcher up from between his legs and shove it through the open window. He pulled himself to a sitting position on the windowsill as dust whipped across his face, lashing his skin with small pelting pebbles.

"Captain," Parker warned. "We talked about this."

Jackson either ignored her or could not hear her through the wind whipping past his face. He brought the rocket launcher to his shoulder, aimed at between the two remaining police vehicles, and pressed the trigger.

The missile shot forward, cutting through the dust cloud to hit and explode in the dirt roadway between the two vehicles. The cruisers swerved. One to the left, the other to the right, avoiding the geyser of fire, smoke, dust and dirt.

One vehicle spun off into a ditch.

The other plowed through the front porch of a house halfway completed. Timbers and boards went flying into the air like so much kindling. The roof framing collapsed, imploding downward as the siren wound down and went silent.

"That's two," Jackson said. "And three down."

Davenport did not let up on the gas. Instead, he sped toward one of the rear exits before twisting around to look at Parker. "Have you got a destination in mind?"

"In fact, I do."

She didn't know how their enemies discovered they would visit Professor Karas at his home, but she could guess. Somewhere, somehow, they had sprung a leak. Had a mole.

Now, on top of everything else, trying to keep them all safe, recover valuable stolen artifacts, and stop a terror attack, she needed to identify and stop a traitor in their midst.

While Davenport waited for an answer, he said, "Airport?"

"No."

Jackson and Davenport twisted in their seats to look at her, inquisitive expressions on their faces.

"We going to just drive around forever?" Davenport asked.

Angry and worried, Parker said, "Just drive. I'll let you know where."

CHAPTER FOURTEEN

Safehouse
Plaka Neighborhood, Athens, Greece

A MIX OF NEOCLASSICAL and contemporary architectural styles, the three-story house had a stone pathway that led to the front entrance framed by an arched doorway. Surrounded by a beautifully landscaped garden of potted plants, small trees, and vibrant Mediterranean flowers, the house was beige with matching blue shutters. It had large windows and balconies on the upper floors lined with ornate iron railings and festooned with flowering plants. A terracotta-tiled roof added to its traditional Greek charm.

The team pushed through the bright blue front door, slamming it closed behind them. They'd abandoned the rental four blocks away. Too close. They wouldn't be able to stay here for long. But it would be enough for them to regroup. To figure out their next move. Then, move on from there.

Inside, a dimly lit foyer with a cool marble floor and walls covered with faded tapestries held a scent of aged wood and incense. The main living area was a spacious room with simple yet comfortable furniture made of dark, rich tones of cherry and mahogany.

"Cool," Lena said, setting her laptop bags on the ornate cherry wood coffee table. She plopped on the sofa. "Whose place is this?"

Karas placed the display case off to one side of the table and sat beside her. A bit shaken but exhilarated by their dangerous escape.

Davenport paced the room, still jacked up with excitement and adrenaline. He found a bottle of brandy—Metaxa Private Reserve—in a cabinet and filled four Waterford crystal tumblers. He passed them around to Parker, Jackson, and Karas. When he reached Lena, he hesitated. "Are you old enough to drink?"

She snatched the tumbler from his hand and downed half of it in a single gulp. "What do you think?"

He shrugged and smiled. "You go, girl."

Returning to the cabinet where he'd found the booze, he poured a fifth drink for himself.

"Someone I used to work with. A friend," Parker replied, answering Lena's question. "We'll be safe here for the time being."

Jackson surveyed the enclosed garden beyond before fully parting the flowing, neutral-toned curtains framing the arched, floor-to-ceiling windows. Unlocking and opening them, he filled the room with light and fresh air. Freshly disturbed dust motes danced on the beams of sunlight.

"Stay away from the street front windows," he said. "I'm going to go check the perimeter."

He left the room. His brandy left untouched on the fireplace mantle.

Davenport strolled over to the hearth. He picked up the tumbler, tossing back his, then consuming Jackson's.

"Lena, work with Professor Karas," Parker said. "See what you can make of his tablet. I'm looking for anything that links it to the Chronicle of Kings tablet, anything that might help us uncover what the damn things say. Sebastian, I need to know who sent those mercenaries after us in Istanbul. Who's got the international juice to turn the entire Athens police department against us? I need to make a phone call. We'll meet up again in an hour."

She left the room, going down a hallway until she reached the narrow winding staircase that led up to a rooftop veranda. Mosaic tiles, weathered by time, covered the deck. The back wall was covered with cascading vines. On the low buttress walls sat terracotta pots overflowing with vibrant bougainvilleas and fragrant herbs. Their colors contrasted against the backdrop of drifting white clouds and the azure Grecian sky.

A scattering of comfortable chairs and cushions circled a rustic wooden table.

Overhead, a canopy of grapevines provided dappled shade. Their lush foliage rustled gently in the breeze. Lanterns were suspended from wrought-iron hooks. As Parker remembered, when lit, they illuminated the veranda with a soft, golden glow as night fell, and the deep purple skies would give way to the velvety blackness of night.

She took a deep, calming breath and over the city beyond. Its labyrinthine alleys and ancient landmarks were bathed in the warm hues of the midday sun. She pulled her cell phone from her back pocket and punched in the top number on her contact list.

With the phone to her ear, she listened to it ring.

"Parker?" Mazz's voice. "Is that you?"

Her voice caught. She held the phone away and cleared her throat. "Yes. It's me."

"Are you okay? We heard—"

"Where are you?" Parker asked. "Can you talk freely?"

"My office. What's happening?"

Parker glanced at the closed French doors behind her. "I don't have a lot of time. Can you loop Secretary Grayson in?"

"Of course. Give me a sec."

When Mazz came back, he said, "I have her. The line is as secure as it can be."

It was the best she could hope for. "Madam Secretary, good afternoon."

"It's only eight a.m. here, Parker. Where are you?"

"I'd prefer not to say, ma'am. No offense."

"None taken," Grayson said. "I tend to get that a lot from my field agents lately. Are you and your team alright? We heard about Istanbul."

"The team is fine," Parker reported. "Thank you for asking, ma'am. But we lost a valuable asset in the incident."

"Yes. We are aware," Mazz said. "The National Intelligence Organization, with the help of some friends at the CIA, they've spun the story, protecting the.. sensitivities around the situation. The authorities have classified the incident as an isolated act of religiously based terrorism. "

"Were you able to secure any useful intelligence," Grayson asked. "Before the loss of our asset?"

Parker swallowed hard at the memory, cautious about how much to reveal. "Yes. She provided a lead. We're pursuing it and will continue to do so."

"And you believe it's necessary to do this on your own?"

"Yes, ma'am. I do. We've been compromised, Madam Secretary. I don't know how or by whom, but the incident in Istanbul and one more recently—"

"An unusual confrontation with the Athens police has just crossed my desk," Grayson said.

Parker smiled. The woman knew all, it seemed. "We've sprung a leak, ma'am. I'm not sure who or how far up the chain, but it's certainly someone in the know."

"That is a serious allegation, Parker," Mazz said.

"Unfortunately," Grayson said. "Such allegations have all too frequently proven to be correct lately. I trust Parker's instincts. She and her team are the ones in the field, in harm's way. They are best suited to determine how to keep themselves safe and complete the mission."

"Yes, ma'am," Mazz said.

"Parker," Grayson said. "We'll rip through heaven and earth to uncover any potential leaks here. In the meantime, I'm assuming you no longer want the services of your pilots, Jason and Jared."

"No, ma'am." With that potential leak plugged, their trail would grow cold here in Greece.

"A word of caution, Parker," Grayson said. "Your Judas could be closer to you than to us."

"I'm aware." That a member of her team—Jackson, Davenport or Lena—was the mole in their operation, the very idea soured her stomach. "I'll suss out if the problem's on my end."

If it was, she'd need to root the mole out. Quickly.

"What else do you need from us?" Mazz asked.

"I'm not sure at the moment. I just wanted y'all to know we're okay. And we're moving forward."

"That's quite appreciated," Grayson said.

"It might be some time before you hear from me again."

Mazz said, "Understood."

"Stay safe and watch your six," Grayson added.

Parker closed the connection and pocketed her phone, taking another moment to survey the bustling Plaka streets. There was a timeless beauty to Athens, filled with solace and strength. Her time spent here, in the city, in this house, filled her with sweet memories and were among some of the best in her life.

But that was a lifetime ago, she thought, before DHS.

Hearing Jackson come through the French doors behind her, she turned.

"Everything alright?" he asked.

She noted the look of concern on the military man's dark face. "Yes, but I had to send our pilots off on an assignment."

He arched an inquisitive eye.

She hated lying to him, but she had no choice. She quickly made up a make-believe lead and laid out her reasons for sending the CIA-provided pilots.

He nodded. "Probably better that way. Any thoughts on who the rat, or rats, might be?"

She should've known he'd confront the problem head-on. Even if he was the mole, trying to keep tabs on her thoughts or throw her off. It would be that sort of response he knew she'd expect.

"That obvious?"

"That we've been compromised?" He joined her by the low buttress walls. He glanced out over the busy streets below. "No other explanation. Few people knew we were going to Turkey. Only *we* knew we were coming here. By we, I mean the four of us and the pilots."

"Isabella told Karas we were coming," Parker said. "Phone could've been tapped. Involving the local law tells us that wouldn't be far-fetched."

"But, not likely," Jackson reasoned. "We were moving way too fast for that. It's one of us. Has to be."

"Which is why we're going off the grid. Cutting off all communications with the outside world. Authorities. Our organizations. Effective immediately, we're radio silent. It'll help narrow it down to—"

"Us or not us."

She smiled. "Hopefully, it's the latter."

"Doubt it," Jackson said.

She hoped he was wrong. But, at the moment, she wasn't very optimistic. "Either way, we need to figure it out fast."

"Before someone gets killed," he said.

Parker sighed. "You mean before someone *else* gets killed."

CHAPTER FIFTEEN

The Summer Garden
St. Petersburg, Russia

ENVISIONED BY PETER THE Great in 1704, and seeing to its planning and development personally, the Summer Garden is home to numerous marble statues sculptured by Italian sculptors of the 17th and 18th centuries. A masterpiece of landscape architecture, captivating visitors with its serene beauty and grandeur. Nestled along the Neva River, the historic garden is a verdant oasis amidst the vibrant cityscape of St. Petersburg.

A symphony of colors and scents greeted visitors stepping through the wrought-iron gates. Meticulously manicured flowerbeds burst forth with vibrant blooms in every hue imaginable. Delicate roses, cheerful daisies, and fragrant lilies vie for attention, creating a kaleidoscope of floral splendor that delights the senses.

At the heart of the Summer Garden stood Peter the Great's first Summer Palace.

Built by the great Italian architect Domenico Trezzini, the majestic Summer Palace, a two-story Dutch-style affair with a high roof and comparatively modest interior—was one of St. Petersburg's first stone palaces. Its golden facades glint in the fading sunlight. A marvel of Baroque architecture, the palace is adorned with intricate carvings and ornamental details, reflecting the opulence and grandeur of Russia's imperial past.

As evening fell, the garden took on a magical aura against the backdrop of the setting sun. Soft lamplight cast enchanting shadows among the foliage. The winding pathways meander through the garden's lush greenery. The sound of trickling water from nearby fountains filled the air. Throughout the garden, secluded alcoves and hidden nooks offered private spots for quiet reflection or intimate conversations.

As Maximilian Stahl wandered through the gardens, he passed other visitors quietly enjoying the beauty of the approaching evening or seated on secluded benches where they could contemplate life and the starlit sky.

The career spymaster sought to take advantage of such seclusion for his meeting with Kuznetsov, whom he spotted traversing the winding pathways toward him. Stahl selected a small atrium off the main path beyond a trestle covered with thick flowery Ivy.

The two men came together in front of a stone bench. Kuznetsov kept his hands in the pockets of his dark overcoat, his head slightly bowed.

"Another failure, comrade."

"It is true the operation in Greece did not work out to our full advantage."

"To our full advantage?" Stahl ground his back teeth in anger. "It was a complete and total disaster. Not only did you fail to secure either the individuals or the information they sought, your actions jeopardized our entire operation to exposure by the West."

"None of it can be traced back to us. I made assurances. Seen as simply a failure of an incompetent police force. A domestic police action gone wrong." Kuznetsov's voice carried no more emotion than if he were reporting on the weather. "But we now know who they were there to see. And why."

"Enlighten me," Stahl said, No less angry, but adding, "old friend."

"They went to see a man named Ioannis Karas. A retired professor from the University of West Attica. His specialties were archaeology and art history, with a concentration in the ancient territories and cultures of modern-day China, Central Asia and the region of Persia."

Stahl nodded. "Oh, That makes it crystal clear."

"The American's interest goes beyond his academic expertise," Kuznetsov explained. "Professor Karas is in possession of a cuneiform tablet reportedly linked back to the Neo-Assyrian Empire period."

"Impossible," Stahl said. "I am aware of every piece of art, every artifact, every worthless chunk of broken pottery that came from that region during that time. I am aware of no such tablet existing."

"Be that as it may," Kuznetsov said, "According to our asset, the spy known as Ebon Sparrow considered this tablet, which you claim does not exist, a valuable artifact. Enough, so she sent the Americans to retrieve it and sacrificed her own life to keep it from us."

Stahl allowed Kuznetsov's sarcasm to slide. "This tablet references what we seek?"

"Unknown at this juncture. But the Americans possess it, and I believe we would be best served to not dismiss it with such disregard."

As if the idea were his own, Stahl said, "Perhaps this *is* the key to unlocking the secrets that have thus far eluded us. The final piece. We need to know more."

"Of course," Kuznetsov said. "Also, Doctor Alhadeff has reported a potential breakthrough in his teams' efforts to decipher the Chronicle of Kings tablet."

Stahl leaned in with intensity. A thrill coursed through him at the prospect his years of work and preparation could finally be coming to fruition. Perhaps the last twenty-four hours were not as disastrous as he'd first thought. "Tell me."

"Among Alhadeff's team, there's... differences of opinions. As there always are," Kuznetsov said. "But Alhadeff reports they've translated a particular set of symbols and related markings. He is confident they refer to a temple. He called it whispering sands. Or, possibly stirring storms."

Stahl wanted more. "And?"

"There is a set of ruins. Recently discovered in an archaeological dig sponsored by the British government and several universities. In the remote desert on the outskirts south of Mosul. Alhadeff believes the ruins might be this temple."

Stahl paced before the stone bench, processing this new information.

The teams of so-called experts he's assembled over the years—whether by force or willing participation—have sent him on wild goose chases before. And yet, it had been some time since there'd been any forward movement on unscrambling the damn cuneiform text. With the news that the American team may have discovered and possesses information they do not have, what initially seemed a setback could well be an important breakthrough.

Stahl struggled to temper his excitement.

Time was running out.

Those who supported his efforts with funding, manpower, and resources were growing short on patience. Stahl feared he could afford to waste no more time. Nor could he afford to endure any more failures from his people. Yet, neither could he ignore potential new information. His grasp on what the tablet and seal told them was too spotty, too fragmented, amounting to little more than educated guesswork.

He glanced hard at Kuznetsov.

He placed a hand on his old friend's shoulder. "We need to know the value of what the Americans believe they have discovered."

"It may be nothing," Kuznetsov cautioned. He had accompanied Stahl down their many false paths over the years. "Perhaps this new tablet is meaningless. After all these years, to have something surface—as the Americans say—out of the blue seems unlikely."

"You speak the truth, brother. But what is also true is after all these years, with all the experts we've utilized, we are now closer to deciphering the tablet's message than ever before. Perhaps this tablet is the missing key we've needed."

Stahl dropped his hand and began to pace once more. "Pressures are mounting. Results must be achieved. There is only one way to ensure we know what value the tablet and this professor might have to offer."

He faced Kuznetsov. "Go to Greece. Take charge of our efforts to secure this tablet and this professor. Eliminate those who oppose us. Once and for all."

Kuznetsov nodded. "I will leave immediately."

"There is no one I trust more than you to take control of our destiny."

"What of the Temple of the Whispering Sands? Though there is debate, there is strong opinion our hunt may well end there."

"I agree. It cannot be ignored. While you go to Greece, I will personally lead our efforts at the temple," Stahl said. "To ensure all goes well."

Kuznetsov nodded. "I will contact you as soon as I have anything worthwhile to report."

"I look forward to hearing from you. Good hunting, my old friend." Silently, Stahl added, *do not fail me a third time.*

CHAPTER SIXTEEN

Safehouse

WITH THE APPROACH OF nightfall, they'd drawn the drapes. A fire crackled in the large hearth. Professor Ioannis Karas paced the front of the room, looking every bit the academic teacher he'd once been. Over a pair of reading glasses, he glanced at a yellow legal pad in his hand. The pages were filled with handwritten notes and doodles. He flipped back and forth, reading them silently, his lips moving.

Lena remained on the couch. She leaned forward, scrutinizing the screens of her two laptops while scribbling notes on a legal pad of her own. When not writing, she clenched the pencil between her teeth. Numerous bite marks indented the wood. Davenport stood by the bar with yet another crystal tumbler filled with booze and ice in his hand. He appeared bored. Jackson stood behind the sofa, tense and attentive.

Parker came into the room. "You have the floor, Professor."

He glanced up. "Ah, Ms. Quinn... excuse me. Parker. Yes, yes, this is most fascinating. First, how much are you all aware of Neo-Assyrian history?"

"Afraid I skipped that class during my misspent youth," Davenport offered, swirling his glass.

Jackson shrugged, indicating he knew not a blessed thing.

"A little," Parker said. "Why don't you start with the pertinent facts? We'll let you know what we need clarified."

"Splendid. Yes." Karas forced a smile. "While I am no expert myself, I've spent the time brushing up on my... Anyway, we need to begin with King Ashurbanipal. You've all heard of him?"

The question was greeted with a round of nods.

"Stupendous. Born into the royal family, Ashurbanipal II ascended to power through a combination of inheritance and strategic maneuvering in 668 BC, following the death of his father, King Esarhaddon. Upon assuming power, Ashurbanipal embarked on a colonizing campaign marked by brutal military conquest. He invaded and conquered various regions, including Babylonia, Elam, Anatolia and Egypt. Extending a Syrian dominance over significant portions of the ancient Near East. He effectively suppressed revolts and rebellions within the empire, maintaining control over unruly providences and those under his rule.

"His military achievements even extended into naval warfare." Karas paused to take a sip of water from a plastic bottle. "Ashurbanipal deployed his naval forces to control trade routes and exert influence over coastal regions, further enhancing Assyrian power and prestige. However, despite his military successes, internal instabilities, external pressures from rival powers, and the eventual coalition of the Babylonians, Metas, and Scythians led to the ultimate downfall of Ashurbanipal's reign and the demise of the Neo-Assyrian Empire in 609 BC."

Jackson said, "That's fascinating, Prof., but—"

"Not really," Davenport said with a yawn.

"But," Jackson continued, "can we fast forward? Say twenty-six hundred years. To today."

"I'm getting to that," Karas said. "Not all of Ashurbanipal's significant contributions revolved around warmongering and brutal territorial expansion or subjugation of his people. He was a notable patron of the arts and literature. Best known for establishing the Library of Ashurbanipal in Nineveh, of course."

"The Royal Library," Parker said. "Where the artifacts that we're chasing were originally recovered from."

"Exactly right," Karas said, excited. "While the ancient Assyrians did not have a distinct concept of modern sciences, they made significant advancements in various fields such as astronomy, mathematics, medicine and engineering. Of importance to us is their work in medicine."

"How so?" Parker asked.

"The Assyrians developed rudimentary knowledge of medicinal plants, surgical techniques, and treatments for various ailments. Medical texts have been found among the clay tablets in the Royal Library containing impressive descriptions of diseases, symptoms and treatments, including a systematic approach to healthcare."

"Not to continually be the dunce in the class," Jackson said, "but I still don't see how any of this is important to us."

"It's significant because the symbols etched in the tablet identified as the Chronicle of Kings and the Guardian of Secrets Seal. While we only have photographs and the work previously done by various FBI experts and scholars, I believe the tablet tells of advanced—for the time—scientific experiments."

"That doesn't sound ominous at all," Davenport said between sips of his drink.

"Agreed," Karas said. "From what Miss Lena and I have been able to extrapolate from the text, we believe there are references to alchemy—the proto-scientific efforts of the day, where efforts were made to combine elements of chemistry, physics, medicine, astrology, mysticism, and spirituality—"

"Mumbo-jumbo." Davenport waved a hand in the air. "Nonsense."

"These early alchemists cannot be so easily dismissed, I'm afraid," Karas said, "If we are correct," he glanced at Lena, who nodded, "under Ashurbanipal's command—perhaps purely by accident—they may have created a biological agent that reshaped the balance of power in the ancient world."

"A biological agent?" Parker repeated. "You're not yanking our pant legs, Professor, are you?"

"I wish I were," Karas said. "Understand, there is a lot of information contained in the tablet and corresponding cylinder seal that is still undecipherable. And thus remains a mystery."

Lena piped up for the first time. "But I believe I know why the FBI and the experts they've consulted have had such difficulty translating artifacts. It is because the symbols and motifs used weren't just from various other languages or known dialects at the time—which was their prevailing theory—but it was written with a complicated cipher—encrypted—more than likely developed for this specific purpose."

"What purpose is that, Lena?" Parker asked.

"To prevent anyone from doing what we're attempting to do. Decipher artifacts. Unlock what the tablet and seal say. To keep what it chronicles a secret."

"Why create a document that can't be read? Understood?" Jackson asked.

"Forbidden knowledge," Lena said. "Locked away. Two of the phrases the FBI believed they translated correctly. And I agree with them. I think the tablet talks of a secret or a hidden—something—and is meant to be understandable, readable, only by those for whom it was intended."

"For your eyes only?" Davenport said. "A top secret designation."

"Yes," Lena said. "For those in power."

"Think of it like a code. Or a combination," Karas said. "If you have the correct key, the message is apparent. Without it." He shrugged. "Unreadable."

"How is it the two of you've made more progress deciphering all this in the last few hours than entire teams of experts over the last decade?" Davenport asked.

"Because of the fragments Professor Karas had," Lena explained. "By comparing a number of the symbols and markings it contains with similar ones on the chronicle tablet and the seal, I was able to use my computerized algorithms and software—some of which I designed and developed myself—to decipher with greater certainty the meanings behind many of the symbols used."

"What we are saying the tablets convey," Karas said, "we can't say with one-hundred percent certainty that we are correct. There is still much to be deciphered. Each new secret unlocked may alter or change what we think is accurate now."

"A work in progress," Parker said.

"Yes. But," Lena said. "I am confident we are on the correct course."

"Not off the mark by much," Karas said, nodding enthusiastically.

"Great. Your asses are covered," Davenport said, pouring himself another drink. "What do we do with all this?"

"Can we get back to the whole biological agent stuff?" Jackson said. "That's the gist of all this, isn't it? That's what Stahl, or whoever, is after."

Karas cleared his throat. "In our best estimation, the tablet records how Ashurbanipal's alchemists experimented with various plants and animals, seeking to understand the nature of diseases that plagued their communities, would be my guess. To create resistance, or possibly even cures, for known pathogens. Through systematic trial and error, they identified specific genetic traits—biological properties—that—"

"You got all that from those hunks of stone?" Davenport asked.

"We are extrapolating," Karas said patiently. "And our… theories of what the tablets say would need to go through thorough, rigorous scientific method analysis. Be scrutinized by peer review. And, I am using modern terminology to explain what they discovered in a very rudimentary way."

He leveled the Englishman with a hard stare. "But yes, Agent Davenport, these tablets do contain a lot of information. They convey how these alchemists discovered—or created—certain pathogens which crossed species barriers and infected organisms previously thought to be immune."

"Like Covid, a few years back," Parker said. "Humans were immune to the strain until it mutated—"

"Intentionally mutated," Davenport said.

"A mutation," Parker continued, "which made it possible to jump from animal to people."

"Yes," Karas said. "Experimenting with propagation techniques, selective breeding and genetic manipulation to enhance the virulence and transmissibility of these pathogens while ensuring its specificity to a desired target species. Such as specific crops, livestock, and or waterways."

"Creating a potent biological weapon," Jackson said. "Unbelievable."

Karas frowned. "I am afraid humanity's hubris and capacity to inflict horrendous harm upon itself is not contained to the modern world, Captain."

"They made it deadly to humans?" Parker asked.

"We can't tell from these tablets. From the small percentage we've translated so far," Lena said.

"But," Karas said. "If we've translated this properly, it's clear they developed something of a biological nature and conducted environmental field tests on farms and animal pens. They observed the effects of the pathogen on crops and livestock. Refined their methods based on the results, and modified the design to maximize its effectiveness and minimize unintended consequences."

"Have you any evidence," Parker asked, "they used this biological agent against people?"

"Not directly from the tablets or seal, no," Karas said. "In history, of course, there are reports of various plagues, viruses, and other pestilence that affected a great many regions and people. It's impossible to attribute such events to the use of an Assyrian bioweapon of this nature with any certainty at this juncture."

"Assuming such a weapon was developed and deployed," Parker asked. "What might the results have been? Symptoms. Side-effects."

"Well outside my area of expertise," Karas said. "But based on the historical record, plagues of the type we're discussing could result in individuals developing severe dermatological manifestations, including widespread implementation of painful lesions, ulcers and necrotic tissue on the skin. Affected skin would exhibit discoloration ranging from reddish rashes to deeper purples, blues and blacks due to impaired blood circulation. The discoloration would be visibly striking and a prominent marker of the severity of the disease. Other symptoms might include open wounds and sores, severe itching and burning sensations, respiratory illness, fever and fatigue. Gastrointestinal discomfort. Often seen as a progression to the central nervous system, resulting in neurological complications, such as confusion, delirium, seizures, and ultimately death."

"Good times," Davenport said.

"Biological weapons are no laughing matter," Jackson said.

He paced behind the sofa. "Okay. Let's slow our roll here for a minute. Assuming everything you've translated is correct—and I'm not questioning your conclusions—the tablets talk about an ancient biological weapon."

He focused his attention on Parker. "So what? I don't mean to be flippant, but all we've learned is the ancient Assyrians were a bunch of asshats. They developed this crap, may have possibly used it twenty-six hundred years ago." He stopped pacing. "Other than historical curiosity, why all this fuss?"

"I don't know," Parker said. "But these terrorists—whoever they are—have spent a lot of time, money, effort, and taken lives to track this all down. There must be more to it than just deciphering the text, to knowing a weapon of this kind existed."

"Perhaps they don't know what it says," Lena offered. "Haven't even translated enough to know even the little we know."

"I would doubt that," Davenport said. "If anything, I'd guess they know more than us. To Parker's point, they've gone to extremes to get to whatever these ancient stories lead."

"Agreed. There's a piece to all this we're still missing."

Karas nodded. "Just knowing the ingredients and method of development of such a… pathogen, virus or whatever we call it, would be quite dangerous. Having access to such a recipe, to develop… By introducing such a contagion into the population today, something not seen on the face of the earth in thousands of years, with no natural immunity or defenses, no prepared vaccine... The potential of such an event could be catastrophic."

The room fell silent.

A minute passed before Davenport said, "This fun little concoction of yours, Professor. It got a name?"

"We've noted several references—as had the FBI—to something called the Breath of Ashur," Lena said. "But of greater concern… "

Karas stepped toward the coffee table.

He pointed at a section on the tablet in the display case.

Lena turned her computer so everyone could see the screenshot of the Chronicle of Kings tablet. She pointed to a similar string of markings on it. Markings that appeared with frequency on both tablets.

"Is this," Lena said, *"Mūtu sāmu."*

Jackson said, "English?"

"In ancient Assyrian, Akkadian," Karas said. "It means… *Scarlet Death.*"

CHAPTER SEVENTEEN

"WELL," DAVENPORT SAID. "THAT sounds charming."

"Then you'll love this," Lena said. "With the professor's help, I managed to translate a few additional markings from the chronicle tablet and the Guardians of Secrets seal that could—emphasizing the word could—be a reference to a location. What's at that location, I can't say. Other than it appears to be of particular importance."

"What makes you say that?" Parker asked.

"This location appears to have been heavily protected. There are repeated notes of warnings as well as references to encoded maps, physical barriers, indications of divine rituals and spiritual safeguards having been performed to ensure that this location remained undisturbed."

"Joy," Davenport said from the bar. "As if Scarlet Death isn't creepy enough, now we've got spiritual voodoo and divine divinations to deal with?"

"Divinations isn't the correct word," Karas said.

"Whatever."

"Comes with the job, English," Jackson said.

"This important location," Parker said. "Where is it?"

"The best we could come up with was a name. The Temple of the Whispering—"

"Or quiet," Karas said.

"Sand or storms," Lena finished.

"Or possibly shadows," Karas said. "It is difficult to be precise, considering the various languages and encryptions used. What is clear is that Ashurbanipal and his alchemists wanted this location to remain a secret. Not to be found or opened by anyone not authorized. Whatever they were hiding—protecting—scared them."

"Why do we care about this location?" Davenport asked. "I thought we were after the stolen artifacts. Isn't that—recovering them—the mission?"

"English has a point," Jackson said.

Thinking out loud, Parker said, "What if this isn't about the artifacts: the tablet, the seal, the statue? The terrorists. They've had them for years. But they've only become important recently. The chatter has only intensified lately. Why is that? I don't think it's about the stolen items at all. But where they lead."

"Directions. Like a map?" Lena said excitedly.

"Like a treasure map," Jackson said.

"What's important now is the where," Parker said. "And the what."

A chill raced down her spine. She leveled them all with a cold, hard stare. "The Breath of Ashur. The Scarlet Death. That's what the terrorists are after. A biological weapon—contagion—unknown to modern humanity with no known immunity or countermeasure. Released, the result could be devastating."

"The recipe for a twenty-six-hundred-year-old bio-weapon," Jackson said. "Or, are you suggesting they're after the actual weapon... Could it even still exist?"

"Again, not my area of expertise, but properly stored and contained," Karas said. "Half-life and all that." He shrugged. "There's no reason it couldn't be as dangerous now as the moment it was created."

"Where do we find this Temple of the Whispering Winds?" Parker asked.

"Sands," Jackson said.

"Storms," Davenport added.

"Whatever," Parker said. "Where is it?"

"The tablets are no help there," Lena said. "At least not until we're able to translate more."

"But," Karas said. "I know of an archaeological dig that began about two years ago. South of Mosul. A British-funded project. They recently reported finding what they believe to be a previously undiscovered temple. It is thought to date back to the Neo-Assyrian Empire period."

"Where?" Parker asked.

"The capital city of Kalhu."

"Let me wrap my head around this," Jackson said. "We're talking about a virus created as a weapon of mass destruction twenty-six hundred years ago, and it's just placed in storage? In a temple? On the outskirts of their capital city. And it might still be there? Intact? That's nuts."

"It's in keeping with what a war-mongering, scientifically forward-thinking despot like Ashurbanipal would do," Karas said. "If he had such a weapon available. And it was as dangerous as we think it was. It makes sense. He'd want to keep it a safe distance from the city. But also close enough his military could get to it. Use it to weaken or destroy his enemies if the opportunity arose. But there's more—"

"Isn't there always," Davenport said.

"The tablet I possess—which I refer to as the Echoes of Empires—Miss Lena and I have determined was written by a man named Nizar Khaldun. A military man from a long line of military commanders. He was one of Ashurbanipal's most trusted aides and confidants. According to his tablet story, he played a pivotal role in advising the king on matters of military strategy and statecraft. In many ways, he was the king's right-hand man. Fiercely loyal to Ashurbanipal."

Karas went on, "The Echoes tablet refers to events following the fall of Ninevah. I think the Scarlet Death virus might have been moved from an original location to an alternative, hidden stronghold."

"Hold your horses for a second there, Prof.," Jackson said. "You're suggesting that as Ashurbanipal faced his greatest military challenge, the downfall of his entire empire, he'd give up his greatest weapon rather than use it against his enemies? Why would he do that?"

"Perhaps by the time he could deploy it, he knew the fight had been lost," Karas said. "Rather than risk the virus being used against himself, perhaps he instructed Khaldun to hide it. Perhaps keep it in reserve. An ace-in-the-hole for future use. Or, maybe dispose of it. We cannot know for sure based on what we've unraveled so far."

"Does the tablet tell us where the Scarlet Death was moved to?" Parker asked.

"We will need to continue… " Karas hedged.

"One possibility is the Temple of the Whispering Sands, of course," Lena said. "But, the Echoes tablet contains symbols we've translated as fire or flames. Possibly as a place of storage or method of destruction. We've translated another symbol that may mean safe storage or vault."

"Crematoriums a thing back in those days?" Davenport asked.

"Or the one has nothing to do with the other." Lena's frustration bubbled forth. "It could all just be conjecture. And wrong."

"What might help," Karas said, "is that the Echoes tablet tells us Khladun, at the time of Ninevah's final defeat, sold or gave away specific items of key importance to the empire. A logical assumption would be some of these items relate to the Scarlet Death.

"And, here's where things get interesting," Karas said. "The items mentioned in the tablet were acquired by a man named Bataar Temujin. A trader known to venture beyond the traditional paths of the Silk Road network. Trading routes connecting China and the Far East to the Middle East and Europe. But were never known to extend into Iraq."

"How do you know this?" Parker asked.

"Here, we *are* getting into my area of expertise." Karas explained, "I have come across Temujin's name before. From what I know of him, he was a determined and ingenious adventurer, well respected by the market merchants and other travelers he encountered."

Karas plopped down in an overstuffed chair and waved for Davenport to pour him a drink.

"Temujin has often been associated with another historical figure. A friendship he had with a powerful nomadic chieftain named Ochir. He was a charismatic leader revered by the nomadic tribes of Mongolia at the time, known for his strategic ability to unite many disparate clans. In a number of missives, Ochir is mentioned as having acquired many items. Statues, jewelry, and the like that, by their descriptions, could be Assyrian. Most scholars dismiss this as impossible because there is little evidence the Silk Road extended as far as the ancient Mesopotamian regions."

Karas leaned forward in his seat. "I believe, and the Echoes tablet confirms, Bataar Temujin was one such traveler. It was that which sparked my interest in the fragments in the first place. I suspected some of the text was Assyrian script, even if corrupted and impure—or, as we've discovered—cleverly encrypted. The experts rejected the possibility. They dismissed the tablet fragments as fake, an incompetent replica."

"Why?" Jackson asked.

"Because it would have been extraordinary. Such a discovery would challenge much of what we think we know about the period. How far did the ancients' movements expand? Their migration. Their regional interactions with others, with distant cultures. All of that could be very different than what we currently believe."

"A reason for all the deniers you encountered," Parker said. "Scholars and experts get entrenched deeply in their findings and don't react kindly to having their established models and theories challenged."

"More than likely, that's what kept it from being noticed by our terrorists friends," Jackson said. "The so-called experts' incompetence may well have saved your life, Prof."

"A sobering thought." Karas visibly shivered and took a slug of his drink. "I know it's based on shaky translations, but it stands to reason. The items Khaldun gave or sold to Temujin could reveal additional information about the Breath of Ashur, the Scarlet Death."

"That does make a certain kind of sense," Jackson said. "Give the treasure map to someone who can take it as far away as possible. But still, this Khaldun must have really trusted Temujin."

"I would agree," Karas said. "And to safeguard the items, Temujin would need someone to trust. Someone who could hide them away. I believe that person would have been Chief Ochir. Like many nomadic chieftains, Ochir would have a stronghold to store his wealth from rival tribes and potential invaders."

"A stash house," Jackson said.

"Treasure room would be the technical term," Karas said. "But yes, a stash house."

"Any chance you've got a line on where this stash house might be?" Davenport asked.

"As it so happens, I do." Karas leaned forward in his chair. "According to an acquaintance—the person who put the Echoes of Empires tablet up for sale—rumors have long spoken of a place that might house Ochir's treasures. Have any of you ever visited the spectacular Flaming Cliffs known as Bayanzag?"

"Mongolia?" Davenport asked.

Jackson looked at Parker. "Where to, boss-lady? A whispering temple outside Mosul or some fire rock formation in Asia?"

"We cannot ignore either lead." Parker sighed. With no choice, she said, "We split up."

CHAPTER **EIGHTEEN**

Archaeological Dig – Ancient Capital City of Kalhu
South of Mosul, Iraq

THE SCORCHING SUN BEGAN its descent behind
the softened ridges of the worn mountain range, casting
an amber hue over the desolate, sandy landscape. The air
buzzed with the almost constant swirl of particle-filled
wind, stinging exposed skin. From the site came the sounds
of canvas tent flaps snapping and the clanging of metal
containers hung from poles or being collected and stored.
Hot, weary workers scurried about. Packing up their tools
before darkness descended over the harsh terrain, the dig
team was anxious to return to town for a warm shower, a hot
meal, and cold drinks.

As the last rays of sunlight stretched across the desert,
casting long shadows that looked like sinister fingers
reaching out from somewhere otherworldly, men and women
dressed in Western safari beige packed several dust-covered
Range Rovers. With them, many dark-skinned men, clad in
long, elegant tunics known as thobes and headdresses called
keffiyehs, climbed into the vehicles.

From a distant ridge, Stahl watched through field glasses.
With him was a team of ten archeologists, scientists, and
military-trained mercenaries.

The Range Rovers left, following rutted trails in the sand, sending billowing dust clouds in their wake. The camp fell silent as darkness crept in, and the quiet desert reclaimed its domain. The only sound came from the distant howl of a hot, sandy wind.

Stahl slid down the backside of the embankment to where his men waited. He spoke to the leader of his mercenaries. A rough-looking, former member of the Israeli MOSSAD. A man named Aryeh Peretz.

"No doubt there will have left a small security detail behind. I would not anticipate much resistance. This dig has been deemed relatively benign and free of controversy. Take your men in and secure any guards swiftly and permanently. Above all else, no calls for help must get out."

"Understood."

Peretz signaled for his men to mount up on their ATVs. Five men, plus himself, dressed in desert sand-colored camouflage with military harnesses and equipment. Their clothing and weapons were void of identifying unit emblems or insignia identification. The dark-colored four-wheel vehicles were surprisingly quiet as they sped toward the encampment a quarter of a mile away. A thick trail of dust in their wake.

Stahl addressed the remaining contingent. Four men, including Dr. Noam Alhadeff. Each an expert in their particular field of archaeology, ancient languages and paleo-civilizations. Clad in lightweight long-sleeved shirts, cargo pants, hiking boots, and wide-brimmed hats, they clutched notebooks and computer tablets.

"Once Peretz secures the camp, we will proceed. We shall not have much time to find what we've come here to find. Should we prove successful, Doctor, you've brought what you need to extract our treasure safely?"

"Yes," Alhadeff said. "Three military-grade, shock-resistant titanium alloy containers, with a secondary containment layer made of reinforced glass and a double-sealing, heavy-duty mechanical locking system with high-grade, reinforced gaskets to ensure airtight and watertight integrity."

"Spare me the details, Doctor. I just need to know if you are ready to go."

"Yes, sir. We are."

Stahl returned his attention to the quiet encampment in the gathering dusk. Distant gunfire split the still air. In the eerie silence that followed, Stahl's walkie-talkie crackled with static.

Peretz's voice. "The camp is secure."

Stahl clicked the walkie-talkie. "Understood."

He said to the men with him, "Get into the truck. It is time to fulfill our destiny."

The men scrambled into the flatbed of an old Mercedes-Benz truck. The tailgate remained down. The bed was lined with hard wooden benches. The containment boxes and other equipment were stored under a heavy green canvas. Stahl climbed into the cab and started the old vehicle up.

Driving into the camp, he had to swerve off the narrow path to avoid a body left dead at a makeshift sentry post. Further in, he pulled the truck to a stop and shut off the rattling engine.

Peretz met him as he exited the cab. "Five guards. All of them have been dealt with. We've also disabled the short-range radio we found in what looks like a communications tent."

"Well done." To Alhadeff, Stahl said, "Tell us how to proceed."

The lead archaeologist conferred with his three experts. After a moment of intense conversation involving different languages, Alhadeff grabbed a lantern off a nearby table.

"This way."

He led them to the large square pit dug into the desert floor.

He paused at the precipice, looking down. A sudden gust of dry, desert wind swirled, whipping sandy clouds around them. The three men of science gathered around him.

"They've exposed the grand entrance. See the lamassu?" He pointed at two colossal statues of winged bulls with human heads poking from the windswept sloping dunes. "There to guard the entrance." A dark opening between them. He said excitedly, "We go in there."

Joining Alhadeff at the edge of the massive pit, Stahl noted the rows of columns to the right and left of the lamassu and a set of wide steps leading downward from the opening only to be buried in sand not yet excavated. So far, only about fifteen feet of the temple's exterior walls were exposed. Jagged, crumbling partitions jutted from the main barrier. More than likely what remained of clerical quarters.

Alhadeff noticed his interest. "The steps lead to the courtyard, I imagine. Once fully excavated, I'd expect them to find small rooms used for storing votive offerings and sacrificial items."

"Nothing of interest to us?"

"No. Our prize—should it be here—will have been concealed deep within the bowels of the temple. I suspect in a secret chamber buried under the ritual crypts."

Stahl glanced at Peretz.

The lead mercenary remained back by the communication tent with his men. At the mention of secret chambers and ritual crypts, they tensed, clearly wanting no part of what came next.

"Oh yes, Peretz, by all means, you will be joining us," Stahl said. "Leave one sentry behind."

Peretz's frown told Stahl the mercenary did not like the idea of accompanying them further. Stahl's own expression communicated a message of his own. To defy his order would not end well for Peretz and his men.

The edge of the first exposed layer of the temple was dotted with ladders, makeshift wooden platforms and temporary scaffolding. Each layer of exposed stonework was etched with intricate ancient glyphs and symbols. A few Stahl excitedly recognized. Similar to some of the text on the cuneiform tablet and cylinder seal he'd stolen from the Baghdad museum all those years ago.

He felt a thrill. Finally, all his work—his years of effort and sacrifice—was coming to fruition. He was close. He felt it. With a smile, he waved at the nearest ladder. "Doctors first."

Led by Alhadeff, the scientists followed him down the ladder. They carried lanterns and shoulder bags weighted down with tools and equipment. In a line, they proceeded toward the grand entrance. Stahl followed, with Peretz and his men bringing up the rear. Alhadeff paused at the entrance. He ran his hand over the sandstone pillar propping up the transom overhead. Shielded from erosion by the centuries of overlying sand until its recent exposure, the etchings were clearly defined.

Fragments of pottery were staged at the bases of each human-headed bull. Some were tagged, while others were arranged beside measuring markers and labels. The scientists paused at each deposit, excitedly exchanging chatter in different languages Stahl didn't understand.

He urged them forward, toward their goal.

"Beyond this opening," Alhadeff said, tour guide for the expedition. "We'll enter the sanctuary Hall."

He raised his lantern overhead.

Inside, the focal point of the chamber was a raised altar made of a single block of stone. Rectangular in shape, it sat on a cracked stone slab, its pieces uneven. Alhadeff ran his fingers along the concave grooves where wine, oil and often blood flowed during ceremonial offerings. Carved panels flanked the walls. Their etchings telling stories of gods and kings, of mystical beasts and epic battles. The lanterns cast dramatic shadows across the engravings, bringing the reliefs to life in eerie motion.

Alhadeff furrowed his brow until he found what he was looking for. "Here. This way."

At the back of the sanctuary hall were openings to stairwells that descended to a lower level. At the bottom, Alhadeff had to duck to clear the low lintel, his outstretched lantern highlighting the cuneiform text and other etchings across its face.

Entering the circular room, they were confronted by another raised dais and twelve alcoves in the curved walls, each housing an ornate stone sarcophagus. On and around them were small, carefully crafted pottery—some shattered—and delicate figurines of gods and mythical creatures: offerings. Their shifting lantern light created deep shadows and contrasting ethereal glows.

"From here, there should be a passage," Alhadeff said. "According to the chronicle tablet, Ashurbanipal's alchemists had a place where they created or stored the Breath of Ashur, the Scarlet Death."

He ran his hands over the reliefs between the alcoves.

"Our translations indicate it is here," Alhadefff said, sounding like he was trying to convince himself. By saying it, that would force it to be true. "The Temple of the Whispering Sands. It must be here. It must be."

Stahl glanced at the group around him. "Spread out. Look for anything that could be a secret doorway or passage beyond this level." To Peretz, he said, "Your men, too. We do not have time to waste. We must find it. And we must find it tonight."

Minutes turned into hours. With each passing tick of the clock, Maximilian Stahl's frustration grew. He had ordered Peretz's men topside to gather shovels and other excavation equipment to dig through the sand that had settled like a carpet over this lowest level. There had to be a passageway. A doorway. To a chamber.

But so far, their efforts yielded nothing.

About an hour before dawn, Stahl reluctantly, begrudgingly, began to accept defeat. His stomach soured at the thought as he prepared to call a halt to the search.

Just then, Alhadeff called out, "Look!"

He pointed toward the northwest section of the room, where two mercenaries stabbed at the sand with long-handled spades, bored and frustrated. It had been nearly imperceivable at first. But the sand around their feet had started to shift.

The ground beneath them was falling away.

Alhadeff shouted, "Get back. Get back! It's a sinkhole!"

The two mercenaries started to run from the corner, but their boots sank deeper into the shifting sands. For a moment, they looked like they were running through quicksand. At first, making progress, albeit slowly. Soon, their running achieved no forward momentum. Perpetual effort with no reward. Their feet were swept out from under them. They fell to the loose sand, clawing at it, only to be pulled into a swiftly widening hole.

Within seconds, they were swept into the void.

Gone.

The others backed away to a safe distance, watching in amazement and horror as the large, gaping hole expanded. When the ground finally stopped shifting, save for a few granules that continued down into the hole, Stahl, Alhadeff and Peretz gathered around the newly formed opening and cautiously gazed downward.

"I can't see the bottom," Stahl said. "Quick! Give me a lantern."

Handed one, he held it over the opening and still could not see the bottom.

He opened his hand, releasing the lantern. It fell into the abyss.

The lantern hit the ground with a dull thud. About ten meters below. Its whitish glow illuminated the two mercenaries sprawled in the sand, unhurt save for a single twisted ankle.

"It must have been a secret passage," Alhadeff said. "Concealed."

"This is it!" Stahl announced.

Stahl snapped his fingers in the air. "Ladders! Ropes! We must get down there quickly." He clasped Alhadeff on the shoulder. "We've done it."

Peretz's remaining men rushed off and quickly returned.

They laid two ladders across the opening and hastily tied bowline knots, hanging the ropes from the rungs. They used a sand-colored tarp as a net and lowered tools, equipment, a medical kit and one of the containment boxes down to the men in the lower chamber.

Stahl watched them work, pacing. He felt they were on the precipice of discovery. The payoff about to be achieved. He even allowed for a poignant moment of disappointment that his old friend, who had been by his side all these years, Kuznetsov, was not there to share in the final discovery.

He wondered how Anton was faring in Greece.

"We're ready for you, Stahl," Peretz said.

It had been decided one mercenary would remain by the ladders stretched across the opening in case there were a problem and the party needed help returning from the pit. Alhadeff and his three-man team were already below. Peretz climbed over the edge, followed by Stahl, the last to reach the chamber floor.

One of Peretz's men tended to the injured man's leg, tying a splint around his ankle. Alhadeff and his team were examining the chamber walls. Their lanterns held high. Their hands gently caressed the symbols and faded inscriptions.

Stahl joined Alhadeff in one corner.

By no means an expert, but having chased the script's meaning for over a decade, Stahl had developed a rudimentary grasp of the ancient language.

"These symbols," he said, "The script. It's straightforward Assyrian."

"You have picked up a thing or two," Alhadeff said with a soft smile. "You are correct. Here, there are no secrets. No tricks."

Alhadeff brushed away loose sand, feeling the symbols and inscriptions. As if he were reading Braille, his lips moved. Silently in his head, he translated the markings.

"What does it say?" Stahl asked.

"It is a warning. Very loosely interpreted, it says, keep out. An 'authorized personnel only' type of alert."

This sparked a new wave of excitement in Stahl. More than ever, he was convinced they were nearing the end of the journey he had started so very long ago. He grinned. "This is it."

"Hey, look," one of Peretz's men called out. "There."

He pointed to the far side of the chamber. His lantern dimly illuminated a large stone door. Like the walls, it was patterned with symbols and other hieroglyphics.

The excited soldier moved forward, rushing toward the door. He had taken just two steps when the chamber filled with a deep, resounding click. Then that of ancient springs snapping, followed by a sharp twang felt through his boots.

The floor under the soldier gave way.

The rest of the team stared in horror.

Gone. The man's screams rebounded from the black void he'd fallen into. The sound faded but did not end for quite some time. This new opening was vastly deeper than the ten-meter descent they'd just made.

It was clear. This opening was a bottomless pit.

CHAPTER **NINETEEN**

Khovuun Hotel
Dalanzadgad, Ömnögovi Province, Mongolia

AFTER A QUICK UPDATE call to Grayson and Mazz, off-book charter jets were arranged to transport Jackson and Lena to Mosul. Parker, Davenport and Karas took a similar transport to the Gurvan Saikhan Airport. Named after the nearby Gurvan Saikhan Mountains, which translates to 'three beauties" in Mongolian. The airport was approximately seven kilometers from Dalanzadgad, where Karas had arranged a meeting with the person responsible for putting the Echoes of Empire tablet fragments up for sale.

"As unscrupulous as they come," Karas assured them when asked if his contact could be trusted. "So, no. But he can tell us how he came to possess the Echoes tablet. And should anyone know where Chief Ochir secured his treasures, it will be Nergui Batbayar."

"If this Batbayar is so unscrupulous," Davenport asked while they sat at an outdoor table near the hotel's entrance. "What makes you think he hasn't already plundered the treasures we hope to find in Ochir's stash house?"

"I don't," Karas said.

"It's a lead, Sebastian," Parker said. "We'll determine if anything in his possession has value for us. If there's anything Batbayar has sold we're interested in, he'll provide that information as well."

"How can you be so sure?"

"I can be quite persuasive. If need be."

She sipped her butter coffee. A strong espresso with a dollop of Mongolian butter. Flavored with cinnamon, cardamom and star anise for a Xinjiang influence. Davenport's impatience mirrored her own. Were they wasting valuable time on a wild goose chase while she sent Jackson and Lena after the real prize, alone and without backup?

Her instincts had told her they'd embarked on the correct course of action. There was no time for self-doubt and recriminations now. She had to trust her team, and she had to trust herself.

"That's him there," Karas said.

All eyes turned toward a grizzled, weather-beaten man with unkept dark hair, graying stubble on his dark face and wearing soiled clothes. He approached the table, pulled out a chair and quickly sat down. Without introduction or preamble, he began to pick through the samsa pastries, vegetable spring rolls and stuffed grape leaves with grubby hands and dirt-encrusted fingernails. He flagged down a waitress as he popped the various delicacies into his mouth.

"A baijiu for me. No, better make that two. And a fresh round for my new friends. It looks like they're having coffee, arak and maotais." To the group, around a cheek-bursting mouth full of food, he said, "I compliment your excellent choices." He glanced up at the waitress and smiled. "Thank you. Thank you."

Batbayar offered Parker a stuffed grape leaf pinched between his grimy fingers.

Parker struggled to conceal her disgust and simply shook her head.

Batbayar clasped Karas on the shoulder. "Professor Ioannis. So good to see you again. What brings you to Mongolia on this fine, beautiful day?"

"You do, Nergui," Karas said. "As you well know. I contacted you."

"Yes. Yes. Just making conversation." He glanced at Parker and Davenport. "As you Americans say."

Davenport's expression soured. "I am *not* American."

Karas cleared his throat. "About the tablet you sold through Aegean Auctions. The one I bought—"

"It is authentic," Batbayur said. "I swear. Whatever they told you as to how it got broken." He put his hands in the air. "That has nothing to do with me. It is genuine and was in that condition when I acquired it. All deals are final."

Parker leaned close and lowered her voice. "Perhaps I should introduce myself, Mr. Batbayur. My name is Parker Quinn. I'm an agent with the US government. The Department of Homeland Security. Specifically, an investigator assigned to their Cultural Property, Art, and Antiquities program."

The color drained from Batbayar's sweaty, weathered face. He put his hands on the table and shot to his feet. "Ioannis. I am shocked. Shocked, I tell you. And less than thrilled with your new friends. And, in fact, disappointed, I would say."

Parker grabbed his wrist. "Let's not get excited, Batbayur. Have a seat. We've a problem and think you can help us."

Batbayur snatched his Baijiu from the arriving waitress. He slugged it down in one gulp and then took the second one from her tray. "I am not in trouble then?"

Parker gave him a reassuring smile. "Not that I am aware of. We're here because you have information we need."

He smiled a crooked teeth grin at Parker and sat back down. "To new business then. And pretty lady agents." Batbayur sipped his second drink. "But before we proceed, may I say. I thought we were better friends than this, Ioannis. I still feel… ambushed."

"We're not here to cause you trouble, Nergui. We need your help, and we don't have the luxury of time to banter and barter in our usual manner. If you help us," Karas glanced over at Parker for approval, "you may be rewarded handsomely—"

"Let's not get ahead of ourselves," Parker said. "Though, I could perhaps be persuaded to not dig too extensively into your past activities."

"Or… any future indiscretions?" Batbayur asked.

"Don't push it."

Batbayur shrugged. "You can't hold it against me for trying."

"I can and I will," Parker assured him. She narrowed her eyes, giving him a long, hard stare. "Give me no hogwash. Tell me no lies."

He popped a spring roll in his mouth. And smiled, albeit nervously. "We are all friends here. Trust comes with friendship. Does it not?"

"We'll see," Parker said, sipping her coffee.

"How can I help you? I am at your humble disposal."

"Nergui," Karas said. "We're looking for Ochir's vault."

Batbayur barked a laugh. "You and everyone else for the last two thousand years."

"Perhaps," Parker said, "But we know you found it."

Bayanzag, the Flaming Cliffs
Ömnögovi Province of Mongolia

IT WAS NEARING SUNSET as their rugged Range Rover bounced over the dunes on the way from Dalanzadgad to Bayanzag. A popular tourist attraction. As they approached their destination, the sun dipped low on the horizon, casting a fiery glow across the vast expanse of the Gobi Desert. Around them, the barren landscape stretched endlessly, marred only by the occasional tough of hardy desert vegetation and the towering silhouettes of distant mountains. Vivid hues of red and orange danced upon the rock faces of the cliffs, giving them their name.

As they drew closer, the first glimpses of the tourist setup came into view. Makeshift stalls selling souvenirs and refreshments alongside small clusters of eager visitors gathering to embark on guided tours of the area.

Batbayur at the wheel. They pulled into a parking area.

Davenport and Karas emerged from the back seats. Parker stepped out of the passenger seat and glanced at the sheer cliff wall. It rose majestically from the desert floor, a towering formation dominating the landscape.

Weathered by centuries of wind and erosion, the rock face bore the scars of time. Its rugged surface marked by intricate patterns and striations. A telltale sign of geological upheaval. Jagged outcrops jutted from the cliff, casting dramatic shadows against the fiery hues of the setting sun.

Light shifted with the passing clouds. The colors of the cliff wall came alive, shimmering and dancing in the ever-changing mosaic of sunlight and shadows. At times, the rock appeared to blaze with an inner fire. A crimson hue glowed intensely, the passage of time etched into the very stone of the Flaming Cliffs.

"Gotta admit," Davenport said. "Expecting real flames, I'm a little disappointed."

Parker slipped on her sunglasses. "Where do we go from here?"

Batbayur rubbed his dirty fingers around his mouth. An increased nervousness was suddenly apparent. "There are rumors… of a small… chasm."

Parker arched an eyebrow. "Rumors? I was under the impression you *knew* where Ochir's stash was?"

"I… " His Adam's apple bobbed. "I might have… embellished a little bit when telling people I… knew where Ochir's chamber was."

"How did you come to… " Karas chose his words carefully. "To understand this was—"

"I have studied this for years. The old texts. Ancient scrolls. They always brought me to this general area," Batbayur explained. "And then several months ago, I heard a story."

"A story?" Davenport rolled his eyes. "This ought to be good."

"There is a chasm in the rocks," Batbayur said. "It was discovered by a young boy from Scotland whose parents were touring the cliffs on holiday recently."

"How recently?" Parker asked.

"Several weeks ago." Annoyed at being interrupted, Batbayur said, "The young boy got bored and wandered off to explore, as seven-year-olds often do. He found the opening and crawled inside."

Batbayur leaned against the front grille of the Range Rover and folded his arms over his chest. "The boy was missing for several hours. The parents, quite understandably, were upset. They made a big deal about their missing boy, enlisting the aid of the attraction's security force, as well as local authorities. It caused quite the stir, as you might imagine."

"Is there a point to this?" Davenport asked.

"I'm getting to it. I never realized the Brits were so impatient. Eventually, the boy came back from his adventurous expedition to the great relief of his parents, the local authority, the media and public, and none more so than the Ministry of Environment and Tourism of Mongolia."

Batbayur continued, "When asked, the boy explained he had found a chasm and was exploring the deep caves underneath the cliffs. Many thought, because he was a fanciful child with an overabundance of imagination—according to his parents—his story of being lost in secret chambers was his way of avoiding a punishment he felt due him for running off."

"Great story, chap," Davenport said. "Where's that leave us?"

"We're here," Parker said. "We'll see it through."

Parker led the three of them toward a touring group just now leaving the parking lot. They tagged along behind them until the tour guide made his first stop. With a welcoming smile, he introduced himself and spoke about the ancient explorers and pioneering archaeologists who first uncovered the secrets hidden within the rocky expanse. Asking the group to move along, the guide led them along a well-worn trail that wound its way along the rugged terrain at the base of the cliffs. They paused at various points of interest. The guide indicated notable rock formations and explained the geological process that shaped the landscape over millions of years.

Gathered at the back of the group, Batbayur tapped Parker on the arm and waved to her and the others to follow him.

They backed away from the group, ducking through the shadows to a small cleft formed at the base of the towering rock formations, hidden from view by cascading tendrils of desert vegetation and shifting sands. It appeared as nothing more than a natural anomaly, a mere crack in the rocky foundation of the cliffs obscured by shadows.

It was a narrow fissure, barely wide enough for a single person to pass through.

They gathered in a tight group. Parker kept an eye on the tour guide, moving his group further away. Batbayur, Karas and Davenport dropped to their knees and crawled into the shadowy recess. Parker brought up the rear.

Once inside the claustrophobic space, the temperature dropped precipitously. The air held a sweet, earthy scent. The passage had rough, uneven walls. The surfaces were edged with faint impressions created by rushing streams of water centuries ago. On their hands and knees, shuffling through the sand, the sound echoed strangely in the confined space and darkness.

Deeper into the cleft, the passageway widened, and the ceiling rose, giving them the room to come almost upright and proceed on foot, if still, stooped over.

Ahead of her, Davenport flicked on a small but powerful flashlight that illuminated the path forward while casting jumbling shadows over the passageway walls. Further on, they gathered in a small chamber that allowed them to stand straight. They paused for a moment.

Here, ancient stalactites hung like daggers from the ceiling. The crystalline forms glinted faintly in the jumbling illumination of Davenport's flashlight. In the center of the space, Davenport glanced about, seemingly unimpressed.

"Now what?" he asked.

Karas and Batbayur walked along the perimeter of the small chamber using the flashlight function of their cell phones, casting the beams to examine the wall like building inspectors searching for defects in the construction of a house. Near the back, they stopped and stared at each other with silly grins on their faces.

"This is it," Karas said, caressing the sandstone wall.

"I believe it is, my friend," Batbayur agreed.

Karas extracted a small brush from his coat pocket and began to sweep away sand particles, quickly revealing a rough-edged square within the rock wall. Carved in its center was an upright rectangle and parallel lines converging to a single point enclosed by a frame.

"The proto-Mongolic peoples hadn't developed a writing system at the time. Passageways were often represented as rectangles, circles or arches," Karas said. "These converging lines could mean an entrance or boundary."

"Perhaps it is a pressure plate," Batbayur suggested.

Karas arched his eyebrow and placed his palm in the center of the square. He turned and glanced at the group, his grin wider than ever. "Here we go."

He pressed.

The square moved a centimeter inward, but nothing more happened.

Parker arched an eyebrow in quiet expectation. The crestfallen expression on Karas' face was almost comical.

Parker heard a faint grinding sound. "Wait. Did you hear that?"

No one spoke. Instead, they all strained to listen, trying to hear what Parker was talking about.

"What was it?" Davenport asked.

Parker held up a finger, silencing him.

The faint grinding had morphed into a muted chunking sound. That of a corroded and rusted mechanism behind thick rock walls grudgingly activating after centuries of neglect and lack of use. Granules of sand cascaded down the stone face near where Karas had pushed on the pressure plate.

He and Batbayur stepped back, as did Parker and Davenport.

To their amazement, the falling sand had revealed the long-hidden rim of a concealed door perfectly camouflaged to match the surrounding rock walls. With a puff of stagnant air, the section of rock receded slightly. Momentarily stuck, the sound of grinding gears came from behind the secret opening.

"Come on." Parker rushed to the door and shoved.

The others joined her. Pushing, using all their strength, until the slab of rock once again started to move. The slab crunched pebbles and sand into deep-laid tracks in the cavern floor beneath it. The gears freed up. The ancient mechanism resumed the heavy lifting of opening the sealed chamber.

"This is all a little too Indiana Jones for my taste," Davenport said.

"Tomb Raider, you mean," Parker suggested.

"Sorry?"

She laughed. "Never mind."

She quickly stepped around the door, snapping on the flashlight function of her cell phone. She crouched and examined the tracks the door had traveled on. They were stone. Cut into precise grooves. Originally, they'd have been lubricated with some kind of oil or animal fat, but any such agent would have dried up long ago.

Her flashlight beam revealed a complex system of ropes, springs and pulleys activated by operating the pressure plate. Such detailed and enduring engineering would have been considered impressive, even if it had been created centuries after this chamber had been built.

"Fascinating," Karas said, joining her.

To Batbayur, Parker said, "Does anyone else know of this chamber? The passage?"

"Not as far as I'm aware," Batbayur said. "As I mentioned, the boy's tale was dismissed as fanciful imagination. I had only begun to collect the necessary supplies and equipment to properly examine this myself. As Ioannis has undoubtedly informed you, finding Ochir's hidden treasure has been a passion of mine for many, many years. And while many legends and stories have told of a great cache of art and antiquities owned by Ochir, none have ever found them."

"Not for nothing," Davenport said. "I find it hard to believe no one else has found that cleft, tiny as it is, until some little boy stumbled on it."

"You are suspicious. I understand."

"Cockamamie stories make me twitchy," Davenport said. "Especially when things seem a little too convenient."

"I am not a geologist but as a seeker of rare antiquities," Batbayur said. "I am aware that several factors can contribute to the development of such a chasm, such as a series of seismic events coupled with a rare, but sudden, flash flooding occurrence which forces rushing water along the base of cliffs, causing them to sometimes collapse, and form new chasms. Especially when weakened by said mild earthquakes."

Batbayur leveled Davenport with a hateful stare. "While what I find uncomfortably convenient is the timing in which you have reached out to me. Just weeks after I became aware of this discovery, just as I'm in the process of gathering tools and supplies and trusted men to come out here. Why don't you explain your timing to me, Mr. Davenport."

"Agent," Davenport corrected. "And, no, we're not here to poach your discovery."

"Aren't you?"

"Stop it. Both of you," Parker said. "We're after something much more important."

"More important than millions of dollars worth of treasure?" Batbayur said, appearing doubtful.

"Yes." Parker left it at that. "How far have you explored in here? No hogwash."

"This far," Batbayur said. "I didn't even know this door was here."

"Yet," Karas said. "You're confident Ochir's treasure room is here?"

"Yes. Everything I've studied about him for years has pointed to the Flaming Cliffs, but until that cleft opened up—"

"Fine." Parker hitched her backpack higher on her shoulder. "Let's proceed. Then we'll know what we're dealing with."

CHAPTER TWENTY

Archaeological Dig – Ancient Capital City of Kalhu

MAXIMILIAN STAHL STARED DOWN into the hole in the sand. The sides were smooth, like a tunnel. The man's screams had faded away, but Stahl had yet to hear the thud of a body hitting anything solid.

Beside him, Peretz's remaining mercenary asked, "Where do you think it goes?"

"No place we want to go," Stahl said.

"What do we do now?" Alhadeff asked.

Stahl stroked the two-day stubble on his chin, still staring down into the hole at his feet. "What can you tell me about this hole, Alhadeff?"

"Nothing."

"That is quite disappointing because I see a hole. One and a half by one and a half square meters. The walls of which are smooth. That tells me this is not a naturally occurring sinkhole, for instance. But instead, a trap. One meant to persuade us not to proceed."

"That would be an acceptable hypothesis," Alhadeff said.

"Shall we test it?" Stahl asked.

Before anyone could react, Stahl shoved the mercenary next to him as hard as he could.

The man shouted. Off balance, he had to skip over the opening in the ground. He staggered several meters to maintain his footing. When he came to a stop, he had his hand on his holstered service weapon. Glaring at Stahl, he said, "What the— "

He stopped mid-sentence when the ground under him began to shift. He leaped to his left as the sand under his feet disappeared. Beside the newly formed hole, he landed on his knees, looking down into the blackness beside him.

Relieved to have not fallen victim to the trap laid out for them, he giggled.

"Are you out of your mind?" Peretz demanded.

"Tell me, Peretz," Stahl said, staring at the pattern of holes he'd uncovered between them and the doorway they needed to get to. "Have you ever played the children's game called Checkers?"

"Not with human beings, for God's sake."

"Heroes of the new world order."

"You can't order my man to continue forward," Peretz said.

"Or mine," Alhadeff said.

"Why not?"

"You don't have enough bodies to throw at it," Alhadeff said. "Look at how much ground you must cover."

Stahl frowned, gauging the distance to the door. "Well reasoned, Doctor. I suggest the rest of you come up with a way to solve this puzzle. Otherwise, that is exactly what I'll do. Throw more bodies at the problem."

It didn't take long for the men of science and the mercenaries to devise an alternate plan. One that didn't involve getting tossed to their deaths.

Peretz ordered the scientists to return topside, to gather as many items as possible with weight enough to proximate a small to average-sized person.

Soon, the men returned, along with the mercenary they'd left at the ladder. Each lugged various-sized sandbags, metal crates, boulders, and other containers, sweating from the effort. They stacked it all beside Stahl and backed well away from him. Fearful he'd change his mind and carry through on his threat to use them as fodder.

Stahl selected a sandbag, hefted it to judge the weight, and then tossed it to the sandy spot beyond the second opening. Holding his breath, he waited, but the ground held. "Toss one of those boulders," he said to Peretz.

The boulder thumped beside the sandbag but didn't collapse the ground beneath it.

Stahl looked to Peretz, who took a step back. The former MOSSAD operative waved his hand forward. "By all means. You first."

Coward, Stahl thought as he exchanged places with the man he'd pushed onto the checkered board puzzle floor. He had Peretz throw him another boulder and sandbag. He tossed them to where the others rested on the square that hadn't collapsed. He leaped to it. Diagonal and forward to where he had stood. He tossed one of the sandbags directly ahead.

And lost it down a trap door chute.

He dropped the boulder to the space next to it.

It held.

He tossed another sandbag to the same square. Again, the ground remained intact. Confident it would hold, Stahl leaped and was that much closer to the door. He repeated the process, losing the remaining sandbags and boulders to newly created holes.

"Give me more sandbags. More weight. Hurry."

Peretz followed Stahl's leapfrog pattern, catching a crate, boulder, or sandbag before tossing them to Stahl. They continued until they had revealed all the stepping stones, arriving on a solid shelf wide enough for the men to gather around the door.

The air in the chamber was thick with dust. Motes hung in the still air like frozen snowflakes in the harsh bluish-white lantern light carried by the remaining men. They gathered around the door, careful to remain on the narrow meter-wide shelf.

Alhadeff ran his hands over the stone door, admiring the craftsmanship of the intricately etched patterns and symbols on the panel surface, smoothed by the passage of time.

◁ ▷ ✳

"*Bābu,*" Alhadeff said. "Gate. Or entrance. Perhaps doorway or passage. This asterisk-like symbol, *dingir*, is a divine determinative. It means protection or sanctity."

His fingers traced the grooves and edges of a locking mechanism embedded in the center of the door. It would most likely activate levers made of bone—human or animal—inside the door. They would then retract like modern-day deadbolts. But, the proper combination or code would be needed to unseal the massive barrier.

Alhadeff traced the inscriptions around the device with trembling fingers. "Another puzzle."

"Can you figure it out?" Stahl asked.

"I am not sure. Without knowing how to manipulate the gears, activate the levers exactly right—these symbols surely hold the clue—but it could take hours."

"Hours we do not have." Stahl snapped his fingers. "The charges. Quickly."

Peretz dug through his backpack, extracting two gray, clay-like bricks of C4 explosives. He handed them to Stahl while he pulled out wires, a detonator and connectors.

Seeing the explosives, Alhadeff put a hand on Stahl's arm. "Are you serious? You're going to blow the door? You can't."

Stahl dropped his arm from Alhadeff's grasp. "Do not attempt to tell me what I cannot do, Alhadeff."

"But the damage. The loss could be incalculable. The significance of such a find—"

"Means nothing to me." He handed the bricks of C4 back to Peretz, who went about the business of placing the charges. "The only thing that matters is what lay beyond this door. And," he added, "our ability to secure it and leave this place before the proper authorities arrive."

"But," Alhadeff protested. "What we seek—the Scarlet Death—could lay right behind this door. Improperly disturbed, we could be exposed. Destroy what we came to retrieve."

"It is a risk worth taking," Stahl said. "Better than being stopped by inaction and fear." He nodded to Peretz to proceed.

Once set, Peretz spooled out the wire and directed everyone to the far corner of the chamber. They turned their backs to the ancient door, hunched down and covered their ears.

Peretz shouted, "Fire in the hole!"

The trigger in his hand clicked. The C4 erupted in an outward burst of fire, smoke and dust, which tore through the chamber with a deafening roar.

As the smoke cleared, the stone door lay in shattered pieces across the sandy shelf like fallen leaves in autumn. Where the door had stood was now a dark opening, beckoning them to the chamber beyond.

Stahl stepped through the rubble, holding a lantern high in the air. Determined to be the first to venture into a passage that had not been visited in thousands of years. Peretz and Alhadeff, and the others, kept a safe distance back but stood on tiptoes to look over shoulders at what lay ahead.

The ruptured opening led to another chamber similar to the one they were in. A second stone door lay at the far end, giving Stahl a disturbing sense of déjà vu.

"Who wants to bet there's another checkered board floor," Peretz asked.

"Or something far worse," Alhadeff offered.

The group stood silently contemplating the dark chamber they faced, illuminated only by their handheld lanterns. Ancient markings adorned the walls. The floor was covered in sand. The large stone door beckoned ominously six or seven meters away.

Considering what hidden dangers may lay between them, Stahl turned to the remaining mercenaries. "You two."

The men exchanged worried glances and cautiously stepped forward.

"Get to that door," Stahl ordered.

The one croaked, "What?"

The second man glanced over his shoulder at the chamber they had just navigated, narrowly and with the loss of life. "It could be booby-trapped."

"It most assuredly is," Stahl said.

"We could be killed," the first one said.

Stahl aimed a gun at his face. "We all die. Sooner or later. You choose when. Later. Or now."

The two men proceeded cautiously. Their hands visibly shook. They moved away from the others.

Stahl, Peretz and Alhadeff watched as the men slowly shuffled onward.

Alhadeff narrowed his eyes and leaned forward. "Stop!"

The first one froze so quickly he needed to pinwheel his arms to arrest his forward motion. The toe of his boot hit a slightly elevated tile under the sand even as he jumped back. The other one grabbed his arm, preventing him from falling to the ground. From concealed compartments in the wall, three stone-tipped darts whizzed past where the man had been about to step.

"Holy crap!" he shouted.

"Careful," Stahl said.

"The whole chamber is a trap," Alhadeff said, as much as a warning to the two men as it was an admonishment to Stahl.

One mercenary glared at them over his shoulder, supporting the other under his arm. "You don't say."

"On the bright side," Stahl said. "One trap down."

The two mercenaries exchanged glances. Their expressions were easy to read. They were ready to defy Stahl, to not proceed, but that meant certain death. They gauged the distance they had come. Calculated the risk of going forward. Fraught with boobytraps, it offered a chance—albeit small—of survival.

Still, the one who'd nearly been impaled stared at the ominous black holes in the wall where the darts had been fired from. He shivered.

"Stay sharp," Peretz offered. "You've got this."

The men cautiously moved forward. Their boots shifted through the thin layer of sand over a stone floor. The others watched, holding their breath. Afraid even a sharp intake of air could bring deadly consequences. A soft, distinct click carried in the quiet stillness of the chamber. The effect of that sound on them was no less devastating than if it had been a resounding boom of a thunderclap.

"Freeze!" the first one ordered.

"What was that?" the other asked. "What did I just step on?"

"Not sure. But it's probably not good."

With his arms spread out like a man on a balance beam, he said, "What was wrong with these people?"

"They were clever," Alhadeff said. "Determined to thwart any intruders daring to enter this level of the temple. Just don't move. Give me a minute to figure this out."

But the chamber was not accommodating.

From behind the walls came a grinding sound, sending vibrations through the darkness. Dust and sand fell from the ceiling as previously hidden ancient mechanisms came to life. Secret panels within the walls slid open. Inside the newly revealed openings, dark compartments containing razor-sharp spikes and more deadly darts were now visible, all poised to strike.

A final warning to not proceed.

Near the far end of the chamber, several massive pendulum blades descended ominously from the ceiling. They locked into position, ready to strike.

"I can't stay here," the one man said. His dirty face streaked with sweat. He literally shook in his boots. "Do something."

"You are in no danger so long as you don't move," Alhadeff said. "There's a pattern to the crossing, just like previously, out there. I just need time to figure it out. I can get you safely through."

"Time is a commodity we're running out of, Alhadeff," Stahl said. His impatience was like a physical presence.

"I *can* figure it out," Alhadeff insisted.

Stahl surveyed the room, noting the dangerous apparatuses poised to strike. His gaze fell on the darts that had already been triggered, now stuck in the opposite wall. His voice low, so only Alhadeff and Peretz could hear him. "Once activated, the traps will then remain inert. Harmless. Would that not be true?"

"More than likely," Alhadeff said. "But there are more. The only way to activate them… " His eyes widened, and his facial expression registered the horror of what Stahl was suggesting. "You cannot be serious?"

Stahl glanced at Peretz, whose expression remained blank. The man was either growing accustomed to Stahl's psychopathic tendencies or had resigned himself to the reality he was powerless to stop him.

"If we do nothing," Stahl reasoned. "All will have been for naught. A decade's work. Billions spent—no—invested to bring about the new world order we envision. You wish to discard that? To throw that all away for the sake of two lives?"

"No, but," Alhadeff bit his lower lip. "I can figure this out. Given time."

Stahl glanced at his watch. He tapped the face. It was less than an hour until dawn. With first light, the archaeological teams would be back. "In case you haven't recalled, we left five dead bodies lying in the sand up there. The time to debate is over."

He unholstered his gun and aimed it at the two mercenaries. "Get to that door. Now!"

One shook his head in defiance while the other glanced at the door, then the traps—revealed as a warning—set to kill them.

Caught between a rock and a hard place.

Stahl fired his weapon. The sound reverberated loudly in the hollow chamber. The bullet pinged off the bronze arm of one of the pendulums. It sparked brightly.

"Go!" Stahl ordered.

The mercenaries exchanged glances. "Like Ninja Isreal?"

The one nodded. "Ninja Isreal."

They leaped forward, leaving the pressure plate they'd stepped on. Three long-shafted spears shot across the room at an incredible rate of speed. One spear whizzed past the lead man's head, narrowly missing him. The second one passed by harmlessly, as well.

But the third one struck its mark.

He cried out.

The sharp bronze tip pierced through his leg just above the knee. He staggered forward. His momentum threw him off balance. He crashed to the ground with a wince of pain. Blood seeped from the wound, staining his cargo pants dark. The other had no time to stop and tend to his fallen friend. Once the traps were activated, they weren't stopping.

"Keep moving!" the man on the ground shouted.

Already, the catch of a pendulum sprang open, releasing the blade. Its surface color was dulled by age and sediment, but not its razor-sharp edge.

The lead man paused for a fraction of a second, grit his teeth, then ran. He started a zigzag run across the terrain with agility and precision, dodging the first of seven swinging pendulums intent on cutting him to pieces.

Behind him, the other one rolled, kicking up a cloud of dust. He shouted out with pain as the end of the spear jammed into the ground, driving the arrowhead deeper into the meaty part of his leg. He got to his knees, sweating and breathing heavily.

"Look out," Stahl shouted with the glee of a spectator at a European football match.

The man twisted. Three darts whizzed past his face. One so close, he twisted his head. The razor-sharp tip nipped his ear. A second one tugged at the fabric of his fatigues.

Peretz shouted, "Run!"

The man pushed to his feet. Limping with the spear shaft still embedded in his leg, he darted past the first swinging pendulum. Timing a leap, he twisted, executing a perfect pirouette around the second pendulum, only to have the third one cleave his back.

It impacted him with the force of a speeding car and sliced him open, sending a splatter of blood across the chamber. The momentum of the deadly axe blade slammed his broken body into the wall. His head lulled to the side, his dead body pinned and inert.

The remaining mercenary continued evading the crisscrossing, swinging pendulums by leaping over, twisting, rolling and finally, dropping to the ground just meters before the stone door. Safe.

His breath came in ragged gasps. He glared back at Stahl and the others. His gaze then focused on his friend's body. His contempt for those waiting on the other side was easy to read.

A quiet moment passed, followed by the slowing swings of the remaining pendulums until they came to a complete stop.

Stahl had the audacity to actually smile. "In your opinion, Alhadeff. Would you consider it safe to proceed now?"

Ghostly white, Alhadeff nodded. "It would appear so."

CHAPTER TWENTY-ONE

Bayanzag, the Flaming Cliffs

WHILE PARKER AND HER team progressed deeper into the bowels of the Flaming Cliffs, their descent lacked any of the manmade traps designed to kill them, such as those Maximilian Stahl and his team had encountered. However, their journey was no less arduous.

She led the way.

Ochir had certainly picked well, Parker thought. As ancient hideaways went, this one was as difficult to get to as any she'd explored in her career. The flashlight apps cut through the darkness like beacons. They've spent the last hour descending along a sloping, narrow passageway. The air grew colder and damper the deeper they went. The cavern walls closed in sharply around them.

The claustrophobic silence was broken only by their shuffling footsteps through the loose terrain, their labored breathing and the steady trickle of running water caught in a small, natural ravine that accompanied their serpentine, downward progress.

Batbayur stuck close to Parker, anxious to be at the forefront of their discovery, while Karas and Davenport followed behind. As the path continued to narrow, they were forced to proceed single file until they reached an opening so small they had to sit and slide through a winding tunnel.

One at a time, they emerged, landing in a chamber the size of a large living room with a vaulted twelve-foot ceiling. Parker panned her flashlight beam around.

As the others joined her, they did the same.

Several old and blackened torches were held in metal holders affixed to the cavern walls. Boulders and smaller rocks were scattered along the sandy floor. Lumpy piles in an otherwise empty space.

"Well, as treasure rooms go, this seems annoyingly disappointing," Davenport said.

"I'm not seeing any way in or out of this chamber other than the slide we just came down." Parker's voice contained her own sense of frustration. "Not the means of entry you'd expect."

"We're missing something," Batbayur said. "This can't be all there is."

Davenport took a torch from one of the sconces and lit the end of it with his Zippo. Dipped in tallow and pine resin back in the day, the linen and wool-wrapped end flared into a bright yellow and orange flame.

"We don't really need that," Parker said. "Our flashlights provide plenty of illumination."

Davenport shrugged. "When else am I ever going to be able to carry a burning torch around?"

Parker gave him a whatever look.

"Ochir amassed a vast treasure. Collected over forty years," Batbayur said. His voice whiny. "It can't not be here."

"Maybe the place has already been pilfered," Davenport said. "It's been thousands of years, after all. Pretty arrogant to think no one else has stumbled across it during all that time."

"I don't think that's the case," Parker said. "Treasure rooms are notable for their wall carvings and cave art. Telling stories of conquest and glory, often of the legendary exploits of the chieftain himself. There would be alcoves carved in the walls to house trophies and jewelry, weapons, and even pieces of armor or tablets cataloging the contents. Perhaps stone or wooden shelves. Tables. Shrines. There's nothing to indicate anything was ever stored here. If marauders had raided the chamber, we'd find bronze and iron fragments scattered across the ground. Broken pottery and urns. Remnants of torn, rotted and scattered clothes or leather goods that would be considered worthless to hunters and left behind."

"An antechamber, perhaps," Karas said.

Batbayur brightened. "Then it must lead to somewhere else." He spun in a circle, looking. "We just have to find the doorway."

"And you have not reached this far?" Karas asked his unscrupulous friend.

"I have not. I swear."

Dust moats danced lazily in the air, disturbed by their arrival. Parker crossed the chamber. She ran her hand over the cavern walls, arching upward to the ceiling overhead. They were cracked and weathered. In places, thick vines of moss clung to the stone. More dangled from above, having snaked their way through small stress fractures in the rocks. Rubble and sentiment coated the ground like a rumpled carpet, forming uneven ripples over a once even floor.

In the middle of the chamber, she noticed a large mound of dirt, sand and chunks of rock debris. She knelt, brushing her hand across a large boulder topping the pile, noting its curvature was too symmetrical to be naturally formed.

Her fingers traced along faint etchings cut in its surface. "Professor, what do you make of this?"

Karas joined her, dropping to one knee. He pulled a small brush from his jacket pocket. With careful strokes, he brushed more sand and sediment from the grooves Parker had discovered. As he worked, uncovering more lines, Batbayur and Davenport crowded in behind them.

Davenport held his torch high while Parker and Batbayur concentrated their phone flashlights on the lines Karas uncovered.

Batbayur pointed at several bumps in the stone revealed by Karas' careful brushing. "What are those?"

"Look like gemstone fragments," Parker said. She scrubbed dirt away from one with her fingers.

"Quartz. Sapphire. Rubies," Karas said, identifying the gems as she cleansed more of them.

When the two of them had finished brushing away the loose dirt and sand, what was revealed was a single piece of polished stone. Dark, black basalt. A volcanic rock both durable and smooth. Though cracked, with missing bits, and mottled with patches of corrosion and mineral deposits that would take more than simple brushing to remove, the precision craftsmanship shone through. Ghostly lines gleamed in the shifting glow of the flickering torch and harsh white flashlight beams. The shadows grew and shrank unnaturally, creating an ominous atmosphere.

"Incredible," Karas said. "It's a representation of the night sky. Stars." His fingers traveled lightly over the lines between small dots—painted with calcite and a bonding agent such as animal fat, egg whites or some plant-based resin—and the embedded gemstones.

"Constellations," Batbayur offered.

"And the gemstones. They're the major stars," Parker guessed.

"Quite right." Karas began pointing out gemstones. "Sirius. Procyon. Aldebaran."

"The Wolf Constellation," Batbayur shouted.

Karas circled the globe. "Vega, Deneb, Capella, and Beta Cassiopeiae."

"Deer Constellation," Batbayur said, following a step behind. "Here's Altair. Epsilon and Zeta Aquilae. With Fomalhaut, they form the Eagle Constellation." He gazed at Parker. "These were sacred creatures and held significant mythical importance to the ancient Mongolian people. The wolf represented strength, cunning, loyalty. The deer, sacred journeys and fertility, and the eagle, dominance and freedom."

"Each constellation would have important seasonal significance and serve as celestial markers to help the Mongolians to navigate at night," Karas said.

"This is a great National Geographic moment, kids," Davenport said. "But, can we get back to why we're here? Treasure room. Scarlet Death. Thwarting terror attacks."

Parker didn't respond. She crouched low, examining a crack she spied near the globe's base. She held her hand out. "Prof., could I borrow your brush?"

"Of course." He handed it to her and crouched alongside her. "What have you discovered?"

Parker went about brushing away dirt and sand from the crack she realized wasn't a crack at all but a seam. "This isn't just decorative," she announced, regarding the constellation globe. "It was built to move."

As she continued to clear the seam, Karas and Batbayur tried to spin the globe. "It's stuck. Won't move."

"There's centuries of gunk built up under it," Davenport said, frowning. "You'll never get it to move."

Parker wouldn't accept that and continued brushing away dust and pulling out small vines and weeds. Soon, she had the seam—which spanned the entire circumference of the globe—exposed and cleared of dirt and debris.

"Even if you do," Davenport said. "What then?"

"It *has* to open a hidden passage," Karas insisted.

"Leading us to the treasure," Batbayur said, his voice full of glee.

"Or to a chamber filled with poisonous gas," Davenport offered. "Or worse."

"I had no idea the English were such a pessimistic lot," Karas said.

"Just been around a bit, mate. Seen a thing or two. Been almost killed by most of it."

Karas and Batbayur grunted and pushed harder. They stopped when they heard a grinding sound like grains of sand being crunched under a heavy weight.

"Did it move?" Karas asked.

"It moved," Batbayur shouted. "It moved."

Parker kept at her work, moving around the globe embedded in the floor on her hands and knees. Her efforts revealed a ring like those around Saturn. Faint etchings embedded in the soft stone.

"Okay," Davenport said. "It moved. Assuming you all are right, and the thing is some… I don't know what, surely, it needs to be set in a precise, correct position. How can we possibly know what that is?"

Parker sat back on her haunches. Breathing heavily and brushing a tangled lock of hair from her face. Batbayur and Karas kept moving the globe, soon getting it to rotate with effort but freely within the band that encircled it, like an old-time school globe.

"This band," Parker said. "There are markings on it."

It appeared to be partitioned into eight sections.

Karas stroked his chin contemplatively, then brightened. "Lunar phases. There are four primary phases: new moon, first quarter, full moon and last quarter."

"With four intermediate phases," Parker said. "Waxing crescent, waxing gibbous, waning gibbous, and waning crescent."

"The positioning of the constellations must work somehow with the moon phases," Karas suggested. "But how can we possibly know… "

Parker frowned. Looking around the chamber, her gaze fell on another pile of rubble. Smaller than the one in the center of the room.

"There." She pointed. "I've seen something like this before."

Protruding from the pile, half buried, was the top section of an oval disc made of bronze. Its face tarnished and dulled by the centuries, covered in sediment and cobwebs and growth. Parker dropped to her knees and dug around it with her hands, digging her fingers through the granular sand and dirt until she could pull the object loose. A large, ragged crack ran through its face.

"It's a reflector disc," she announced excitedly. "We're dealing with a celestial shadow alignment lock."

"Come again," Davenport said.

Even Karas and Batbayur remained puzzled.

"It's a sophisticated, clever locking system. I found a variation of one in a Nabataean temple years ago." Parker explained, "The ancient people who built the city of Petra. In modern-day Jordan. Anyway, this disc. It's meant to catch a light source, most likely the sun."

"Nar," Batbayur said. "The sacred sun. But how?"

Parker looked toward the ceiling, where the chamber arched to a central point. "I imagine at one point there was an opening up there. Long since covered over, clogged. Sunlight would stream down, reflect off the disc, and illuminate the celestial globe at certain times."

"To what end?" Davenport asked.

"Open the entrance to the treasure room," Karas said. "Hopefully."

"Okay. So how do we do that?" Davenport asked. "There's no hole up there. No sunlight streaming in."

"We improvise. Sebastian, cradle the torch." Parker used her hand to clean the surface of the disc. Holding it in one hand, she held her cell phone out. "Take this and stand beside the globe. You and Prof. Karas shine our four flashlight beams at the disc." Hoping that the beams would provide a light bright enough, she held the disc up like a shield in front of her. "Batbayur, when I tell you, slowly rotate the globe."

"Wouldn't you require the light to come from the opening above," Batbayur asked. "If it were still there, to achieve the correct angle?"

"Normally," Parker said, "But since the disc is no longer affixed to its stand—I'm assuming there had once been a stand—and the globe rotates, we can adjust the angles as needed."

Davenport and Karas aimed the lights at the disc, doing their best to concentrate the beams into a single point of light. Parker jiggled the disc, adjusting the angle until the harsh light appeared on the globe, like a white laser pointer—or sniper's sight.

Batbayur slowly rotated the globe. As gemstones crossed the path of light, they glowed brightly, casting their own colored beam of light on the cavern wall. White quartz. Sapphire blue. Ruby red. But nothing more happened.

What did any of it mean?

Parker lowered the disc, her shoulders sore from holding its weight. "We're missing something. The constellations. The moon phases. They all must mean something. Work in conjunction. But how?"

"The gemstones are the major stars in the constellations," Karas said. "The wolf, the deer, the eagle, right?"

"Sure," Parker said, agreeing.

"And their glow hits the wall," he continued, reasoning out loud. "They must interact with something on the wall then."

"But what of the lunar ring?" Batbayur asked. "We determined it plays a role in unlocking the combination, have we not?"

"Lunar phases, constellation alignments, seasonal indicators," Parker mused. "Like a combination lock, each must be in perfect synchronous alignment." She put her hands in the air like she was hanging items. "Moon. Sun. Stars. Earth. Each must be in their exact right positions. On a specific day."

"What day?" Davenport asked.

"A date chosen by Ochir," Parker said. "An important day to him."

"Spring or Autumn Equinox," Karas suggested.

"Summer and Winter Solstice," Batbayur said, adding, "The full moon in midwinter. It's called the night of the wolf's call."

"We try them all," Parker said.

"How do we figure out... " Davenport frowned. "I don't even know what I'm asking. Where the sun, the moon, the stars were in the sky 2600 years ago. It's different now, right? Alignments or whatever." He pointed at the ceiling. "Especially with no sun hole?"

Karas snatched his phone from Davenport. "Maths. It is all calculatable."

His thumbs began typing. "Pick one," he said.

Parker shrugged. "Autumn Equinox."

A minute later, Karas said, "Got it."

He went about adjusting the lunar ring. Then he moved the globe. Several times, he stopped and looked at the cavern wall, like an artist contemplating his canvas before consulting his phone again, making minute adjustments each time. "Okay. That should do it."

"Parker." He took her by the shoulders and placed her a dozen feet from the globe. "Squat down, low."

She did as he directed, picking up the disc. He adjusted it in her hands.

Karas then positioned Davenport ten feet to the left of the globe, facing Parker. He remained by the agent's side. "Here goes." Together, they raised the four phones until their light beams were once more pinpointed at the disc.

When their reflected light appeared on the globe, Karas gave Batbayur careful instruction. "Move the globe—slowly—dipping it to the southeast, but go slow, only a degree or two at a time."

Parker stared at the cavern wall until her eyes watered.

When the reflected red light of a ruby appeared on the wall—nothing happened.

"We go again," she said. "Spring Equinox."

They ran through the process once more with the same result. Then again and again.

When they'd failed their fifth time, Karas sat wearily on a boulder. "I don't understand. I must have made a mistake. My calculations. They must have been off, but I can't see how."

"Or it was all a fool's errand," Davenport said. "There is no entrance. There is no treasure room."

While it galled her to have to agree with the agent, she felt forced to—

"I have another date we should try," Batbayur said.

"Waste of time," Davenport said.

"What have we got to lose?" Parker asked.

Batbayur gave Karas a particular date in January.

"The waning gibbous," Karas said, noting the moon phase corresponding to the date. "We haven't tried that one."

Once more in position, adhering to Karas' fastidious direction, the flashlight beams hit the reflector disc, bounced to the globe where they lit up the sapphire gem representing the star Sirius, the wolf's eye, before redirecting it to the cavern wall.

The antechamber became unnaturally quiet, and Parker felt a chill. She held the reflective disc as motionless as she could, her shoulders aching from its weight.

"Hold it steady," Karas said. "Nergui, slow rotation—just a bit to the northeast. Slow. Slow."

The blue dot on the wall grew brighter. More intense.

"That's it. Hold it there."

Suddenly, the gems closest to Sirius began to glow, to brighten. They began to cast beams of crimson and sapphire and white light toward the cavern wall on their own. There, as the beams struck, others began to magically illuminate, like an unseen switch had been flipped. Lines of white phosphorescence cascaded outward, bringing to the surface— to light—the outlines of the eagle and deer constellations across the massive stone wall. A larger, brighter representation than what was carved in the basalt globe.

The entire wall began to shimmer with light, to glow, a dizzying mix of red and blue and white.

Soon, the final constellation appeared: the wolf. Completing the mural. A more magnificent sight, Parker could not recall seeing. She stared, awed by its beauty.

A low, resonant rumble filled the chamber. Growing louder, it reverberated through the rocky floor. The vibrations caused particles of dust to rain down from the ceiling. A muted, grinding gear sound reached their ears. A noise in harmony with the faint tremors they felt.

It came to a stop with a soft thunk. A weight or perhaps a counterbalance hitting the ground.

Incredibly, the light from the mural intensified. Filling the room, it cast them in an ethereal blue and red and white glow.

An indented section beside the breathtaking mural split along a previously invisible seam. Faint, weathered lines, once hidden, appeared, blending with the wall's existing cracks and folds. With a shudder, jagged pieces of rock crumbled away from the freshly formed lines.

Once revealed, two massive stone panels swept open.

Heavy stone scraping against stone echoed through the chamber, bringing a sweeping kiss of cold air into the antechamber. Parker wrinkled her nose at the scent of moist earth, aged stone, and something faintly metallic.

A dark, ominously black passageway lay beyond.

Parker lowered the disc and came to her feet. The need to illuminate the cavern wall was gone. "We did it."

"It actually worked," Davenport said, pocketing his phone and grabbing the still-burning torch from its cradle. "What was that date you used?"

Sheepishly, Batbayur said, "When Ochir reportedly was born."

"Bollocks," Davenport said. "One of the first passcodes ever in history, was a damn birthday?"

"You really think there's a treasure room in there?" Karas asked.

"Whatever's in there," Parker took her phone from Davenport and aimed it toward the black maul ahead of them, "has been waiting for over twenty-six hundred years to be discovered. I say it's time we go take a look."

CHAPTER **TWENTY-TWO**

Archaeological Dig – Ancient Capital City of Kalhu

JACKSON PULLED THE OLD tan Land Rover to a stop near a cluster of tents, their canvas flaps fluttering in the predawn breeze. He put the vehicle in park and stepped out. Lena joined him at the front of the vehicle. Its hot engine ticked as it cooled.

The sun inched slowly into the sky, rising slowly over the horizon, painting the surroundings in fiery orange and deep, sunburnt red hues. The ground beneath their feet was parched and cracked. The air stirred, sending swirls of sand and dust around their boots.

"It seems quiet," Lena noted.

"Yeah. Too quiet." Jackson went to the back of the Rover and extracted a Colt M4A1 carbine rifle from the boot. He pocketed a box of 5.56x45mm NATO rounds in his khaki-colored field jacket. "Keep sharp. I'm not sure what we can expect."

He slipped on a pair of sunglasses and surveyed the camp with a practiced eye. Made up of eight clusters of tents and rickety, makeshift structures. One large tent stood dominant over the others. The desert silence was a familiar sound to Jackson, who'd spent the better part of the last ten years in Iraq, Afghanistan and covertly in Syria.

Beside the largest tent sat an ancient Toyota Land Cruiser and two dusty ATVs.

The Toyota was likely the transport vehicle for whatever watchmen had been left behind to guard the dig site overnight. How big that contingency was was anybody's guess. What disturbed Jackson most was the abundance of tire tracks around the area in front of the tents. They were fresh. The gently stirring breeze had yet to obscure them entirely.

And then there was the large dark brown spot.

Jackson had spent enough time in the desert to recognize how blood dried in the sand.

They moved cautiously toward the large tent. Jackson took the lead with the rifle gripped low, ready to use. Casually, he asked, "You know how to use a gun?"

"What? No." She hurried a step closer. "Is something wrong?"

"No. Just asking. But stay behind me. Stay close."

At the first tent, Jackson pushed back one flap with the barrel of his gun.

Inside were several tables littered with maps, notebooks, closed laptops and other reference and research materials. Scattered around were folding metal chairs and kerosene lanterns. Noting nothing of concern, they moved on to the next smaller tent.

This one appeared to be used for supply storage; excavation tools, trowels, brushes, measuring tapes and sticks occupied most of the space with a single folding table that contained scales and other sample collecting and examining paraphernalia used by the excavation team to analyze and catalog their findings.

"Jackson. Here." Lena called out. Her voice low with intensity. "Come here."

He found her standing outside yet another tent, staring inside. Her features were ashen.

He came up behind her and saw what she'd found.

Five bodies stacked like crisscrossed sacks of laundry. Each had either been shot or stabbed or both. He knelt to be sure but found each of them dead. Coming to his feet, he slung the rifle over his shoulder and drew his Glock 19. Back at the tent's entrance, he glanced around the camp with a renewed sense of apprehension.

"They must have been the overnight security personnel. Stay close. This time, I mean it."

Lena stared at his gun. "How hard is it to shoot one of those things?"

Jackson couldn't help but smile. From a pancake holster pressed into the hollow of his back, under his khaki field jacket, he withdrew a small Smith and Wesson 9mm pistol. His backup piece. He handed it to her.

"Point. And squeeze the trigger."

She nodded, clearly apprehensive. "There are no other vehicles. Whoever did this must be long gone."

He noted the hopeful lilt in her assertion. He believed she was correct but did not want to lower her state of alertness, so he didn't comment.

They entered the next tent, one of the smaller ones.

Inside were two filing cabinets next to a small table with a short-range base station radio. It had been smashed beyond repair. The sand under an overturned folding chair in front of the equipment was stained dark with blood.

"The security people must have been ambushed. The radio destroyed before they could call for help."

Back outside, Jackson found more scuffle marks in the sand. His gaze followed the drag marks to the tent where the bodies had been piled. Along the way, a haphazard attempt had been made to cover the bloody streaks with kicked over sand.

Trying to assess what they were up against, Jackson reasoned, "I figure three, possibly four people were involved with moving the bodies."

Lena had moved away from the tents and stood at the lip where the dig began.

The gentle desert breeze stirred at her loose-fitting brown trousers and the sleeves of her safari jacket. At her feet, the sand swirled around dozens of footprints. Many of them were still crisp, meaning they were fresh. They pointed in several different directions.

"A lot of activity here, too."

Jackson joined her. The boot prints suggested several trips had been made in and out of the excavation site. "Four or five more," he confirmed. "Not bad."

She smiled. "Determining the movement of people from impressions made thousands of years ago isn't much different than your skill set."

Jackson chuckled. "No, I suppose not." He pointed to a ladder leaning against the sandstone wall, their way down.

"I guess we need to go down there, huh?" she said.

He climbed down the ladder first. Stepping off to the next level below, he held it steady for Lena.

The rising sun cast the pit in deep, shifting shadows.

Three more levels down, they reached the pit floor. Jackson pointed at the big hole formed in the northwest corner. "I'm no archaeologist, but that doesn't look right to me."

"It's a sinkhole," Lena said. "Caused by people carelessly stomping around this level."

"Mercenaries who don't give a crap about preserving historical artifacts," Jackson said. Ladders crisscrossed the opening with ropes tied to the rungs left to dangle into the hole. "Used the ladders and ropes to get down there."

Together, they crossed to the opening. Jackson dug a large flashlight from the side pocket of his cargo pants. Edging closer to the sinkhole, he aimed the beam down into the darkness.

Sand flowed past his boots into the hole.

"Careful," Lena warned.

Jackson backpedaled to keep from being swept into the hole. Back on solid ground, he said, "Looks to be about ten or twelve feet." With his sidearm holstered, he pocketed the flashlight and adjusted the Colt rifle, strapping it across his chest. "Let me check it out. Wait here."

On hands and knees, he climbed across to the middle of the ladder. There, with incredible agility for a man of his size, he swung over the side and quickly climbed down the rope. He reached the bottom. With flashlight and sidearm in hand, he twisted at the waist, surveying the chamber, finding it empty.

He called to Lena, telling her it was safe to come down.

When she joined him, they moved cautiously forward.

Panning the flashlight ahead of them, Jackson crossed the threshold into the enclosed chamber beyond. The beam, cloudy with sand and dust particles, picked up the checkerboard pattern of missing tiles across the rest of the floor.

"What do you make of that?"

"Booby-trap." Lena's voice was high with excitement. "Many ancient cultures protected sacred and other important chambers with such traps to prevent unauthorized people from gaining access… " She pointed across the chamber to the large section that had been blown open. "Like that!"

"Said sacred and important chambers possibly housing a deadly biological weapon," Jackson suggested. "To keep it from falling into the wrong hands."

"Exactly."

Jackson frowned. "You think those intact tiles are safe to walk on?"

"That would be the purpose."

Feeling less confident than he appeared, Jackson stepped on the first tile, ignoring the missing tiles on either side. Then, he glanced downward. "I can't see the bottom."

He ignored the tingle of adrenaline—or was it fear—that surged through him as he stepped on the tile diagonal to the first one. Taking his full weight, it held. He exhaled a breath. Annoyed by the hammering in his chest.

Lena took his place on the first one, following him.

Jackson proceeded across the chamber floor, hopscotching from one sand-covered tile to the next. He assumed those in pursuit of the Scarlet Death—whom they were pursuing— were responsible for the ad hoc and destructive progression he and Lena were following. "I wonder how they determined which tiles were safe."

"It's possible the traps were triggered by previous explorers before today," Lena said.

Jackson eyes the boulders and sandbags that zigzagged a path to the other side. "More likely, they used the sandbags and large rocks. Trial and error to trigger the non-supportive tiles."

At the far end, his nose picked up the acrid and telltale scent of detonated C4 explosives. Fresh. Still caustic. Previous explorers were not responsible for the terribly damaged door lying on the floor of the next chamber. "They were a little less nuanced here."

As Lena came up behind him, he panned his flashlight around the opening that lay ahead. Stepping inside, It was here they confronted the horrific reality that was their enemy.

Lena gasped.

He put a comforting hand on her shoulder.

A body remained pinned to the wall. In black fatigues, he must have been one of Stahl's men. A large, sharpened pendulum embedded in his back. His face pressed against the stone wall. Half turned. It held a painful expression frozen forever in death.

Jackson gently cleared his throat. "Do you think it's safe to cross?"

Lena forced herself to look away from the dead man, to ignore the various darts and spears embedded in the walls. The other pendulums, hanging inert. "They appear to all have been triggered."

She focused on the opening on the opposite side and nodded. "Looks like they made it to the other side. I doubt we'll encounter any more hidden traps."

"You doubt." Less than thrilled, Jackson knew they had no choice but to proceed.

She clung to his arm as they began their trek across the chamber floor. "What type of monsters would sacrifice their men in such a way?"

"The same that would unleash a biological WMD on the world," Jackson answered. "This is why we must stop them. At all cost."

They eased around the last of the pendulums, reaching the opening without further incident. There, they paused and looked inside.

The chamber walls showed signs of crumbling decay. In one corner stood a clay furnace. Its back hearth ladened with ash and other charred remains. Dust-laden torch sconces lined the walls. Their flames extinguished long ago. Empty shelves carved into the walls lined the chamber. Fragments of ancient pottery littered the floor. In the center was a casket-shaped container on a centerpiece of stone. The container's top slab had been tipped over. It lay on the ground, split in two.

Moving away from Jackson, her expression one of sheer awe, Lena said, "This must have been the alchemists' laboratory. Thus, the elaborate protection."

Jackson strolled past the overturned slab. He noticed its dust had been disturbed recently. There were fresh boot prints in the sand and disturbed cobwebs in the corners of the shelves. "Our friends were here. Searching. Frantically, I'd say."

"But was there anything to find?" Lena asked. The shelves lacked the telltale impressions in the dust and sand of jars or containers having been removed recently. She moved around the chamber, gingerly moving clay shards of pottery with her toe. "It looks like the place was empty. And that it had been for some time."

"If that's the case, that'd be a blessing."

Lena strolled past the clay furnace. Squat and cylindrical, it was about four feet high and the same in circumference, with bands of iron riveted by skilled blacksmiths of the time. An obvious vent hole—now clogged and closed—fed into a manually operated bellows system. She traced her fingers across the reliefs of winged bulls, deities, and cuneiform inscriptions engravings. Clay bricks littered around the raised base were cracked and blackened. She dropped to one knee near the back of the furnace.

She asked Jackson for his flashlight.

"Find something?"

"Not sure yet." She pointed the flashlight beam at the rubble wedged between the wall and the back of the furnace. Fallen rocks, discarded bricks, and broken clay fragments. A few oxidized iron rods and weapon parts.

She picked through the remnants, displacing a few of the rocks and shards of clay and weapon parts until she sat back. "Huh."

"Huh. What?"

She held a small clay container in the air, the size of a modern-day mason jar. Intact.

"What's that?"

Rather than answer, Lena brushed away layers of sand, glass-like slag and dust. Her fingers traced along the ancient script on the container's surface.

"I can't read all of it but these symbols here." She pointed with her finger. "And here." She indicated a second etching. "They say 'death' and 'plague.'"

"Death and plague."

Lena shrugged. "Or paradise and love."

"Stop," Jackson said. "You're not serious?"

"Unfortunately, I am. Letters in modern languages, arranged in a specific order, form a single word or words. With exceptions, they mean the exact same thing. Ancient symbols, pictographs, hieroglyphics, on the other hand, tend to have multiple meanings depending on a variety of circumstances. A picture of a bird, for example, will mean different things in different cultures, in different regions and times, even as drawn by different authors."

"I get it. Translating is hard."

She climbed to her feet. The jar cradled in her hands. "But I'm leaning more toward death and plague."

"And what? You think that... contains the actual virus." Jackson took a step back. "That they missed it?"

"I don't know." Lena squinted, bringing the jar close to her eye. "There could have been other jars like this one here. Maybe hundreds or thousands of them. Maybe they got them all and just missed this one."

"That's a cheery thought."

She shook the jar.

"Jesus. What are you doing?"

"Checking the seal. Making sure it's intact."

Jackson's eyes went wide. "And if it's not? You're risking exposing us to—"

"If it were compromised and a gas, it would've dissipated centuries ago."

"Isn't there something... like the way they measure radioactive decay? A half-life?"

"Then we'd already be exposed. Contaminated. If it contains a solid or liquid, it's probably not harmful unless we touch it."

"Well, stop doing that. Makes me nervous. What do we do now?"

"We get a forensic team down here. Get the CDC to examine this place," Lena said. "And we seal off this dig site. Immediately."

CHAPTER TWENTY-THREE

Bayanzag, the Flaming Cliffs

BATBAYUR RUSHED INTO THE dark chamber, holding his flashlight high overhead. He panned the beam wildly around in the darkness.

"Guess he's going first," Davenport said.

Parker shrugged. With an excited smile, she glanced at Karas. The thrill of discovery ran through her. Her early ambition had been to become an archaeologist. Her youth spent digging around in the dirt looking for fossils on her grandfather's ranch. A bachelor's degree from Brown, an MPhil from Oxford, fieldwork—then a PhD in archaeology and anthropology from the Australian National University followed.

In the late 2000s, while working at the Kaimana Ruins in Western Papua, Indonesia—believed to be the fabled Kingdom of Kalana, a ceremonial hub of a lost civilization thought to inhabit the region a thousand years ago—a vicious band of tomb raiders attacked the site. Items of historical importance stolen that day included jade masks, gold and gem-studded ceremonial daggers and crowns, important scrolls and an amulet thought to be used by the high priest or village shaman, rumored to grant protection, power or eternal life.

Under cover of a moonless night, masked and armed men came through the dense jungle. A team of five dressed in all black. Three men quickly made their way to a storage tent where items were waiting to be cataloged, including several Obsidian blades, a golden death mask and a jade amulet recovered from a burial chamber.

The other two men held guns on those sitting around the campfire, including a not-yet-twenty-year-old Parker Quinn. Their guns glinted in the dim light of the lanterns and the flickering flames from the campfire. They forced the explorers to the ground. Made them press their faces into the dirt.

The leader of the dig, Professor Alistair Wentworth, a distinguished archaeologist from New Zealand, tried to reason with the men. "Please. Take whatever you want. Just don't hurt anyone."

"Everyone's safety is up to you," the leader said.

From the storage tent came a gunshot.

A second ticked by, then a young student named Sarah stumbled out from inside the tent, clutching at the flaps as she fell. Shot in the stomach. She hit the ground, motionless. Parker would never forget the expression on the young woman's face as she died. As the light left her eyes.

The three men came outside carrying bags and backpacks laden with stolen goods.

"Idiots," the leader hissed. "Move! Move out!"

He glanced at those on the ground around the campfire. He aimed his gun at each. A silent warning for them to stay put and not interfere with the tomb raider's escape. None did.

When they were gone, the working students and archaeological team came to their feet. Shaking, many of them crying, they came face-to-face with the ugly and terrifying reality of the black market trade. A harsh introduction to the deadly, multibillion-dollar business of illegal smuggling of art, artifacts and other precious antiquities.

Parker vowed at that moment to dedicate her life and career to preventing such tragedies from ever happening. And to bring those responsible for such atrocities to justice. Six months later, she was an agent with Homeland Security Investigations, working in their Cultural Property, Art, and Antiquities program.

About to take a step toward the entrance, she stopped when, from inside, Batbayur let out a blood-curdling scream.

Parker instinctively reached for her sidearm, unable to conceive what danger Batbayur could have encountered. In her other hand, she held her phone app flashlight high in the air, trying to peer into the darkness. Karas stepped in behind her with his light as well.

The space before them appeared to be a short, tunnel-like foyer.

Batbayur suddenly appeared in their lighted glow, running at them. Dancing a drunken, chaotic jig, he waved his hands frantically. Screaming.

The twin flashlight beams picked up a large, yellowish-brown nest built out from the far chamber's archway. It had a rough, textured appearance with visible layers of a paper-like material. Chewed-up wood fibers mixed with the saliva from a hive of worker hornets.

In his rush to explore the chamber beyond, Batbayur must have disturbed the nest.

Buzzing, angry hornets swarmed around the man as he tried to swat them away.

"*Vespa mandarinia.* Asian giant hornets," Karas said, backing away. "The world's largest species of hornets. Quite venomous."

"Stand back."

Davenport pushed past Parker and Karas, holding his torch high and out in front of him. He grabbed Batbayur by the shoulder and pulled him away from the opening as he touched the torch to the enormous nest. It flared into an orange and red glow. A thick, blackish plume of smoke filled the chamber with the smell of burning wood fibers and hornet saliva, charring the nest, which began to crumble away while the swarm of angry hornets intensified.

Batbayur fell to the ground and crawled toward Parker and Karas. Large, discolored welts from multiple stings covered his face and the back of his hands. He whimpered in pain.

Davenport frantically waved his torch. It swished through the air, filling the antechamber with thick, noxious black smoke.

Coughing, with the back of her hand over her nose and pulling Batbayur further away from the swarming nest, Parker shouted, "Is he going to be okay?"

Karas helped her tug the whimpering man across the sand. "I cannot say. Asian giant Hornet stings are quite venomous. Also painful. A few shouldn't be fatal unless one is allergic."

"Nergui," Parker said. "Are you allergic?"

He rocked on his hands and knees and waved his hands in the air like he was trying to dry them. He moaned and shook his head. "No. It hurts. God, it hurts."

Parker heard a hornet buzz near her ear and followed it as it landed on her sleeve. Two inches in length, the insect had a dark brown body with interesting yellow-orange markings on its head and a nasty-looking stinger. She smashed the insect, killing it.

Davenport, still waving his torch but less frantically now, backed away from the main entrance. "It should be safe now. I think."

He knocked a hornet to the ground and squashed it under his boot. "Guess having a lit torch with us wasn't a bad idea after all."

Parker didn't respond, annoyed by his smugness and maybe a little bit by the fact he was right.

She and Karas helped Batbayur to his feet. The professor extracted a first aid kit from his backpack and handed Batbayur a tube of hydrocortisone cream, a packet of Benadryl tablets, and a container of ibuprofen.

With trembling hands, Batbayur applied the cream on the angry welts covering the back of his hands and face. He dry swallowed a handful of Benadryl and ibuprofen pills.

"You good to go on?" Parker asked.

Weakly, Batbayur smiled. His lower lip puffy from being stung. "Try... try and stop me."

Davenport took the lead, stabbing at flying hornets to keep them at bay while they passed the smoldering black husk of the nest, now on the ground. Each time a hornet buzzed near him, Batbayur flinched like a man with PTSD.

Davenport crossed the threshold and stopped abruptly. "Whoa!"

Parker and Karas stepped up beside him. Batbayur remained a step behind them, still swatting at the occasional hornet. With Davenport's torch held high, Parker and Karas aimed their flashlights into the room, further illuminating the ancient chamber.

Karas gasped.

Davenport whistled.

Stunned, Parker simply said, "Wow."

PARKER STOOD IN AWE, staring at the vast cacophony of hoarded treasures and artifacts before them. The air held an earthy aroma mixed with the noxious smell of the burnt hornets' nest and the burning creole-soaked torch. She stood still for a moment, letting the thrill of discovery wash over her. The beams from her teams' flashlights and the torch cut through the gloom, revealing jagged shadows and the outline of objects that hadn't seen the light of day in over two thousand years.

The chamber was immense. Its walls were carved with intricate symbols and petroglyphs of dragons, mountains, and fierce battles. Their flashlights flickered over chests and urns adorned with ornate carvings and symbols. Some were set on stone shelves; others occupied almost every square foot of the chamber. Many of the storage containers were overflowing with gold and silver coin trinkets and intricately crafted jewelry. Their lights and flickering red-orange torchlight illuminated a golden warrior statue astride a horse, weapons sheathed in delicate scabbards that shimmered with precious stones. Ceremonial armor hung from the stone walls.

Parker's heart raced as she and the others moved cautiously forward. Their shuffling footsteps kicked up puffy clouds of dust. She scanned the chamber, trying to take in everything at once.

To her right, she noticed a collection of scrolls lying atop a gilded table. The papyrus was cracked but meticulously preserved. "Unbelievable," she muttered under her breath, her voice a mixture of reverence and amazement.

"Ochir's treasure room," Batbayur said. "I've found it. After all these years."

Davenport found an iron cradle embedded in the wall and set his torch in it.

Karas picked up various items that appeared to be early manufactured tools, plates, and eating utensils. He moved onto an open vault that gleamed, Full of gold, silver and various gemstones. "This is incredible. These glass beads are Phoenician. This ring," he held it in the air, "is from the Sassanian Empire. The goblets and chalices over there are also Persian. We've got gold and ivory bangles from India. Roman necklaces, brooches and rings. Even Greek coins—"

"Turtles?" Parker asked. He flipped her a silver coin. It featured a sea turtle on one side, representing the Aegina island's maritime strength.

"Yes," Karas said. "This discovery could rewrite history as we know it."

"Is any of this what we're looking for?" Davenport asked.

"All of it is." Batbayur grinned gleefully despite the obvious pain he was in. His welts wept.

Returning her focus to the mission, Parker fought the urge to be distracted by the enormous cultural find surrounding them. There would be time enough for that later.

For now…

"We need to find anything that appears to be Assyrian in nature," Parker said. "Look for familiar cuneiform script, symbols and glyphs similar to those of the tablets and seals we have."

She and the others began to move about the chamber like shoppers at a street bazaar. Observing, occasionally stopping, picking up an item of jewelry or some other artifact. Examining them before putting them down and moving on to something new.

A piece of bronze glinted in the light, catching Parker's attention.

It turned out to be a beautifully crafted ceremonial dagger. The blade was marked with intricate inscriptions and symbols Parker couldn't decipher, but she recognized. They were similar to etchings on the Assyrian tablets and seal they'd been studying. She felt that familiar, tiny tickle at the back of her brain. The one she'd come to accept as a warning.

And had learned to listen to. There was something about this dagger. Something important about it, but she couldn't put her finger on it.

"Here," Karas said. "Take a look at this."

Disinterested, Davenport wandered the chamber like a board husband while his wife shopped.

Parker slipped the dagger inside her backpack and joined Karas and Batbayur.

The professor had been digging through an old chest when he'd brushed aside a gilded bracelet, and his fingers touched something cool and smooth. It wasn't the feel of polished metal or the roughness of carved stone, but something else—something almost too perfect to be natural.

He pulled it from the chest.

Square at the bottom. Approximately seven inches in height and five inches at its base. It tapered toward the top, giving it a pyramid-like shape but stopping several courses from being a complete point. Made up of several layers of translucent stone or glass, it had intricate inscriptions etched in the top surface and on the thickness of each layer.

"At first, I thought it just a small container." Karas placed the artifact on a nearby table. "But the material intrigued me. Too smooth to be natural. The etchings are clearly Assyrian. Yet, the inscriptions are unlike the usual offerings found on other Assyrian artifacts."

"They look different," Parker agreed. "Similar but not exactly like what we've seen on the tablets and seal."

"No," Karas said. "I've never seen anything like it. But as I've said, my expertise is not ancient Assyrian. Nergui, you?"

Batbayur frowned. "It is not like anything I've seen or heard about from ancient Asian findings."

"I wonder," Parker said, reaching out. Gently, she brushed some of the stubborn dirt away from the sides of the strange, layered box. She held it in place on the table and attempted to push at one of the courses with her finger. With little effort, it began to spin. Excited, she said, "It's a puzzle box. Align the courses in a certain way and the script can be read, not horizontally like normal, but vertically."

"Like aligning the colors on a Rubik's Cube," Karas said.

"Then read it in columns," Batbayur said. "Like kanji."

"Exactly."

Parker and Karas leaned in closer, examining the box, their fingers lightly tracing the symbols.

"This one," Karas said. "Lena believed it meant Kalhu."

"Where we think the Whispering Sands Temple is," Davenport said, approaching, seemingly suddenly interested. "Where the Scarlet Death was maybe created or stored."

"Yes," Karas said.

"And here," Parker pointed at a symbol on another side. "Isn't this Nizar Khaldun, Ashurbanipal's military guy?"

"It is. Exactly as it's found on the Echoes of Empires tablet." And most chilling of all, Karas pointed to a top-layer inscription.

✳ ⊢ ⟪ ⬦⊟

It was one they'd all come to recognize: *Mūtu sāmu.* The Scarlet Death.

"This is what we came for," Parker said excitedly. "Ioannis, can you read any more of it?"

"Sadly, no. Not without Miss Lena's assistance and her wonderful computer program."

Davenport glanced at his watch. "Well, I suggest we collect what we came here to get and take our leave."

"Loot the treasure?" Karas asked. "Are you mad, man?"

"I've heard worse ideas," Batbayur said, scratching at a welt on his cheek.

"You want to save the world? We can't risk getting caught down here," Davenport said. "It's well past closing time for the cliff attraction. Our vehicle's still in the car park. It is sure to be noticed by now."

To Parker, he said, "We don't have time to quibble about rightful ownership with the Mongolian government at the moment."

"No. You have only time to put your hands in the air and not resist arrest," said a heavily accented voice that stressed the first syllable of each spoken word. The dark-skinned man now standing behind them rolled his 'R's.

Several other dark-skinned men crowded around behind him. They wore dark blue uniforms with insignias of rank and division, a national flag of Mongolia patch on their upper sleeves, and badges on their chests. Their hands were on holstered weapons. Having not drawn leather yet, their narrow glares and no-nonsense expressions said they were ready.

The General Police of Mongolia.

Parker and the others slowly raised their hands into the air. "Well, this wasn't part of the plan."

CHAPTER TWENTY-FOUR

The Vergeltung
Somewhere Under The Mediterranean Sea

MAXIMILIAN STAHL SAT AT a sleek and streamlined central console in the compact room called the Communications Nexus. Surrounding him were ergonomic workstations, each equipped with high-resolution displays and various communications terminals capable of transmitting and receiving encrypted data streams at high speed via satellite and radio, all utilizing cutting-edge encryption algorithms and secure protocols.

A soft hum emulated from the electronics. The monitors and touchscreens glowed faintly in the soft blue ambient light. Stahl faced a high-resolution screen, which he thought pointless, as the figure he was talking to was shrouded with AI-assisted manipulation and his—or her—voice digitally altered to keep the individual's identity secret.

Stahl had no idea who he worked for.

Over the years, he'd made several attempts to find out. But each time he felt he was getting close, he found himself on the wrong end of a gun barrel. He'd grudgingly accepted his station and let it go, so long as their end goals remained the same.

So far, they had.

A soft knock on the Nexus' door a moment before it opened interrupted Stahl's train of thought.

Anton Kuznetsov entered, remaining in the shadowy corner to avoid detection by the computer system's cameras.

Stahl returned to his conversation.

"I do not believe this is our best course of action. We have only enough of the virus to make one warhead operational. We are better served to use the sample recovered from the Whispering Sands Temple for study. Re-engineer it so that when we are ready to strike, fully armed, we will achieve the maximum impact we desire."

"What you are suggesting could take additional months or even years to accomplish," the robotic voice broadcast from the tinny equipment speakers.

"We can find more of the virus," Stahl said, though the words sounded hollow even to him.

"By your own admission, you don't know where additional stockpiles of this so-called scarlet death could be or if it even exists at all. That is not in our best interest. This... quest of yours has already lasted for far too long, having stretched both our resources and patience. The target has been selected. Carry out your orders."

The signal was cut off with the definitive click.

Stahl stared at the blank screen. "Fools! Idiots!"

Surprised by the news, Kuznetsov, treading carefully, asked, "You secured samples of the Scarlet Death? Your trip to Kalhu was successful?"

Stahl stared at his long-time comrade with an angry glare. "It bore fruit, yes. Unlike your efforts in Mongolia."

"The Americans were much closer, giving them a head start. By the time we arrived, the Mongolian authorities were already on site and had them in custody. There was nothing we could do."

Stahl sighed, tired of the failures and the setbacks, of the unreasonableness of those he had chosen to work for. "Luckily, my proximity to Kalhu allowed me to reach the temple before our enemies. Not to our favor, the alchemist lab was mostly empty, with only one clay container left behind. Most probably missed when the Ashurbanipal's military shut it down and the virus transported elsewhere."

"This is what I came to discuss with you," Kuznetsov said.

Stahl shook his head and mouthed the words *not here*. He came to his feet. He put an arm over Kuznetsov's shoulder and steered him toward the exit from the Nexus. "Come, old friend. I am weary and in need of a drink."

Outside the Nexus, Stahl steered him through the dimly lit corridors of the submarine, humming with a quiet vibration and the sounds of metal hatches clanging closed. They passed an open hatchway where compact bunks were made with thin, coarse brown blankets and starched white sheets. The narrow passageway was so tight they had to walk single file and press against the wall whenever they passed someone.

At the next hatchway, Stahl spun the center wheel and opened it, leading Kuznetsov to the central command hub.

The hub was full of crew members in utilitarian steel grey jumpsuits, void of military rank or country affiliations. They sat at stations, their gazes slavishly fixed on holographic displays of projected maps, systems outputs and other streams of data.

Stahl and Kuznetsov ascended a narrow ladder that led to a closed overhead hatch. Stahl twisted the handle and pushed through. Kuznetsov followed closely behind. They climbed out onto the submarine's compact conning tower.

The distinct scent of the sea hung heavy in the nighttime air. The sky overhead was a brilliant canvas of white stars against a rich black background. Gentle waves whispered against the dark hull.

The advanced submarine had been made available to Stahl by his mysterious and unidentified benefactors. Not a maritime man, on his first inspection of the vessel—he'd been informed it had a length of fifty meters, a beam of eight, and a draft of six. The *Vergeltung's* displacement was seven-hundred twenty-five metric tonnes submerged—he'd noticed an amalgamate of technologies on board originating from various nations such as China, Japan, the European Union, Russia, and even the United States.

The hull had a graphite composite with an advanced absorbent and deflective polymer coating, rendering it nearly invisible to enemy sonar. He'd also been told the propulsion system was powered by a combination of fuel cells and lithium-ion batteries, giving it a maximum speed capacity of forty knots submerged. The advanced submersible crewed with fifteen and could accommodate up to ten mission specialists.

The vessel had teeth as well.

Six vertical launch system tubes capable of firing various guided missiles, including anti-ship, land attack and anti-aircraft targets. Along with that, four reloadable torpedo tubes armed with supercavitation anti-sub and anti-surface vessel torpedoes. They were also equipped with deployable surveillance and attack drones with aerial and submersible capabilities. The sub's low profile design and compact size allowed it to navigate through narrow passages and shallow waters undetected.

Stahl placed his hand on the moist railing, feeling the subtle vibration of the submarine's engines through his fingertips. In the distance, the vibrant lights of Barcelona were visible in the darkness. The iconic Sarada Familia stood out. Its soaring spirals lit up like beacons in the night. Stahl could just make out the flickering of lights along the famous La Rambla and the W Barcelona Hotel. Shaped like a sail, it stood out on the coastline. Its facade reflected the bright, bluish moonlight.

The Mediterranean breeze carried the distinct sounds of the distant city's nightlife. A muffled symphony of music, laughter and life reached out to them from across the waves. Stahl extracted a pack of cigarettes and shook one out. He lit it with a gold-plated lighter and inhaled sharply.

"Here, we can talk freely."

"While we were too late to stop the Americans in the Mongolian desert," Kuznetsov said, "I have learned what their objective was. A cuneiform tablet from the final days of the Neo-Assyrian Empire was given to a traveler of the Silk Road."

"Impossible." Stahl exhaled a cloud of cigarette smoke. "I have spent a lifetime studying and acquiring everything that came from that period. There is no tablet that I am not aware of."

Kuznetsov shrugged, indifferent. "According to my source, it tells of the fall of Nineveh, as recounted by Ashurbanipal's most trusted general, Nizar Khaldun."

The name piqued Stahl's interest. Familiar to him, it lent credence to Kuznetsov's claim. "Tell me of this supposed tablet."

"From what I have learned, it was discovered in Mongolia a few years ago and dismissed by scholars as either a fake or irrelevant to Assyrian history. My source suggests the tablet and other pertinent items from the fall of the Neo-Assyrian Empire were transferred to a trader who brought them back to Mongolia."

"Sounds far-fetched." Yet Stahl puffed heavily as he stared at the twinkling lights of Barcelona in the distance.

"Perhaps. But the Americans did find an unbeknownst, hidden treasure cache belonging to a Mongolian chieftain named Ochir, discovered deep inside Bayanzag, the Flaming Cliffs."

Stahl ground his teeth. The thought, the idea, that important, pertinent artifacts and information had been out there all these years, and he had learned nothing of them, not even of their existence, perturbed him greatly. Dismissively, he said, "A wild goose chase."

"I do not believe so," Kuznetsov said. "Items were found inside the treasure room appearing to be Assyrian in origin."

"These items. What were they? And where are they now?"

"The main item of interest has been described as a puzzle box. A multi-layered artifact of unknown material with distinct Assyrian writing and symbols on it. As for where it is now, fortune smiles upon us. The Mongolian authorities captured the Americans before they could spirit away any items from the site. The treasure room and all of Bayanzag are now under heavy guard twenty-four-seven while an in-depth investigation is being conducted."

Stahl looked out over the dark sea. A slow smile formed on his face.

He had inside people in almost every major country's intelligence services. Especially those that dealt extensively with black marketing and tomb raiding of artifacts and antiquities. If there were items that could aid in their continuing effort to secure the Scarlet Death—beyond the measly amount recovered from the Temple of the Whispering Sands—he would quickly know what information they offer and how any of it would fit into his plans as they advanced.

He took a final drag of his cigarette and flicked it into the dark sea.

"This is excellent news, Anton. We will continue with this idiotic test run the powers that be have ordered. We'll fire their silly missile and play our hand early. But now, with this grand news you bring me, it will not matter."

He turned.

"While the world focuses on this great distraction, believing this attack is a one-off, we shall continue our efforts to find and secure a stockpile of the Scarlet Death. Then, we will show the world who is really in charge. At that moment, my friend, we bend world events to our favor. It will be you and me who change the world order forever."

CHAPTER TWENTY-FIVE

Muwaffaq Salti Air Base
Azraq, Zarqa Governorate, Jordan

THIRTY-SIX HOURS AFTER THE Mongolian authorities had apprehended them in the secret treasure room of Chieftain Ochir, Parker and Davenport were at the Muwaffaq Salti Air Base in Jordan.

After being handcuffed and provided free transportation to the nearest national police substation, Parker had successfully negotiated a meeting with the police colonel in charge. That led to contacting the U.S. Embassy in the 11th Micro-District of Ulaanbaatar. What followed were numerous phone calls to Washington, D.C., including the State Department, the Department of Homeland Security, and the White House. Secretary of State Bennett Sinclair, Secretary Director Elizabeth Grayson, and the president's chief of staff, Amal Haddad, efficiently expedited the swift release of all parties involved.

Professor Karas and Batbayur remained behind with no charges filed. However, Batbayur felt little gratitude as he witnessed his substantial payday slip through his grubby fingers due to the Mongolian government's immediate seizure of any claim to Ochir's treasure.

Davenport clasped the dejected tomb raider on the shoulder, giving it a squeeze. "Cheer up, mate. Perhaps there will be a finder's fee."

"Crumbs and scraps. All I've ever received."

"And the gratitude of two grateful nations," Parker said.

"As I said," Batbayur grumbled. "Crumbs and scraps."

At the American air base located in Jordan, Parker and Davenport were given the opportunity to eat, shower, rest, and a change of clothing.

Now, they sat in a secure briefing room in a secluded part of the air base. Furnished with comfortable chairs arranged in a semicircle, they faced a large bank of digital screens at one end of the room. Typically, the screens would be used to display mission data, flight plans, and other critical information to be analyzed during a briefing or debriefing process. Currently, they were blank.

Parker could see their reflections on the grayed-out screen. The room was silent, giving Parker an uneasy feeling.

"Why'd they bring us to Jordan?" Davenport asked.

"I have no idea. They've given me no more information than you, Sebastian."

The door behind them opened. Secretary Elizabeth Grayson strolled in.

Behind her were Jaques Jackson and Lena Rodriguez, wearing big grins.

Parker jumped to her feet, and even Davenport stood.

Relieved her team was safe, and together again, she gave Lena a big hug and shook Jackson's large hand. Even he and Davenport exchanged cordial greetings. Grayson remained a step removed, allowing them a moment to reunite before asking them all to take seats.

"Ma'am," Parker said, "I wasn't aware you would be here."

"I flew in this morning. There's been a number of significant developments. One in particular I need your help with." The lights were lowered. Grayson clicked on the large central display screen.

An image of the Mediterranean Sea at night appeared. Lights illuminated the coastlines, making them visible. Beyond that, the picture revealed little.

"Since your travels through Turkey, Greece, Mongolia, and Iraq, sources have picked up a significant increase in chatter regarding the terrorist attack we've been fearing. The intel suggests—strongly, I will add—a strike could be imminent. Perhaps just days away."

"Means and methods?" Jackson asked.

"Target?" Parker asked.

"Unknown," Grayson admitted. "What we do have is this. Twenty-four hours ago, AeroSentinel drones detected the presence of an unidentified submarine in the Mediterranean Sea."

Parker had read about the AeroSentinel X-700 series drones. They were state-of-the-art unmanned aerial vehicles designed and released by a Defense Department contractor called SkyWatch Dynamics. The latest models were equipped with advanced radar, sonar and infrared cameras, coupled with advanced AI-driven algorithms, giving the small drones the capacity to differentiate between natural phenomena and man-made objects, thus being able to detect submarines, for example, amid cluttered maritime environments even miles away.

The image Grayson displayed shimmered before seemingly transparent layers were systematically stripped away. The picture became less dark until underneath the gossamer layers of water revealed the distinct outline of a man-made object.

"Looks like a submarine to me," Davenport said. "You have no idea whose?"

"No," Grayson said. "From the data gathered, we can tell its length is approximately fifty meters, with a narrow eight-meter beam. It is not a design we're familiar with. And that's after conducting extensive research with the help of NATO, the CIA, other intelligence agencies, friendly and otherwise, and even DARPA. No one's seen anything like it. In production or even in a developmental stage."

"You suspect this has something to do with what we've been chasing?" Parker asked.

Grayson didn't answer directly. "With assets stretched thin due to the ongoing and numerous threats here in the region, and at home," she added, "the President has decided to press you into service."

"Surely there's other, better-qualified resources that can do this, ma'am," Jackson said. "With all due respect. NATO's Naval Striking Forces command over five thousand U.S. sailors and marines here. The USS Bataan Amphibious Readiness Group is assigned to the Mediterranean. That alone—"

"That's true, Captain," Grayson said. With the thinnest of smiles, she changed the image on the display screen.

Once again, it was a view of the Mediterranean Sea. This time centered on a long and narrow, black, cigar-shaped object. Everyone in the room recognized it for what it was. A surfaced submarine with its conning tower exposed.

"An hour after the sub was first detected," Grayson said. "An X-700 drone took this image."

Standing on the conning tower were two silhouetted figures dressed in dark clothes. The lights of Barcelona in the background. Bright moonlight shimmered on the dark water. The conning tower would've been invisible to the naked eye. Grayson scrolled through several more images. Each grew closer to the figures, offering different angles of the two men. All were blurred with low resolution, making a positive identification impossible, even with the flair of a lighter lighting a cigarette.

"These images have been examined every which way from Sunday," Grayson said. "The most sophisticated facial recognition programs on the planet have failed to confirm— and most of my colleagues disagree with me—but I believe in my gut—"

Parker came to her feet and took a step closer to the image. "The smoker. That's Maximilian Stahl."

Grayson nodded. "And I believe the man with him is his long-time cohort, Anton Kuznetsov."

"Reynolds and the FBI believe they're responsible for the Baghdad museum heist," Parker said.

"And if that's true... " Grayson flicked off the display to ensure all attention was on her. "Look. You've all done great work so far. And I know you haven't yet had a chance to debrief and compare notes regarding your recent trips and discoveries. But if these two are Maximilian Stahl and Anton Kuznetsov, they are behind this pursuit of the Scarlet Death. And I believe the increased chatter we're picking up is about them and whatever they're planning. If I'm right, this lone submarine is the target we need to neutralize to bring an end to *Operation: Ashur.*"

"But not everyone agrees with you," Davenport said. "It is not a lack of resources in the region that brings you here, Madam Secretary. It's a bureaucratic spat between agencies."

Davenport came to his feet. "Your President hasn't decided to press us into service, has he?"

"Officially? No. But he's aware I'm here."

"Typical of your American arrogance. You believe you are right, and everyone else is wrong."

"You're absolutely correct, Agent Davenport," Grayson said. "Not even your Prime Minister—a charter member of NATO—would grant my request for assistance. They barely were on board when we first came to them with the idea that a twenty-six hundred-year-old biohazard weapon could pose a formidable threat to us here in the 21st century."

She stood in front of the dapper agent, nose to nose. "You can sit this out if you'd like, Agent Davenport." She looked at the others. "Any one of you can. But if you think I'll sit on my hands and do nothing while I can make a difference—do nothing because risk-averse world leaders, afraid of their poll numbers, refuse to act—you've got another thing coming. If that's American arrogance, so be it."

Jackson cleared his throat. "So, no getting the Wasp-class amphibious assault ships?" He was speaking of the USS Bataan, of course. The flagship of the Naval Striking Forces' Amphibious Readiness Group.

"No," Grayson said.

"Okay, then," Parker said. "What *do* we get?"

CHAPTER TWENTY-SIX

TCG Selçuklu
The Mediterranean Sea

TWELVE HOURS LATER, PARKER, Jackson and Davenport found themselves standing on the bow of a Turkish Navy Barbaros-class frigate called the *Selçuklu*. Lena had remained at the air base in Jordan, tasked with translating and deciphering the multi-leveled puzzle box they'd recovered from Ochir's treasure room in Bayanzag.

It had taken a lot of wrangling, called-in favors, and political capital, but Secretary Grayson convinced the Mongolian government to allow them to remove the puzzle box for continued examination. Parker had smiled at the gleeful jubilation Lena displayed upon laying her eyes and hands on the artifact.

While it was not the Wasp-class assault ship Jackson had hoped for, the *Selçuklu* was impressive in its own right. Built in the last decade, the ship boasted a length of three-hundred-eighty-three feet and a forty-foot beam. Powered by two General Electric turbines and two MTU diesel engines, the ship could reach thirty-two knots and had a range of forty-one hundred nautical miles. It crewed with twenty-four officers and one-hundred-fifty-six enlisted personnel.

As for weapons, the *Selçuklu* had two MK 29 Sea Sparrow launchers, two RGM-84 Harpoon quad-pack launchers, one five-inch, 54-caliber gun on a Mark 45 mount, three Sea Zenith four-barrel 25mm close-in weapon systems, and two Mark 32 surface vessel torpedo tubes capable of firing 12.75-inch torpedoes.

The warm hues of the setting sun painted the sky in shadows of orange, pink, and purple. The seas shimmered with the reflected light of the sunset. The air was warm, carrying a salty tang of the sea, mixed with the fresh scent of paint, motor oil and diesel fuel.

The frigate cut through the water with a steady hum of power, creating a white, frothy trail. The Mediterranean stretched out in all directions around them. A seamlessly endless table of blue. The wind tugged at Parker's green jumpsuit and whipped her fiery mane of red hair into a frenzy. She used the crook of her finger to drag a lock of hair from her mouth.

"I am Captain Demir," said an imposing figure, approaching in a white dress uniform. "Welcome to the *Selçuklu.*"

His immaculately maintained jacket was double-breasted with gold buttons, each engraved with the emblem of the Turkish Navy. The gold stripes on his epaulets denoted his rank. On the left side of his chest, he wore a row of ribbons, commendations, and service medals. His name tag was pinned over his right jacket pocket. He wore a traditional naval officer's cap. The visor adorned with intricate gold embroidery, and the cap band bore the ship's name: *Selçuklu.*

His weathered face reflected years of service at sea, and sharp, eagle-like eyes sparkled while seemingly missing nothing. His hair was salt and pepper, cut military short, and he sported a neatly trimmed beard.

Introductions were made.

"What can you tell us, Captain?" Parker asked.

"I'll take you inside." He smiled apologetically. "Easier to hear that way. Follow me."

Parker started to walk beside him, Davenport falling in step behind them.

She stopped short.

Jackson stood rooted on the deck. His attention was elsewhere.

Noticing the object of his rapt adoration, a smile tugged at Parker's lips. He reminded her of another serviceman she'd recently met with a similar love and respect for high-tech military toys, a coastie named Skyjack McMurphy.

The *Selçuklu* had, on loan, an Aegis Skyblade XH-99 attack helicopter from the U.S. Navy.

Demir and Davenport joined them. The captain beamed with pride at the sleek but formidable attack helicopter. It had a streamlined, aerodynamic silhouette. Its fuselage was coated with radar-absorbing materials, giving it a matte finish. Painted in a gradient of sea-foam green and deep blue. Its camouflage mimicked the ocean depths, designed to visually blend with the oceanic environment. It featured a five-blade main rotor and shrouded tail rotor. The cockpit glass provided a broad, panoramic view for its pilots.

"Ah, *Neptün*. A beauty, isn't she?" Demir said. "One of only three manufactured by Boeing utilizing cutting-edge technologies developed by your own DARPA scientists and engineers."

"*Neptün*. A fitting name," Jackson said.

"She's equipped with a phased-array radar system, capable of scanning the ocean surface and can penetrate water to detect submerged vessels. It can also track multiple targets simultaneously. Along with that, it has ultra-sensitive sonar arrays." Demir pointed to the underbelly of the helicopter. "Their advanced algorithms can analyze underwater sounds. Useful when searching and trying to pinpoint submarine locations. All of it's controlled by an AI system that collects the data from all sensors, making it capable of predicting movements and adjusting the helicopter's flight plan accordingly.

"As you can see, the airframe incorporates advanced composites that absorb radar waves and reduce its signature. The rotor blades are specially designed to minimize noise. The *Neptün* can execute rapid turns, evasive maneuvers, and hover for longer periods than most standard choppers out there."

"What's its weapons platform?" Jackson asked.

Demir's grin grew even larger.

"As a military man, you will love this, Captain. The *Neptün* carries an array of precision-guided missiles capable of striking from various distances. These missiles can penetrate the water's surface and hone in on submerged targets as deep as twenty-five fathoms. It's also equipped with retractable torpedo pods that house lightweight, high-speed projectiles that, once released, can track and engage enemy targets using AI-predictive modeling. Additionally, there's also a forward-mounted, high-energy laser system capable of locking onto and burning through a ship's hull to disrupt critical systems."

"Like phasers from *Star Trek,*" Davenport said.

Demir laughed.

"The concept is similar. Finally, the ship crews with just a pilot and co-pilot. AI handles the sensor fusion, target tracking, and defense systems, and can even patrol predefined areas, detect submarines and other enemy combatants, and engage them all without direct human intervention."

Visibly impressed but frowning, Jackson said, "Guess it's true then. Eventually, we will be fighting wars with robots."

"I can think of worse ways to put you out of a job, Captain," Parker said. "But for now, come on. We've a submarine to find."

Demir led them across the deck to a heavy steel door.

"We arrived at the target's last known coordinates approximately nine hours ago. There's been no sign of your friends nor any indication of where they've gone. We began a search pattern using our AI's predictive modeling based on the sub's last known position. Inputting projected speed capabilities, environmental conditions, feasible coastal destinations, and prophesized potential courses ranked by probability assessments. Our sonar arrays have been sweeping the area in concentric circles, and we're utilizing satellite imagery and drones to scan deeper thermal layers. We're factoring in ocean currents, potential hiding spots along the seafloor, and nearby underwater features that might provide cover. But so far, we've come up dry."

He held the steel door open as Parker, Jackson, and Davenport stepped inside a narrow corridor.

With the door closed again, the sound of the sea was replaced by the hum of the ship's interior. The overhead lights cast a stark white glow. The smell of oil and fuel was strong. The walls were lined with pipes and dials, and the poly-future tech flooring provided a slight give under their boots.

They moved through the superstructure's main corridor, passing several large hatches that led to the lower decks, which housed the crew's living quarters, mess halls, and other off-duty, entertainment-focused areas.

Next, they ascended a series of ladders to reach the bridge.

They passed through the CIC—Command Information Center—already abuzz with activity. Officers monitored various screens displaying real-time information about the ship and their surrounding environments. Finally, Demir had them climb to the superstructure's highest point: the radar and surveillance station.

"The radar system is continuously scanning our surroundings on the surface, and even in the air, while the sonar system is probing the depths below us, listening for the telltale sounds of underwater objects," Demir explained. "Namely, your sub."

The room crackled with the soft symphony of electronic hums, beeps, and whirling sounds.

"Is there anything more we can do to narrow the search?" Parker asked.

"We've tapped into every available satellite feed and have been deploying aerial reconnaissance drones since we arrived on site," Demir said. "But so far, nothing." His demeanor and the pronounced pulse of a vein in his neck made it clear he was dissatisfied with their results and desperate to change that. "And with all due respect, we've been given very little to go on."

Parker felt her back stiffen at the criticism, but she knew he wasn't wrong. "Only because we know very little. Nothing has been withheld from you, Captain. I assure you."

"Not saying it has. But without information such as destination, course direction, or potential targets to narrow the search parameters...

"The Mediterranean Sea covers 965,000 square miles, stretching from the Atlantic Ocean in the west to Asia in the east. That's over four thousand kilometers," Demir said. "With its 800-kilometer north-south extent. That's a lot of sea to search."

"Not to mention they could have hightailed it back out to the Atlantic by now," Davenport said.

"Or made port," Jackson added.

"That's forty-six kilometers of coastline," Demir said.

"In twenty-five countries, "Jackson said. "Not all of them friendly to us allied types."

"Any of you wanna dig in deep and come up with some good news instead?" Parker asked.

Davenport shrugged. "There's a better than even chance this is all a wild goose chase."

In her gut, Parker knew that wasn't true. Every fiber of her being told her Maximilian Stahl and Kuznetsov were on board that submarine. She knew that it—and they—were the source of the increased chatter, the architects of any potential terror threat, and the endgame of this global pursuit of the Scarlet Death.

About to speak up again, not knowing what to offer, she was interrupted by a crewman seated at a high-tech computer console. He wore headphones. His intense concentration on a display screen conveyed a sense of urgency. "*Kaptan. Sanırım bir şeyim var.*"

Parker didn't understand what the young man had said, but the inflection of his voice told her he was excited. She rushed over, reaching the sailor almost before Demir. Jackson and Davenport crowded in quickly behind them.

"*Söyle bana.*" Demir said.

"Something... I've been tracking." The young man shifted to hesitant English.

Parker gave him an encouraging smile, appreciating his efforts. "What? What is it?"

"*Denizalti.* The submarine," he said. "I found it. They're in the Adriatic Sea."

CHAPTER TWENTY-SEVEN

The Aegis Skyblade XH-99 Helicopter Neptün
Over the Adriatic Sea

TWENTY MINUTES AFTER SPOTTING the sub on radar, the *Neptün* launched and sped ahead of the *Selçuklu*, streaking low across the Mediterranean Sea. With a streamlined, stealthy design, the *Neptün* cut through the sky like a hungry predator.

Jackson stood in the cockpit, wedged between the pilot and copilot seats. In the back was a six-person contingent of the Sualti Taarruz, a Turkish Navy maritime underwater attack squad. The hastily hatched plan was to attack the sub from the air and disable it, forcing it to surface. With the *Selçuklu* on its way at top speed, they would rendezvous. The Sualti Taarruz team, Jackson with them, would coordinate with a second team from the *Selçuklu* to execute the difficult task of boarding and taking control of the submarine.

Jackson stared intently through the anti-glare glass at the vast expanse of the Mediterranean Sea, which stretched out below them. A blue canvas hiding an enemy beneath its calm surface. A headset connected him to the bridge of the *Selçuklu*, her captain and Parker Quinn. "Initiating search pattern now," he advised.

The *Neptün's* smooth, glass console was lit up with data.

Jackson watched as the sonar sent out pulses, scanning the depths for any sign of Maximilian Stahl's tiny submarine. The infrared sensors swept the surface, looking for heat signatures that might betray the sub's position.

With his eyes fixed on the monitors, the co-pilot, a lieutenant named Kerem Ergin, announced, "All systems are green. Starting grid search now."

"The computer is doing all of this?" Jackson asked.

"Pretty much," said Baran Sezer, the pilot. A lieutenant commander. "I'm not even flying."

Jackson frowned. He was no Luddite and had nothing against technology as a tool. But, turning everything over to computers, to AI, made him nervous. Sure, they could calculate faster, process more data, and predict outcomes with stunning accuracy, but what happened when something went wrong? A glitch or a hack could cause chaos. Over-reliance on AI might make soldiers complacent, weak, lazy, lose their abilities to function independently, cause their skills to atrophy.

Strip away the human element, and what's left?

It's not all about speed or efficiency. A soldier's greatest strength—their tactical advantage—is their capacity to adapt, to improvise, to be unpredictable. What happens when soldiers need to operate unaided by AI? Need to act using their guts? Their knowledge? Must rely on instinct and intuition, rather than being told what to do by a computer? If critical thinking becomes a lost art, if real-world problem-solving becomes obsolete, pull the plug and people become helpless, like cutting the strings on a marionette.

What if the real danger wasn't AI becoming too powerful but rather humankind's inability to function without it?

Jackson felt useless. All he could do was wait while the *Neptün* banked, gently following her preprogrammed search pattern, covering a wide swath of sea with each pass. The sonar pinged rhythmically, each pulse graded on Jackson's nerves.

Sezer said, "Infrared and visuals are clear. Nothing unusual on the surface."

"Same goes for radar sonar readings," Ergin said.

Jackson balled his hands into fists, struggling to push aside his growing frustration. Waiting was always the worst part of an op, but he knew patience and thoroughness were critical. If they slipped past and missed the submarine, all could be lost.

Trying to be encouraging, Jackson said, "We'll find it."

Silently, he added, we have to.

The minutes stretched into an hour and then two as the *Neptün* continued her methodical, AI-driven combing pattern of the calm, tranquil water. The sea appeared deceptively peaceful. Jackson knew better. The submarine was out there, and it was their job to find it before Stahl could initiate any attack.

The console beeped with a sudden, louder tone.

"Sonar contact!" Ergin called out.

Jackson leaned over his shoulder, seeing a bright yellow dot blinking on the screen, distinguishing it from the usual sounds of the sea.

"Confirming contact," Sezer said. His fingers danced over the glass touchscreen, bringing up the unmistakable shape of a submarine on the infrared camera display.

Holding the mic from his headset close to his mouth, Jackson informed Demir and Parker. "Got him. We've got him!"

"They're moving east-northeast at approximately thirty-five knots," Sezer said.

"They're just below the Italian coastline," Jackson said, speaking into his mic. "Entering the Adriatic Sea." Addressing Sezer, he asked, "How far ahead of us are they?"

"Seven to ten nautical miles."

"Time to intercept?" Jackson asked. "Till we can engage?"

Sezer offered a cold smile. "Minutes, Captain."

In his ear, Jackson heard Demir's voice. "The *Neptün's* computer has relayed the coordinates. We are inbound to the location."

"Carrying a bone in our teeth," Parker said, an old sailor's expression meaning they were moving so quickly they were kicking up a spraying foam at the bow, resembling a bone in a running dog's mouth.

Jackson smiled and shook his head. Parker and her folksy, homespun expressions. "Just don't be late to the party."

Jackson felt the *Neptün* change course and surge forward, increasing speed. "What happens now, Commander?"

"Enjoy the flight while the computer activates its advanced sonar and infrared systems. It'll gather data from all the available resources: drones, infrared cameras, radar, sonar, and satellite GPS tracking information. All that will be needed to get a pinpoint fix on the sub's position. Setting us up to make an attack run."

"System's adjusting course to intercept location," Ergin announced. "All readings are green. Weapons are hot and ready."

"Who decides to fire, and when?" Jackson asked. "Us or the computer."

"Will need to give it the go-ahead," Sezer said. "But after that, it's sit back and enjoy the show."

"Parker, Demir," Jackson said. "What's the play here?"

"Standby," Parker said.

A minute passed.

Lieutenant Ergin broke the silence. "We are in range."

"Awaiting orders," Sezer said.

The helicopter slowed. Not overtly noticeable, but Jackson felt the slight change of vibration where he gripped the back of the pilot and co-pilot seats. Any time now, he groused silently.

He heard a soft blast of static in his ear, then Demir's voice. "You are a go, *Neptün*. I repeat. You are a go."

"Confirming, *Selçuklu*. Mission is a go. I repeat. The mission is a go."

"Affirmative, *Neptün*," Demir said. "Fire at will."

Jackson patted Sezer's shoulder. "Let's rock and roll."

"Patch audio and visual displays in real-time to the *Selçuklu*," ordered Sezer.

Speaking to the computer, Jackson guessed.

Ergin called out, "Target acquired."

Jackson glanced at the gleaming glass console. The three-dimensional map of the Mediterranean Sea glowed brightly with swirling blue and green hues. The helicopter's position was displayed in the lower right-hand corner, while the target submarine, marked in red, was located near the center of bright yellow concentric circles, forming a crosshair targeting pattern.

To the left of the screen, smaller panels flickered with quickly moving streams of data, flashing too rapidly for Jackson to follow.

"Trajectory locked," Ergin said, getting verbal data from the computer through the comm system. "Weapons systems ready."

Below the central touchscreen was a series of brightly colored buttons and digital sliders, some simply lit up, others pulsating upward and downward.

"Release manual overrides," Sezer said.

"Manual overrides released," Ergin confirmed. "Target lock confirmed. Submarine trajectory stable. Weapons systems fully operational. Firing solution optimal. Initiating missile launch."

Ergin was simply repeating information fed to him by the computer. Jackson felt redundant and his presence—their presence—in the chopper's cockpit unnecessary.

"Missiles away," Ergin announced.

Jackson watched the missiles streak out from the belly of the chopper and curved left before plunging into the ocean. Their streamlined casings cut through the surface with hardly a splash.

The *Neptün* put itself into a wide, circular holding pattern around where the missiles entered the sea. Jackson did his best to steady his breathing, not hold it. His gaze skimmed across the console, checking monitors and displays tracking the progress of their attack.

Seconds felt like hours while Jackson's heart thumped in his chest. All of them waiting anxiously for confirmation of a strike.

It came not from the computer but as an underwater explosion erupted beneath the surface, sending first one, then a second, massive plume of water skyward. The *Neptün* captured the spectacle in high definition, forwarding the images to Demir and Parker on the *Selçuklu*.

The violent churning of the sea sent twin concentric waves rippling outward.

"Direct hit," Ergin announced. He twisted in his seat, smiling. "We did it. Took 'em out."

"Assessing damage," Sezer said. His gaze on the touchscreen. His fingers danced across the controls. He knitted his eyebrows.

Jackson's gut knotted. He sensed something was off.

He'd been in enough combat situations, including naval warfare operations, to wonder at the lack of foam and wreckage where the plume of water had indicated a successful strike. His mind rejected the possibility they might have failed, an outcome contrary to AI's confirmation.

But if they'd caused significant damage, the sub should have surfaced by now. Distress calls should've been broadcasting over all the emergency frequencies. But they were all clear.

Jackson leaned forward between the seats. He gazed at the Mediterranean Sea, watching it slowly return to calmness. The dissipating concentric circles of the initial explosions were the only fading indication anything out of the ordinary had happened.

"Something's wrong."

The words barely escaped his mouth when the sea churned violently, bubbling and frothing, erupting as a monstrous force pierced the surface at a steep, forty-five-degree angle. Dark and menacing, the submarine became more pronounced as it shot upward. Sheets of water cascaded off its black hull in torrents.

Like an angry leviathan rising, the submarine breached with a final massive heave and broke free. Settled on the surface, it sent a surge of displaced water fan tailing outward in all directions. The waves slapped against its sides. The submarine remained a dark, ominous presence, floating, a sight of raw power and eerie resilience, appearing free of damage.

"Impossible," Sezer said.

"We scored a direct hit," Ergin said. "There's no question about it."

"Didn't even make a dent," Jackson said.

"What the hell is that thing made out of?" Sezer asked.

"Doesn't matter," Jackson said. "We need to disable it. Now."

Before anyone could react, the submarine's missile tube covers retracted. Two projectiles launched. Jackson watched as the missiles shot into the air. They shuddered and turned, their contrails corkscrewing about. Reacting to their onboard guidance control systems, the missiles changed direction.

The *Neptün* targeted, the two missiles course corrected and streaked toward the helicopter.

"Incoming!" Ergin shouted.

Sezer yanked the controls, attempting evasive maneuvers. The *Neptün* veered sharply. Its engine strained against the sudden surge and change in direction. Jackson's stomach lurched as they dipped and swerved. The pilot doing his best to outmaneuver the impending attack.

The cockpit erupted with a cacophony of alarms.

Jackson's eyes darted between the controls on the screens and the incoming missiles directly ahead. His mind raced, searching for options and finding none.

He shouted their status to the *Selçuklu.*

"We cannot outrun them." Ergin's voice grim.

"And we can't outmaneuver them," Serer added.

He pulled back on the stick, raising the helicopter intensely, throwing them off balance.

Jackson wrapped an arm around the copilot seat to keep from being thrown to the back of the cockpit. When the first missile struck the *Neptün's* tail rotor, it spun them violently around. Jackson lost his grip. Thrown into the bulkhead, he grunted. The wind knocked out of him. Warning lights flashed across the flickering display panel. More alarms filled the small cockpit cabin. Smoke billowed from the copilot's console. Sparks flew from an overhead panel. The space quickly filled with an acrid and choking stench.

"We're hit!" Jackson shouted. "*Selçuklu.* Mayday! We're hit! I repeat, we're hit!"

The fire suppression systems activated, filling the cockpit with Novec 1230 gas. A clean, odorless, colorless agent that quickly doused the flames.

Sezer continued to struggle with the controls while the chopper blocked and shuttered.

Seconds later, the second missile pierced the *Neptün's* composite skin and exploded in the rear cabin. Jackson heard, only for a split second, the painful, final screams of the six soldiers as they died. Overhead, the main rotors thumped unevenly, creating a rhythmic, chaotic, metallic, clashing sound.

The helicopter pitched nose first as it spun. Sezer wrestled with the controls, trying to urge the doomed helicopter toward the Italian coastline. Keep them in the air, trying to reach shore.

The altimeter spun down in a dizzying spiral. Sezer fought for control of the ship. His teeth gritted. His knotted arms trembled. The *Neptün's* descent became a frenzied freefall. The water of the Mediterranean Sea rushed up at them at a horrific rate.

"We're going down!" Ergin shouted. "Brace for uncontrolled water landing."

Jackson shouted into his mic. "We're going down, *Selçuklu!* I repeat. We're going down."

The Italian coastline was in sight. Scattered along the shore were quaint coastal towns. Their red tile roofs and white-washed walls stood against the rolling hills' lush greenery.

All of it in stark contrast to the chaos inside the cockpit.

As the chopper descended rapidly, strapped into his seat, Ergin shouted to Jackson over the alarms and whining engines. "Grab on to something! Hang on!"

Sezer battled desperately with the controls. He white-knuckled the helicopter across the water's surface, doing his best to bring them as close to the coastline as possible.

The *Neptün* hit the water with a bone-rattling crunch.

The impact sent a spray of seawater high into the air. The windshield cracked and then shattered inward. With the force of a waterfall, a cascade of water rushed into the cockpit. The fuselage came apart. The sound of tearing metal filled the wrecked cabin.

Sezer and Ergin were tossed about, straining the five-point canvas harnesses strapping them in.

Thrown off his feet, Jackson sailed across the cockpit. Rushing water slammed him into the bulkhead. He hit his head. Blood blurred his vision as the crashing waves battered him relentlessly around the small space.

The helicopter bobbed on the surface then began to sink.

CHAPTER TWENTY-EIGHT

The Vergeltung

BATHED IN A DIM glow of red, with flashing green indicator lights, the cramped bridge of the submarine buzzed with the low hum of machinery and the hushed interaction of the crew. Each member hunched over control panels, focused on their tasks.

Maximilian Stahl stood in the middle of this activity, his gaze fixed on the central monitor displaying the skies above.

Anton Kuznetsov stood behind him along with the short, dark-skinned Iranian captain, a demure two steps behind them both. Dressed in a nondescript, utilitarian grey jumpsuit, much like the rest of the crew, Captain Amir Sadeghi's uniform lacked any country-specific affiliation patches, badges, or even rank designation. In the presence of Stahl and Kuznetsov, his stance was passive and one of quiet deference.

"A direct hit," Sadeghi announced needlessly as they watched the missiles strike the Turkish airship on the display feed. "They are struggling."

"They are attempting to reach the coastline," Kuznetsov said.

"It is doubtful they can make it," Sadeghi said.

Stahl watched the screen intently, his expression a mask of cold indifference. He had learned long ago not to underestimate his enemies, especially the allied forces, whilst operating in conjunction under the unified NATO Treaty.

"They are losing altitude quickly," Sadeghi reported as if Stahl did not have eyes. "What are your orders?"

"Maintain a pursuit course."

Sadeghi repeated the order, and the crew around them responded with practiced efficiency.

Stahl leaned closer to the monitor, catching every detail of the attack helicopter's desperate struggle. He smiled grimly with every dip and sway the chopper made as the pilot fought for every precious second to keep them in the air. Stahl silently commended the pilot's skill and his enemy's valiant determination.

With the Italian coastline visible in the distance. Stahl murmured more to himself than anyone else. "So close, and yet so very far away."

Executing his final, last-ditch effort, the pilot yanked up on the helicopter's cyclic stick, angling the machine to skim across the surface. The sea erupted in a violent splash as the chopper hit, sending a plume of water skyward and shattering the windscreen of the impressive Aegis Skyblade XH-99.

"They've crashed. Approximately one nautical mile from shore," Sadeghi reported. "The helicopter is sinking."

"Any sign of survivors?" Stahl asked.

Sadeghi held up a hand. "A moment." Conferring with several crewmen, he spoke in Farsi and hushed tones. To Stahl, he said, "Satellite imaging confirms at least one life raft has emerged from the wreckage. It's moving toward shore."

"Maintain current course and speed," Stahl ordered. "We're not done yet." The captain relayed the orders to the crew. Stahl turned to Kuznetsov. "You know what to do."

Kuznetsov nodded and stepped smartly from the *Vergeltung's* bridge.

The dimly lit, cramped space buzzed with tension. The crew moved about quietly, performing their duties. Precise and controlled, Stahl thought. He commended the Iranian captain for his competency in training and supervising the rogue crew recruited from a multinational consortium. The low hum of machinery and the rhythmic beeping of instrument panels and computerized output provided a soothing white background noise.

"Now, Captain, the real work begins."

Sadeghi step forward, filling the void left by Kuznetsov's departure.

Stahl handed him a simple scrap of paper. Scrolled in his precise handwriting were a set of coordinates. His voice steady and emotionless, Stahl said, "Initiate launch sequence."

Sadeghi glanced at the set of coordinates and furrowed his thick, dark brow. "What is the target?"

"That is none of your concern, Captain," Stahl snapped.

Sadeghi visibly flinched. "No. Of course not. Understood."

He snapped his fingers and handed the paper to his executive officer. They exchanged several hurried words in Farsi before the XO nodded and scurried off.

"Excuse the interruption, sirs." A technician monitoring the submarine's internal sensors and activities approached the two men. "The deck department is reporting the launch of two RHIBs. Sirs."

Having given no such order, Sadeghi glanced at Stahl. His bushy eyebrow raised.

"There might be someone very important to the success of our mission among those survivors," Stahl explained, though he was under no obligation to do so. "How does the launch prep proceed?"

Sadeghi dismissed the technician and glanced at several screens to his right. "Missile is prepped and ready to fire."

"Then why have you not launched?"

Sadeghi issued orders to his men on the bridge in Farsi, then waited. A voice—in English—announced over the submarine's comm system, "Missile away. Tracking systems are fully functional."

The voice belonged to the weapons officer. A former US Navy Missile Technician named Ranger. He had an expertise in handling, targeting, and launching ICBMs intercontinental ballistic missiles. An imposing, intimidating Texan Stahl had recruited personally for this mission.

"Trajectory stable," Ranger reported.

Sadeghi directed Stahl's attention to a digital camera display. On it, he watched as the missile ascended into the sky unchallenged. The weapon's smoky white contrail was visible behind a flare of yellow-white fire.

"No interference detected," the technician from earlier announced.

Stahl's mouth formed a tight smile. The target, known only to him and Ranger, who had input the coordinates given him, was Minsk, the capital of Belarus.

With its close alliance and extensive military cooperation with Russia, Stahl's chosen target would be a shock to the Kremlin. He felt a surge of cold superiority as the strike would undeniably ignite already simmering tensions between Russia and the United States.

Russia will accuse the allies of the unprovoked attack. The US would understandably and naturally deny the accusation. Still, public favor would be lost when the remains of the missile's outer casing and guidance systems were forensically examined and determined unequivocally to be American-made.

The missile rocketed skyward. Its path was unwavering and unchallenged.

While he felt this test was unnecessary and risked potential unwanted complications, Stahl knew now that the culmination of his meticulous planning and ruthless efforts was coming to fruition. He watched with a cruel smile as the missile, now a dark silhouette against the vast sky, soared higher, a powerful visual of the destructive force at Maximilian Stahl's command.

CHAPTER TWENTY-NINE

TCG Selçuklu
Ionian Sea En Route To The Adriatic Sea

PARKER STOOD ON THE bridge, horrified. Her eyes were glued on a bank of monitors. The atmosphere around her was thick with tension, a mix of horror, disbelief, and rapidly mounting rage. The muted hum of the ship's systems seemed incongruous against the charged silence.

Jackson's ominous final transmission haunted her. "We're going down, *Selçuklu*. I repeat, we're going down." She couldn't stop hearing it.

One monitor displayed the *Neptün* on fire. The rear cabin was decimated, trailing thick, black smoke. She watched as the pilot heroically struggled against gravity, the loss of power, and additional explosions. She silently willed him success in getting the aircraft within striking distance of the Italian shoreline.

Beside her, under his breath, Davenport said, "Come on. You can make it."

Even as he spoke the words, a second monitor showed an even greater threat.

A missile launched from the black, unmarked sub. It shot upward. A blinding burst of propulsion trailed it. Making it look like an inverted candle. Its ascent was rapid, almost graceful. A stark contrast to the *Neptün's* agonizing descent.

A cold sweat broke out across Parker's forehead. Her eyes followed the missile's trajectory, a terrifying arc. Its destination unknown. She glanced at Captain Demir. "We have to stop that missile."

Demir was already on it. His fist squeezed the mic in his hand. "Weapons Room. Şahin, prepare to launch two Sea Sparrow counter strike-intercept missiles." He shouted, "Nav, I need tracking coordinates now!"

"Transmitting to your screen as we speak," the navigations officer reported.

"Missiles ready to launch, Captain," a voice called out over the intercom. Parker assumed it to be the ship's weapons officer, Astsubay Başçavuş Levent Şahin. A petty officer, first class.

"Inform me when you have weapons lock," Demir ordered.

A silent second followed. It felt like an hour. Demir squeezed his fingers on the back of the navigations officer's chair. A death grip.

Davenport continued to look grim.

Parker nervously tugged at a lock of her red hair.

"We have target lock," Şahin announced. "I repeat. We have target lock."

"Fire!" Demir ordered.

"Sparrow's away," came the response.

The bridge fell silent. Demir pointed at a cluster of monitors. Each had a different view of the enemy's weapon and the Selçuklu's twin ballistic missiles streaking toward it.

Praying, Parker felt her breath catch as the RIM-7 Sea Sparrows arched toward their target. Sleek with four rectangular rear fins, their fiery exhaust trails were bright white with grayish smoke. The screens were filled with ever-changing angles, measuring the distance between target and interceptor missiles. Traveling at Mach 2.5, there was no doubt the *Selçuklu's* missiles were gaining, closing in—until the trailing missile started to fall short.

The lead interceptor continued to close the gap, inching closer. Seconds passed. Then, the screen flared with a brilliant white light. An explosion. The sky filled with a fiery bloom.

"Direct hit!" the navigations officer announced with a broad smile.

Those on the bridge cheered, but the celebration was short-lived as the target missile emerged from the black smoke and fireball, continuing its ascent. Its trajectory remained steady and unwavering.

"How?" Parker asked.

Demir grabbed a spare chair and sat. Furiously, his fingers flew across the keyboard in front of him. As he input information, he shouted to the weapons room, "Şahin, fire Sparrow three and four. Prepare the Harpoon quad-pack. Fire when ready."

"Sparrows away, sir. Awaiting Harpoon targeting coordinates."

"Transmitting now," Demir said, hitting what Parker assumed was a send button. The Turkish captain stood up and wiped his hand across his chin. "Fire at will."

To those on the bridge, he said, "We've done all we can do. *Insha'Allah.* If God wills."

On the screens, they watched as one RGM-84 Harpoon missile ignited, bursting forth from the launch tube in a bright plume of flame and smoke. Three more Harpoon missiles fired in quick succession, creating a staggered line of bright exhaust trails across the sky, racing toward the target.

Ahead of them, the Sparrows continued their flight, and the bridge crew was again forced to wait with held breath. This time, both Sea Sparrow missiles hit their target. And yet, like before, the enemy missile continued on its path. The only difference this time was its erratic trajectory. The onboard guidance system, if not disabled, had undoubtedly been damaged enough to throw the missile off course.

Meanwhile, the Harpoon missiles reached the target. They exploded around it but failed to knock it from the sky.

"We need to get more missiles in the air," Davenport said.

Demir frowned. "It's too late. We only carry four Sparrows. Even if we had more, the distance is too great. Nothing else aboard has the speed... "

The bridge fell silent, like being inside a steel coffin. Parker felt trapped. Helpless. There was nothing else she could do except make the call. She hit the speed dial on her sat phone, connecting to the only number programmed in it.

It rang just once before being picked up.

"Ma'am," Parker said. "You're aware of our situation here?"

"I am."

"I'm sorry, ma'am. There's nothing more we can do here. Can you give us an update?"

"Understood. Standby."

The tension could be cut with a knife as they waited for word, knowing the news could be nothing short of crushing.

It came a few minutes later when Grayson returned to the line. Her voice shaky with rage and sorrow. "I have confirmation. The missile has struck. All evidence points to the target being... Minsk, the capital of Belarus."

A cold shiver ran down Parker's spine. "What is the extent of the... devastation?"

"Impossible to tell at this time," Grayson said. "Responders and emergency units are en route. Most industrialized nations have plans and protocols in place for such an event. But, considering Belarus's strained relationship with the West, we can't know how prepared they are for such an incident."

"Surely the Russians will allow for... humanitarian assistance," Demir said.

"Our people are reaching out to the Russian government," Grayson said. "To the Federal Assembly now, but I wouldn't hold my breath. Based on Belarus' strategic relationship with Russia, I've no doubt there are secrets there neither country wants discovered. No matter how many lives it costs."

Parker asked the question she wasn't sure she wanted the answer to. "What is the population of Minsk?"

"Two million souls," Grayson said. "God help them."

CHAPTER **THIRTY**

TCG Selçuklu, Fast Patrol Boat
Monopoli, Italy

UNABLE TO DO ANYTHING to help the citizens of Minsk and unwilling to sit on her hands and do nothing, Parker boarded the fast patrol boat commissioned by Captain Demir to make the trip to the coast of Italy—a search and rescue mission to aid survivors of the downed *Neptün.*

Cutting through the night and the dark sea, she rode the bow of the fast-moving patrol boat, wearing borrowed lightweight, quick-drying maritime combat fatigues in a dark blue and gray camo motif. She clutched an MPT-76 battle rifle, the equivalent of the U.S. Armed Forces' M16. Goggles protected her eyes from the intense water spray. Davenport sat one seat behind her. With them was a squad of six elite commandos from the **Su Altı Taarruz**, which translates to "underwater offense" or "attack." The SAT unit was similar to the British SBS or U.S. Navy SEALs.

A special corporal led the mission. At the controls of the patrol boat, he steered, bouncing them at a high rate of speed as they raced toward the sandy shore of Monopoli.

"Approaching the shoreline," he called out over the roar of the engines and the slapping of the rubber hull rigid inflatable patrol boat against the whitecaps. "ETA two minutes."

The coastline stretched out a mix of golden sandy beaches and rugged rocky outcrops, reminding Parker of her recent trip to the New England seacoast of Maine and New Hampshire. She squinted, scanning the dark beach. A white ribbon of frothy water ebbed and flowed where the tide gently broke against the shore.

The downed helicopter lay partially submerged in the surf. A bent rotor angled into the air, the crew cabin glowed yellow, still on fire. The flames licked around the metal husk and the shattered windscreen of the cockpit. Black, oily smoke billowed skyward.

Further up the sandy beach, Parker spotted a bright orange life raft, partially deflated.

The pilot angled them away from the wreckage and aimed the swift boat toward the raft on shore.

When the nose of the swift boat scraped along the sandy bottom, Parker leaped out, splashing through knee-high water toward where emergency responders in bright, reflective uniforms moved swiftly around the life raft. Already on-site, medics were working diligently on two bodies lying prone in the surf.

From Jackson's last transmission, Parker and the crew of the *Selçuklu* knew the SAT team aboard the *Neptün* had perished instantly. The only hope of survivors remaining was for the pilot, copilot, and Jackson. But she saw only two figures lying in the sand.

Parker shouted. Her voice tight with concern. "Are they alright?"

"We are assessing now, *signora,*" one medic said.

Barann Sezer sat up, looking toward her. "Agent Quinn."

The medic had cut away the sleeve of his uniform, tending several deep lacerations along the man's arm. They bled profusely.

Parker lowered herself to one knee and touched the man's shoulder. The fabric soaked from his escape from the downed chopper. "Lieutenant Commander. How bad is it?"

"This man has lost a lot of blood, *signora,*" the medic said. "But with proper care and rest, I believe him to be fine."

Davenport joined her. Together, they helped the pilot to his feet. Unsteady, he reached out, catching Davenport's supportive grasp. Only then had Parker noticed the long, ragged tear along his thigh. Wet from seawater and dark with blood. A piece of metal shrapnel still embedded in his thigh. Blood leaked from the deep gash.

"The entire assault team," Sezer said. "They're gone. The *Neptün* took a direct hit to the crew cabin. All killed. Instantly."

"We know, Commander. We're so sorry."

"Ergin? How is he?"

Parker looked down the beach to where a pair of medics tended to the copilot.

"Pretty much the same as you," Davenport said. "Cuts and lacerations. A bump to the head. A couple of broken bones in his left leg. Probably will require surgery, pins, that sort of thing. But he's alive."

"Commander," Parker said. "Captain Jackson. He's not on the beach. Where is he? Did he make it? Do you know?"

"Not soon after we landed the raft on the beach, barely making it," Sezer said. "Two black-hulled RHIBs came after us. I can only assume it was dispatched from the sub. They came in heavily armed. We were weaponless. Defenseless. They grabbed your captain. They took him."

"Took him?" Davenport asked. "Or did he go with them?"

Parker glared at the lanky Englishman. Her annoyance apparent.

"What are you asking?" Sezer winced, putting weight on his injured leg.

"Did it appear... " She had trouble articulating the question. "Did he fight them? Or did he go willingly?"

"You're asking, was he... a part of this? Working for them?"

"It's a question," Parker said simply.

Sezer shook his head. "I... I can't say. Did he put up a fight? No. He was weaponless. Outmanned. Outgunned. Exhausted and injured. How much resistance can you expect?"

"Come on," Davenport said, pressing. "Were they rescuing an asset or taking a prisoner? Surely you can tell the difference."

"The man was barely conscious. They grabbed him and dragged him to the RHIB. What his status to them was, is, I've no idea. If they wanted a prisoner, why him and not Ergin or me? I can't say. What I do know is this. My co-pilot and I are alive because of Captain Jackson. He got us to the beach. Does the enemy do that?"

Parker thanked the man and stepped away.

She looked out over the smooth, quiet Mediterranean Sea.

If they took him prisoner, why? For what purpose? What would make the effort, the risk and the extra time to get him worthwhile? Recovering an asset? Preventing such a person from falling into enemy hands? Simply rescuing a fellow agent all made more sense to her. And yet, having worked with the man over these last few days, the man had saved her life on multiple occasions, and his act of heroism saving the pilot and co-pilot was enough to give Parker pause.

From the very beginning of this mission, she and her team have been plagued by the possibility that one among them was a mole. Maximilian Stahl had been kept annoyingly up-to-date about their activities. He knew of what leads and clues they had uncovered almost instantaneously. There was no question in her mind: Someone very, very close to them was feeding intel to their enemies.

The question of whether Jacques Jackson was that mole, a traitor to them and his country, would remain unanswered for the time being.

CHAPTER **THIRTY-ONE**

U.S. Coast Guard Patrol Forces – Southwest Asia
Persian Gulf, Bahrain

INITIALLY DEPLOYED IN 2003 to support Operation Iraqi Freedom, the Pacific Forces Southwest Asia (PATFORSWA) was now a permanent presence in the Kingdom of Bahrain, under the command of U.S. Naval Forces Central Command (CENTCOM) with a mission to equip, deploy, and support mission-ready Coast Guard forces for maritime operations in the region. The fleet comprises six 154' Sentinel-class fast response cutters with a 150-member support detachment, including a Maritime Engagement Team (MET) that worked closely with the Royal Bahrain Naval Force and the Royal Saudi Navy.

Located within the archipelago of the Persian Gulf, east of Saudi Arabia.

Perched atop a rugged cliff face. The military base offered an unobstructed view of the Gulf. Parker stood looking out over the water, clutching a borrowed Coast Guard windbreaker jacket against the salty breeze that whipped at her arms and legs and tossed about her loose mane of red hair.

Below the cliffs, she watched the bustling harbor where Coast Guard cutters bobbed at their moorings. Crew members scurried about securing lines, checking engines, and loading supplies.

Secretary Elizabeth Grayson stepped up beside her. She brushed her silver-gray hair from her face. "Mind if I join you?"

Parker glanced at her. "I'm surprised you can stand to look at me?"

The older woman raised an eyebrow.

"I failed. I failed miserably. You sent me out to prevent a catastrophic terrorist event, and I couldn't come close to stopping it. People are dead that shouldn't be. I've had a traitor in my midst this whole time and still can't tell you who it is. I'm supposed to be this hotshot antiquities agent, and I can't find a simple storage vault."

"Hmm." Grayson stared out over the Gulf, watching the busy port, bustling mainly with coach guard personnel who ultimately worked for her. "I knew you were a strong, confident woman, Parker, but had no idea you had such an inflated sense of self-importance. That you thought so much of yourself, you could rest the entirety of all the world's woes solely on your shoulders. I wish someone had told me. I'd have been happy to dump my burdens on those broad shoulders of yours."

"You're making fun of me."

"No. I'm not," she said. "I'm putting you in your place, where you belong, Parker. You're an agent for the Department of Homeland Security. A highly skilled, very competent, smart and valuable agent, but you are just one of thousands. In a law enforcement organization, that is one of hundreds working for the United States government. Working toward the goal of keeping our country and its interests safe. Not one of us is so all-important that all the bad things in the world can be laid at our feet. Not you. Not me. Not even the President of the United States."

She finally turned to look at Parker.

"I'm telling you to get over yourself. What you are considering failures, I—and the many people in power I work for—are looking at it in awe and gratitude. You and your team failed to stop a missile armed with a warhead from launching with a payload containing a catastrophic ancient biohazard weapon of mass destruction."

"Sounds like failure to me," Parker said, adding, "Ma'am."

"Except you're leaving out what you and your team *did* manage to do." Grayson's voice was stern. "You successfully altered the course of that missile. Because of your efforts, that missile was diverted two hundred twenty miles southwest into the Carpathian Foothills. An area with a population of under fifty thousand people, where casualty rates are projected to be one to two thousand, depending on Russians' response capabilities. Not hundreds of thousands, which would have been the cost if that missile had been allowed to get to Belarus unaltered. I'm not popping a bottle of champagne over that, but in my book, the number of lives saved far outweighs those lost. Maybe not a win, but certainly no failure."

"Ma'am—"

"No, Parker. The senior officer is talking now. What you also managed to accomplish—though you're too self-absorbed at the moment to see it—is that you and your team may well have prevented the start of World War Three. Our intel tells us the missile casing and several other components discovered in the impact area were U.S. manufactured. We believe it was stolen, of course, but in today's political and social climate, neither the Russians nor the public would accept that explanation. Stahl orchestrated this in an attempt to ignite the already smoldering tinderbox of Russian-Western tensions into a full-blown war.

Grayson pushed back a lock of hair from her eyes. "That is what you accomplished, Parker, so far. Where I do agree with you is the job isn't done. We've not even reached the ninth inning yet, much less gone into overtime."

"Baseball doesn't have overtime."

Grayson smiled. "Whatever."

"What about Jackson?" Parker asked.

Grayson sighed. "God knows I wish I could say I've never had an agent turn under me. That I've never been blindsided by it when it's happened. The truth is it's more common than we'd like to admit. And that is me speaking from personal experience. Still, all we know for now is that Maximilian Stahl grabbed Captain Jackson. We don't know why, and we have no firm evidence to support he's our mole."

"Do you truly believe that?"

"I want to. And I will until somebody shows me indisputable evidence to the contrary. The man deserves at least that much from us."

Parker wanted to think Grayson was right about Jackson and that he was not the mole. Not a traitor. She told herself to believe that, but she also knew she needed concrete proof. And that would only come when she could confront Jackson and Stahl face-to-face. Hear it from them for herself. Like Grayson, she needed indisputable evidence. Whether that exonerated or condemned remained to be seen.

Parker nodded her gaze out across the gulf once more. "Why are we here in Bahrain, Madam Secretary, and not out there, searching for Stahl?" She silently added: *And Jackson.*

"And where is out there, Agent Quinn? Have you any clue? If you do, now would be a great time to share it." Grayson paused. Her tone softened. "One added benefit of your efforts, Parker, is we now have plenty of assets assigned to the area. The entire might of NATO's resources in this region are now at my full disposal. We've allocated every available resource to finding Captain Jackson and neutralizing whatever Maximilian Stahl has planned next."

"You're operating on the assumption he has more of the contagion?"

Grayson shrugged. "Until we know otherwise, it seems the most prudent course of action."

"What is the situation on the ground in the Carpathian Foothills?"

"Accurate intel is difficult to get. It being Belarus and the geopolitical situation there. What we do know is the missile's warhead had the destructive power of approximately five hundred kilograms of TNT. Estimates are that the initial blast radius was approximately two hundred meters, destroying buildings and causing severe structural damage. The shockwave extended further out, blowing out windows, causing additional structural damage to buildings and igniting fires within a radius of approximately three hundred meters beyond that. We can't begin to estimate at the casualties to come because we have no clue what the ancient toxic contagion is. We're assuming the dispersal of the biological agent to be airborne, but it could also be a surface contact contaminant."

Parker felt tears welling in her eyes, Grayson's admonishment echoing in her head. Yes, they had saved potentially hundreds of thousands of people, but she could not escape the feeling of responsibility gnawing at her gut. She had still failed thousands of others. While she had not caused their deaths, their suffering—that onus rest solely with Stahl—it was an irrefutable fact she had not prevented them either.

In that moment, she vowed to avenge those deaths and all that suffering. She asked, "Have you contacted Agent Reynolds? Has he followed up on my request?"

"He's working on it," Grayson said. "They've not turned anything up yet."

"Thanks." Parker pulled at her lower lip. "There must be something else I can do." Her resolve apparent in her firm tone. "I can't just remain here and do nothing."

"And you won't be." Grayson faced her. "I didn't come out here to give you some kind of Knute Rockney pep talk. But, to let you know, while you were on the *Selçuklu*, Miss Rodriguez found something."

"The prism puzzle box? She cracked it?"

Grayson smiled. "Come on. I'll let her explain."

THE CONFERENCE ROOM IN the heart of the naval support activities base was cavernous. Yet the centerpiece wasn't large. A sleek table made of dark, polished teak. It sat only eight people. Built-in control panels and displayed devices embedded within its surface. The walls around the room were dominated by large, high-definition screens that were blank when Grayson and Parker arrived.

Typically, they would display a variety of mission-critical information, including maps and nautical charts, radar data, weather tracking information and other video feeds from satellites or surveillance drones. The floor was a blue-gray composite tile. The walls were covered in a battleship-gray fabric foam material that was soundproof and sound-absorbent. The room was so quiet their footsteps were like whispers across the floor.

Already in attendance were Lena and Davenport, sitting beside each other along the far side of the table. Facing them was a large, broad-shouldered man in his mid-forties. He wore a formal U.S. Coast Guard captain's uniform. He had a full salt and pepper-colored beard. His white cap—did they call it a lid like they did in the marine, Parker couldn't remember—sat on the conference room table.

"Agent Parker Quinn. This is Captain Ezekiel Styles." Grayson introduced her as she took the seat next to the man. They shook hands. His was calloused and weathered with a firm grip.

"A pleasure to meet you, Captain."

"Call me Easy," the man said with a pleasant smile. "Since it seems we'll be working very closely together."

"Will we?" Parker directed the question at Grayson with a curious arch of her eyebrow.

Grayson smiled. "We've got a lot to cover. You'll understand in a minute, Parker. Miss Rodriguez, why don't you get us started."

Lena came to her feet, a smile on her face. Her shaggy hair still looked like it had been chopped up by Edward Scissorhands, an intentional style that suited the petite woman. Since Parker last saw her, the young Latina had changed into a black Rosalía concert t-shirt, distressed blue jeans with intentional tears ripped through the thighs and knees, and black Converse sneakers. She wore a delicate gold chain around her neck with a milagro, or little miracle, charm. Parker hadn't noticed her wearing it on the plane in Teterboro; perhaps she'd just missed it. She knew the heart-shaped charm symbolized faith, protection, and blessings in Latin American and Spanish cultures. A green hoodie with a Razer logo hung from the back of her chair.

Lena reminded Parker of herself as a young grad student preparing to give and defend her final dissertation. Nervous, but extremely confident in her work.

Lena clutched an electronic tablet and began to pace the room, swiping across its surface. As she did, it dimmed the lights, and various display screens flickered on around them. On one appeared the same pictures that Parker had first encountered when FBI Agent Reynolds initially shared them in the New York office of the DHS.

The Chronicle of Kings cuneiform tablet.

The Guardian of Secrets cylinder seal.

The bronze statue of King Ashurbanipal.

Another screen illuminated. On it were the two fragmented pieces of the tablet Professor Ioannis Karas possessed and had named the Echoes of Empires tablet.

"As you all know." Lena paused. "Apologies, Captain. Are you—"

"Yes. Director Grayson has brought me up to speed." He smiled. "I should be able to keep up with the class."

"Oh, okay. Good, then." Lena continued, "Translating these tablets and the seal has been frustratingly challenging. But with the help of Professor Karas and the puzzle box we recovered from the Ochir Treasure Room, I've made quite a bit of headway translating both King Ashurbanipal's tablet and the seal, and that of his chief confidant and military commander, Nizar Khaldun."

She illuminated three more screens.

They each displayed the two tablets and the seal once more, but this time, they were overlaid with red circles highlighting various points found on the ancient artifact. Red lines directed the eye to superimposed descriptions of what the circled symbols or images represented. Some was the result of a decade's work done by the previous FBI analysts, no doubt. The rest, the bulk of it, had come from Professor Karas and Lena's collaboration and hard work.

"Quickly," Lena recalled. "We know that the Chronicle of Kings and the Guardians of Secrets seal are the recordings of events that took place prior to and leading up to the fall of Nineveh in 612 BC. The text details the development and chilling use of a biological toxin they called the Breath of Ashur. Other times, referred to as the Scarlet Death. What we today would call a biological weapon."

"We know all this," Davenport said. "Can we get on with it?"

"Since last we were all together, I've managed to translate enough of the tablets and seal to determine this devastating weapon was likely developed in the alchemist's secret chamber discovered in the Temple of the Whispering Sands. We now know Maximilian Stahl found at least a small sample of the Scarlet Death there before Captain Jackson and I arrived. Able to secure a sample of our own—"

A chill ran down Parker's spine. "We... we have a sample?"

Yes," Grayson said. "Miss Rodriguez recovered a small clay jar from the temple. It's been forwarded to the CDC in Atlanta. It is being analyzed as we speak." Grayson held up a hand, halting any questions. "They've not reported what, exactly, it is. Yet. We're still waiting. Miss Rodriguez, please continue."

"What we also learned from the tablets," Lena said, "Particularly, Nizar Khaldun's Echoes of Empires fragments, was that the alchemists' lab was not the final storage place for this contagion. The Scarlet Death was moved."

"We know there's more of this stuff out there?" Parker asked. "You know for sure?"

"Let's not get ahead of ourselves," Grayson said. "Go on, Miss Rodriguez."

Lena switched off all the screens, then tapped her pad.

The room filled with a soft, luminous, bluish-white light. In the center of the conference table appeared a holographic image of the pyramid-shaped prism puzzle box. It floated a few inches off the table surface and slowly rotated. Its ethereal radiance reflected on the faces of those gathered around it.

Parker marveled at its beauty.

Square at the bottom. Seven layers. Each contained a row of small, square panels. Each panel—comprised of some kind of translucent stone or glass—had an inscription, symbol or other marking on it. Some glowed white as if lit from the inside. The brightness contrasted with the icy blue panel they were etched in.

Parker had not had a chance to examine it thoroughly at the scene. The untimely arrival of the authorities had prevented that. But now, she noticed not all the markings and symbols were Assyrian. At least not known Assyrian etchings. The prism box tapered toward the top, making it look like a flat-topped pyramid. The uppermost courses were missing, or the artifact was simply incomplete. Whether by design or not was anyone's guess.

As if reading her mind, Lena said, "The prism box is complete at just seven layers."

"The symbols," Parker said. "They're not all Assyrian. I'm seeing Hittite hieroglyphs, Elamite Cuneiform, and is that Cypro-Minoan?"

Lena smiled. "Also, there's some Phoenician alphabet, Babylonian, Aramaic, Egyptian, and even Hurrian writings. You see, the prism box is a translation key. We determined earlier that the tablets and seal had been written using some sort of complex encryption strategy."

"Explain," Grayson said.

"With a few exceptions, our translation efforts, and that of the FBI, returned results that were—to use a scientific term—gibberish. We knew some combination of other languages were used."

"I recall that conversation during the FBI's initial briefing with us in New York."

"And if it had been a matter of a simple substitution cipher, using an Egyptian hieroglyphic in place of a Cypro-Minoan etching, we'd still have been able to decipher it, even allowing for languages we had no record of Assyrian having ever been exposed to. But it was so much more ingenious. Brilliant in its complexity. There's a combination of substitution and transposition ciphers. There are also position-based arrangements and numerical substitutions. They even used false traps. It's all actually quite impressive. Something we've not seen, at least not to this level of complexity in anything so old. This would've taken the most sophisticated code-breaking computer programs and algorithms—I don't know—years, maybe decades to crack."

Styles raised his hand. "Okay, the slow kid in the class is lost now. I admit it."

Lena explained. "Position-based subterfuge involves using the same symbol to mean different things depending on where it is used in the section of text or if it is upside down or right side up. For example, this symbol," she pointed to what looked like a bird on the prism box, "when found on the tablets in the fifth position, the fifth symbol in a line, it doesn't mean 'bird.' It means 'fish.' If it is inverted on its side but not in the fifth position, it means 'wind.' Additionally, other characters are placed within the text that have no meaning to what the line refers to at all. Just randomly placed symbols to confuse a reader."

"Turning the line into gibberish unless you have the key," Captain Styles said.

"Exactly." Lena continued. "The same type of applied confusion was also employed using symbols and markings from other languages, as we discussed, Egyptian, Elamite, Babylonian, and Aramaic. Among others. And numbers."

"Great," Davenport said, ever the impatient one. "So, how'd you crack it?"

"The prism box," Parker said. "Lena, how does it work?"

"The layers. They spin, like we surmised in Mongolia. The Rubik's Cube analogy was quite good. Except rather than just matching colored sides, when the layers are properly lined up to decipher a particular line of text," she beamed, "It's done vertically, not horizontally, which took some doing to figure out... Anyway, when I got the vertical rows to line up correctly, read up and down, the prism began to glow," Lena beamed, still fascinated by what she'd discovered. "Deciphering the lines of script on the tablets and the seal... making them, well, readable. There was a lot of trial and error, let me tell you—"

Davenport leaned forward. "What's it tell us?"

"The location," Lena said. "Which is why I'm confident Stahl has only gotten a small amount of toxin. Afraid it would fall into enemy hands, the Scarlet Death was spirited away from the Whispering Sands Temple."

If a pin dropped in the soundproof, sound-absorbent room at that moment, it would have sounded like a cannon going off. Lena left-swiped her pad. A satellite image of what looked like a lake in the desert appeared.

Lena announced, "To here." She zoomed in on the irregular blue shape on the map. "This is where we'll find the Scarlet Death."

"I enjoy a little suspense as much as anyone, Lena," Parker said. "But, where exactly is here?"

Lena painted a red circle, outlining the blue lake on the satellite image. "The Mosul Reservoir. Buried in its depths, I give you the Vault of Doom."

CHAPTER **THIRTY-TWO**

The Vergeltung
Somewhere Under The Black Sea

AFTER LAUNCHING ITS DEVASTATING missile attack against Belarus, the *Vergeltung* dove deep. Leaving the Mediterranean, they traveled through the Aegean Sea to the sixty-one-kilometer-long Dardanelles Strait—a natural waterway separating European Turkey from Asian Turkey and one of the world's narrowest straits. An essential naval and commercial shipping lane, it's heavily patrolled by Turkish naval forces. Passage required stealth maneuvering along the narrow channel. With an average depth of only fifty-five meters, they had to navigate the treacherous bottom at near silent running conditions to avoid detection.

From there, their route took them across the Sea of Marmara, where they passed through the Bosporus Strait. Another narrow shipping channel with an average depth of sixty-five meters and a scant three-point-six kilometers at its widest point. From there, they emerged undetected in the Black Sea.

The bridge of the *Vergeltung* was strictly utilitarian. And cramped. The metal walls and diamond-plated floors reflected the sterile, clinical lights from overhead. The control room was filled with the hum of machinery, and the thick air had a subtle tang of oil and metal.

Half-carried, half-dragged, two men in dark combat fatigues dropped Jackson at Stahl's feet. On his hands and knees, Jackson grunted. He clutched his waist, sure he'd broken at least one rib. He had a laceration the length of his thigh, where a ragged piece of metal had sliced deep. His jumpsuit was soaked with a mix of blood and seawater.

Stahl glared down at him. Like he was a mongrel dog. He noticed the deep, bloody gash over Jackson's eye. "Bet that stings? I am Maximilian Stahl."

"Great to put an ugly puss to the psychopath behind all this."

"American witticisms will get you nowhere with me, Captain Jackson. But, I, too, wished to meet the person who so valiantly thwarted my best efforts lately more often than I've been comfortable with. Unfortunately, Agent Parker Quinn wasn't on that helicopter. I'm stuck with you."

Jackson forced a grin, deepening a cut in his lip. "Happy to disappoint, Maxie."

"Insolent dog!" Stahl backhanded Jackson across the face. The blow knocked him sideways to the deck. Stahl's men grabbed Jackson before he could launch a counterattack. They stood him up, holding his arms behind his back.

His breathing labored. Each inhalation was a struggle against Jackson's broken rib. His facial cuts leaked blood, and his leg wound puddled a mix of blood and seawater on the deck.

"Why am I here? Why didn't you just kill me?"

"An artist," Stahl said. "Does he paint for himself, or does he do it for an audience?"

Jackson scoffed. "That's what you think you are? Some sort of terrorist Michelangelo?" He spit blood on the deck at Stahl's feet. "A terrorist is just a terrorist. Small, impotent men with delusions of grandeur. Angry, little people bent on tearing down instead of building up."

That earned Jackson another backhanded fist across his face. He spit more blood while Stahl rubbed his bruised knuckles. Jackson grinned, revealing bloody teeth. "You're just a garden variety narcissist. A cliché."

Stahl chuckled. A low, menacing sound. "You think you know me, Captain. Can psychoanalyze me based on your battlefield experience? You think this is all about me?" Stahl shook his head like a teacher schooling a dull-witted student. "How small you think, Captain."

"Isn't it? You've got some petty beef with the world, and you think you can get revenge for this preconceived slight in your past."

"You could not be further off the mark," Stahl said. "Captain."

"No? Enlighten me, Maxie. What is this then? What twisted ideology do you follow that justifies the horrific slaughter of thousands?"

Amused, Stahl said, "Thousands? You really do think small, Captain. Think tens of thousands. Hundreds of thousands. That's what it will take to get the incompetent leaders of this world to wake up. To listen."

"To what? A new world order? World domination with you at the helm. Is that it? You've got a Messiah complex?"

"Not me, Captain. Men.. and women far greater than me."

"Women, huh? I didn't know terrorist scum could be so progressive."

Stahl shook his head. "Simpleton. I am not some maniacal madman who believes himself to be greater than his station. Twisting my villainous mustache."

"Just my luck," Jackson said. "I get the world's only humble terrorist. If what you're saying is true, then you're just a puppet. Serving men... and women—good for you—who are using you as a tool. And when it becomes necessary, cannon fodder."

"Does that make me any different than you then? Serving the great United States of America. Truth. Justice. The American way."

"We don't slaughter hundreds of thousands of innocent people?"

"Don't you? Afghanistan. Iraq, twice. Vietnam. Korea. Shall I go on?"

"Defending democracy."

"And the same can be said of us," Stahl countered. "Fighting against the invasion of enemy forces. We are a necessity. A harbinger of change. The world needs guidance, Captain. United control. Without it, humanity is destined to remain mired in its current state of crisis. Bogged down in chaos and conflict. Which can only lead to its inevitable conclusion: destruction."

Stahl paused, getting a second wind. "Power, Captain. True power—in the hands of people not afraid to use it—can reshape this world. Our future order and stability will reign supreme."

"A better world," Jackson said. "Form-fitted and forced to your twisted version of what that should be. And death to anyone who dares to think differently than you, speak out against you, who might dare to want more than you're willing to provide. All challenges to that are to be struck down in the name of order and stability. Sounds like subjugation to me. And a pathetic God complex, whether held by you or the idiots above you."

Jackson shook his arms away from the two men holding him. "Now, tell me why I'm still alive, or for mercy's sake, put a bullet in my brain so I don't have to endure one more minute of your inane philosophical crap."

"Fortunately, I, too, tire of the debate," Stahl said. "As for why you still live, you are simply a bargaining chip. A chess piece to ensure I encounter no further obstacles from your friends while I claim the final prize. That which I have sought for too many years."

"The Breath of Ashur," Jackson said.

"Yes. The attack on Belarus was only a simple appetizer of what is to come, of what we will be capable of once we obtain the full cache of Ashurbanipal's secret toxin, the Scarlet Death."

"Well, if you think I'm going to help you in any way, you might as well just kill me now and save yourself some time and trouble, Maxie. And so we're clear, as far as I know, Ashurbanipal's storage place was the chamber in the Whispering Sands Temple. And you already raided that."

"Oh, don't you wish that were the case, Captain? No, the prize was moved. Centuries ago. But don't fret. I know exactly where the Vault of Doom is. Thanks to Parker Quinn's intrepid team and their efforts."

Jackson's breath hitched. His mind raced despite the fog of pain that dulled his thoughts and the soreness radiating through every part of his body. Parker had been right all along. There was a mole, and whoever it was, they were very, very close.

"Vault of Doom?" Jackson said. His reaction indifferent. Nonchalant. "A little dramatic, don't you think?"

"Tell that to the Assyrian people. It was they who named it 2600 years ago."

"Well, that's all news to me," Jackson said. "But again, it looks like I won't be much help to you."

"For now, perhaps," Stahl agreed. "But once we arrive at Mosul Reservoir, that situation will change."

Mosul Reservoir, Jackson thought. Where the hell did that come from? "I'll die first."

"Yes, you will die, Captain," Stahl said. "You, and Parker Quinn, and all the rest who stand in my way. But not before the Scarlet Death is mine."

CHAPTER **THIRTY-THREE**

USCG Chinook Helicopter – Sea Breeze
Over Mosul Reservoir, Iraq

THE CH-47D CHINOOK HELICOPTER thundered across the surface of Mosul Reservoir. Its twin rotors cut through the air with a deafening chuffing sound. A heavy-lift helicopter, the Chinook could handle a 19,500-pound load with a top speed of 170 knots. Dark matte-gray, the machine was a beast as it skimmed the calm waters of the reservoir below.

Slung underneath was the massive Oceanic Research and Command Platform, known as *Osprey's Nest*, dangling from a myriad of thick, reinforced steel support cables. The weight of the platform pushed the helicopter to its operational limits. Cutting through the air, it swayed underneath, putting an additional strain on the suspension system. The pilots fought to maintain a steady course, carefully watching their various gauges and navigational instruments.

Parker, Davenport, and Lena were strapped into their seats in the crew cabin, the rhythmic thrum of the routers loud in their ears. Parker's thoughts took her back to the conference room several hours earlier.

"The Mosul Reservoir. Buried in its depths, I give you the Vault of Doom." Lena's words still echoed in her ears.

"These idiots sunk this stuff in a reservoir?" Davenport asked.

"The dam was constructed in 1986," Grayson said.

"Before that," Parker said, "the area was mostly rural land and a few scattered villages."

The loss of archaeological sites such as Basetki and Qasr Shamamok was of concern at the time of the dam's construction. With a cadre of international archaeologists, the Iraqi government conducted extensive salvage excavations of the two cities to recover and preserve as many artifacts as possible before the dam's completion, which resulted in their flooding.

"It was before my time," Parker said, "but from what I read, the construct of the dam and reservoir still led to significant archaeological losses."

"Located north of Nineveh and Nimrud," Lena said. "Ashurbanipal must have thought it was a considerable enough distance away to keep it safe should Nineveh fall, yet close enough to retrieve if using it as a weapon was a viable option."

"And now it's underwater?" Davenport said. "That's just great."

"Which brings us to why I'm here," Captain Styles said. He activated several screens, taking over the presentation from Lena Rodriguez with an endearing smile. "As mentioned, the Mosul dam and reservoir were created in 1986, previously known as the Saddam Dam. It is Iraq's largest dam. Located on the Tigris River about fifty kilometers north of Mosul, it was built to control flooding, provide water for irrigation and generate hydroelectric power."

He enlarged one image of the reservoir with the impressive dam in the background. "The dam is a remarkable structure in terms of size and capacity. It stands at approximately three-hundred-seventy-one feet. That's one-hundred-thirteen meters for the metric users in the room. It spans two miles and can hold back three trillion gallons at full capacity. Our interest, of course, is the reservoir. It extends twenty-eight miles north along the Tigris and has a maximum width of almost nine miles. Its max depth is two-hundred-forty-six when at full capacity."

"Don't suppose we could drain it to get to our Vault of Doom," Davenport inquired.

"Not likely," Styles said. "it provides seven-hundred and fifty megawatts of power, providing electricity to millions."

Davenport frowned. "Wishful thinking."

"You afraid to get wet, Agent Davenport?" Grayson asked.

"Just not a fan of drowning, ma'am."

"We have something Stahl doesn't," Parker said. "The prism box and the location of the Vault. No way he can know that. So, how do we proceed?"

"I'll let the Captain explain," Grayson said,

The holographic prism box in the middle of the table disappeared. Replaced by…

"*Osprey's Nest*," Styles said proudly. "This is a versatile, next-gen oceanic research and command platform designed for ocean exploration, scientific research, and, when necessary, a mobile military command center."

"Which it's now commissioned as, effective immediately by order of President Kingsley," Grayson said.

Styles continued, "This platform is thirty feet in length and twenty feet wide. It has a height of twelve feet and a total operating weight of fifteen hundred pounds. Constructed of high-strength, low-alloy steel and lightweight composites with corrosion-resistant coatings. It has a multi-level retractable equipment base and fold-out observation decks. Its deployable outriggers are gauged to ensure stability in the face of a category two storm. Powered by a hybrid solar and wind energy system with backup diesel generators. The platform has a propulsion system that allows for minor adjustments and positioning while deployed."

"That oil rig wannabe is sitting in the Mosul Reservoir?" Davenport asked.

"No, of course not. That would be ridiculous," Styles said with a wide grin. Parker wondered if the man ever didn't smile. "The *Nest* is completely mobile. It's airlift transportable. We'll be using a CH-47D Chinook helicopter to transport—"

"You're going to *fly* it to the reservoir," Davenport said. "And I'm the one being ridiculous."

"We'll have it in position and fully operational in under six hours," Styles said.

"Crewed with a team of scientists and researchers, yourselves," Grayson nodded toward Lena, Davenport and Parker, "and a fully trained MET team commanded by Captain Styles to assist in your dive and search for the Vault of Doom."

Now, as the Chinook neared the designated drop zone and the pilots began their descent, Lena gripped the edges of her seat. Her dusky features were flush from motion sickness. She gasped when the chopper banked sharply, getting into position to air-drop the massive research structure cradled beneath them.

Parker leaned to her right, looking through the open door. She watched as the reservoir's surface came closer. The chinook's twin engines roared with their relentless fury. The blades overhead a blur of motion. The downwash from the rotors churned the water and kicked up spray, creating a misty rainbow-infused halo around them.

The pilots adjusted their position, bringing the Chinook to hover a mere ten feet above the water. Orders began to ping pong through their headsets as the Coast Guard team initiated the task of lowering *Osprey's Nest* into the reservoir.

The helicopter hovered steadily, gently rocking, while the crew painstakingly worked to ensure the platform settled properly into the water with a gentle splash. The cables slackened as the weight transferred from the helicopter to the water, where the platform now bobbed gently on the surface. Next, the six-member MET team was repelled to the platform below. Specifically trained in the deployment of the ORCP platform, they went quickly and efficiently about the task.

Over her headset, Parker heard Captain Styles' voice. "It won't be much longer, Agent Quinn."

"It's Parker, Captain."

"Aye, aye, Parker, ma'am."

The team detached the dozens of cables, now swirling underneath like dangling snakes. The chopper gently banked, entering a holding pattern over the platform, giving Parker, Davenport and Lena a bird's eye view of the ORCP as it was brought to operational readiness.

While the Chinook crew secured and stowed the support cables, Parker and the others watched through the open doors, wind whipping in their faces. Below, the platform's side decks unfolded like mechanical wings from the central structure, expanding the platform's operational area significantly.

Once the decks locked into place, the *Nest*'s exterior lights snapped on. They illuminated the brush gunmetal steel decks and superstructure in a warm, bluish-white glow. The lights rimmed the edges of the deck and highlighted key operational areas, casting wide, reflecting pools of yellow light on the settling water's surface. Control panels, equipment bays, and walkways were outlined in glowing yellow lines like one sees on an airport runway. A section of the lower deck opened, and from it, a portion extended outward smoothly as heavy-duty ballast tanks stabilized it.

"The landing pad," Davenport said.

The deck had an illuminated yellow circle and flashing running lights to guide incoming helicopters. The platform was now ready to receive them, and the supplies still stored onboard the Chinook.

The final stages of activating the platform included the extension of antennas and satellite dishes used to establish communication links and data connections. Within twenty minutes, the *Nest* was a hive of activity as the MET moved with purpose and professionalism.

The Chinook continued with one final circle before descending to the platform below.

Excited, Parker said, "This is it."

She gave Lena an encouraging smile, noticing how the young woman clutched her laptop bag with a death grip. Green around the gills, the analyst was clearly anxious to set foot on solid ground—such as it was.

IT TOOK AN HOUR to completely unload the Chinook and another two to go through the safety briefings set up by the MET team—too important to skip, Styles demanded—for the civilian scientific and research members brought on board to assist in the search for the Vault of Doom.

In a compact conference room with walls of sleek brushed steel integrated with LED panels and a large clear glass window that took up most of the far wall, the team selected to make the dive assembled. Beyond the glass, the reservoir's deep azure surface glimmered. Soft ripples catching the sunlight. Yellow-white glints of brightness reflected across the walls and battleship gray table. The serenity of it in stark contrast to the hazard concealed somewhere beneath its shimmering calm.

Besides Parker and Davenport, there would also be four MET team members and two scientists specifically selected for their expertise in their chosen disciplines and extensive underwater diving experience.

The first was a man named Doctor Rajesh Patel. A geologist from MIT whose past work involved groundbreaking research on tectonic plate movements, underwater volcanic activity, and mapping undiscovered cave systems. An expert in analyzing rock formations, sediment layers, and thermal anomalies. And also an acclaimed certified cave diver with over twenty years of experience.

Of concern, Mosul Dam is on a foundation of soluble rock, including gypsum, anhydrite, and limestone, in a seismically active region. Although not at the level of major tectonic plate boundaries, the weight of the water could induce seismic activity. A phenomenon known as Reservoir-Induced Seismicity (RIS).

With them would also be Dr. Emily Carter, a highly respected expert flown in from the Centers for Disease Control and Prevention. With a PhD in toxicology and environmental health sciences from Johns Hopkins University, she was a specialist in the study of hazardous substances and their effects on human health, earning her a superlative reputation in the field of biosecurity. She'd been involved in a number of high-stakes CDC missions to identify and neutralize biological threats, including outbreaks of rare pathogens, investigating chemical spills with the potential for mass casualties, and mitigating the spread of highly contagious diseases.

She'd led the team dispatched to the alchemist's chamber in the Whispering Sands Temple, where she'd secured the area and initiated a thorough search for additional stored pathogens. She supervised the meticulous examination of the scene for signs of contamination and other hazardous materials before overseeing the decontamination process to ensure the safety of the dig site and the surrounding environment.

Her assignment now would be to keep the team from unwittingly exposing themselves to or releasing a devastating biological pathogen onto the world.

No pressure, thought Parker.

The MET team would include Captain Ezekiel Styles, as on-site command authority was his prerogative. Parker had learned the man was thirty-five and a highly decorated officer who had served in the Coast Guard for over fifteen years. Grayson assured Parker that Styles's dive skills, underwater demolition expertise, and tactical combat abilities were second to few in the service.

With them would be team leader Lieutenant Sarah Mitchell, Petty Officer Alex Ramirez, and Ensign Bruce Chang. Each had extensive chemical, biological, radiological and nuclear threat training focused on identifying, containing, and decontaminating hazardous materials and environments during maritime missions.

While Lena Rodriguez would remain on board *Osprey's Nest*, she was included in the briefing. It was her interpretations and translations of the various ancient texts that had brought them to this point, after all. Her continued involvement via commlink during the dive could determine their success or failure depending on what they found under the calm blue waters of Mosul Reservoir.

Introductions were made, and the briefing began.

CHAPTER **THIRTY-FOUR**

Fifteen Fathoms under the Mosul Reservoir

CAPTAIN STYLES HAD INSISTED on taking the lead of the dive team. Parker and Davenport were in formation behind him, followed by the two scientists, Dr. Patel and Dr. Carter. The rest of the MET team brought up the rear. Parker was a practiced and competent diver but not an expert anywhere near the level of her Coast Guard escorts. She had come to learn these people basically lived on and in the water.

The surface rippled gently overhead, lit by the morning sun, while the depths below promised cold and darkness. The deeper they swam, Parker could feel the water pressure pushing against her body, compressing her chest and making every breath feel heavy and labored. Her ears popped painfully, forcing her to equalize. She swallowed hard and wiggled her jaw. The silence, other than the sound of her breathing and the rhythmic hiss of her regulator, coupled with the murky darkness and the unknown, caused her to shiver.

As her eyes adjusted, Parker began to make out the sunken remains of the ancient city of Bassetki. A once vibrant regional hub for the crucial trade routes connecting the Assyrian heartland to the northern territories. The tops of ancient columns and portions of the fortification wall, softened by time and sediment, loomed below, draped in a veil of algae and aquatic plants. Schools of fish darted like silver missiles in the divers' shoulder-mounted lights. A part of her mourned the loss caused by the flooding of these great landmarks.

Parker shook away the thought.

She focused her concerns on the mission as they descended deeper, approaching an area of the reservoir's western wall. Lena, with the assistance of Doctor Patel and the prism box decipher, felt she could get the team within a hog's breath of the so-called Vault of Doom. Still, finding the exact location of a cave hidden for over twenty-five hundred years and then flooded by the formation of a reservoir would be anything but a cakewalk.

Parker reacted when something hit her leg. She twisted to see Patel. He'd tapped her with the edge of his underwater tablet to get her attention. Swimming up beside her, he pointed at the screen. Then he pointed toward a layer of sloping rock ledges.

"You are aware we're micced up, aren't you, Doctor?"

"Oh, right. Sorry. Old habits. I don't often get to dive with such sophisticated equipment. Anyway," Patel pointed at the screen again. "According to the 3D subsurface modeling we created from the existing tomography maps and previous GPR data collected of the area, along with existing historical maps and known archaeological landmarks, and using Dr. Rodriguez's translated texts, I believe… "

Patel pointed toward the sloping wall to the right.

"We shall find the access we seek somewhere along that shadowy crevice there."

Ahead of them, listening in, Styles veered to the right and down, following Patel's directions.

After four false starts, Parker's excitement over each new lead had begun to wane.

According to Patel, over time, the reservoir water has seeped into cracks and voids, interacting chemically with the highly soluble sedimentary rock, likely forming many such cavities and fractures. Even minor seismic activity in the region could create or expand such fissures. A process called karstification. What they needed to find was one that would lead them to a specific natural karst feature—an underground cave, sinkhole, or void—formed long before the dam's construction. The one the Assyrians built called the Vault of Doom.

Yet, despite their lack of success so far, Parker remained optimistic. They were on the right track. She could feel it. It would just take time and patience, which she feared were both in short supply. They had a jump on Maximilian Stahl, but for how long?

As for her patience, that was scarcer than a hen's teeth. Parker nodded and gave Patel a thumbs up. "Let's check it out."

She kicked her finned feet harder, nearly overtaking Styles. He glanced at her through his face mask. She saw his expression warning her to back off—putting her in her place. This was his team, it said, and he would lead it.

Parker bit back a retort but let the captain swim a foot or so ahead of her.

They neared the dark void Patel had pointed out in the rock formation, obscured by a tangle of underwater vegetation. The group converged, their lights passing over the jagged edges of an opening. It looked narrow, barely large enough for a person to squeeze through.

Parker's pulse quickened. Her excitement charged her nerves like a live electrical wire. This was it. She was sure of it.

"Lieutenant Mitchell, you're with me," Styles said. "We'll go in and check things out. The rest of you remain here until we signal it's safe to come in."

"Absolutely not." Parker's green eyes narrowed with barely contained fury. "You're in charge of your people, Captain. But this exploration is mine."

With no interest in continuing the conversation—argument—Parker swam past the group and shimmied between the rocks like a timber rattler scurrying to safety. The narrow opening required her to swim sideways to fit her shoulders through. Her heart pounded as she pressed her hands against the rough rock wall inches from her face.

"Parker!"

She ignored Styles and kicked her legs, propelling herself deeper into the crevice.

Her shoulders and air tank brushed against the cave walls. The darkness ahead of her seemed to swallow her flashlight beam. Yet she could still make out the craggy path angling through the narrow passages, the twists and turns the deeper she went into the cave system.

"We are going to have a conversation about this, agent," Styles's voice said over the commlink.

Noticing the occasional flicker of light behind her as the captain and presumably the rest of the team followed behind her, Parker didn't reply.

Continuing on, fish darted away from her waving beam of light.

She noticed tiny crustaceans scurrying across the rocks the deeper she went. Her breathing and the hiss of her regulator sounded louder in her ears. She struck her knees and scraped her gloved knuckles against the rock walls, narrowing and closing in on her. Kicking up salt and detritus, a sense of panic settled in her chest.

Could this have been a mistake?

Might the cave narrow too close for them to pass? Could it be a dead end? In either case, was it possible they could not get turned around? Get stuck with no way forward and no way back?

Parker concentrated on her breathing. Focusing on the steady rhythm of her regulator, she forced it to become a comforting reassurance. She began to relax.

Told herself to take it one kick at a time.

Just then, her flashlight picked up a section of passage ahead that widened slightly.

She motioned to Styles, now close on her heels, to stop. She pointed. "I see an opening ahead."

Parker shimmied herself upright through the opening, snagging her air tank for a frightening moment before she wiggled it free. The crevice opened into a large, watery space. The walls around her disappeared into darkness. Parker could see nothing beyond the muted beam of her flashlight.

She consulted her digital compass and depth gauge. Each emitted a soft, greenish glow. She kicked and slowly adjusted her buoyancy to be slightly positive, rising with a controlled, gentle lift. Soon, the darkness felt less oppressive. Perhaps it was her imagination, but it gave her a sense of growing relief.

Parker broke the surface and slowly turned, panning her flashlight beam over arching rock walls that formed a sizeable vaulted cave. They glistened with moisture and bioluminescent marine plankton, vibrio bacteria and glow worms clinging to the rocky, dry ledges.

The cavernous space immediately relieved Parker's growing sense of claustrophobia.

"It's a tight squeeze, but there's a lagoon once you're through."

She took off her facemask and took a deep breath. The air smelled earthy and damp and held a faint sulfurous odor—like rotten eggs—coupled with a metallic, tangy taste. "And a cave. With a breathable air pocket. It's beautiful."

Parker swam for the small beachhead where the trapped water—disturbed by her swimming—lapped onto a horseshoe-shaped beach. Plopped down on the sandy inlet, she watched as Styles and Patel and then Davenport surfaced. Soon after, the others popped into view, breaching the water, with Lieutenant Mitchell bringing up the rear.

Parker dropped her facemask and stripped off her air tank, BCD vest, and weight belt. She stepped out of her fins. As the others swam toward the beach, she unzipped her wetsuit top. Wearing a white tank top with a USCG logo underneath, she let the neoprene suit hang from her waist.

With her back turned to the others, she adjusted her bra, the straps biting uncomfortably into her shoulders. Sure everything under her shirt was secure, she turned and shook out her damp red hair.

Styles climbed out of the water, looking around. His mouth open. "This is incredible. But how is it possible?"

Patel came to his feet next to him. "Geographical features such as this are not all that uncommon. With the completion of the dam and the formation of the Mosul Reservoir, the rising water levels pushed through the siphons and vertical shafts present in rock formations such as these, trapping air in chambers and caverns and, thus, forming air pockets. The created pressure prevents them from flooding. There are probably many other such caverns close by."

"Any chance they lead to a way out that doesn't involve," Davenport held up his face mask and fins, "these?"

"Well, it's a perfectly lovely beach," Parker said. "I suggest we use it as a staging area, Captain. It's time we got this show on the road."

While the others emerged from the water and stripped out of their scuba gear, Styles seized Parker's arm and pulled her to a secluded corner of the beach.

She glared down at his hand. He released her arm and apologized, but his easy smile was gone. "That was unacceptable and completely out of line. The safety of this party. Including you and the others, whether you like it or not, is my responsibility."

Parker met his intense stare. "Which was why I was happy to have you and your team join us. I've recently learned the value of having a few well-trained, competent coasties riding along shotgun. But understand this, Captain, this expedition is mine. I am in charge. And I don't need a babysitter. If you've got a problem with that, take it up with Grayson or President Kingsley."

She flashed Styles an engaging yet smug smile.

He lowered his voice. "I might if I could get through to them. We lost contact. And I've been trying to get through for the last ten minutes."

"Lena. She was supposed to be standing by," Parker said. "Be available if we needed her assistance with any translation issues that came up."

"The problem's bigger than that. A comms officer is supposed to be manning our channel 24/7. Which means—"

Parker concluded, "There's a serious problem topside."

CHAPTER **THIRTY-FIVE**

Mosul Dam
Wadi al-Murtibah, Iraq

WHILE PARKER QUINN AND her team had been preparing for their dive into the depths of the Mosul Reservoir, Maximilian Stahl, Anton Kuznetsov, and a small contingent of combat fighters arrived at Mosul Dam. Ten armed and well-trained mercenaries in scuba suits arrived in three sand-colored, deuce-and-a-half trucks. Using a naturally formed lime and sandstone ramp, they unloaded and prepared to launch seven two-man, submersible assault watercrafts.

Underwater sleds, the crafts were four meters in length, with a one-point five-meter width and one meter in height. Constructed of lightweight composite materials painted in a matte black finish, they were equipped with dual electronic propulsion systems, allowing them to glide silently for a maximum speed of ten knots and a distance of forty nautical miles before needing to be recharged. The machines were equipped with acoustic modems, micro-LED technology and live data processing, establishing a secure, high-frequency commlink, transporting advanced sonar and GPS navigational information to heads-up, integrated 3-D displays in each diver's mask.

Jackson's wounds had been superficially treated. Now, forced to don a scuba suit, he was secured with zip ties to the back of the craft Anton Kuznetsov would pilot. As the last of the assault team slipped under the smooth surface of the reservoir, Stahl glanced at Kuznetsov.

"I would prefer the captain arrive at the platform alive," Stahl said. "Until I'm assured he will be of no further use to us." He glared at Jackson. "But should you find it necessary, his remaining alive is not mission critical."

Jackson spat at his feet.

Kuznetsov nodded. "Understood."

Stahl launched his craft without another word or thought.

Confident Kuznetsov and his prisoner would be behind him, he plunged into the crystal clear blue water, leaning forward on the craft like one might ride a racing motorcycle. The water around him quickly darkened to an ominous purple-black the deeper he went. Despite the five-mm full-body wetsuit he wore, a shiver ran through him as the water temperature dropped from 18°C to 10°C, where he skimmed along the reservoir floor.

Over him, a pale cerulean ceiling rippled. The sled's control panel glowed red and green, as did the display readouts on his face mask. Through the darkening water, he could barely make out the silhouettes of his assault team further ahead.

They moved in perfect formation.

Each pilot expertly maneuvered their submersibles, proceeding low and close to the bottom. Each observed the strictest silent running protocols.

Fifteen minutes later, the first faint crackle of static transmitted over the closed commlink. Korhonen, the team leader, announced, "Approaching target location. ETA one minute."

Stahl's lips curled into a grim smile. After all these years, he was so close.

All his efforts. His sacrifice and necessitated subservience that ate at his soul had brought him to this moment. To this point in time. And to think, what he had sought all these years, the pursuit that had taken him around the world more than once, begun all those years earlier with the nighttime burglary of the Baghdad museum, the goal of this treasure hunt lay just four hundred kilometers from where it all began.

As they reached the underside of the research platform, the team slowed their approach. The enemy had no reason to suspect Stahl was this close or that he was even aware of this very operation. They expected little in the way of station fortification and minimal resistance once their assault began.

The floating platform's lights cast a bright white glow into the water, creating an eerie, almost surreal tapestry. A school of fish darted through the lights. Below, the ruined remnants of the bustling city of Bassetki lay. A fortified city with the outlines of a surrounding wall, buildings, temples and towers surprisingly well preserved and visible through the sediment, the algae and aquatic plants that waved like green tendrils. Carp, shabut, tilapia, and other fish, silver and gray flashes, darted through the nooks and crannies. Crayfish scuttled along sections of the fortification wall.

Stahl slowed his approach. The assault team gathered in a tight group hovering just below the platform's large rectangular moon pool.

"Standard positioning," Korhonen said through the commlink. "Prepare to breach."

The underwater sleds were equipped with an advanced buoyancy control system managed by each vessel's onboard computer. The ABCS calculated the optimum buoyancy based on water density, depth, and currents to maintain a stable, unmanned hover, even in turbulent waters.

Which these were not.

Like leaving a herd of horses to graze in a field, thought Stahl, watching his men swim upward, leaving the sleds behind. Clad in black scuba gear, armed, they swam toward the moon pool and began to ascend two at a time, using the ladder rungs conveniently illuminated with yellow caution lights.

Stahl noticed Kuznetsov's arrival with his prisoner from the corner of his eye. "Remain below," he ordered. "I will signal you when it is safe."

He caught Kuznetsov scowl through his facemask. Angry at missing the action.

"Everyone plays their part, Anton."

Stahl swam to the pool opening and quickly climbed up the ladder.

The overhead sun cast a warm, pleasant light across the impressive platform surface. The ingenuity of the Americans never ceased to impress him. *Osprey's Nest*'s three-story superstructure loomed above him, casting a section of the platform in deep shadow. His mercenaries advanced in formation, moving like phantoms through the shadows. Their presence at the moment remained undetected.

That advantage evaporated quickly.

A mercenary named Tomer Raziel to Stahl's right cried out as his head snapped back. His face erupted in a gore-filled mess of blood, bone, and brain matter. Stahl dove behind several stacked metal crates and drew his weapon. He spotted the Coast Guardsman sniper on the roof of the superstructure.

Too distant for Stahl to do anything, being armed only with a Soviet-manufactured SPP-1 underwater pistol. Essentially, a 4.5mm dart gun. All he could do was remain hidden and wait for his team to do their job.

The mercenaries on the deck scattered. Most ran for cover at the base of the towering superstructure. An alarm sounded from inside as they charged through open doors, entering the structure with a rushed but practiced precision.

From inside, gunfire erupted, shattering the tranquil quiet.

Orders and counter-orders filled Stahl's ears from his commlink as his men moved through the structure, killing military and civilian personnel without hesitation or remorse. Stahl remained where he was, hiding. He heard a scream. Looking over the crates, he watched the sharpshooter fall through the sky.

He landed on the platform with a bone-shattering thud, bloodied and dead.

"We have control," Korhonen reported. "The platform is secure."

Stahl rose tentatively. "Well done. I want every inch of this platform searched and secured. Find me the redheaded woman, Parker Quinn."

"Understood. Commencing search now."

Stahl emerged from behind the crates and tapped his commlink, switching channels. "Anton, you can bring our reluctant guest topside." He stared at the sniper's broken body, now in a puddle of blood, and the mercenary who had lost his face to gunfire. "There's plenty up here I want to show him."

CHAPTER **THIRTY-SIX**

Osprey's Nest
Mosul Reservoir, Iraq

IN THE ARTIFACT EXAMINATION and preservation room located on the second level of the *Nest's* superstructure, Lena Rodriguez sat at a table staring at three computer screens. The room was well-lit. A spacious work area designed specifically for researchers and scientists assigned to the ORCP. Bright, overhead LED lights cast a clean white glow over polished steel countertops and high-tech examination equipment. One wall was filled with glass-front preservation chambers designed to protect and preserve recovered delicate artifacts and specimens.

In the center of the room sat several large examination tables. Cabinets and shelves around the room were clustered with digital display microscopes, spectrometers, high-resolution cameras, and more than a dozen computer monitors, keyboards, and printers. Upper-level bookshelves held an assortment of reference materials: books, journals, and digital tablets.

A large observation window spanned the main wall, providing a spectacular view of the reservoir beyond. The opposite wall provided a plate-glass view of an interior corridor.

Lena jumped as the sound of gunfire reached the research room.

With her were several scientists and research assistants assigned to Dr. Patel, the geologist from MIT and Dr. Emily Carter, the toxicology and biological pathogens expert from the CDC. As the one most connected to the events that had brought them to this spot, those in the room looked at Lena with quizzical expressions.

Their unspoken question: *What do we do?*

Her blood ran cold with fear. All she could suggest was, "Find somewhere to hide."

Even as she spoke the words, she knew it was too late. Shadows of approaching soldiers moved across the corridor walls outside. The first round of shooting had brought her to her feet. Now, she dropped to her knees and crawled under the polished steel table.

She could just see a gap in the window from her hiding place.

Lena counted three men wearing dark clothes and black masks that only revealed their eyes. Wearing neoprene wetsuits and weighed down by tactical gear Lena was becoming all too familiar with, they stopped outside the panoramic window. Facing the research room, they raised their assault weapons.

They sprayed the room with automatic gunfire.

The windows shattered and crashed to the floor.

Lena covered her ears and bit her lip, trying not to cry out.

Across the room, the scientists and researchers ran screaming for cover. Seven innocent people were senselessly mowed down. With their shouts cut short, their bodies crumbled to the ground, their white lab coats covered in blood.

The roar of the automatic fire continued. Bullets pinged off metal, shattered touchscreen consoles, and nicked conduits and wires, causing them to spark and start small fires.

On her hands and knees, Lena crawled through the gummy shards of glass littering the floor—fragments from exploded computer screens, the preservation chambers, and the reinforced safety windows.

She reached a dark computer console workstation.

Lena pulled it from the wall and climbed behind it, drawing her knees up to her chin and making herself as small as possible in the dark recess she'd created. Exposed conduits and wires sparked around her. Shaking, she waited for the gunfire to stop.

When it did, she still didn't move.

The lab door opened, scraping shattered safety glass across the floor. Footsteps entered the room. Debris crunched under boots. They're looking for survivors, Lena presumed.

One found. A single shot rang out.

A deep voice said, "Alright. Alright. Let's go. We're done here."

Lena listened as the assault team withdrew and moved on.

Still trembling, a mix of fear and adrenaline, she gave herself a moment to exhale, then, gathering the strength and will to move, she crawled out from behind the console. Lena gasped. One of the researchers lay staring up at her. A bullet had pierced the forehead of a young college student, an intern assigned to the CDC for the summer. She'd introduced herself to Lena—her name was Patty—she'd been so full of excitement and... life.

Lena remained low and made her way to the door.

Left open, she cautiously leaned past the frame and looked up and down the corridor. The assassins were gone. She'd been lucky. But now she had to do something. Had to call for help. Had to contact Parker and the dive team. Warn them the platform had been overrun.

A tiny voice in her head warned her against taking such action. "You're a linguist. A researcher and a computer genius. Not a soldier."

Lena ignored the voice. People needed her help. Her friends needed her help. She brushed a tear from her cheek. Her eyes burned from the acrid smell of gunpowder, melted plastic and wispy fires. Her legs felt weak as she stood, and her breath came in ragged sobs.

She needed to get to the communications room.

Enter the corridor. Stay low, she told herself.

Looking both ways, she crept along the wall. Her fingers brushed the hard, smooth surface to maintain her balance. Every sound seemed amplified. The shuffle of her rubber-soled sneakers on the tile. The faint murmur of distant voices. Even the occasional pop of a gun being fired.

Those made her jump.

At the nearest junction, Lena pressed herself flat against the wall. She peered around the corner. Ahead of her were two men talking in low voices. They had on the same scuba-clad fatigues as worn by the death squad that executed everyone with her in the research center. They held rifles loosely by their sides.

She drew a breath and waited to see if they would move on, hoping she would not have to backtrack and find another way around. Luckily, their radios squawked. Orders were given using a 10-code she was not familiar with. The two men grumbled and moved off down the corridor.

Lena ran swiftly to a ladder that would take her to the next level. She paused at the upper rim, checking to make sure the corridor above was deserted. It was. She stepped out of the alcove. The communications room was just across the way.

She raced to the door, noticing the access keypad had been shot away. The wall around where the wrecked keypad hung from colorful wires was charred black and smelled of burnt plastic. She tried the door. To her surprise, it slid open.

Lena rushed to the main console and steeled herself at the sight of the radio operator slumped over in his chair. The back of his neck was a bloody crater of gore, ragged skin, and exposed bone.

Her breath hitched as she rolled the chair with the dead body away from the console.

Upon arriving on the *Nest* and at Captain Styles's insistence, they were given a rudimentary briefing on the platform's operations, including instructions on how to use the communications systems. She now cursed herself for not paying closer attention while they'd been told how to use the equipment.

"Stupid. Stupid. Stupid," Lena muttered under her breath. She scanned the controls, annoyed at how foreign all the buttons, dials, and keypads looked. "How hard can this be?"

She saw a red switch, recalling Styles pointing to it. She remembered him saying, "This is the emergency broadcast system." He told them it was monitored continuously 24/7. She toggled the switch and was rewarded with a low squelch of static and a steady hum.

Whispering, she said, "Coast Guard command. Bahrain. Come in. This is Dr. Lena Rodriguez. I'm on *Osprey's Nest*. Do you copy?"

The silence that followed was deafening. Each second stretched into an eternity. Lena strained, listening for approaching soldiers or any indication she'd made a connection on the communications frequency.

She tried again. "Coast Guard base Bahrain. This is *Osprey's Nest*. Dr. Lena Rodriguez. DHS. Do you read me?"

She waited, holding her breath.

More silence and then a crackled response. "*Nest*. This is Coast Guard base Bahrain. Identify yourself with proper rank and clearance code. Do you copy?"

"I don't have any damn clearance codes. I'm a civilian analyst assigned to DHS. My name is Dr. Lena Rodriguez. Talk to General Grayson about my clearance." She unleashed a flood of fear, adrenaline, anger and frustration on the radio operator. "This facility has been attacked by heavily armed men who have killed any number of your men and scientists and researchers assigned here. *Osprey's Nest* has been attacked and is in the hands of terrorists."

"Understood, doctor. We have Secretary Grayson on the line. Are you in the communications room?"

A wave of relief washed over her. "Yes. But I don't know how long I can stay here. They've got roving death squads searching for survivors. Killing them. I don't even know if anyone is still alive. Except maybe the dive party."

"Doctor, it's me." Grayson's voice came on the line. "Did you say the dive party?"

"Yes, ma'am. Parker and the others began their dive about a half hour before we were boarded."

"Maximilian Stahl? Is he there?"

"I don't know. I haven't seen him. All I can tell you… wait."

"What is it?" Grayson asked. "Lena."

She lowered her voice below a whisper. "Someone's coming. I can't stay here."

"Help is on the way," Grayson said. "Get out of there, Lena. Find someplace safe to hide."

Before Lena could respond, she heard the faint crackling static that had been an ever-present part of the background noise throughout the call cut out.

Silence. The connection was dead.

Her relief at getting a warning out was short-lived as she crouched low behind the console, hearing the muffled sounds of approaching footsteps and the low murmur of voices getting closer. She glanced over the console in time to see two soldiers half carrying, half dragging, a battered and shuffling Jackson between them.

Her breath caught in her throat.

His clothes were torn and bloodied. His face swollen and bruised. One eye appeared blackened and half closed. She caught in his eye one good eye, a fierce defiance that still burned. His gaze swept the corridor as they approached. She was sure he was looking for a weapon or a means of escape.

He caught sight of Lena, crouched and hiding.

Their gaze met briefly, and for a moment, time stood still for her.

Without warning, Jackson surged forward, ramming his shoulder into one of the guards. The impact sent the man staggering back. A surprised curse—in a foreign language—escaped his lips. The second guard reached for his holstered sidearm, but Jackson was faster. He swung his handcuffed arms in a desperate attempt to knock the gun from the man's hand.

The one guard shouted, "Grab him, Mendez!"

"You think I'm not trying?" Mendez responded.

From further down the corridor, a third guard appeared, running at the sound of the commotion.

Jackson was thrown face-first against the wall, where he was punched and kicked and pistol-whipped across the back of the head. Yet he continued to fight. His face turned, he locked his gaze on Lena and mouthed the word: *Go!*

She felt rooted to the spot, but at his urging, with a second nod, she was pushed into action.

There was a side door to the communication center.

She moves swiftly and silently, crouched below the consoles. She reached the door and eased it open. About to silently slip around the hard metal frame, she paused once more, watching Jackson through the windows as he fought valiantly, handcuffed and outnumbered.

They pinned him to the wall.

Their fist pummeled his already battered and beaten face. Blood course down his cheek and sprayed from his mouth as he roared against his attackers. They grunted, savagely beating his face and body until a gunshot reverberated loudly off the metallic walls.

Jackson's body stiffened. A look of relief and calmness crossed his face. In those final seconds, Leona saw a defiant smile flicker across his lips as his body slumped.

Lena gasped, "No."

She whispered a choking sob, covering her mouth to stifle the sound.

Jackson had bought her the time she needed to escape. To remain free. His sacrifice gave her the chance to be able to do something—she didn't know what yet—to save their friends.

And possibly the world.

She ran down the corridor behind the communication center in the opposite direction from where Jackson had violently died. She promised she would not let his death be in vain. The echo of a second gunshot reminded her of the price of their fight. She vowed to find a way to survive.

To make Jackson's sacrifice worthwhile.

CHAPTER **THIRTY-SEVEN**

Subterranean Cavern

PARKER WATCHED AS CHANG and Ramirez lugged three large black bags from the water's edge and dropped them heavily on the sand. They set up two tripod work lamps. The bright halogen lights operated off two fully charged batteries, giving them sixteen hours of power. One bag contained all sorts of offensive and defensive munitions and weaponry, most of which she had thought would prove unnecessary.

The coasties overplaying their motto: *Semper Paratus.* Always Ready.

In light of Captain Styles's disturbing revelation, her opinion changed.

"How do you wanna play this?" Parker kept her voice low, their spat unimportant now.

"Part of me wants to take Mitchell and the others back topside and see what the hell's going on," Styles said. "But that would leave you and the team vulnerable and exposed."

"Davenport and I can handle ourselves."

"I've no doubt you can. But, the bottom line is," Styles said, "this—down here—is the mission. I have to trust that the people I left behind are up to the task of keeping the platform safe."

"And if they're not?"

Styles frowned. Stoic and working to prioritize and compartmentalize his tasks, she could see the worry in his eyes. "We'll deal with it when we're done here."

Parker realized she liked his easy smile much better than his worried frown. "Then let's do this and get back up there."

Styles nodded.

Carter and Patel had brought bags of goodies of their own. From the waterproof cases, they pulled out a handheld-size mass spectrometer, a portable gas chromatograph, and other biohazard detection equipment used to search for traces of biological contaminants, as well as a portable seismometer, an accelerometer, geophones and a GPS station to detect ground movements. Busying themselves, they set up the equipment. Patel hummed softly while he worked.

Styles rummaged through one of the USCG bags and pulled out several Batman-style utility belts and sidearms: Glock 19s. Parker accepted an offered belt and cinched it around her waist. She tied the neoprene arms of her wetsuit around her waist and adjusted her bra straps under her t-shirt, where they kept pinching her shoulders.

Davenport hitched a belt around his waist, uncharacteristically quiet.

There was a hollow quality to the cavern. The softest of sounds were amplified. The unsnapping of buckles, the faint ripping of Velcro, and the slow unzipping of gear all seemed unnaturally loud in the stillness. The air was moist and stagnant, thick with an earthy, damp scent. Each inhaled breath wrinkled Parker's nose, leaving a stale, metallic taste on her tongue. Greenish algae clung to crevices in the rock walls. Small pools of still water pooled in some of the pockets.

A relatively comfortable 68°F, Parker guessed, checking her Glock's magazine. She holstered it.

Emily Carter knelt in the sand, setting up a bioaerosol sampler. The device was black and compact, about the size of a small briefcase, encased in a rugged, waterproof container with rubberized corners. The sampler pulled air through an inlet, forcing particles to collide with a sticky surface, where they were captured for analysis.

Carter started the device.

It emitted a soft hum as LED indicator lights flashed and cycled through a pattern before settling to a steady green glow. She adjusted several settings on the touchscreen. The device produced a high-pitched beep, similar to the sound of an EKG machine flatlining.

"Are we good, Doctor?" Parker said.

Carter examined the readout. "The data indicated no anomalous peaks that would indicate known toxic substances in the air."

Davenport looked worried. "Known?"

"Readings all fall within the baseline parameters commonly established for a safe environment. The absorption spectra show no detectable hazardous volatile organic compounds or measurable traces of weaponized toxins or chemical agents."

"Known. Detectable. Measurable. Doesn't fill me with confidence," Davenport said. "We don't have any idea what these ancient voodoo witch doctors cooked up."

"While it is true I can't say with one hundred percent certainty—"

Parker held up her hand. "Doesn't matter. We can only test for what we know. If you want to stay behind, Sebastian, that's your call." She looked around at the others. "That goes for everyone. Anyone else want to sit this out?"

Styles didn't wait for an answer. "Let's go, people."

Ramirez and Chang each shouldered a bag and stood up, ready to go. Patel and Carter nodded at each other. Parker glanced at Davenport. He sighed and waved a hand. "After you."

They proceeded in a single file toward a triangular fissure. Parker took the lead.

Beyond was a narrow, constricting tunnel of jagged rock. Another passage barely wide enough for a single person to pass through. The walls were rough, covered in ancient deposits of calcium and materials that glistened in the jumble of their flashlight beams.

As they progressed, the passageway widened into a larger chamber. There, they found a partially collapsed corridor. Rubble and rock strewn across the sandy floor slowed the team's progression. The air was damp and cool. Heavy with the scent of wet stone and earth with a distant sound of dripping water.

A half-hour in, they paused for a breather.

Parker worried that they might be on a wild goose chase again. This one costing them a lot of valuable time and effort until Lieutenant Mitchell said, "Does this mean anything?"

Styles and Parker joined her.

Mitchell pointed at carved renderings she'd discovered on the wall. Her flashlight beam aimed at the deep etchings.

Parker ran her fingers over the markings but felt frustrated at her lack of expertise in the ancient Neo-Assyrian language, though the symbols did look familiar. She wished she could consult with Lena. That thought caused her gut to constrict, reminding her they were cut off from the surface and that the people left up there could be in grave danger. "I can't say for sure, but some of this does appear to be Neo-Assyrian in style."

"So, we're in the right place?" Styles said.

"It's an encouraging sign," Parker offered. "Only one way to find out."

She pointed at the narrow passage to their right.

"Saddle up, boys and girls," Styles said. "We are going in."

Parker took the lead, ignoring Styles's frown.

Ten minutes later, they reached the top of a stone staircase framed by massive stone pillars.

Parker put her hands on her hips. "Huh."

She counted twenty-seven steps to the bottom. They stopped at a large stone door. The steps were cut stone. Uneven and covered in a layer of silt and detritus. Reaching the bottom, Parker moved her hands over the etchings, marveling at what it felt like to run her fingers over something that had not been touched in twenty-six hundred years.

"Dr. Carter, can you take an air reading, please?"

Carter set her bag on the bottom step. Once more, she pulled out and activated her equipment.

Parker shined her light on the door. It was intricately carved with symbols and representations of several deities. These Parker recognized as Assyrian. She panned her beam over the door's heavy stone lentil, highlighting more inscriptions that no doubt warned of dire consequences for any who dared enter.

"I've picked up a little since we started all this. These symbols. They are a warning, meant to deter intruders."

"Like 'keep out, authorized personnel only,'" Styles asked.

"Something like that," Parker said. "The doors are heavy stone, constructed to contain whatever lies within."

"Like a vault," Davenport offered. "A Vault of Doom."

That sent a shiver down her spine.

A few minutes later, Carter gave them the all-clear.

"One challenge down," Styles said. "What do you want to do about the door? We've got explosives and torches back at the staging area."

Still gently caressing the door's surface, Parker smiled. She'd found what she was looking for.

"That won't be necessary." With her slim fingers, she delicately brushed the sand, dust and sentiment from a small opening in the door's center. A slit, caked with dirt, hardened sand and silt. She brushed at the edges, flicking away crusted flakes, enlarging the hole, revealing what it was.

Styles said, "That looks like a... keyhole."

"Because that is exactly what it is." Parker reached behind her back, under her tank top. She'd fashioned a makeshift sheath, wearing it at the small of her back. She withdrew the ceremonial dagger she'd swiped from Ochir's Treasure Room.

Parker held it up in the air.

The blade was forged from a shimmering bronze alloy with a hint of gold, copper and iron, giving it an earthy sheen in the harsh flashlight beams. The cross guard was shaped into intricate, stylized wings embedded with tiny lapis lazuli and carnelian gemstones. The handle was wrapped in old leather, cracked, worn and stiff with age. And finally, the base was formed into an intricately carved lion's head.

A slightly raised groove ran the length of the blade. An oddity that caught Parker's attention when she'd first laid eyes on it. She carefully inserted the blade, aligning the raised groove with the narrow indentations she'd uncovered. The wings of the cross guard fit perfectly into the recesses on either side of the slot. She twisted the dagger.

It resisted.

The blade made a crunching sound inside the lock. The sound of centuries of caked debris breaking away. But it stopped turning.

Parker tried to force it.

Afraid she'd snap off the blade or break the locking mechanism, she paused. Then, with a smile, she noticed by twisting the dagger back half a turn, counterclockwise, the lion's jeweled eyes would line up with markings on the door. Doing so, through the artifact in her hand, she felt the internal locking mechanism thunk into place.

"Give me a hand," she said.

With the dagger key in position, she, Styles and Davenport pulled at the door.

Dust and sand—undisturbed for thousands of years—sprinkled from the transom. Caked-up dirt broke free as time and history gave up its grip on the door. It moved. Slowly, grinding, it scraped across the dirt floor as they swung it outward.

Parker grinned, enjoying that warm, fuzzy feeling.

That thrill she got when she was close to recovering a lost or stolen artifact, putting a smuggler or black marketer in jail. The journey was over, and she had won. The reward at hand. She pushed past Styles and Davenport to be the first to enter the chamber.

A large, rectangular room with stone walls and a vaulted ceiling. About twenty feet long and fifteen feet wide. Three of the four walls were lined with wooden or stone shelves. Filled with ancient clay vases, stone and wooden crates. One shelf was stacked with cuneiform tablets and cylinder seals. The information they contained would be invaluable to scholars, historians and archeologists the world over. The reliefs over the shelves were covered with additional symbols, etchings, and inscriptions.

Torches hung from iron sconces throughout the chamber. The air was cool and dry, unlike the cavern and narrow passageways they'd come through. But with a tainted, foul odor Parker couldn't place.

"Check the air quality, please," Parker said. "Would hate to think we just walked into an incubator of toxicity."

Carter set up her equipment near the doorway. Unpacking the bulk of the equipment she'd brought with her, staging it on a stone table near the back. She went to work.

Parker went about lighting the torches as the others came through. The old bitumen flared to life, filling the ancient chamber with a heavy, smoky odor and a warm, flickering amber glow.

In the center of the room, on a platform, stood a large stone, coffin-shaped container.

"Think there's a body in there?" Styles asked.

It certainly was large enough, but Parker suspected what was inside was much worse. It was her belief they had found the final resting spot for the Breath of Ashur. The Scarlet Death.

Final, until now, anyway, she thought with a bit of trepidation.

"That," she said, "I suspect is the motherlode, Captain."

As the others spread out, exploring the chamber's shelves and other nooks and crannies, Parker cautioned, "Don't touch anything. Any containment seals could be degraded and fragile. We don't want to cause a leak."

The shelves were littered with mortars and pestles, vials, and other ancient alchemical tools—a treasure trove of valuable neo-Assyrian artifacts in and of themselves. But it was a particularly unassuming container that caught Parker's eye. Made of a semi-translucent alabaster, about the size of a moonshine jar, its smooth surface had a faint, milky white sheen to it. Intricately decorated with cuneiform inscriptions. The bronze lid—tarnished with age—appeared to be fused shut with a band of dark resin. With it were other smaller ceramic, bronze, and clay amphorae. All were sealed with the same type of waxy resin. All had an identical string of markings:

《⊨𝄐 ◁⊣⧻

"We're sure nothing's escaping from these jars?" Davenport asked.

"If anything is," Carter said. "It's not registering on any of my detection equipment."

"So," Davenport said. "We could be exposed and not know it? Again."

"Aren't you the cheery one?" Styles asked.

"You learn to live with it," Parker said with a smile.

She jumped at the sudden sound of a gunshot.

Beside her, Sarah Mitchell's head snapped to the side. A spray of blood and brains spurted from her temple. She collapsed to the ground with barely a gasp.

Parker spun toward the vault door. Her hand on the Glock she'd thought she wouldn't need. Styles and the other coasties reacted similarly. And just as quickly. But, like her, they were all too late.

Maximilian Stahl and three others stood at the vault entrance. Having effectively gotten the drop on them, he, his righthand henchman, Anton Kuznetsov, and two serious-looking men dressed in black scuba gear crowded through the entrance and spread out. Holding rifles trained on Parker and the others, they appeared more than willing to use them.

"Agent Parker Quinn," Stahl said with a sardonic smile. "It's a pleasure to finally meet you in person. Now, everyone, put your weapons down so I don't have to kill you all. At least, not yet."

CHAPTER **THIRTY-EIGHT**

Osprey's Nest

WHILE PARKER AND HER team made their way into the Vault of Doom, Elana Rodriguez had managed to avoid detection for a full hour after Jackson's brutal murder. His selfless sacrifice to save her life. Thinking about it made her eyes sting with tears. But they also renewed her determination. To fight back. To ensure his death wasn't in vain.

She emerged from her latest hidey-hole. This time from under the steel cabinets in the platform's mess hall. Her heart raced as she crept through the quiet, shadowy corridors. The air was foul with the smell of smoke and burned wires. Tense, and jumpy, as if jacked up on too much caffeine, she paused frequently, listening, hearing approaching mercenaries, ducking into a closet or some other small space to remain out of sight.

Eventually, she'd move on, still in search of a plan.

She found herself once more in the communications room, only to find it in ruin. The consoles and equipment were a twisted mess of torn-out wires, shattered screens and scorched metal. Some of the hanging electrical conduits flickered and sparked. Stahl's men had been thorough. They'd left no chance anyone not yet caught could transmit a message to Parker and her team down below.

Grateful she'd been able to get out a call for help earlier, Lena now cursed under her breath.

She had to find a way to tell Parker about what had happened. To warn her, Stahl and his men were here. That to return to the *Nest* would mean certain death.

Lena edged closer to the bank of windows. Through the broken glass, she scanned the corridor outside. She heard voices approaching.

"They must have it with them. We find them, we find it. The reservoir isn't that big."

The second voice—heavily Russian—said, "The team's standing by. Ready to dive. The rest will remain here."

"Keeping an eye on things," the first voice said. "Good. Let us finish this, old friend."

Lena remained crouched under the window. She watched as the two men passed. The taller of the two, his hand on the stocky one's shoulder.

Stahl and Kuznetsov, Lena assumed. Damn it. Rather than simply wait for Quinn's team to return, they were going after them.

She had to act quickly. Every second counted.

Lena sprinted from the wrecked communications room. Her steps were silent and deliberate, but she needed to get to the dive locker quickly. The room where wetsuits, air tanks, BCUs and other underwater equipment were stored. She'd heard the coasties call it that.

She could hit the water ahead of Stahl and Kuznetsov if she were fast enough.

To her advantage, they didn't know the location of the Vault of Doom, while she had, if not the exact location, a pretty good idea. She ran, energized by the thought that she could get to Parker first. Warn her and the MET team. Maybe in time to mount a viable resistance against the armed goon squad on their way to them.

She reached the dive locker without encountering any more of Stahl's men.

Lena rifled through the equipment lockers, scanning the shelves while quickly stuffing things into a waterproof bag: a multipurpose tool. Some zip ties. A small first aid kit. She snagged an extra pony bottle—a small auxiliary air tank.

Next, Lena found a scuba suit hanging neatly on a rack.

She slipped into it. The neoprene fabric was cool and tight against her skin. Zipped up, it fit snugly. Her fingers worked swiftly, securing the wrist and ankle seals, double-checking the integrity of the suit. At the gear bench, she attached a regulator to an air tank, listening for the reassuring hiss as it locked into place. She checked the pressure gauge, confirming a full tank. Her fingers moved over the dive computer, setting it to monitor her depth and air supply. With mask, fins, and a buoyancy control vest in hand, shouldering the stuffed waterproof bag, she made her way to the *Nest's* exterior moon pool.

She stepped from the shadows of the superstructure only to jump back again.

Stahl, Kuznetsov, and three others were gathered around the open hatch. Like her, they were prepared to dive. The men checking each others' equipment for proper fit and functionality.

To a man with a rifle slung over his shoulder—Lena recognized him as one of the men who'd killed Jackson—Stahl said, "Korhonen, I anticipate no additional interference from the Americans, but remain vigilant. Everything depends on the next hour or two."

"Yes, sir."

"An extraction helicopter has been dispatched for us from Amman, Jordan. Ensure it is here by the time we return. Timing is crucial to our escape."

"Understood."

To Kuznetsov, Stahl said, "Everyone ready? Let's go."

Lena watched them slip from sight as the remaining soldier named Korhonen strolled back toward the superstructure. She was too late.

The Vault of Doom

PARKER STARED DAGGERS AT Maximilian Stahl. How?

She knew the answer, of course. Their mole. She knew now it couldn't be Jackson, which brought with it its own small sense of relief. He'd been away from the team since before Lena had revealed the location of the Vault of Doom. He couldn't have known.

"Take your hands away from your weapons." Stahl ordered Kuznetsov, "Move them all to the corner. Disarm them and do not hesitate to kill any of them if they are foolish enough to act heroic."

Taken by surprise and outgunned, Styles had no choice but to wave his people toward the back of the chamber. Parker nodded to Patel and Carter to join them. Stahl's men moved through the chamber, disarming her, Davenport, and the MET team with professional efficiency, herding them to the chamber's back corner.

"You two," Kuznetsov snapped at Parker and Davenport. "Go."

"Not, Agent Quinn," Stahl said. "I'll be needing her assistance."

"Best go on and pull the trigger now 'cause you'll get no help from me."

Quicker than she could react, Stahl crossed the space between them and seized her throat, forcing her to arch over the coffin-like stone container in the center of the room. His fingers squeezed. A vein pulsed in his temple.

Davenport and Styles took steps forward but were stopped by the raised weapons pointed at them. Kuznetsov shoved them back with the others. Stahl released his grip on Parker and stepped back.

"Still prepared to play the arrogant bi—" Stahl asked.

"*Osprey's Nest*?" She flung sand-coated locks of damp hair from her face. "What have you done?"

"The platform?" He pointed over his head. "Up there? Oh, they're all dead. Or will be. If they're not already. Nice toy, that. It will be quite the consolation prize for my side."

"You killed everyone?" Styles asked, outraged.

Stahl glared at him. "I don't repeat myself, Captain." He turned to Parker. "Now, let's get started."

"Tell me something first," Parker said.

"How I came to be aware of the Breath of Ashur?" Stahl asked.

"It traces back to the loss of Russian influence over Ukraine in 2005. The so-called Orange Revolution. When Yushchenko stole the nation from an impotent Russian Federation and a weak Putin. Failure after failure after that. Their soft South Ossetia response. The lack of decisive action in Moldova and Transnistria. Tragically missed opportunities in Central Asia. Each failure an indictment of a government unwilling or unable to make decisive, bold decisions, to take brutal control."

He paced the chamber. "Disgusted, I withdrew, retreated. A frustrated patriot who knew there had to be a different way. A better way to achieve the changes the world so desperately needs. The catalyst came to me through a scholarly article I read in the Journal of Near Eastern Studies, discussing the peculiarities of recently recovered artifacts from the Royal Library of Ashurbanipal. The Chronicle of the Kings tablet and the Guardian of Secrets seal specifically. The authors hinted at the possibility of them containing hidden meanings, even sophisticated encrypted messages.

"My curiosity was piqued by the conflicting translated passages—phrases such as 'winds of death,' 'locked away, forbidden knowledge,' the 'Breath of Ashur,'" and my personal favorite, 'the Scarlet Death.'

"I, of course, became obsessed. Scoured every source. Learned everything I could about the Neo-Assyrians. That period. Their leaders. The more I read and researched, the more I realized Ashurbanipal's military victories were due to more than a superior force, military acumen or strategy. Specifically, I focused on the reports of plagues, widespread epidemics, and diseases that accompanied many of his military campaigns or swept through the conquered lands shortly after.

"It couldn't be a coincidence. I was convinced they had a biological weapon of some sort. I conferred with top agencies and institutions like the WHO, the UK's Ministry of Defence, France's Institut Pasteur, and even VECTOR, Russia's Novosibirsk Research Institute. Spoke with leading microbiologists, epidemiologists, immunologists and toxicologists. They all agreed. In the hypothetical, of course. An ancient biological pathogen, long dormant or extinct. If introduced into the populist today, would be nothing short of total devastation."

Stahl sneered a sinister grin.

He looked around the room and spread his arms like someone in a ticker-tape parade with confetti raining down from the sky, having won the lottery.

"Typical narcissistic male ego. Going on about themselves, like anyone cares," Parker said. "I just wanted to know who your spy is?"

"Ha. I prefer to get down to *my* business." He yanked her arm, turning her to the coffin-like centerpiece in the chamber. "Bowing to your expertise, agent. I think the prize we're all after is inside here. Don't you agree?"

Parker set her jaw, remaining silent.

"How do we open this thing while making sure we're not at risk of exposure?" he asked.

"You bring down a few Level A PPE suits?"

"Hum." Not amused, he said, "Surely the Assyrians would have safeguards in place so as to not expose themselves."

"Or boobytraps to keep something so deadly out of the wrong hands."

"Such as?"

"I'd guess maybe a drop trap or false latch system. Probably with a trip line."

"Explain."

"A drop trap activates when a lid is improperly lifted. A weighted mechanism inside releases a heavy stone or other object, smashing the contents within. Releasing whatever's inside."

"And a false latch?"

"Like it sounds. Activate the wrong latch or a series of them in the wrong order—a trip line inside triggers a secondary lock. Often, these boxes contain a collapsable inner lid. Triggered, it drops, damaging the contents within."

"Releasing the pathogen," Stahl concluded.

"That would be my guess."

"How do you archaeological types get around such traps?"

"X-ray imaging. Electromagnetic scanners. Laser Doppler Vibrometry. Other acoustic and imaging equipment." Parker patted her neoprene scuba pants. "Which I don't happen to have on me. Ruins the lines of my girlish physique."

"But, they are all readily available on your *Osprey's Nest,* I would guess."

Parker remained silent. It was true. All the equipment she mentioned was on the research platform, along with an MRI, thermal imaging cameras, mass spectrometers, fiber optic scopes and borescopes. Not to mention the hermetically sealed, negative pressure room, with a double airlock entry and exit system and multiple HEPA and ULPA filtration systems designed for just such excavations and examinations. Everything they would need to safely contain, transport, and study the contents within.

"What do we do?" Kuznetsov asked, stepping closer.

Stahl stroked his chin, thinking.

"Opening it down here," Parker said, "is a death sentence."

He stared at her. His cold eyes sizing her up, determining if he could trust anything she said.

"A gamble," he said. "Certainly." He strolled along the length of the large container. His hand gently ran along the underside of the lid, caressing the rough-hewed surface, feeling the texture of the pitted stone for a latch or trigger plate.

He reached the narrow end and quickly drew back his hand. "Ow."

Parker noticed a dollop of blood on his index finger. Something had pricked his finger.

"Oh, didn't I mention," she said. "They might've used a poison needle trap."

Stahl stared at his finger. "Poison needle?"

"Spring-loaded needles coated with some kind of poison."

"Poison," Stahl said again.

"Probably aconite," Parker said. "Commonly called monkshood or wolf's bane. But it could be hemlock. Both cause respiratory failure, paralysis, and cardiac arrest. Less likely, but possibly it's belladonna. Known as nightshade. That's a fun one—causes hallucinations in addition to the previously mentioned paralysis and respiratory failure. You get to see all kinds of *crazy* things while you can't move, stop breathing, and ultimately have a heart attack and die. Wild stuff."

"You bitch!"

Stahl rushed at her, but Parker was ready for the attack.

She yanked her t-shirt up with her left hand. With her right, she grabbed the grip of her Seecamp, stainless steel .32. An old pocket pistol she'd picked up from a manufacturer in Connecticut years earlier. Protected in a sealable plastic bag, the gun was contained in a bra holster strapped between her breasts. The slim, six-shot autoloader cleared the hard Kydex shell with a snap.

Parker swung the weapon toward Stahl, but he'd advanced too quickly.

Trying to shoot through the plastic bag, she fired an awkward shot. The bullet tore through his upper arm. Not a fatal or even incapacitating wound.

It certainly didn't stop his freight train-style assault.

With an animalistic growl, he slammed into her, driving her backward.

Lifted off her feet, they hit the hard, gritty ground, kicking up a cloud of dust and a breath-deflating grunt from Parker. His full weight knocked the wind from her lungs.

But Stahl's tackle wasn't the only thing she needed to worry about.

An explosive force boomed through the chamber. It vibrated through the walls and floor. Dust and sand rained down from above. The resonating blast rang in their ears, deafening. A slab of limestone knocked loose, fell from the ceiling. It smashed to the ground less than a foot from where Stahl and Parker had landed.

"Earthquake!" someone shouted.

CHAPTER **THIRTY-NINE**

Osprey's Nest

ANGRY AT HERSELF FOR being too late, Lena waited a beat to ensure the deck remained empty before she snatched a pistol-size speargun and leg holster with two spare spears from a rack on the wall. She moved quickly to the moon pool, where she descended the ladder, pausing for another moment to give her racing heartbeat a chance to slow down.

With her arm slung through a ladder rung, she strapped the leg holster to her thigh and inserted the spear shaft into the muzzle until it locked into the trigger mechanism. She pulled back the bands, hooked them into the shaft notches, disengaged the safety, and then slipped on her mask. After checking her regulator and BCD, she slipped into the tepid water below.

Sinking under the gentle waves and prepared to face resistance, Lena twisted and turned as she emerged in the open water, aiming the speargun in every direction at once, alert for any enemy.

The only movement was a silver-scale Tigris bream swimming past her facemask.

Stahl and his goons had wasted no time getting on their way. They were nowhere in sight.

To Lena's delight, what was left was one of their underwater sleds. It's dark cowl and chrome trim illuminated by the *Nest's* lighting.

She slipped onto the seat. Pleased to find the control panel incredibly intuitive, Lena started the engine, feeling its vibrating thrum through her thighs squeezed against the machine's flanks. She leaned forward and quickly maneuvered the sled away and down, plunging herself headlong into the dark depths and toward unknown danger.

She knew the general location of where she believed the vault to be. She tapped the coordinates into the watercraft's onboard GPS. She wondered if she could get out ahead of Stahl, given she had more specific information than he did.

It wasn't to be.

By the time she reached the crevice that served as an entrance into the cave system, Stahl's three underwater sleds hovered around the fissure. The crafts were abandoned, except for one mercenary left behind to guard them and deal with any unexpected arrivals.

Lena turned away from the cave entrance.

Concealed by the gloomy darkness, she aimed her sled down and to the left, diving until she was near the bottom. She believed she'd escaped unnoticed as she hastily hatched a plan. For this to work, she needed the element of surprise.

Staying deep in the shadows, Lena turned her sled, facing it upward toward the guard. She slid low to one side, hanging off it so the machine was between her and the mercenary guarding the cave entrance. She goosed the throttle, surging upward from the dark reservoir floor.

She aimed the speargun over the cowl. A short-range weapon, she needed to get close.

The sled sped upward at its top speed of nearly ten knots.

The guard heard the sled's approach. He twisted in time to see the machine barreling toward him, up from the reservoir floor. His eyes went wide.

She cautioned herself to wait.

Wait...

Wait...

At the last possible moment, she pulled the speargun's trigger.

She felt a slight resistance, then a smooth release. The recoil was barely noticeable. The water absorbed most of the force. The spear shot forward. She watched it glide toward the diver, bubbles trailing behind it as it tracked silently and swiftly through the water.

The razor-like tip pierced the hollow in the man's throat, just below his jaw. His hands clutched at the bolt sticking out of his neck. He yanked, doing even more damage. A trail of dark blood clouded the water around his now slack face.

Unmoving, he floated in neutral buoyancy. His arms hung limp.

Dead.

Lena pushed off the sled. It traveled away from her, slamming into the other sleds, sending them scattering, like underwater pins struck by a bowling ball. With her bag clutched to her shoulder and the speargun tightly gripped, she swam for the black fissure, ignoring the submersibles wildly cascading about, their auto buoyancy commands jumbled.

It didn't take her long to navigate the narrowing chasm and finally surface in the inlet lagoon.

There, she found the bags of equipment, air tanks, BCUs, and discarded scuba suits left by Parker and the others. The relatively cool temperature made the moisture in the air uncomfortable and sticky, lending a stale, earthy odor to it.

Lena followed the footprints to the next narrow fissure in the rocks and quickly reached the stone steps. She started to descend when she heard voices from below. Parker's voice.

And Stahl's voice. Angry.

"I've got to do something," Lena whispered.

But what, she wondered.

When an idea struck her, she smiled, convincing herself it would work.

She raced up the steps and made her way back to the inlet. It *could* work, she thought, quelling the self-doubt rising up inside her like bile. She gathered up two fairly full air tanks and a bag left behind by the coasties.

Inside it, two exothermic cutting torches. "Just what *el doc recetó!*"

She lugged her haul back to the base of the stairs. There, she quickly went to work.

She knelt in the corner near the large open door and set the first air tank down. Attaching a fresh rod to the cutting torch handle, she opened the valve on the oxygen tank. Hearing the hiss of gas, she adjusted the torch handle valve.

The raised voices inside the chamber covered what little noise she made.

The rod burned brightly. An intense flame burning white-hot. She jury-rigged it so it would continue to burn and positioned it at the end of the air tank. She repeated the process with the second torch and air tank, then ran to the top of the stairs for cover.

She had no idea how long it would take to heat the tanks so the pressure inside—set to three-hundred-forty-five psi—would reach their stress limits and explode, but she wanted to be well clear of the area when they did.

"Come on. Come on." She put her fingers in her ears and leaned against the rock wall, holding her breath. She gasped when she heard a gunshot from inside the chamber.

Seconds later, the first air tank exploded.

Twenty-seven seconds after that, the second air tank blew.

The Vault of Doom

A SECOND EXPLOSION ROCKED the chamber, seemingly more deafening than the first. Or that might have been because Parker's ears were ringing so loud from the first one, coupled with her .32 going off so close to her ear, she couldn't tell.

The fallen chunk of limestone startled Stahl. "What the—"

On top of her, Stahl's distraction was Parker's opportunity.

She rolled him off and darted for cover around the far end of the stone container. There, she ducked, grabbed a random clay jar from the floor and pitched it at Stahl's head. "Think fast."

He flinched.

She fired off two shots from her Seecamp pocket pistol. Three left.

Stahl dove to his right. One bullet whizzed past his ear. The other grazed his already wounded arm but barely drew blood. He reached for his ear. "Damn."

STYLES AND ENSIGN CHANG exchanged a glance. Each chose an opponent and leapt at the two gunmen. Styles dove like a linebacker making a tackle, getting in under the mercenary's attempt to swing his assault rifle around.

Locked in a bear hug, they hit the ground. Hard.

Chang hadn't been so lucky.

A step slower and with his chosen target a greater distance away, the man got his rifle lined up with the charging Chang and fired, putting a 7.62x39mm round in the young ensign's face, arresting his charge with a grunt and spatter of blood and gore.

Against the wall, Carter screamed. Patel took her in his arms while turning his back to the gunfire, shielding her with his body.

Ramirez made a play for the pile of guns Stahl's men had taken from the coasties. Chang's killer sprayed a rapid-fire staccato of gunfire. Ramirez took a round in the shoulder but got a hand on one of the Glocks. He hit the ground in a puff of dust, squeezing off several rounds.

His opponent flinched, then his body jerked. A round catching the man's throat. Blood spewed from his neck like scarlet water from a punctured garden hose. He released his rifle, clutched at his throat and dropped to his knees. Ramirez pumped two more rounds into his head as the mercenary fell forward.

He twisted onto his back, but Kuznetsov stood over him, his Stechkin automatic pistol pointed at his face. Kuznetsov pulled the trigger. Dead instantly, the bloody hole in Ramirez's forehead barely leaked any blood.

WHEN THE SHOOTING BROKE out, Davenport ran toward the doctors, but with the automatic fire spraying across the chamber, spitting up little geysers of rock chips and dirt from the cavern walls, he dove to the ground and Army-crawled toward the exit.

Davenport noticed a round had clipped Patel in the cheek, drawing blood. Too shallow to even scar, in the MI6 operative's opinion. He and the woman, Carter, were crouched against the base of the wall, trying to get out of the line of fire but having nowhere to go.

Of greater concern to Davenport was the rumbling he felt through the chamber floor. A vibration, barely perceptible. Like a buzz under his feet. Dust and small bits of debris continued to fall from the ceiling. His chest constricted with an odd feeling of uneasiness, certain he could hear a deep, muffling growl between the staccato of automatic fire and the sporadic pop of pistols.

The initial explosions, their cause unknown, had triggered a seismic event.

The sort Patel had warned them about.

PARKER REMAINED CROUCHED BEHIND the stone container, mindful of the chaos around her and wary of what Stahl might do next. To her left, Patel and Carter were crouched in the corner. Styles was exchanging gunfire with Kuznetsov and the one remaining mercenary. Stahl, at her twelve o'clock, was moving steadily toward Kuznetsov.

To regroup and unify against them.

Parker couldn't let that happen.

She fired a shot. Down to two.

It nicked a shelf over Stahl's head and ricocheted off a clay urn.

Stahl ducked. He returned fire. The bullets pinged off the large container. His wounded arm hung limp as he ran.

Parker looked around the chamber for Davenport but couldn't find him. He was gone.

"Captain," Parker shouted. "Get the doctors out!"

Crouched in a crevice created by a fold in the sandstone wall, he nodded. He fired a shot at Kuznetsov, who'd sought cover by overturning a stone workbench. Rusted tools, mortar and pestle, and clay jars slid to the ground in a jumble.

Parker popped up. Double-tapped. She hit the remaining mercenary in the neck and his ear. He went down instantly. "Where the hell's Davenport?"

"Ran." Styles urged Patel and Carter to their feet, pushing them toward the door.

"I'm out." She tossed her pistol aside.

Styles tossed her his AK-74 even as Kuznetsov sprayed a round of bullets at the retreating group, stitching the wall behind them before Parker returned fire, spraying the room with wild abandonment. That sent the Russian back behind his cover. One round caught Stahl in the leg. He dropped to his knees with a grunt.

Styles and the doctors were through the door and in the clear.

"It's over, Stahl," Parker shouted.

Stahl used the overturned workbench to pull himself to his feet. Blood soaked his wounded arm and trickled down the side of his neck where she'd nicked his ear. More blood leaked through the hole in his trousers, just above his boot.

"You might think you won, Quinn. But this?" Stahl winced. "Just the opening salvo in a war to come."

"Perhaps," Parker said, cautiously stepping backward toward the entrance. "But your campaign's over today. And you lost."

A deep rumble rolled through the chamber. A low growl but louder than the previous ones.

Parker felt it in the soles of her feet. The entire place seemed to vibrate. Stone dust and sand trickled from the vaulted ceiling. The wooden shelves quivered. A few clay jars tipped over.

The tremors grew more violent. The ground heaved. Loose tiles in the floor shifted. Their jagged edges jutted the centuries-deep layer of sand and dirt. The chamber filled with a jarring, grinding noise. Cracks snaked up the ancient walls, cutting through the intricate carvings and inscriptions, while chunks of limestone broke free overhead, plummeting to the floor amid a cascade of dust and debris, clouding the air in a choking plume of dust.

"Cave in!" Styles shouted from the doorway. "Parker! Move it!"

She reached the entrance as Kuznetsov popped up like a deadly jack-in-the-box. His Stechkin automatic pistol clutched in two hands. His face an ugly, twisted expression of anger and fear.

Before he could fire, Davenport appeared beside Parker.

He grabbed her shoulder and yanked her back.

He fired an AK-74 held in his hands. With the trigger squeezed tightly, at a rate of ten rounds per second on full-auto mode, he obliterated a large, basalt stone urn set on the shelf over Kuznetsov and Stahl.

The container shattered into a thousand shards. Stored inside, a dark, sickly green, semi-liquified sludge splattered like a burst water balloon.

Under it, Stahl looked up.

The gelatinous, syrupy substance splashed over him, coating his face and fatigues. The slime formed tiny bubbles that popped like water coming to a boil. Each tiny eruption released a glowing vapor of gas.

A sickening hiss filled the air.

Stahl clawed at the goo and screamed.

Turned red and bubbling, his skin slacked off his face where his fingers revealed long trails of exposed, molten flesh. His eyes were wide, bulging where his eyelids had melted away. The goo ate through the fabric of his uniform. The material blackened, hardened, and turned brittle, crumbling away in flaky tatters as the liquid underneath continued to eat away at his flesh, muscles, tendons and veins.

He staggered around the chamber, limping on his one good leg, clawing at his body, renting skin and cloth away. His flesh smoldered, and his veins burst, popping bright red geysers of blood. His eyeballs melted while his fingers were reduced to blackened skeletal claws. His head became a discolored, sizzling, darkened skull.

Stahl collapsed to the floor, thrashing and screaming.

"Close the door!" Parker shouted. They couldn't let the toxin escape.

She, Styles and Davenport gathered together, shouldering the door closed.

Inside the chamber, Kuznetsov tossed his gun away, shouting, "Don't leave me here. Please."

Nearest to the door frame, she watched Kuznetsov rush around the stone container. He ran for the door.

Parker shouted, "Push! Push!"

His skin already turning red and getting splotchy. Boils formed on his cheeks and his hands. The biggest one erupted, emitting a puff of ghostly white vapor.

"No!" he shouted. The door almost closed. "Don't let me die. Not like this."

With the door sealed, Parker twisted the dagger key and extracted it. Even if the door had a way to be opened from inside, Kuznetsov alone wouldn't have the strength to do so.

The cave continued to rumble.

"We've got to go!" Styles shouted.

At the top of the stairs, Lena was ushering Patel and Carter ahead of her, shouting, "Go. Go. Go."

Parker raced up the stairs after Styles and Davenport. Several of the steps had begun to crack. Chunks of rocks and brown dirt fell from the rough-hewed ceiling. Dust filled her lungs and coated her tongue. The tremors filled her ears as she prayed the narrow passages they'd taken hadn't collapsed.

She pleaded with whatever entity watched over them they could get to the lagoon.

Get there before the whole damn place came down around them.

Get there and get out alive.

CHAPTER FORTY

Osprey's Nest

UNDER THE MOON POOL, Parker hung back, ensuring her team made it safely topside.

The crawl through the narrow clefts had been harrowing. A pile of small rocks and boulders had blocked the passage ahead, but they were able to dig through the obstacle, even as the tremors lessened in both intensity and frequency.

At the lagoon, Patel warned, "The seismic activity may have subsided for the time being, but I can make no guarantees they are over. We should go."

"You'll get no argument from me," Parker said.

The others began to properly suit up, adjusting air tanks and BCUs. With the casualties they suffered, there was enough equipment to make the dive back through the submerged tunnel, even without the two air tanks Lena had used in her brilliant rescue effort.

The swim out to the waiting watercrafts had been uneventful.

They'd made it.

As the last of her people ascended through the moon pool, Parker sighed, kicked, and reached for the first ladder rung. Slowly, she made the bone-weary, achy climb. When she broke the water's surface, she heard a familiar but unexpected voice boom overhead.

"Let me give you a hand, Red."

She glanced up.

A pale arm with thick red hair and a meaty grip reached down to her. Beyond the freckled arm, a large walrus of a man wearing a green aviator's flight jumpsuit grinned down at her. He had red hair as vibrant as hers and a round, ruddy face.

"Skyjack!" She took his hand.

The big man effortlessly hauled her from the moon pool. After a deep embrace, she glanced at a dark helicopter half-submerged at an angle in the water. Its cabin was ablaze with bright yellow and red crackling flames. Dark smoke curled from its smashed windows, a column of oily black against the clear, blue sky.

"What's the story with that?" she asked.

"Stahl's extraction plan."

"Your handiwork?"

With a sly smile, Skyjack McMurphy said, "I might've had something to do with it. At least it's the bad guy's ride this time."

The last time she'd seen the big man, he was explaining—poorly—to Secretary Grayson how a twenty-eight-million-dollar H225m Airbus helicopter, entrusted to his care by her, had ended up on the destructive end of a savage LAWs rocket attack. A blackened and burned-out husk on the sandy beach of Versteek Island. One of an archipelago of islands on the New Hampshire-Maine border called the Isles of Shoals.

A bright red Sikorsky MH-60T Jayhawk helicopter sat on the platform, a mainstay of the Coast Guard's aviation fleet. She noticed several bullet holes in the chopper's skin. A small price to be paid for the Coast Guard's liberation of the platform from Stahl's men.

"How... why are you here?" she asked.

"Lizzie called. Said you were up against it. I happened to be in the neighborhood. Had a little downtime on my hands."

Thrilled at the news, Parker asked, "Brice and Tara? They're here, too?"

Brice is," McMurphy said. "He's off dealing with a… thing. Not Blades. The Middle East is problematic for her."

Parker could see why a return to the Middle East would be an issue for the woman.

Tarakesh Sardana, Blades, as McMurphy called her—a woman of Egyptian origins—became a rogue mercenary during the U.S. conflicts in Iraq and Afghanistan. Doing so, she'd gone AWOL and, on the run, had been forced to adopt several identities over the years. Now living in the States, she worked with Coast Guard Commander Brice Bannon and McMurphy. They were a close-knit, very effective band of operatives assigned specifically to Secretary Grayson.

McMurphy slipped on a pair of Ray-Bans. "Your team's in good hands."

"The ones that made it back."

Parker saw medics treating Dr. Patel's cheek. The others were stripping out of their gear and wetsuits and dressing in offered shorts and dry shirts. They downed bottles of cold water. Their exhaustion was apparent.

"How many?"

"Three. All coasties."

"I'm sorry," McMurphy said.

"Yeah. Sucks."

She spotted Dr. Carter. "Excuse me a minute, Skyjack." She extracted the small alabaster jar she'd pinched from the Vault of Doom and handed it to the woman. After a short conversation, she returned to McMurphy. "You're working on that V.P. thing y'all rushed off to last I saw you?"

McMurphy glanced at the moon pool, avoiding the question. "Heard you had a posse after you down there. Anything still needs worrying about?"

"They won't be coming back up."

McMurphy grinned, looking like a proud father. "You little spitfire from Oklahoma, you."

Parker slipped her arm through McMurphy's. They strolled toward the superstructure. "Well, I'm chuffed to hear all about what you and Brice are up to."

"Unfortunately, you're up first. Lizzie wants to debrief. Forthwith."

"Grayson's here?"

"Naw. She's on a plane back to the States. They're trying to get a feed linked up."

Parker sighed. "Fine. Afterward, then."

McMurphy patted her hand in the crook of his arm. "Sure, Red."

By the way he said it, Parker knew there'd be no time. He'd be gone. Reunited with Brice and Blades once more. The three of them would be off to lord knew where to save the world again. But for now, it felt good to spend time with her friend.

He led her to the conference room where Parker and Styles had debriefed the team hours earlier. She gasped at the condition of the room now. It had been trashed. The LED panel had a spiderweb crack through it. Chairs had been knocked over, some of them broken. The touchscreen had been ripped from its console. Wires were pulled out, left cut, dangling and exposed. The acrid scent of burnt plastic fouled the air.

The large glass window overlooking the reservoir had been smashed.

Concentric cracks spread across multiple points. Each a dark, chipped circle where bullets had struck the reinforced glass. Rippling outward in distorted patterns, the fractures connected to other splintered lines, then spun out in wildly different directions. The damaged glass now reflected the streaming rays of sunlight in a chaotic kaleidoscope of white-yellow patterns across the walls rather than the calming ripples of gentle waves she'd noticed her first time here.

McMurphy righted a couple of chairs on the table's far side, opposite the damaged LED panel. He patted the seat on one while he sat in the other. "Take a load off, Red."

She sat, noticing the blue and white cooler between the chairs.

He flipped the top open and rooted through the jumble of ice, digging under a layer of bottled waters and soft drinks to extract two cans of Fort Point Ale. He popped the tops and handed one to her.

"From the very fine Trillium Brewing Company," he said. They clinked cans. He took a sip. "Both floral and citrusy, perfect to celebrate the successful conclusion—"

"That's not a beer. On a Coast Guard platform, is it, John?" Grayson asked. Her stern, thin face had suddenly appeared on the cracked LED screen. Larger than life. Her features were distorted from the displaced display glass and the staticky feed of the link.

McMurphy gulped, then sputtered. "That would be a regs violation, Lizzy."

Neither confirming nor denying. Parker held her open can under the table, out of sight.

"Yes, John. It would. And shouldn't you be someplace else right now?"

"That sounds like my cue to get the fleet out of here." Holding his can against his thigh, he got up, leaned down and kissed Parker on the top of her head. "Great to see ya again, Red."

At the door, off camera, he downed the last of his beer and gave Parker a wink.

"Is he gone?" Grayson asked.

"Yes, ma'am."

Grayson shook her head, unable to suppress her smile. "I swear, that man."

The cold can of Fort Point Ale held under the table chilled Parker's fingertips. And made her mouth water for it.

"Okay," Grayson said. "In the spirit of full disclosure, Agent Quinn. The visual quality of this link is sporadic." She made a tsk, tsk sound. "Difficult for me to see through all the snow and static the techs can't seem to clear up."

"Ma'am?"

"I'm saying if that scoundrel of a chopper pilot gave you an unauthorized alcoholic beverage. One you might be holding under the table right now. I'd not be able to see you consume such a beverage—as richly deserved as it would be—while we debriefed."

"Understood, ma'am." Parker took a long, cold and grateful swallow. "Thank you, ma'am."

"Now, Agent, fill me in."

CHAPTER **FORTY-ONE**

PARKER REMAINED ON OSPREY'S *Nest* for the following two weeks.

Soon after the briefings, debriefings, and reports were completed, Captain Styles, Parker, and the remaining members of her team, Davenport and Lena, gathered at the edge of the helicopter pad at dusk. With them were doctors Patel and Carter and the Coast Guard personnel assigned to the *Nest*.

The reservoir's waters were calm and dark. A warm, gentle breeze carried the dry, crisp fragrance of the desert across the platform. Without access to formal wear, the civilians were dressed in practical, weathered clothing, while the Coast Guard personnel wore their ODUs. Their hats off and cradled under their arms. The atmosphere was somber yet resolute, the fading sun painting the sky in hues of amber and crimson that reflected softly on the reservoir's dark, glassy surface.

Styles stepped forward, his sharp and commanding voice softened but still firm, carrying the weight of the moment.

"We gather here tonight to honor Lieutenant Sarah Mitchell, Ensign Bruce Chang, and Petty Officer Third Class Alexander Ramirez." His words remained steady while a vein pulsed along his jawline, just under the surface, belaying his stoic demeanor. "They gave their lives in the line of duty. Far from home. Protecting others and standing for something greater than themselves. Though we cannot bring them back, cannot bring them home, their sacrifice will never be forgotten."

Parker felt a tear track down her cheek.

"They were more than just our teammates," Styles said. "They were our family. Out here, facing a hostile and unrelenting enemy, they stepped up to the challenge, unwavering, prepared to give their all." His voice crackled. "We relied on them. And they did not falter."

He paused. His hands squeezed into tight, white-knuckled fists. Then he held his head higher. "We honor their bravery, their dedication, and their selflessness. They deserve more than this, but this is what we can give, for now."

The Coast Guard members came to attention.

Davenport narrowed his eyes and cast his gaze to the deck. Beside him, Lena, her eyes shimmering with unshed tears, perhaps as much for the fallen coasties as for Captain Jack Jackson, took Parker's hand and squeezed. Dr. Patel and Dr. Carter, though civilians, stood solemnly among the team, their respect and shared sorrow evident in their expressions.

Parker spoke softly, breaking the silence. "In our line of work, we talk about sacrifice. But today, we honor its true meaning. Sarah Mitchell, Bruce Chang and Alex Ramirez stood for what that meant. The best that we can be. In them, we must find the inspiration to press on and stand firm. In our darkest times, we must find the strength and ensure their light never fades. Only then can our fallen heroes' sacrifices have not been in vain. That is how we honor them and carry their memories forward all the days of our lives."

She concluded, "We owe them—as does the world—a debt that cannot be repaid."

Styles nodded his appreciation. He lifted a flare gun, its crimson casing gleaming faintly in the twilight. He aimed it skyward. His voice carried over the sound of the rising wind, "Fair winds and following seas."

The flare shot into the sky, bursting into a brilliant scarlet flame that illuminated the fading dusk. The glow reflected off the still waters of the reservoir, casting long shadows across the platform and highlighting the somber faces of the gathered mourners.

As the flare faded, the group observed a moment of silence. The only sounds were the distant lapping of the water and the faint rustle of their clothing in the desert breeze. Each stood lost in thought, remembering the camaraderie, the bravery, of their fallen comrades.

Finally, Styles spoke. His voice firm but tender. *"Semper Paratus."*

Slowly, they turned away from the platform, their mission calling them back to duty.

During the days that followed, a myriad of personnel came and went.

Under the eagle-eye supervision of Easy Styles, Coast Guard repair crews worked day and night to clean up and make repairs to the platform. Far from a solo endeavor, the U.S. Navy provided technical expertise and logistical support, while the host country of Bahrain contributed skilled labor and essential resources, showcasing their commitment to ensuring the platform's swift return to full functionality. Representatives from other member nations of the International Maritime Organization (IMO) collaborated closely, lending their specialized knowledge and equipment to tackle the wide-ranging challenges posed by the undertaking.

The operation also saw active participation from the commercial shipping industry and private sector stakeholders. Maritime companies supplied advanced tools and machinery, while engineers and technicians from private enterprises worked together to transform *Osprey's Nest* back into a fully operational and regionally strategic maritime asset.

Dr. Patel remained, bringing in a team of seismologists, geophysicists, geologists and geochemists to analyze the seismic data recorded by the local and global monitoring stations. He explained to Parker they were highly-trained specialists assigned to study the implications of the quakes— examine the tremor patterns, the changes in rock formations, evaluate soil stability, and determine how the geological shifts could impact the region's existing ecosystems.

Collaborating closely with them were a contingent of Army Corp of Engineers, government and civilian structural and geotechnical engineers, there to analyze data from the seismic and geophysical teams to assess how the tremors might have negatively affected the dam's stability and the integrity of the Vault of Doom. Their findings would determine whether additional reinforcement or emergency measures were necessary to prevent a catastrophic failure of either structure.

Meanwhile, Emily Carter brought in a fresh CDC team to work with the Iraqi Ministry of Health, the Ministry of Environment, and other concerned agencies. They made full use of the *Nest's* bio-containment labs and specialized equipment. Their priority was to determine whether any of the Scarlet Death pathogen had escaped and might have leached into the reservoir, potentially compromising the dam's water supply and surrounding ecosystems.

Drones equipped with advanced water sampling equipment gathered specimens from various depths and locations within the reservoir, particularly near the cavern's entrance. Simultaneously, a second team of military and civilian engineers deployed remotely operated vehicles (ROVs) equipped with sonar imaging and high-definition cameras to inspect the structural integrity of the submerged cavern's passageways and fissures, looking for any fractures, leaks, or weaknesses that might suggest a breach.

At the two-week mark, the area had been cleared and deemed safe. However, cooperative teams would remain and continue to monitor and analyze for the foreseeable future.

Parker steered clear of them mostly, having little to offer their efforts other than to answer a question here and there, when asked. She spent most of her time with Lena Rodriquez.

The container she'd given Dr. Carter had been inscribed with a particular cuneiform inscription. It had bothered Parker when she'd first seen it in the Vault of Doom. She'd had a feeling it was somehow important. Though it had been on several jars, Parker had only managed to swipe the one before Stahl's arrival and their fight to escape.

Over the two weeks, she and Lena had spent days analyzing the Akkadian text:

《⮞⫽⊟ ◁⌐⫽⫿

Finally, they concluded the first half to be transliterated as *nūrum* or a variation thereof, which meant "light" or "fire." The second half they determined was *šamāmu*, "sky" or "heaven." Putting it all together as *nūrum šamāmu,* they came up with "Heavenly Fire" or "Light of the Sky."

"What does it mean?" Carter asked once Parker and Lena brought the information to her.

"Akkadian can be highly nuanced," Lena warned.

Maximilian Stahl's attack on Belarus had been intended to orchestrate a catastrophic incident with a singular, chilling objective: to maximize casualties with its rapid and widespread dissemination. To create an apocalyptic event that would send shockwaves around the world.

The confirmation that the Breath of Ashur pathogen was used came from extensive on-the-ground analysis by multiple agencies, including the CDC and WHO, assigned to the rugged, affected areas in the Carpathian Foothills after the attack. Their conclusion relied heavily on comparisons to the sample recovered by Lena and Jackson from the Whispering Sands temple.

Stahl and his shadowy benefactors had unleashed the pathogen in an aerosolized state—derived from the sludge-like goo encountered by Parker and her team in the Vault of Doom. Unlike in its original gelatinous form—which melted Stahl's skin off and dissolved his body in mere minutes of contact—the aerosol version proved less immediately deadly.

The CDC and other world health organizations like the WHO, OPCW, UNEP, and a dozen other national agencies concluded the method used to alter the pathogen into a gaseous state had diluted its lethality. While many victims in Belarus died horrific and swift deaths, hundreds, perhaps thousands more were affected by a slower-acting, milder exposure, resulting in less extreme symptoms over a longer period of time.

Meaning—unlike in the case of Kuznetsov and Stahl—in Belarus, there were survivors.

Survivors that could be helped with a...

"A cure," Parker said. "I believe. Inside the canister… I think it's an antidote or vaccine or something. It's hope. Like a beautiful, glorious, sun-filled sky after a terrible storm. Heavenly fire."

EPILOGUE

Pier 1 Café - Central Park
New York City - One Month Later

PARKER AND LENA SAT at a wooden table by the railing overlooking Central Park Lake. Mid-morning, the air was warm though heavy with moisture. A gentle breeze rustled the nearby trees, carrying the scent of rich, brewed coffee and freshly baked pastries. A cappuccino for Parker, while Lena drank a smoothie and picked at a blueberry muffin.

Birds chirped, and a motorized toy sailboat glided past, leaving ripples on the lake's surface. Sunlight reflected off the water where children threw breadcrumbs for the badling of ducks. Around them, parents and other adults conversed and shared croissants and morning beverages.

A jogger in shorts and a moisture-wicking t-shirt ran by. He glanced up from his smartwatch to give Parker and Lena a second look. He smiled at them.

Parker leaned to one side. From behind oversized sunglasses, she watched his backside as he jogged away. "Have you given Secretary Grayson's offer any more thought?"

Lena mimicked Grayson's clipped, precise manner of speaking. "'You have performed in an exemplary manner, Miss. Rodriguez. Above and beyond. The mission's success is due in no small part to you.' Was there an offer in there?"

Parker smiled. "That's practically a standing ovation, shouted from the rooftops. The best I get from her is usually 'well done' and 'good job.' And yes. She wants you to join the team."

Lena ran her thumbnail along the length of her cup. Her eyes clouded with doubt. "So this... offer would be to work for... "

"DHS. CPAA," Parker said. "The Cultural Property, Art, and Antiquities program could use your skill, your level-headedness and courage, Lena. You've proven yourself capable, and the need is there."

It's been on my mind," Lena admitted but looked worried. "And the idea... it's exciting."

"But?"

"I... Parker, I killed a man. Shot him in the throat with a speargun."

"That's not sitting well with you? Can't reconcile taking a life, no matter how justified it might have been?" Parker took a minute to size her up. "No. That's not it. You're not looking for the 'he was a bad guy and would have killed you or us' justification, are you?"

"I'm not sure." Lena forced a smile. "I worry it's not affecting me like I think it should. I don't feel strongly about it either way. I should be sick over it, shouldn't I?"

"I get it." Parker clasped her hand. "Maybe because deep down, you know, in your soul, they were responsible for all those deaths in Belarus. Would have killed tens or hundreds of thousands more if we hadn't stopped them."

"Does that help you?" Lena paused. "Justify it?"

"I don't know. Doesn't always sit well with me all the time either. I guess I do believe it's a 'greater good' thing. So long as I'm sure what we're doing, what *I* do, is... right. All I can do is trust that the cosmic scales properly sort it all out."

"Truth is," Lena fingered the Miracle Heart charm at the end of the delicate gold chain around her neck. "That's not the only reason I'm hesitant to join up with the DHS. It's noble work, and if I can do some good, make a difference—"

"You would. Of that, I've no doubt."

She could see the conflict in Lena's eyes as she turned, her attention on a duck flapping its wings and taking off from the lake. Her thoughts were so much farther away.

"Jackson," Parker guessed.

"I feel nothing, just hollow, about Stahl and Kuznetsov and their ilk. But the others. Jackson, Isabella Arroyo, the slaughtering of our team in the vault, the innocents killed on the *Nest*. I don't know if I can deal with that… all that death, destruction. That level of grief, of sadness and despair all the time."

Parker understood. She forced a smile, no stranger to those very same struggles. "I get it. Whatever you decide, Lena, know you have a place with us. Know you'll be welcome."

"Thank you."

Parker watched as Davenport approached from the far side of the park. Dressed in a soft-lavender dress shirt under a navy blazer. A black tie with a matching pocket square, severely creased trousers and comfortable-looking loafers. A gold Rolex and engraved cufflinks winked, catching the sunlight from under his blazer's sleeves. "There they are. The two prettiest ladies in the Big Apple."

"What?" Parker asked. "No umbrella, Steed?"

Davenport flashed a put-upon smile. "Can't say I miss your biting American witticisms, Parker." He glanced around the park. "Is it too early to order a proper drink?"

"I'm so glad you could make it, Sebastian," Lena said.

"Of course, I wouldn't miss Jackson's memorial service for all the tea in the Boston Harbor."

Captain Jacques Jackson had family in Harlem. A small, family-and-close-friends-only gathering had been scheduled for that afternoon. The family would never know the details of Jackson's death, nor would he be afforded every top military and government honor he deserved. The powers that be had determined there would be no upside in disclosing to the world just how much worse the attack on Belarus could have been or how close the world had come to a global catastrophe.

Parker argued the public deserved to know. Had the right to know how dangerous the world really was. But she could also concede their point. Fear, despair, and mistrust already mired the world and its citizens. Collectively, aware of only a fraction of the dangers and threats, the atrocities humankind was capable of. Full disclosure. Full transparency. It could only result in total and worldwide panic.

Jackson's family, his friends, and other loved ones would be told in no uncertain terms what sort of hero he had been.

"I owe that yank my life, as you know."

"We all do." Parker came to her feet and faced Davenport, nose-to-nose. "Which is why I'd never sullen his sacrifice, his reputation or memory by allowing the person responsible for his death to be anywhere near his memorial service."

"What are you saying?" Davenport said. "Have you gone daft, woman?"

Lena stared at the two of them, open-mouthed, as if she thought Parker had gone insane.

"You were Stahl's inside man." She poked Davenport in his chest. Pushed him a step back.

Behind his sunglasses, Davenport narrowed his dark eyes but said nothing.

"When I first met Agent Reynolds," Parker said. "Over a beer, he meticulously, in painstaking detail, broke down the Baghdad heist for me. Explaining to me how the crew, other than Kuznetsov and Stahl, consisted of three individuals. A German nationalist, Nico Müller, and an American mercenary named Mike Harper. Both of them are dead now. Killed less than a year after the heist."

"You said three," Lena came to her feet. Her expression a mix of confusion and suspicion.

"The third was a young Chinese girl named Li Xinru, who went by Lilly."

"What are you getting at, Parker?" Davenport said.

"Five years ago, a young Chinese hacker doing a job in North Korea got picked up by MI6." Parker slammed her finger into his chest. "By you. You were the one who caught her. In North Korea."

"This Lilly person," Lena guessed. "That was the woman who arrived with you at Teterboro airport?"

"The woman at Teterboro airport," Parker confirmed. "Careless of you, Sebastian, but you figured none of us would be smart enough to put it all together. And to ensure that, you never mentioned who she was, what her connection to Stahl had been."

"You said the girl was picked up," Lena said. "By MI6. If she was in their custody—"

"They lost her. Reynolds's inquiries were stonewalled. He believed the woman had escaped, and the Brits were too embarrassed to admit it, or she was shipped off to some black site, maybe forced to use her skills on behalf of the British government. Was that it, Sebastian? You flipped her. Servitude. To pay for her crimes. What? Earn her freedom?"

"I don't know what you're prattling on about, Parker."

"A double agent?" Lena asked.

"Triple more like," Parker said. "She was your pipeline to Stahl."

"I've had about enough of this. I'll not stand here and take—"

Parker grabbed his arm. "We monitored every call, every outgoing contact between the team and the outside world. No one blinked twice over your communications with Ms. Xinru. Not until I asked Grayson to have Reynolds look into it. Once that happened, the communiques were examined. The contents revealed. And your lies were exposed. Lilly's in custody and singing like a—"

Davenport shook his arm loose. "I'm done here."

"Yes. You are. Once the connection was made, Sebastian," Parker said. "It was a simple matter to trace the money." She whistled. "Lots of money."

He spun on his heels to leave. His path blocked by two men who grabbed his arms. He struggled to pull away, but their grips – and determination – were too strong.

"Allow me to introduce you to Chad Mazzarelli. My boss at the DHS. And FBI Agent James Reynolds."

The men held their badges in front of Davenport's face. "You're under arrest, Sebastian Davenport, for espionage and conspiracy to commit espionage."

Mazz added, "And conspiracy to commit terrorism, providing material support to terrorists."

Davenport twisted against their grip. His smug, overconfident demeanor replaced by an expression of concern, bordering on fear. "I'm not an American citizen. You have no authority,"

"But I do, mate."

A third man with a clipped English accent approached them from behind Parker. He smoked a pipe and had his hands in the pockets of a light trench coat. "You'll be facing charges of war crimes, crimes against humanity and treason against the crown, as well."

"This is Sir Percival Beaumont-Smythe. Senior Director of Counterintelligence for MI6," Mazz said, introducing England's top spymaster.

Beaumont-Smythe removed his pipe and extended a hand, giving Parker a slight bow. "A pleasure to meet you, Agent Quinn."

He pulled Davenport from Mazz and Reynolds and turned him over to three waiting uniformed NYPD police officers. By pre-arrangement, they cuffed Davenport and led him away.

Lena looked visibly shaken, all of this a surprise. "What will happen to him?"

Beaumont-Smythe smiled. "He'll be held at the British Consulate General for now. Full access will be granted to your agencies for as long as you deem necessary to extract whatever intelligence you believe him to possess. Thereafter, he'll be flown home to face the Crown's full fury and the international authorities as appropriate."

He shook hands with Parker again, and this time with Lena as well. "And let me add bravo. It's an honor to meet you both. If not for your actions… well, I don't believe it to be hyperbole to say you saved untold lives and quite possibly prevented the start of World War III."

"I'll accompany you back to the consulate, Sir Percival," Reynolds said. "I'd like to get started right away with… debriefing Davenport."

"Smashing." He clasped Mazz on the shoulder. "Agent Mazzarelli, well done, mate. Well done." Beaumont-Smythe clenched his pipe between his teeth once more.

"Appreciate that, sir."

"Ladies." Beaumont-Smythe nodded as if reluctant to leave. Finally, to Reynolds, he said, "Come along, old boy. We've got a spy to break."

When they were gone, Lena said, "Was that for real?"

Mazz smiled. "Yeah. Smitty is a bit of a character. Part Sherlock Holmes. Part Winston Churchill, I think." He pointed at the two of them with a stern look. "As for you two," he warned. "Don't let that stopped World War III stuff go to your heads. It's not gonna cut any slack with me. Understand?"

"Wouldn't think that it would, boss." Parker smiled and gave Lena a wink. "So, what's next?"

Mazz smiled. "How do you feel about Arizona?"

PARKER QUINN WILL RETURN

Thank you for purchasing this book. We hope you enjoyed it.

If you'd like to stay informed about new releases, special events, and exclusive content only available to subscribers, sign up to get David DeLee's newsletter

https://www.subscribepage.com/daviddelee

And don't forget to check out David DeLee's companion series, the pulse-pounding Brice Bannon Seacoast Adventure series.

ALSO BY DAVID DELEE

Grace deHaviland Bounty Hunter Series
Too Far
Stare at the Moon
Takedown
With Intent to Deceive
Pin Money
Fatal Destiny
Runners

Brice Bannon Seacoast Adventures
Crimson Storm
Siege at Tiamat Bluff
The Yakuza Gambit
Strike of the Stingray
The Oceanic Princess
Facing the Storm

Dark Justice Crime Thrillers
Between Truth and Lies
Cold Cases
While the City Burns
Moral Misconduct
Out of the Game
Crystal White

ABOUT THE AUTHOR

David DeLee is the award-winning author of the Grace deHaviland Bounty Hunter series. In addition to the novels, he's written many short stories featuring Grace, most notably *Bling, Bling*, which appeared in the anthology *The Rich and the Dead*, edited by Nelson DeMille.

David's other work includes his Nick Lafferty thrillers. The first-in-the-series, *Crystal White*. SUSPENSE MAGAZINE called "...a dark portrayal of the evil that men—and women—can do." He's also written the Flynn & Levy police procedurals and the Brice Bannon Seacoast Adventures, the latest being *Crimson Storm*.

A member of the Mystery Writers of America and the International Thriller Writers Organization and a former licensed private investigator, David also holds a Master's Degree in Criminal Justice. He makes his home in New Hampshire.

For more information, join David's newsletter: https://www.subscribepage.com/daviddelee

Dark Road
PUBLISHING